Legacy of Lies

I0563768

Martine Daniel

chipmunkapublishing
the mental health publisher

Martine Daniel

Published by
Chipmunkapublishing
PO Box 6872
Brentwood
Essex CM13 1ZT
United Kingdom

http://www.chipmunkapublishing.com

Chipmunkapublishing gratefully acknowledge the support of Arts Council England.

About the Author

Martine Daniel was born in York in 1981, and always dreamed of being a published author. Despite suffering mental health difficulties herself, her hopes of seeing her name in print never dimmed, and her dreams came true when her first novel, The Fire in Your Eyes, was published by Chipmunka Publishing in 2009.

Martine hopes that by bringing the experience of mental illness alive in her works of fiction she can contribute to the on-going battle to reduce the stigma surrounding mental health issues.

You can find out more about Martine Daniel on her website www.martinedaniel.co.uk.

Martine Daniel

Legacy of Lies

Author's Note

In the first decade of the twenty-first century, thanks to public campaigns like the *Time to Change* campaign, the stigmatised attitudes towards mental illness finally began to shift. Although stigma still exists, and there is a long way to go before negative attitudes towards mental health problems are eradicated, it is becoming more acceptable to admit to having illnesses such as bipolar affective disorder (manic depression) and schizophrenia.

A hundred years ago – and even as recently as forty years ago – the idea of mental illness being acceptable would have been inconceivable. Psychiatry and psychiatric treatment were still in relative infancy, and the most common solution to the problem of mental illness was to keep people with illnesses like manic depression locked up in the old Victorian asylums – out of sight and out of mind of the general public. Mental illness was a shameful subject, one which was rarely spoken about – and it was in the shadow of the silence that the myths and misconceptions about mental health problems grew up. Out of the silence came the mistaken belief that all schizophrenics are dangerous. Out of the silence came the myth that people with mental illness can never live normal lives.

Only in the latter decades of the twentieth century did psychiatric care begin to change for the better. The old asylums have gradually been closed down in many areas, being replaced by modern units that promote better recovery. The focus has shifted to keeping people with mental illness out of psychiatric units and supporting them in their own homes. The change is good – but for those people who were locked up in the asylums in the 1930s, 1940s and 1950s, it has come too late.

In writing *Legacy of Lies*, I wanted to highlight the appalling state of psychiatric care in the first half of the twentieth century, to remember the forgotten generation of people suffering mental illness who were offered no hope of recovery, and contrast psychiatry then with the hope for the future.

Martine Daniel

Dedication

This one's for Holly and Theodore, my beautiful niece and nephew!

Martine Daniel

Legacy of Lies

PROLOGUE
JULY 1968

Lies had become the cornerstone of the community. Lies built upon lies, built upon lies. They penetrated deep, infecting every single person who stepped inside the 'chapel' to hear Pastor Tyrell preach his poison every evening. His voice haunted Elvina's dreams, amidst her sister's screams. There seemed to be no escape from her daily nightmare.

'Elvina, open the door this minute!' The door handle rattled ominously, but the door didn't budge. There was no way anyone was getting into the attic bedroom, not with the heavy oak dresser pushed right up against the door. Elvina cowered in the corner of the room, her wet hair dripping droplets of icy-cold water down her back. Her dress was torn, the bodice ripped open to expose her pale flesh. There were vivid stains where the pastor's fat fingers had pinched her; her head rang still from the stinging blow he had dealt her after she tried to bite him.

'You will open this door, Elvina, or, God help me I shall have it broken down!'

The voice outside the bedroom door belonged to her grandmother – the one person she feared as much as the pastor. They worked their evil together, the two of them, always in the name of God, so that the whole brainwashed community hung from their every word. Georgina Warburton was a formidable woman – stout and sharp-tongued, with a heart that Elvina knew to be so cold it was as if she wasn't human at all.

'I am warning you, Elvina!' Georgina shrieked. 'The ceremony is not complete. You must be cleansed of the evil – or do you want to share in your sister's fate?'

At that moment, Elvina would have gladly given her life to be with her twin again. Her heart ached with the raw pain of losing her 'other half' without even the chance to say goodbye. An agonised sob tore from her lips and she crumpled in on herself, rocking back and forth in anguish.

'Let me speak to her, Mother.'

There was no comfort to be found in her father's voice, either. Walter was as much a pawn in his mother's hands as any of the faithful sheep who practiced Pastor Tyrell's barbaric take on Christianity.

'Come on now, Elvina. Open the door,' Walter cajoled. 'Let me in. I can't talk to you through the door, now can I?'

Elvina continued to rock, her fist stuffed into her mouth to stop her sobbing aloud. If she closed her eyes, she could see herself back in that room again, with her father standing by and watching – as he surely must have stood by and watched them do the same to Isabella. The thought that her sister had endured this horror before she was dragged screaming away – never to return, despite Walter's false promises – brought bile rushing up into Elvina's mouth. It was inhuman, the things that the pastor did whilst claiming to do God's work. Elvina had studied the Bible at length – at her grandmother's insistence – and nowhere could she find mention of the vile acts practiced by the Church of the Glorious and Great God.

As footsteps faded away down the stairs, Elvina unfurled herself and tiptoed across the room to listen by the door. She could hear nothing, but that didn't mean that someone wasn't waiting on the other side for her to throw caution to the wind and try to escape. Not that she was stupid enough to try it. Instead, she stripped off her dress – torn when she made her bid for freedom – and pulled on a pair of slacks and a jumper, shivering as she tried to wring some of the water out of her long chestnut hair. Her teeth were chattering still with shock.

The attic was at the very top of the house – three storeys up – and so the last thing Elvina expected was for someone to try to climb in through the window. She heard the dull thud against the wall as the ladder was raised, but took little notice, feeling almost safe barricaded inside the room. She lay curled up on Isabella's bed, clutching in her hands the one photograph – of the two of them together – that Georgina hadn't burnt in a ritual 'cleansing of evil'. Tracing Izzy's face with her fingers, Elvina allowed the tears to fall freely.

When the sash window was hurled open, Elvina screamed, cowering back on the bed and dropping the photograph. It slipped down the back of the bedside chest as the pastor heaved his bulky body through the window and into the room.

'There is evil in this house and it is my duty to cleanse you of it!' Tyrell bellowed, slamming the window closed again. 'I *will* exorcise the devil from your soul, Elvina.' He shoved the dresser out of the way of the door with little effort, such was the strength behind the great monster of a man. 'Will you come willingly, or do I have to drag you?' he asked, turning on Elvina with a malicious glint in his eye.

Elvina folded her arms across her chest in a gesture of defiance. She tried not to show the pastor that she was afraid of him, but her heart was pounding so loudly she felt sure that he must be able to hear it.

'Very well,' Tyrell said, smiling maliciously. He crossed the room in two long strides and seized Elvina by the shoulders, pinning down her arms as he manhandled her, struggling as best she could, towards the door.

It was no accident when Tyrell knocked Elvina's feet from under her as they descended the steep wooden staircase. She tumbled and rolled down the remaining stairs, landing in a bruised and shaken heap at the foot of the attic staircase. Tyrell didn't so much as spare a thought of concern for her; wordlessly, he hauled her back to her feet and continued the descent down to the ground floor of the house.

The hallway was lined with prominent people from the Church, all dressed identically in a strange black attire that marked them out as the Trusted Elders. Georgina and Walter, of course, were amongst them, as well as Elvina's aunt Louisa, her father's sister, the post-master Mr Musgrave, Mr and Mrs Denton from the village shop, Mr Crossgate the dentist, the three Misses Silk and their brother who between them ran the village school, and Mr Falsgrave from the old Manor House. They each crossed themselves as Pastor Tyrell marched Elvina past them to the front door, and then they formed a sombre procession through the village to the old chapel that had been home to the Church of the Glorious and Great God for four centuries.

The interior was dark and dank, lit only by flickering candles that guttered as the procession filtered in and took their seats, arranged in a circle around the stone altar. The inner circle of twelve plush-upholstered chairs was reserved for the Trusted Elders, with the hard wooden chairs for the rest of the congregation arranged in two outer circles around the Elders. For ceremonies such as this, however, only the Elders could be present.

'Kneel and repent!' Tyrell snapped, forcing Elvina to her knees before the altar, on which was placed a stone urn half-filled with water that Tyrell had blessed earlier. Elvina bowed her head, but she refused to repeat the words of repentation that the pastor had tried to force from her lips before she had fled the chapel earlier. She would not – could not – renounce her own twin as a servant of the devil. Izzy had not been evil, or possessed. Reckless and wilful, yes, but her only crime had been to rebel against Georgina's iron rule.

'Repent!' Tyrell repeated impatiently.

'*Never,*' Elvina whispered.

Tyrell grasped a handful of Elvina's hair and twisted it in his hand. From his pocket, he produced a pair of scissors and began hacking at Elvina's hair. He didn't stop until all that was left of her once-beautiful curls were inch-long tufts that stuck up from her scalp.

'The devil feeds on vanity,' he snarled, throwing down the scissors. 'On vanity and sin. You are a vain and sinful child, Elvina, and I fear for your mortal soul.' He picked up the urn and poured it over Elvina's shorn head – thus restarting the ritual he had begun earlier, before Elvina had escaped. The pastor placed his hands on Elvina's bowed head and turned his face towards the domed ceiling of the chapel, on which was painted a fresco of the Stations of the Cross.

'I command thee evil spirit, along with all thy minions now attacking this servant of God, by the mysteries of the incarnation, passion, resurrection and ascension of our Lord Jesus Christ, by the descent of the Holy Spirit, by the coming of our Lord for judgment, to depart, transgressor. Depart, seducer, full of lies and cunning, foe of virtue, persecutor of the innocent. Give peace, abominable creature, give way, thee monster, give way to Christ, in whom thee found none of your works. For he has already stripped thee of thy powers and laid waste thy kingdom, bound thee prisoner and plundered thy weapons. He has cast thee forth into the outer darkness, where everlasting ruin awaits thee and your abettors!' Tyrell's voice rose as he uttered the final words of the exorcism; he raised his arms heavenwards and then brought them crashing down upon Elvina's shoulders, making her cry out in pain. 'Be gone, Satan, be gone!' Tyrell screamed, shaking Elvina by her shoulders. He released her without warning, so she slumped forward, banging her forehead on the base of the altar. Blood began welling from a cut just above her right eye.

'Get up,' Tyrell snapped. 'Let me see your eyes.'

Shivering so hard her teeth felt as though they were rattling in her skull, Elvina raised herself slowly up. Her vision was blurry, her head was pounding, and she felt as though she was about to pass out, but Tyrell wouldn't care about any of that. He caught her chin in his hand, forcing her head further up, and he stared into her eyes so intensely, it felt as though he was trying to see straight through to her soul. After several long minutes, he released her with a curt nod.

'Is it done?' Georgina asked sharply.

'Time will tell,' the pastor muttered, wiping his hands on his trousers as if he'd been forced to handle something unpleasant. 'Take her out of my sight, Walter. We shall soon see if she has been cleansed. And if not, well then we shall have to try some other means of ridding our community of evil.'

Walter stepped forward to help his daughter to her feet; Elvina shook his hands off her, repulsed by his touch. Not once had he tried to defend her – just as he had failed to defend Isabella. He had willingly sent Isabella to die alone – and Elvina would never forgive him for it.

'Let's get you home and out of those wet things,' Walter said timidly, casting a nervous glance towards his mother.

'Don't you *dare* pretend you care,' Elvina hissed bitterly. 'Don't you *dare!*' Once outside the chapel, she broke away from him at a run, only to have to wait at the front door, which Georgina insisted always be locked.

'Run up and get out of those wet clothes,' Walter said. 'And then let me take a look at that cut. It might need a little stitch.'

Elvina stopped at the foot of the stairs, turning slowly to stare at her father. 'You stood by and watched while he... he *exorcised* me, and suddenly you're all worried about a little cut?' she cried. 'You let them send Izzy away, let everyone think she had TB because of the shame of the truth, and you let her die, all on her own, but you still think you can make it all right with a little bit of sympathy? You repulse me, Father. You make me sick, you and *him* and *her*, and all the rest of them. Exorcising *me* and *Izzy*, when the only evil in this community resides in that bloody chapel!'

'Elvina!' Walter gasped, his face blanching white.

'How do you sleep at night, Father?' Elvina asked. 'Knowing that you sent your own daughter to her death?'

'No!' Walter cried, reaching out and trying to grab hold of Elvina's hand. 'It wasn't... I didn't...'

'You let them do it. That makes you responsible,' Elvina snapped, struggling to keep a traitorous tremble from her voice. She turned and ran up the stairs before she broke down completely. The pounding of her footsteps on the stairs drowned out her father's whispered words: 'If only you knew.'

***

The attic bedroom that had once been a safe haven for her and Isabella now felt like a prison to Elvina. She doubted she would ever feel safe again – at least not whilst her grandmother and the pastor ruled dominion over her and the rest of the community. There would, she knew, be no let up. They had driven people from the village before, with accusations of devil worship, but what they had done to Isabella was a step too far.

All Elvina had to hold onto was the hope of escape. For Izzy's sake, she had to escape her grandmother's clutches. That was the promise she had made her twin the moment Georgina broke the news that Isabella had died. There was no chance of revenge, as much as Elvina wanted to see her grandmother in hell. The whole community had come out to pay their respects to Isabella's young life lost, never knowing that the coffin that was lowered into the ground was empty: Georgina had refused even to allow Walter to bring his daughter's body home to be buried. Izzy had been interred as she had died: alone, and hundreds of miles away from home.

Were it possible, Elvina would have fled the night of her exorcism, but she had to bide her time until, three days later, she passed her sixteenth birthday without celebration. The police would not waste time looking for a sixteen year old runaway, but they would have been obliged to search for a fifteen year old. Being found was a risk Elvina couldn't take. When she left the prison she had once called home, she didn't intend to ever come back.

The moment she heard first her grandmother's and then her father's bedroom doors click closed at precisely 11:30pm, Elvina, fully dressed in a pair of bell-bottom jeans that her grandmother had forbidden her to ever wear and a sweater that had belonged to Izzy, slipped out of bed and tiptoed across the room. Her bag – a battered canvas holdall that had once belonged to her mother – had been packed and hidden in the bottom of the wardrobe for days, just waiting for the moment when she could make her bid of freedom. Carefully, she lifted it out and undid the buckles that held it closed, checking that everything – especially the little money that she'd been able to save from her weekend job in a cafe – was still inside. About to slip on her coat and shoulder the bag, she hesitated, and put the bag down again. Tiptoeing across the room, she crawled into hers and Izzy's cubby hole and opened the trunk at the back, pulling out the tin box that she and Isabella had found several years before.

It had belonged to their mother – the only thing of Medora's that had survived their grandmother's 'purge of evil' after Medora's death. Crawling out and closing the cubby hole, Elvina forced the box on top of her clothes and struggled to fasten the buckles again. She couldn't leave the last remnant of her mother behind.

She had planned her escape carefully so as not to risk being caught. She had memorised every stair that creaked, and every door that squeaked, so she could be certain to make it downstairs without being heard. She even knew that once her grandmother took a sleeping tablet, it was exactly twelve and a half minutes before she was snoring like a pig. Waking Walter was the least of her concerns. He would not stop her. He wouldn't openly defy his mother, but neither would he stop Elvina escaping – she was almost certain of that.

For the five minutes it took her to travel from the attic to the back door – the front door made too much noise – Elvina hardly dared to breathe. Even when she was safely outside, she didn't dare relax. She wouldn't feel safe until she had left the village far behind.

She walked through the night, never stopping to rest, so that by the time the sun began to creep over the horizon, she was walking through the outskirts of Sheffield. Tired, cold and overwrought, she stumbled and almost fell, holding onto a low wall to steady herself. Her shoulders shook as great sobs began to wrack her body. She'd left behind everything she knew; she had nowhere to go, very little money, and not the slightest idea what she was going to do now. She'd not been able to think past escaping from home.

The sound of a milk float rattling down the road towards her soon roused Elvina from her self-pity. Swiping angrily at the tears dribbling down her cheeks, Elvina straightened her shoulders and started walking again. When she got to the railway station, she boarded the first train that pulled into the platform, not even caring where the train would take her. As long as it took her away, she didn't care. As long as she never had to go back, nothing else mattered.

CHAPTER ONE
Friday 23RD May 2008

It was ridiculous to be so nauseatingly nervous about meeting her grandfather. Standing in front of the bathroom mirror, Luci Rushden scowled at her pasty-faced reflection and splashed cold water on her cheeks. He was just an old man – a senile old man at that – but knowing that couldn't stop her stomach churning like a hyperactive washing machine. At the back of Luci's mind was the niggling question that had been troubling her since she first discovered that her mother had lied about Luci's grandparents both being dead. Walter was very much alive – but Elvina wasn't, leaving Luci wondering what had made her mother lie. *Something* had happened – that much Luci had gathered from her mother's cousin, Ted – and Walter was the only hope she had of discovering exactly what it was. When he'd suffered a stroke at the end of February – just before Luci had been due to visit him – she'd thought she might never get an answer. Thankfully, he'd made a good recovery, but now Luci was less than twenty-four hours away from getting her answer, she wasn't sure she actually wanted to hear it.

'Right, that's the car loaded up. Are you nearly ready?'

Luci started like a skittish colt when her fiancé Alex poked his head around the bathroom door. 'I guess,' she murmured, forcing a smile to her lips. It took more effort than usual. 'Actually, no. What if this is a really bad idea, Alz? You know what they say about some skeletons being best left in the closet?'

'It's not a bad idea,' Alex said firmly, drawing Luci into his arms. 'Stop worrying – those furrows in your forehead don't suit you, and if you don't stop frowning, you'll make them permanent.'

'And what, you won't want to marry me if I've got frown lines?' Luci shot back, trying – and failing – to keep the tremble out of her voice. She tilted her head to look up at Alex, blinking hard to keep the tears from her eyes. Sometimes, she could hardly believe that Alex had stuck by her after everything she'd put him through. He was so devastatingly handsome, he could have had the pick of the girls; that he'd chosen *her* was something Luci had never been able to understand. But he hadn't really known what he was letting himself in for when he asked her to marry him. Nobody had known.

'Stop it,' Alex said sharply, narrowing his eyes at her. 'I can tell what you're thinking just by the look on your face. How many times do we have to go through this, Luce? I love you just exactly as you are, frown lines and all.'

'It's not the frown lines you should be worried about,' Luci said darkly, pulling away and sidling past Alex out of the bathroom. The trouble was, Alex knew her *too* well. There was a downside to having grown up almost as brother and sister – Alex was one of the few people she couldn't fool with a practiced smile.

'I'm not worried about anything,' Alex retorted, following her into the nursery, where their five-month-old identical twins, Matthew and Theodore, were sleeping, curled up together in one cot like a pair of puppies. 'Except you torturing yourself over what happened last year. You were ill, Luce. And nobody got hurt.'

Luci's shoulders quivered. 'I know,' she murmured, sighing. 'But...' It was only a year since she'd been diagnosed with Bipolar Affective Disorder, after an episode of psychotic mania that could have ended far more badly than it had done. Everyone had been so understanding, so accepting. For a while, Luci had almost come to terms with it all herself. But for the last couple of weeks, the dark thoughts had been creeping in. That nobody had been hurt during that last episode wasn't the point. The point was, they could have been. How was she supposed to trust herself again after what had happened? She leaned over the cot and stroked Matty's cheek with her finger. He woke, blinking trustingly up at her. A sob caught in her throat. She'd been pregnant with the twins back then, but she hadn't given the lives growing inside her a single thought. What kind of mother did that make her?

'But nothing,' Alex said softly, turning her to face him and wiping away her tears with his thumb. 'You've got to stop going over and over what happened, Luce. You're going to make yourself ill again if you carry on.'

'I can't just forget it, Alex. I can't just pretend it didn't happen. I could have...'

Alex put his finger across her lips. 'No,' he said firmly. 'No more "what ifs". I mean it, Luci. You'll make yourself ill, and for what? Thinking about it all the time doesn't change anything.' He drew her back into his arms, resting his chin on the top of her head. After a moment of resistance, Luci snuggled against him, sighing heavily.

'I know you're right,' she said, her voice muffled by his sweater. 'I just wish I could shut my brain off sometimes.'

'If I find the switch, I'll let you know,' Alex teased, pretending to scour her head for the off-button.

A sudden squawk of protest from the cot behind them broke the moment. Pulling away from Alex, Luci bent over the crib as Matty, robbed of his mother's attention, grew red-faced and wind-milled his little fists in outrage, working up to a full blown wail. Scooping him up in her arms, Luci kissed his button nose, feeling the lump growing in her throat. Alex pretended to scowl, prodding Matty lightly in the chest.

'I can see you and me falling out, little man,' he said, laughing as Matty grabbed a tiny fistful of Luci's long hair. 'You're nothing but a little attention seeker – *and* you've got your mummy wrapped around your little finger.' He glanced at the clock on the wall. 'I'll go get their bottles, Luce, and then we should really be making a move. We're late as it is.'

Luci wandered across to stand in front of the window, giving Matty her finger to suck on in lieu of his bottle. It still rankled that, because of the cocktail of medications she took to stabilise her mercurial moods, she couldn't even breastfeed her babies. Though they no longer rooted at her breasts for what she couldn't give them, for the first few weeks it had been hell having to refuse their instinctive search for her milk. Though the health visitor assured her that many women chose not to breastfeed, she somehow still felt less of a mother. The twins were no more dependent on her than they were on Alex.

'I *know* you're hungry,' Luci murmured as Matty grew frustrated with her unrewarding finger and started to cry again. His impatient cries woke Theo, who protested loudly about being left alone in the cot. As their wailing reached a crescendo, Luci put Matty back into the crib and leaned her forehead against the wooden bars as the familiar feeling of helplessness crashed over her. 'I'm sorry,' she whispered, her words inaudible above the babies' crying.

'Have no fear, Daddy's here,' Alex called out as he ran up the stairs and back into the nursery. 'What's all that noise…' The words died on his lips as Luci straightened, her shoulders shuddering.

'I can't even be a proper mother,' she choked out, snatching one of the bottles out of Alex's hands. Picking Matty up again, she carried him through into the master bedroom, kicking the door shut behind her. Matty had finished his bottle and Luci had burped him before Alex ventured in with a fed and content Theo strapped into his baby-carrier-cum-car-seat. He was carrying Matty's carrier in his free hand. Setting both carriers on the floor, he wordlessly took Matty from Luci's arms and strapped him in.

Kneeling in front of Luci, Alex took hold of her hands, squeezing them reassuringly. 'We're going to pretend you didn't say that,' he said gruffly. 'Because we both know it's nonsense.' He waited a beat. 'Right?'

Luci shrugged, pulling her hands away. 'If you say so,' she muttered.

'I do say so.' Alex sighed heavily. 'Listen, if you don't... feel up to meeting Walter, we can always put it off. I can call Ted. He'll understand. There's no pressure. No need for you to put yourself under stress. We can still have the holiday without the visit.'

It would have been easy to put the blame for her low mood on the impending visit, but Luci knew it went deeper than that. She shook her head. 'No. I want to meet him. I'm just...' She ducked her head. 'I'm just... struggling a bit.' She hated having to admit it, hated that she wasn't coping as well as she thought she should be. Never mind that she'd been warned about her susceptibility to postnatal depression, or that the support worker who visited once a week kept reminding her that there was no shame in needing help nor asking for it. There was still the niggling voice at the back of her mind shouting – loudly – that she *should* be able to cope.

'I wish you wouldn't say it like that – like it's some heinous crime,' Alex said softly, cupping her chin and making her look at him. 'You wouldn't go into a hospital and tell someone who had pneumonia that they shouldn't be ill, would you?'

He'd got that one off Rebecca, the support worker. Luci sighed. 'No, of course not,' she said dutifully.

'Well then,' Alex said. 'Stop being so damn hard on yourself.'

'Yes, oh lord and master,' Luci said, smiling weakly.

Alex shook his head. 'I give up,' he said, mock seriously. 'At least you're smiling.' He traced her lips with his finger. 'Come on then. Let's make a move. I'd rather like to get there before it gets dark.'

'I'd be a lot happier if you'd actually tell me where "there" is,' Luci said, narrowing her eyes. 'You know I don't like surprises.'

'You'll find out soon enough,' Alex replied, standing up and grabbing Theo's carrier. 'The whole point of surprises, Luce, is that you *don't* know. I've given you a clue, anyway – it's not far from Walter's nursing home.'

'Which could be anywhere within a twenty mile radius of Bakewell,' Luci muttered. 'As clues go, it's pretty vague.'

Alex smiled. 'Like I said, you'll find out soon enough.' He glanced pointedly at his watch. 'If we ever get there.'

Luci rolled her eyes, picked up Matty's carrier, and followed Alex down the stairs.

***

'You've just driven past the exit for Sheffield,' Luci said, leaning forward and frowning.

'We're not going to Sheffield,' Alex replied.

'No, but when we came to Ted's before, we always came off the motorway at Sheffield,' Luci retorted.

'We're not going to Ted's, either,' Alex said.

'You're being deliberately obtuse now,' Luci grumbled.

'Relax, will you? I know where we're going, *and* how to get there.'

Luci sat back, drumming her fingers against her arm-rest. Tiredness was making her tetchy; she'd missed the nap she usually had when the boys were sleeping in the afternoon, and whilst Matty and Theo had slept for most of the journey, Luci had forced herself to stay awake. She gazed out of the window, the traffic flashing by almost sending her dizzy. Alex pulled across into the left hand lane and began to slow as they passed the sign for Woodall Services.

'Please tell me you haven't booked us into a motorway motel,' Luci begged.

Alex laughed. 'What do you take me for? We're coming off at the next exit.'

Luci sat up sharply as Alex pulled over into the middle lane to allow traffic from the service station to join the motorway. 'I swear that was Dad's car you just let out,' she said, grabbing the arm-rest as Alex swerved swiftly back into the left hand lane.

'Because Jack's the only person in the country with a red Vauxhall Zafira,' Alex said dryly.

'Ha, ha, bloody ha,' Luci retorted. 'The last three letters were the same. How likely is that, huh?'

'You've memorised Jack's license plate?' Alex teased. 'I am impressed.' He pulled off the motorway at Junction 30 and took the first exits on the next two roundabouts. Luci frowned at the road signs.

'Worksop?' she read. 'What's at Worksop?'

'We're not going to Worksop,' Alex replied.

'Argh!' Luci groaned. 'Why won't you just *tell me*?'

'Because that would spoil the surprise,' Alex said, grinning infuriatingly.

'You are seriously testing my patience, Alexander Freeman,' Luci ground out. At another roundabout, Alex turned right. '*Lincoln*? What is this? A magical mystery tour of the Midlands?'

'No. We'll be there in quarter of an hour. Patience never was one of your strong points,' Alex replied. 'I tell you what – close your eyes and I'll tell you when we get there.'

'Alex...'

'Indulge me. Please.'

'This is crazy,' Luci muttered, but Alex was making puppy-dog eyes at her and after a moment she dutifully closed her eyes. She was asleep within minutes, lulled by the rhythmic purr of the engine and the sound of the twins' tiny snores.

***

'Wakey wakey,' Alex whispered, his mouth close to Luci's ear. 'Magical mystery tour's over. We're here.'

'Huh?' Luci opened her eyes and blinked drowsily. 'Where's here?' She stretched, knuckling the sleep out of her eyes. Disorientated, it took her a minute to take in their surroundings. Alex had parked the car in front of a two-storey lodge-type building, in the shelter of a cluster of trees. There was a red Vauxhall Zafira parked alongside.

'Surprise,' Alex said softly.

'Where are we?' Luci asked weakly. 'Alex, please tell me we're not where I think we are!'

Alex looked away. 'CenterParcs Sherwood Forest,' he said. 'Luci...' He tried to take her hand, but she snatched it away, curling her knees up to her chest and wrapping her arms tightly around them.

'How could you do this?' she whimpered. 'A surprise, you said. This isn't a surprise. It's like waking up in the middle of a *nightmare*!'

'It was your dad's idea,' Alex said. 'And Rebecca agreed that it was a *good* idea to get you to maybe face some of your demons. Just to prove to you that what happened last year doesn't have to set the trend for everything; that you can have a good time without things spiralling out of control.'

'And did you stop to think about what you were doing? What if... what if the staff remember me, Alex? What if they look at me and think, "Oh, look, there's that crazy woman that abducted her brother and sister, went swimming in her clothes and drove away from here wearing nothing but a bathrobe"?' Luci cried, hysteria in her voice. She was shaking so hard, her teeth were rattling together, and her chest felt so tight it was impossible to breathe normally.

'Calm down,' Alex pleaded. 'Luci, please. Look at me. *Look at me*. Nobody's going to remember. It's over a year since. Hundreds of people come here. The staff aren't going to remember one person.' As Luci continued to panic, frantically trying to draw air into her lungs, Alex reached across her to pop open the glove box. It was months since she'd had a full-blown panic attack, but there was still a supply of paper bags in the glove box. Alex shook one open and forced it over Luci's mouth. 'Come on. *Breathe*. Nice deep breaths. You know the drill, Luce.'

Tears rolled down Luci's cheeks as her breathing gradually steadied. Alex crumpled the paper bag and hurled it out of the car window, cursing under his breath.

'I'm sorry,' he said, brushing Luci's hair back off her face. 'I thought it might help to come here, to give you something positive to think about instead of all the bad stuff. We don't have to stay. I'll find us somewhere else.'

'We've got an audience,' Luci murmured, jerking her head towards the lodge. Her father had come out onto the porch, followed by the rest of hers and Alex's complicated family. It took a lot of explaining to strangers, because Alex had been Luci's step-brother long before he became her fiancé. His mother, Ruth, was married to Luci's father, Jack, and they shared three half-siblings – thirteen-year-old Danny, and nine-year-old twins Zack and Zoe. But that was only the half of it. Ruth's brother Mike and his wife Hannah were also out on the porch, their adopted son, seven-year-old Charlie, standing between them. Luci was Charlie's birth-mother, a fact that the little boy had only recently learned. That they were all there, watching, only made the situation worse. Luci buried her head in her hands, feeling sick.

'I'll sort it,' Alex said quietly. 'You stay here.' But Jack was already striding towards the car; before Alex could get out, Jack had opened the passenger-side door.

'Luci, sweetheart, what's wrong?' Jack demanded. 'Are you ill?'

Luci raised her head. 'I'm allergic to CenterParcs,' she said hoarsely. 'Do me a favour, Dad. Next time you have a good idea, could you actually think it through, first?'

'We're not staying, Jack,' Alex cut in. 'I'll have to find us somewhere else to stay.'

'It's half-term,' Jack pointed out. He crouched down to Luci's level. 'The kids have been really looking forward to this, sweetheart. Think of it as a chance to do things properly. What's the worst that can happen, hey? It can't possibly be any worse than what happened before, now can it?'

Luci sighed. 'Thanks for that, Dad. Was that you trying to make me feel better, or worse?'

'Can we go to the adventure playground now, Dad?' Zack demanded, running up to the car. 'You said we could once Alex and Luci got here, and they're here now.'

Jack straightened. 'Give us chance to find our way around, buddy. We've got a whole week to explore,' he said, placing a restraining hand on Zack's shoulder.

'But we already know our way around. We explored loads last time!' Zack protested, peering around his father's legs. 'Will *you* take us, Luci? This is near the lodge we stayed in last time, isn't it? I remember it, don't you?'

Luci glanced at Zack's eager face, marvelling at the way he seemed to have disregarded all the bad bits of the impromptu 'holiday' last April. 'It was somewhere around here, yeah,' she heard herself saying.

'So can we go? *Please*, Luci. Pretty please with cherries on top!' Zack was hoping from one foot to the other impatiently.

Luci sighed. 'Oh, hell, why not.' She scrubbed her hands over her face. 'What's the worst that can happen?'

Zack paused to consider that, a cheeky grin lighting up his face. 'It's okay, Luce,' he said earnestly. 'I don't think you're going to go swimming in your clothes again, are you? 'Cos you were poorly then, and you're better now.' He pivoted, beckoning Charlie and Zoe. '*C'mon*, or it'll be *dark*.'

Alex caught Luci's arm as she made to get out of the car. 'We don't have to stay, not if you don't want to,' he said.

'I think maybe we do,' Luci said, drawing in a steadying breath. 'Maybe I need to make it up to the kids before I can start forgiving myself.' She hesitated. 'I just wish you'd warned me. Maybe if it hadn't been such a shock…'

'If I'd warned you, we wouldn't be here,' Alex replied.

Luci smiled ruefully. 'True.' As Zack bobbed impatiently in front of the car, she got out, running her fingers through her hair. 'All right, I'm *coming*,' she said, smiling down at Charlie as he slipped his hand into hers. The scene could easily have been from thirteen months ago, with one difference. This time it was Zack who was running wildly ahead – not Luci.

CHAPTER TWO

Breakfast time turned into a battle-zone as the kids bickered over the activities they wanted to try out. Danny declared himself 'too old for dumb kid's stuff', and Zack and Zoe almost came to blows in the battle between Laser Combat and Falconry. After less than five hours sleep – Matty and Theo hadn't taken well to the disruption to their routine – Luci was more than glad not to have to get involved. She and Alex were due to meet Ted at Walter's nursing home at ten. She excused herself from the breakfast table as Jack launched an attack of his own.

'Quiet!' he roared. 'Right, first things first. Daniel, you are part of this family and you *will* participate, whether you like it or not. Second, we're here for a week, so there's plenty of time for *everyone* to choose an activity. The world is not going to come to an end tomorrow. Since Charlie's the youngest, I think he should pick first – and before you start, Zacharias, you'll get your chance soon enough.'

'How come Luci and Alex don't have to stick around for this charade?' Danny grumbled. 'They're part of "this family", too.'

Luci closed the bedroom door and leaned back against it, blocking out Jack's reply and the chaos downstairs. Though the trip to the adventure playground yesterday had gone without a hitch, the thought of playing happy families for the rest of the week made Luci's head ache. So much for the quality time with Alex and the babies that she'd been banking on. Alex had even taken the twins out in their double buggy whilst she was in the shower; sometimes his ideas of 'helping' were the antithesis of hers.

Sighing, Luci sat down on the end of the bed and lifted a metal fireproof box out of her suitcase. The box had once belonged to her grandmother Medora, Walter's late wife. Luci had found it seven years ago, in the chimney breast in the attic, hidden there by her mother – who by then had been dead seven years herself. Besides the locket that Elvina had always worn, the box was full of old photographs, diaries and letters written to Medora by her sister Violet. It was a long shot, but Luci was hoping that showing Walter the photos might help to jog his memory. Since his stroke, the dementia had worsened. Ted had warned Luci that Walter might not even understand who she was.

Luci flipped the catches on the box and lifted out the photos, shuffling the ones that showed Walter and Medora together to the top. Her gaze lingered on one photo from 1952 – from her mother's Christening. It was that photo that had started Luci's search for answers about her mother's mysterious past – because Elvina had never once mentioned that she'd had a twin sister.

'All set?'

Luci flinched at the sound of Alex's voice from the doorway. She closed the box and dragged her fingers through her hair in a vain attempt to tame the wild chestnut curls she'd inherited from her mother.

'Do I look okay?' she asked anxiously, frowning down at her jeans and checked shirt. 'Maybe I should've packed something smarter. I don't want him to think I haven't made an effort.'

'You're meeting your grandfather, not going for a job interview,' Alex pointed out. 'You look fine. Come on. I've put the boys in the car already. We don't want to be late.'

'No,' Luci agreed dutifully, tucking the box under her arm and following Alex down the stairs.

***

'I feel sick,' Luci murmured as Alex pulled into a parking space in front of Walter's nursing home. Ted was already waiting, sitting on a wooden bench by the main entrance. He smiled and waved; Luci didn't wave back.

'You'll be fine,' Alex said firmly. 'But I've been thinking. Maybe I should take the boys down to the river and feed the ducks or something. It might be a bit much for your granddad if we all go in. It's more important that you see him and get to know him.'

'Maybe.' Luci unfastened her seatbelt as Ted approached the car. He looked very dapper in a dark steel-coloured suit that almost matched the colour of his slicked back hair. His blue eyes were crinkled in a smile as he opened Luci's door.

'I got here a little early and went in to see Uncle Walter,' he said. 'He seems to be having one of his better days.'

'That's good,' Luci murmured, not sure whether she meant it.

'I'm going to take the boys off for a bit, rather than overwhelming Walter,' Alex said. 'Give me a call when you're done, okay?' He leaned across and kissed Luci lightly on the cheek. 'Relax,' he murmured quietly so Ted couldn't hear. 'He's your grandfather, not an axe murderer.'

Legacy of Lies

Luci forced a smile. Walter might well be a harmless old man, but that didn't explain why her mother had run away from home at sixteen and claimed that her parents were dead. Ted had been deliberately evasive about what had happened almost forty years ago. Luci was sure he was hiding something.

Her stomach was churning, threatening to reject the slice of dry toast she'd forced down for breakfast, as she followed Ted into the nursing home and along the rabbit-warren of corridors that led to Walter's room.

The old man was sitting in an armchair in front of the window, looking out over an impressive vista of Derbyshire moors. He was smaller than Luci had expected him to be; he appeared almost shrivelled, like a grape on the verge of becoming a raisin. His hair was white and wispy; the hands gripping the arms of the chair were gnarled and liver-spotted. Luci faltered in the doorway, shocked by her grandfather's appearance. Somehow, despite what Ted had told her about Walter's failing health, she had expected him to be different – to at least bear some resemblance to the man she'd imagined him to be – a man capable of causing his daughter to flee and never speak his name again.

'Uncle Walter?' Ted spoke loudly and slowly, as if to a small child, sitting down in the chair opposite Walter. The old man reluctantly turned his gaze from the window. 'This is Luci. Remember, I told you she was coming? Elvina's daughter.'

'Elvina?' Walter's face lit up as he peered short-sightedly past Ted.

Luci stepped forward. 'Elvina's *daughter*,' she corrected.

'Where's Elvina?' the old man demanded. 'You told me Elvina was coming!'

'Some chance of that,' Luci muttered, sitting down on the edge of the bed whilst Ted tried to placate the old man.

'I told you, Uncle,' Ted said. 'Elvina was involved in an accident. She died some years ago. But Luci's come to see you instead.'

'You said *Elvina* was coming,' Walter repeated petulantly, reminding Luci of a child having a tantrum.

'My mother jumped in front of a train fifteen years ago,' Luci snapped. 'She won't be coming.'

Walter's eyes widened and filled with tears. 'She promised,' he cried. 'She *promised*.'

'To come and see you?' Luci asked sharply. 'When? When she ran away? But she didn't, did she? She told me that you were dead.'

'No!' Walter tried to rise to his feet, but soon fell back; the stroke had all but robbed him of the ability to walk, and he looked pathetic as he howled his frustration.

'Why would she say that?' Luci pressed. 'What did you do to her to make her run away and tell everyone that you were dead?'

'Luci,' Ted began, a warning note in his voice.

'I'm only asking,' Luci muttered.

'She's a good girl really. It isn't her fault. I had to let her go,' Walter said, but it was as if he was talking to himself. He was staring out of the window again. Luci leaned forward, ready to question him, but Ted cut in before she could speak.

'Luci's brought something to show you, Uncle,' he said. 'A box of Aunt Medora's things.' He nodded to Luci to bring the box over.

At the mention of his wife's name, Walter looked around. Luci perched on the arm of Ted's chair and flipped the catches on the box, opening the lid. With the box balanced on her knee, she pulled out the christening and wedding photos, offering them to her grandfather. He took them with a trembling hand, tracing his fingers over the faces of his wife and daughters. After a moment, he looked directly at Luci, startling her when he reached out and snatched the box from her hands.

'Where did you get this?' he demanded. 'Who gave it to you?' Grabbing handfuls of black and white photographs, he allowed them to cascade to the floor, along with the bundle of letters tied with a ribbon.

'I found it. My mother hid it before she... died,' Luci said, glancing anxiously at Ted.

'You stole it!' Walter cried, banging his fist against the chair arm. He tipped the box out onto his lap, flipping to the back of each of the diaries in turn, growing increasingly agitated. 'Where is it? What have you done with it?'

'With what?' Luci asked in bewilderment, shrinking back as Walter lunged forward in his chair and grabbed her arm, his grip surprisingly strong.

'You've no right!' the old man shrieked. 'Where is it? Give it to me!' His nails dug into Luci's arm, breaking the skin. As blood welled, Ted intervened, easing Walter's fingers from Luci's arm and forcing his uncle back.

'Do you think you could find your way back to reception, Luci?' Ted asked quietly. 'I think we could all do with a cup of tea. Ask for a tray.'

Luci stood up shakily, backing out of the room. Out in the corridor, she leaned back against the wall, drawing in a deep, steadying breath. Walter was still shouting, despite Ted's attempts to calm him. Luci pulled a tissue from her pocket and dabbed at the scratches on her arm. Walter's fingers had left vivid marks. For a frail old man, he was surprisingly strong. And if he was strong now, after having a stroke... Luci wondered if her mother had run away because Walter was violent.

The care-worker who came out of the kitchen when Luci rang the bell at reception offered to bring the tea-tray through to Walter's room, but Luci declined the offer. She was in no hurry to go back. 'I'll wait and take it myself,' she said, sitting down on the edge of a sagging sofa in the lobby. Her heart was still hammering in her chest, as Walter's words ran on a loop through her mind. What had he been looking for? What was missing from Medora's box that had worked the old man into such a frenzy?

'Here you are, lovey,' the care-worker said brightly, emerging again from the kitchen with a rattling tea-tray. Luci stood up and took it from her, hoping the rotund woman wouldn't notice that the tray rattled more violently in her trembling hands.

Walter was settled back in his chair, quiet and calm, when Luci returned with the tea-tray. Ted was kneeling on the floor, gathering up the photos and letters that Walter had spilt out of the box.

'Tea's up, Uncle Walter,' Ted said brightly, nodding towards a small table where Luci could put the tray down.

As Walter turned his gaze from the window, all the colour drained from his already wan face, and a rasping gasp ripped from his lips. His hands came up to cover his mouth, and he stared at Luci as if seeing a ghost.

'Uncle?' Ted stood up sharply, taking the tray from Luci's hands.

'It wasn't my fault!' Walter cried. 'I had no choice.'

Luci took a step backwards as Ted quickly poured out a cup of tea and offered it to his uncle. With a sweep of his arm, Walter knocked the cup to the floor.

'Tea!' he shrieked. 'I don't want tea at a time like this!' He held his hands out towards Luci. 'Forgive me,' he begged. 'I only agreed because there was no other way. It was for the best. Otherwise...'

His voice cracked and tears dribbled down his cheeks. 'It was happening again, but I couldn't let you go to one of those places. What I did, what I let them do, it was out of *love!*'

Ted glanced at Luci. 'He gets confused sometimes,' he said. 'I think maybe we should try this another day. Why don't you go and wait in the lobby?'

Luci didn't hesitate. As she left the room, Walter cried out after her, a desperate, raw edge to his voice. 'No!' he wailed. 'Izzy! Don't go! IZZY!'

Luci stopped in the doorway. 'Izzy?' she repeated.

'Wait for me in the lobby,' Ted said quickly. 'He's confused, that's all.' But as Luci turned again, she noticed that Ted had pressed a call button to summon one of the staff.

***

Ten minutes passed before Ted joined Luci on the sagging sofa in the lobby. His smile was strained as he handed her the box of her grandmother's things. 'He gets so easily confused,' he said. 'Since the stroke, he's been deteriorating fast. I'm sorry you had to see him like that. I was hoping... well, I suppose I was hoping you might get a glimpse of the man he used to be.'

Luci picked at the scratches on her arm. 'I think I did,' she said. 'I think I know why my mother ran away.'

'No,' Ted said quickly. 'No, Luci. He was never violent. I never once saw him lift a hand to strike anyone, let alone your mother or Isabella. He wasn't like that.'

'Then why did she run away?' Luci asked.

'I don't know,' Ted said, sighing. 'It was after Isabella died...'

'He thought I was her, didn't he? He thought I was Isabella,' Luci said. 'He must be *really* confused if he thinks his dead daughter could pay him a visit.' She paused. 'What did he mean when he said "forgive me"? Forgive him what? Isabella died from T.B., didn't she? Why would he want her to forgive him? He didn't infect her with it, did he?'

'He's just a confused old man, Luci. I don't think he means anything – or even knows what he's saying most of the time,' Ted said hastily. 'Although...'

'What?' Luci prompted when Ted fell silent.

'It's not the first time he's said those things. He had a home-help when he was still living semi-independently last year; she looked a little like Isabella, and he became very distressed then. I don't think he ever got over losing her.'

'Why would he want her to forgive him, though? What did he do?' Luci pressed.

'Perhaps he felt guilty for sending her away to recover, and not being there when she died,' Ted suggested. He smiled. 'I shouldn't worry about it, Luci. It most probably means nothing.'

'Did he tell you what he was looking for in the box?' Luci asked.

'He kept asking where "the other one" was, but what he was looking for is anybody's guess,' Ted said. 'I'm sorry. I know you were hoping he could answer your questions. But you're here for a week, right? We can try again another day. He *can* be incredibly lucid sometimes. It's just a matter of catching him on the right day at the right moment.'

'Yeah, I guess,' Luci said dubiously, unable to shake the feeling that Ted wasn't being entirely honest with her. He had a shifty look in his eyes that reminded her of the way her mother used to look whenever she or her twin brother Luke asked any questions about Elvina's past. She sighed, fishing her mobile phone out of her jeans pocket to call Alex.

'We're done here,' she said the moment he picked up.

'How did it go?' Alex asked.

'It didn't,' Luci said flatly. 'It was a complete waste of time.' She hung up before Alex could say anything else. Ted smiled again – but the smile didn't come close to reaching his eyes. He was hiding something. Luci would have put money on it.

CHAPTER THREE

Whilst Alex and the boys snored in synchronized oblivion, Luci slipped silently out of bed, tired of watching the minutes on the digital alarm clock ticking slowly towards dawn. Sleep had danced tantalizingly out of reach since her visit to Walter, three days ago; his words seemed to be forever churning around in her mind. Though both Alex and Ted had tried to reassure her that the old man had just been confused and rambling, Luci wasn't convinced. Stooping, she retrieved Medora's box from the suitcase and padded softly down the stairs into the kitchen.

After flicking the kettle on, Luci sat down at the table and emptied the contents of the box, sorting the photos and letters into separate piles and arranging the diaries in date order. For what felt like the millionth time since Walter's outburst, she scoured the empty box for signs of a secret hiding place that she might have missed. Nothing. No false bottom or hidden partition. Sighing, Luci shoved everything back inside – everything but a picture of Walter in his RAF uniform, circa 1944.

'What were you looking for, Granddad?' she asked the serious-faced, handsome young pilot. 'What did you mean, "the other one"?' She rested her chin on her upturned palms, as if staring at Walter's photograph might somehow reveal the answers to her.

She was still sitting at the kitchen table, nursing a third mug of coffee, when Alex came down to prepare the boys' bottles for their six o'clock feed. He didn't seem surprised to find her there; but then it was where he'd found her *every* morning since her visit to Walter. He wrapped his arms around her shoulders from behind, resting his chin on the top of her head.

'You need to sleep,' he chided gently. 'It's been *days,* Luce. And you *know* what happens when you don't sleep.'

Luci sighed. 'Mania?' She laughed bitterly. 'Right now, I'd gladly *pay* for mania.'

'You don't mean that,' Alex protested.

'I do, Alex,' Luci retorted. 'Believe me, I *do*. I'm tired of feeling like I'm downing in quicksand. If I thought it would make a difference, I'd gladly inject coffee directly into my *brain*.'

'Maybe, when we get home, you should make an appointment to see Dr Fielding,' Alex suggested tentatively. 'If your medication isn't doing the trick...'

'Oh, yeah, blame it on the meds,' Luci muttered. 'But what if it isn't down to the meds? What if the problem's *me*, Alex? What then?'

Alex sighed. 'We've talked about this, Luce,' he said resignedly. 'You *know* it's a balancing act getting the medication right.'

Luci pulled away from Alex's embrace. 'I *hate* it,' she snapped. 'I hate that everything comes down to this, this *balancing act* between mania and depression. It rules my life, Alex – it rules my life, and I *want my life back*. I just want to be *normal* again.' Standing up, she snatched the bottles up off the kitchen counter and started spooning in the milk formula. Her hands were shaking; more of the white powder ended up on the counter than in the bottles.

'Come on, let me do it,' Alex said gently, gripping her wrists to stop her. When he smiled, the smile didn't reach his eyes, which were shadowed with worry. 'What *is* normal, anyway, huh? I love you just as you are. I wouldn't want you any other way.'

'Not everything's about what you want, Alex,' Luci said wearily.

'You're exhausted, Luce. You can't think straight when you're so tired. You need to sleep. Go on back to bed – please. You're worrying me,' Alex pleaded.

'Heaven forbid,' Luci muttered. Alex shot her a look, and she sighed. 'All right. I'll go.'

'I'll bring the boys down here, so we don't disturb you,' Alex said, shaking the bottles hard to mix the formula. 'And then I'll take them out later, so you can get some proper rest.'

'Proper rest?' Luci repeated dubiously.

'Just try, please, for me?' Alex set the bottles down on the counter and squeezed Luci's shoulders. 'You'll feel better for it. I'll even tuck you in.'

Luci forced her lips into the ghost of a smile. 'How can I possibly refuse?' she murmured.

Alex kissed the top of her head and took her by the hand, leading her up the stairs like an obedient child. He stood over her until she climbed into bed, and tucked the duvet up under her chin.

'Now *sleep*,' he commanded, mock-sternly. He bent over the cot, lifted the boys out and strapped them into their carriers. 'Mummy's going to have a nice long rest,' he whispered conspiratively, before closing the bedroom door firmly on his way out.

Luci rolled over so her back was to the mocking display of the digital alarm clock, and curled her knees up to her chest. She sighed heavily. Sunlight was streaming through the thin material of the curtains, making sleep ever increasingly unlikely. Rolling back onto her back, Luci pushed herself up onto her elbows and pounded the pillows irritably before falling back against them. Her eyes felt gritty and sore with tiredness; she even tried counting sheep as a last resort, but sleep still danced tauntingly out of reach. With another heavy sigh, Luci sat up and opened the bottom drawer of the bedside chest, pulling out her vanity case. Inside a concealed pocket was the box of sleeping tablets Dr Fielding, her consultant, had prescribed a month ago. Alex didn't even know about them; Luci had been resolute in her determination not to have to resort to taking them. Now, though, her resolve was faltering. Alex was right on one thing: she *needed* to sleep. Her fingers trembled as she pushed one of the tiny pills out of the foil and tipped it into her mouth, washing it down with a gulp of water. It felt like admitting defeat; yet another aspect of her life that she was handing over control of to chemicals. Sinking back against the pillows, she closed her eyes and miserably waited for the cotton-wool oblivion she always associated with sleeping pills. It wasn't long in coming.

***

'Feel better?' Alex asked, sitting down on the edge of the bed and putting a mug of tea on the bedside chest. 'The tea might be a bit cold. I was beginning to think you'd never wake up. Every time I've come up, you've been dead to the world'

Luci blinked blearily up at him, still heavily under the influence of the sleeping pill. 'Huh?' she mumbled. 'How long have I been asleep?'

'Hours,' Alex replied, smiling. 'I told you you were exhausted.'

'Yeah,' Luci murmured, knuckling sleep out of her eyes. 'I had the weirdest dream. Mum was here, rooting through Medora's box, and she was trying to tell me something, but she was speaking in tongues and I couldn't understand her. It was something about Walter, and Isabella.'

'That's because you've been thinking of nothing else for days. Forget about it,' Alex said. 'You must be hungry. Jack's gone for take-out for us all.'

'I got the feeling that it was important, what Mum was trying to tell me. She seemed really agitated,' Luci said. 'I think I'll go and see Walter again. Maybe that was what Mum was trying to tell me to do.'

'It was a *dream*, Luce,' Alex said cautiously. 'It's just your subconscious talking; you've been so preoccupied these last few days, it's no *wonder* you dreamed about it too.' He handed her the mug. 'Drink. And then you could jump in the shower before Jack gets back with the food.'

Luci accepted the mug with a grudging smile. 'All right. But I'm still going to visit Walter again tomorrow. You and the boys can come with me.'

Alex sighed. 'Shouldn't we check with Ted first? He might be busy.'

'I'm not even *telling* Ted,' Luci retorted. 'He's hiding something. I want to visit my grandfather without Ted being there to keep him quiet. It's the only way I can get to the truth.'

Alex opened his mouth, paused, and closed it again, as if thinking better of whatever it was he was going to say. 'All right. Tomorrow it is, then.' He bent to kiss Luci's forehead. 'I suppose it would be nice for Walter to meet his great-grandsons. I just hope Ted doesn't think we're being funny.'

'Why should he?' Luci asked, frowning. 'Walter's *my* grandfather. I shouldn't have to make an appointment to visit him!'

Alex sighed again. 'Of course not,' he agreed, but Luci got the feeling he was only on a mission to pacify her. She took a gulp from the mug, pulled a face and spat the cold tea back into the mug.

'I'll pass on the tea,' she said, sliding off the bed and grabbing the towel that was hanging on the back of the bedroom door. 'I'll just have a quick shower, okay?'

'Sure. I'll give you a shout when Jack gets back,' Alex said, following her out of the bedroom. Luci paused in the doorway of the bathroom, watching him walk downstairs. As she closed the bathroom door, Ruth's voice drifted up to her.

'Is Luci okay?' her stepmother asked Alex.

Alex lowered his voice, but Luci still heard his reply. 'God knows,' he said, sounding resigned. 'Apparently, we're going to visit Walter again tomorrow. She's got another bee in her bonnet about him and thinks Ted's hiding something.'

Luci leaned against the bathroom door, squeezing her eyes tightly shut. So much for Alex's pseudo-supportive act. He was just trying to pacify her. She moved towards the shower, then stopped, flinging the bathroom door open again. When Alex shouted up that her father was back with the food, Luci ignored him. His footsteps sounded on the stairs, but when he poked his head around the door, Luci was feigning sleep. He closed the door quietly, and Luci rolled back over onto her back. For a moment, she hesitated, then reached into the drawer for the packet of sleeping tablets. One tiny pill ensured that she wouldn't have to look at Alex until the next morning.

***

'You needn't bother coming,' Luci said testily as she finished fastening Matty and Theo, both asleep in their carriers, into the back of the car. 'I can manage. I'm sure you'd rather be off doing Laser Combat with the kids than traipsing to a nursing home with me.'

'*What?*' Alex stared at Luci as if she'd sprouted a second head.

'You heard,' Luci snapped.

'What's got into you this morning?' Alex asked. 'You've been stomping around like a bear with a sore head since you got up! If that's what too much sleep does to you...'

'It's not too much sleep that puts *a bee in my bonnet*,' Luci retorted sharply.

Alex sighed. 'Oh, come on, Luce, it's just a turn of phrase. It doesn't *mean* anything.'

'If it doesn't mean anything, why did you say it?' Luci demanded.

Alex wrapped his arms around her from behind. 'I told you, it's just a turn of phrase; you know, one of those things that people say without thinking about it.'

'Alex, I'm not stupid. You told Ruth that I'd got *another* bee in my bonnet. You think I'm getting carried away, like I've done before, and you think it's a waste of time. That's okay. You can think what you want. But I'd rather you told me to my face. And I certainly wouldn't want you thinking that you've got to traipse around with me, when obviously you don't want to.'

'I'm coming with you,' Alex said firmly, prising the car keys out of Luci's hand.

Luci glowered at him, but she didn't argue. She climbed into the passenger seat and stared stonily out of the window for the duration of the journey. The moment Alex stopped the car in the car park of the nursing home, she jumped out and hauled the double buggy out of the boot, refusing Alex's help to fix the carriers onto the frame. 'I can manage,' she snapped, pushing the buggy ahead of him into the nursing home.

There was no one at the Reception Desk, but Luci didn't bother ringing the bell, just pushed the buggy down the corridor to Walter's room. The door was open; the old man was sitting by the window, as if he hadn't moved since the first time Luci had seen him.

'Granddad? It's me, Luci. Do you remember? I came the other day, with Ted,' Luci said, pushing the buggy towards her grandfather. Walter started at the sound of her voice, turning to look at her with an expression of bewilderment on his face. His gaze took in the buggy, and then came to rest on Alex as he walked into the room. Luci smiled at the old man. 'I've brought my fiancé, Alex, to meet you, Granddad, and these two little monkeys are Matty and Theo – your great-grandsons.'

'You!' Walter cried, pointing a shaking finger at Alex. 'How dare you come here, as bold as brass, like you've done nothing wrong, after what you did? I should call the police on you!'

'No, Granddad, Alex is with me. He's not done *anything*,' Luci explained patiently. She bent over the buggy and unstrapped Theo, who'd woken at the sound of Walter's raised voice. 'Can I sit down?' she asked, not waiting for an answer before sitting down in the chair opposite Walter, with Theo on her knee.

Forgetting his tirade against Alex, Walter turned his stare on the baby. Sudden anguish crept across his face and tears began dribbling down his cheeks. 'They let you keep him,' he whispered. 'They let you keep him and they didn't tell me! I would have had you back. I didn't *want* to send you away. They said it was for the best, and I didn't know what else to do.' He stretched out his hand towards Theo, and smiled a watery smile when the baby clutched his tiny fist around the old man's finger. 'Forgive me,' he whispered. 'Please forgive me!' His voice rose in anguish as he gazed imploringly at Luci, his shoulders shuddering with grief.

'Of course I forgive you,' Luci said, shooting a puzzled look at Alex. Whatever it was that was upsetting Walter, it was better to pacify him than question him.

But her words didn't pacify her grandfather. Walter's distress only increased, his sobs shaking his thin shoulders pitifully. 'I should have stood up to them,' he cried. 'I lost both my girls because of *them*.' He eased his finger out of Theo's grasp and brought the finger to his lips. 'But you're here now. You're here now, my darling Izzy.' He smiled again, through the tears.

Izzy? Luci frowned. 'Granddad, I'm not Isabella. I'm Luci. Elvina's daughter, remember? Isabella *died*, a long time ago.'

Walter's face crumpled. 'Dead?' he cried. 'No! Oh no, NO! Please, *no*.' He covered his face with his hands, tears dribbling between his fingers. As Luci watched helplessly, he seemed to crumple in on himself, rocking back and forth, still moaning a long, drawn out 'nooooo'.

'Granddad?' Luci handed Theo to Alex and touched Walter's shoulder. He pushed her away with more strength than she would have thought he had. She stumbled back as Walter overbalanced and tumbled to the floor, landing in an undignified heap and letting out a howl of pain.

'Granddad?' Luci repeated, bending over the old man. She made to help him up, but Alex put out a hand to stop her.

'He's hurt, Luce. We shouldn't move him, just in case.' His gaze travelled around the room, searching for a call or panic button. There was a pull-cord hanging at one side of the bed; in two long strides, Alex crossed the room and yanked the cord. Moments later, footsteps could be heard along the corridor and a care-worker came rushing in.

'What's happened?' she demanded, looking from Luci and Alex to Walter lying prone on the floor. 'I'm sorry, but who exactly are you, and what are you doing here?'

'I'm Walter's granddaughter,' Luci snapped. 'He fell; I think he's hurt himself. Are you going to stand there asking questions or are you going to get some help for him?'

The woman scowled and went to the door. 'I need some help in here,' she yelled, with a voice like a fog-horn. Turning back into the room, she pressed her lips into a thin line of disapproval. 'Can you wait in the lobby, please,' she said – an order barely disguised as a request. Luci opened her mouth to protest, but Alex caught her eye and shook his head, strapping a protesting Theo back into the buggy and pushing it towards the door.

'Let them do their jobs, Luce. We'll only be in the way,' he said, and after a moment's hesitation, Luci followed him. In the lobby, Alex sat down on the sagging couch and gave Theo his dummy to quieten the baby. As soon as Theo fell silent, his twin woke and started crying. Alex groaned as a passing care-worker frowned in disapproval. 'I'll take them outside, push the buggy around a bit and see if I can get them off to sleep again,' Alex said, squeezing Luci's shoulder. She was gazing down the corridor where Walter's room was, anxiety etched across her face. Alex hesitated. 'Do you think I should call Ted and tell him what's happened?'

'It's not my fault he fell,' Luci snapped defensively.

'I didn't say it was,' Alex protested.

'No, but that's what *they* think, and what Ted will think,' Luci retorted.

'Don't be daft,' Alex said mildly. 'I'll call Ted, anyway, tell him what happened.'

Luci shrugged, gnawing on her thumbnail as a care-worker came rushing out of Walter's room and snatched up the phone behind the Reception Desk.

'Ambulance, please,' she said urgently into the handset.

Luci's stomach lurched and she stumbled to her feet, following Alex out of the building. 'Let's go,' she said, panic in her voice.

'What?' Alex turned and stared at her.

'I want to go, now,' Luci said, looking suddenly close to tears.

Alex hesitated, then shrugged. 'Let me call Ted first, and then we'll go, okay? You be putting the boys in the car while I ring.'

Luci nodded numbly, fumbling with the catches on the buggy. Alex walked away to make the call; he came back frowning.

'I had to leave a message,' Alex said, sliding in to the driver's seat. 'He was on another call.'

'Probably *them*,' Luci murmured, 'telling him I walked in without telling anyone and assaulted Walter.'

'Don't be so melodramatic,' Alex said, fighting to keep a straight face.

'Just drive, Alex, please,' Luci said tightly. Her hands were shaking as she clasped them in her lap, and there was a sick feeling of dread in her stomach. Alex started the engine and pulled out of the car park onto the main road.

'Calm down,' he said softly. 'Walter'll be okay. And you didn't do anything. He fell, that's all. It could have happened whether we were there or not.'

'But I was there. And if I hadn't been, he... he wouldn't have been in such a state,' Luci said, her voice trembling. 'If... if he's not all right, they're going to blame me, anyway. For harassing him, or... or something.' Suddenly, tears were spilling down her cheeks. Matty and Theo, picking up on her distress, started wailing, and Luci buried her head in her hands. Alex pulled in to the side of the road, turned off the engine and drew Luci towards him. She sagged in his embrace, sobbing pitifully. 'I just wanted to talk to him, that's all, to find out about Mum and Isabella, and I know… I know you think I was reading too much into everything he said last time, but I just wanted to know, that's all. I wanted to know what made Mum like she was, because… because I don't want to be like her. I don't want to do to Matty and Theo what she did to me and Luke, but what… what if it's genetic, what if it's like some family curse…?'

'Shhh,' Alex soothed, smoothing Luci's hair back off her face. 'There's no need to get yourself so worked up. For what it's worth, I don't think you're a bit like Elvina.'

'But I'm like my grandmother,' Luci whispered. Medora had died in a psychiatric hospital, suffering from manic exhaustion. Medora's diagnosis of manic depression was something that Elvina had kept secret, but her final words to Luci had been full of fear – the fear that Luci had inherited more than just a casual resemblance to her grandmother. Elvina had spoken of the fire in Luci's eyes – the same fire that Elvina had once told Ted that she had seen in her mother's eyes. That her illness was in some way genetic was something that had troubled Luci since her psychiatrist had first given her a diagnosis. Already she feared that Charlie's reckless streak was more than just 'pushing the boundaries'. If Elvina had seen fire in Luci's eyes, then Luci had seen it in Charlie's, too. Matty and Theo were too young – but already Luci often found herself staring into their trusting eyes for some early sign – and she could remember her own mother staring at her and Luke in the same way.

'Stop it,' Alex chided. 'You're upsetting the boys. They don't like seeing their mummy crying her eyes out.'

'Sorry.' Luci gulped and pulled away from Alex's embrace, scrubbing her cheeks with the sleeve of her sweater. Twisting in her seat, she smiled weakly at the twins and tried to pacify them with their dummies. 'Mummy's just being silly,' she said, her voice shaking ever so slightly. It seemed as though both boys were regarding her suspiciously, their blue eyes wide as they blinked at her.

'All right now?' Alex asked, squeezing Luci's thigh.

Luci shrugged, returning her thumbnail to her mouth and gnawing anxiously. She didn't speak again for the rest of the journey back to CenterParcs.

Legacy of Lies

The holiday lodge was empty, the rest of the family out enjoying themselves. After settling Matty and Theo down for a nap, Luci lay down on the bed and curled her knees up to her chest. Alex brought her a mug of coffee, but she could barely swallow past the lump in her throat. She dozed fitfully until Alex came back up, clutching his mobile phone and looking worried.

'Ted just called. He's been at the hospital, with Walter,' he said.

'And?' Luci sat up, hugging her knees.

'Walter's fractured his hip,' Alex said. 'And he's had another small stroke.' He sat down on the edge of the bed as Luci crumpled in on herself. 'But he's going to be fine, Luce. Just a few weeks in hospital and he'll be just fine.' He hesitated. 'Ted's told me what ward Walter's on, if you want to go and visit him.'

Luci shook her head miserably. 'What, so I can go and finish him off?' she choked out. 'No. I'm not going to risk going anywhere near. I just want to go home. We should never have come here. This place... it's got some kind of bad omen. Only bad things can happen, and I don't want to spend another *minute* here. What if something happens to the boys, or to you, or... or the roof collapses, or...?'

'Nothing's going to happen,' Alex soothed, hugging Luci close to him and feeling the vibrations of her silent sobs. 'But okay, we can go, just as soon as we've packed everything up, we can go, all right?'

Luci nodded weakly. 'I'll be all right once we're away from here,' she whispered, pulling away and yanking the cases out from under the bed. She started throwing clothes inside haphazardly, until Alex eased her away and took over, leaving her to gather together all the baby paraphernalia that had to accompany Matty and Theo everywhere they went. Half an hour later, the car was loaded up and they drove away, after Alex had spent ten minutes reassuring Jack that he was more than capable of taking care of Luci. By the time Alex pulled out onto the motorway, Luci was asleep beside him, worn out by the emotional toll the morning had taken on her. Neither she nor the twins stirred until they were almost home.

CHAPTER FOUR

Ted rang daily with an update on how Walter was progressing, but once Alex was back at work every day, Luci stopped answering the phone and let Ted leave his message on the answering machine. She couldn't face speaking to him, knowing, as she did, that she was responsible for Walter *being* in hospital.

At first, it seemed that the old man was progressing well, but then, on the Thursday, a week after Luci and Alex returned home, Ted left a more sombre message: Walter had suffered another stroke and had been moved to a high dependency unit in the hospital. Luci replayed the message several times, the dread settling like a rock in her stomach. If he died... That same thought chased around in her mind, guilt making her feel physically sick. She should never have gone back to visit Walter, knowing that her presence had upset him so much the first time. If not for her stupid conviction that Ted was hiding something and Walter was keeping secrets, her grandfather wouldn't be hovering on that thin line between life and death.

When Alex came home from work, Luci had already bathed the twins, settled them in their cot, and gone to bed herself, leaving Alex a note on the kitchen table. Ignoring her request to be left alone, Alex charged straight upstairs and into the bedroom, flicking the light on on his way in. Luci her drawn the curtains and was huddled beneath the duvet, just the top of her head poking out.

'Can't you read?' she murmured, her voice thick.

'I'm not leaving you alone when you're like this,' Alex said sharply.

'Like what?' Luci asked flatly.

'Depressed,' Alex replied, snaking his hand beneath the duvet and grasping her hand. 'I've been worried about you since we got back – but when you start taking to your bed in the middle of the day, I know it's serious.'

'I'm just tired,' Luci muttered, snatching her hand away.

'I know you too well to buy into that, Luce,' Alex retorted. 'I'm going to call Dr Fielding's office tomorrow – see about getting you an appointment.'

'I've got an appointment,' Luci said wearily.

'Yeah, for the end of July,' Alex replied. 'That's too long to wait. I think your meds need adjusting. You've not been right for weeks. I'm not going to stand by and watch you sinking lower and lower.'

Luci rolled over so her back was to Alex. 'I'm fine,' she said woodenly. 'I just need to sleep.'

Alex sighed. 'Don't, Luce.'

'Don't what, sleep? Why shouldn't I sleep? I'm tired.'

'That's not what I meant – and you know it,' Alex said sharply.

'Then what did you mean?'

'Don't shut me out like this. Please.'

'I'm not shutting you out. I'm trying to sleep. There's a big difference.' Luci groaned as a wail rose up from the nursery. 'Can you see to them? I've had enough today.'

Alex squeezed her shoulder. 'Sure,' he said softly, a catch in his voice.

'And if you're going to come to bed late, maybe you should sleep in the spare room,' Luci added, drawing her knees up to her chest.

'Luce...' Alex let his voice trail away, gave her shoulder another squeeze and left the room, closing the door tightly behind him.

Luci rolled over onto her back, biting the inside of her cheek as she heard Alex singing to the twins in the nursery. The tears she'd been valiantly holding back since Alex came home trickled dejectedly down her cheeks, soaking into the pillow as she sobbed.

***

'Mum's downstairs,' Alex said softly the next morning, sitting down on the edge of the bed. Luci edged away from the hand he tried to put on her shoulder. 'She's happy to take the boys if you want a break.'

'Why, do you think I'm not capable of looking after my own babies?'

'It's not that,' Alex said hastily. 'I was just saying if you *did* want a break... I'm going to have to head into work in a bit – I'm due in court at eleven.'

Luci sighed. 'Tell her thanks, but I can manage,' she murmured, swinging her legs over the edge of the bed. Her eyes felt sore, her head was throbbing, and her throat ached from too many tears, but the last thing she wanted was her step-mother hovering over her all day, offering sympathy Luci didn't think she deserved. Shunning the thought of a shower – too much effort – Luci pulled on the same clothes she'd been wearing the day before, despite the baby-sick stain on the shoulder of the sweater, and padded downstairs in a pair of slippers that should have been thrown out long ago. Alex called out to say that he was leaving; seconds later, the door slammed behind him.

'You look dreadful,' Ruth commented when Luci walked into the living room. Matty and Theo were happily rolling around on the floor under their jungle-gym, whilst Ruth tackled the pile of ironing that Luci had been studiously ignoring for a week. Everything was too much effort.

'Thanks,' Luci said dryly, slumping down on the sofa.

'You should go back to bed. I can take care of things down here for you,' Ruth said, her smile not quite reaching her eyes.

'I'm fine,' Luci snapped. 'I'm quite capable of taking "care of things". I'm not that incompetent that I can't look after *my* house and *my* children.'

'I'm just trying to help, Luci,' Ruth said quietly.

'Yeah? Well I don't need your help. I don't need *anyone's* help. I'm *fine*,' Luci retorted. 'I can do my own ironing, thank you very much.'

'I'm worried about you,' Ruth persisted. 'And Alex is, too.'

'I'm *fine*,' Luci said again, rubbing her hand across her eyes.

'No, you're not,' Ruth said softly. 'You're really not fine, sweetheart. I'm not leaving you on your own like this.'

Matty started crying suddenly, and Luci bent automatically to pick him up, struggling not to cry herself as he looked up at her with trusting eyes. She stroked his downy hair and blinked hard against the mist of tears.

'It's okay to admit that you're struggling, Luci,' Ruth said. 'You're under a lot of stress.'

'I'm not struggling,' Luci said woodenly.

'But you *are*,' Ruth insisted. 'Sweetheart, I know you too well.'

The phone rang, and Luci flinched, staring at it like it was a deadly creature that had invaded her living room. The answering machine clicked straight on – Alex had obviously never turned it off from the day before.

Ted's voice filled the room, too loud, too oppressive. Luci stood up, still rocking Matty in her arms, but she hadn't even made it to the door before Ted dropped his bombshell. 'Luci, are you there?' he asked, barely pausing before he rushed on. 'I'm afraid it's bad news. I've just had a call from the hospital. Uncle Walter died a little while ago. I thought you'd want to know right away. Call me when you get this.'

Luci stood frozen, halfway across the room. The silence after Ted rang off was deafening.

Dead. Walter was *dead*. A sick feeling lurched its way up from Luci's stomach and she thrust Matty at Ruth before fleeing from the room with her hand clamped over her mouth. There was nothing in her stomach to bring up, but she retched violently for several minutes, kneeling on the bathroom floor with her hands gripping the porcelain bowl in a white-knuckled grasp.

When she stood up, her legs felt wobbly and weak, and she leaned against the wash basin, staring at her reflection in the mirror.

'He's dead,' she whispered. 'He's dead, and I killed him.'

'Of course you didn't.'

Luci turned; Ruth was standing in the doorway, worry etched in the deep lines on her face.

'I did,' Luci said flatly. 'I upset him. I made him fall. I made him have a stroke. And now I've made him die, just because I was curious.'

'It was an accident, and he was very old, and very frail, Luci. You're not responsible for what happened. He'd had a stroke before and that wasn't your fault,' Ruth said.

Luci shook her head. She couldn't expect Ruth to understand how she felt, and she didn't have the energy or inclination to try and explain. She shrugged. 'I guess,' she said, the lie slipping easily off her tongue.

'Let me make you a cup of sweet tea – for the shock,' Ruth suggested, leading the way downstairs. But whilst her stepmother busied herself in the kitchen, Luci picked up the twins, strapped them into the double buggy, and left through the front door, leaving the door blowing open in the breeze.

She tried valiantly to hold back the tears, knowing that the boys would pick up on her distress, but her shoulders shook with the effort of smothering the sobs, and in the end, she gave in and let the tears rain in rivers down her cheeks.

'Why does it always happen?' she whispered. 'Is it me? Is it because of me that people keep dying? Am I cursed?'

There had been too much death already. First her mother, then her twin brother Luke, her fiancé Ben, and now Walter. It felt as though death had been stalking her for nearly all of her life. She shuddered, stopping and crouching down in front of the buggy. The boys gazed at her with wide, trusting eyes, sucking on their soothers in syncopation.

'What have I done?' Luci whispered, placing one palm against Theo's cheek and the other against Matty's. 'I'm not safe to be around people. Everyone dies. *Everyone dies!*' The thought of anything happening to her babies made her feel sick with fear. 'Please, God, no,' she moaned. 'What have I done that's so terrible that I deserve this?' Straightening, she grabbed the handles of the buggy and turned it around, running pell-mell towards the only place she could feel safe.

***

'I've put plenty of sugar in – they say that's good for shock,' Ruth said, carrying two steaming mugs into the living room. She stopped dead in the doorway. 'Luci?' Putting the mugs down on the coffee table, Ruth backed out of the room, turning towards the stairs and noticing the front door standing open. 'Luci!' Running out onto the driveway, Ruth looked up and down the street, but there was no sign of Luci and the twins. Ruth tore her fingers through her blond, shoulder-length hair, fighting a losing battle against panic. Panicking wasn't going to help, but Ruth couldn't stop herself. She knew only too well how unpredictable Luci could be when she wasn't well – and Walter's death was enough to push her over the edge.

Back inside, Ruth snatched up the cordless phone and dialled Luci's mobile. It was a long shot, but she had to at least try. The call didn't go straight through to voicemail, and Ruth held her breath, letting it out in a sigh as the ringtone sounded from the kitchen. Ending the call, Ruth dialled another familiar number.

'I need to speak to Alex,' she told her son's secretary sharply. 'This is his mother. It's about Luci.'

'He's in court,' the woman said. 'I can take a message.'

'A message is no good,' Ruth snapped. 'I need to speak to him. Now. Is he on his mobile?'

'He's in court,' the secretary repeated, a note of exasperation creeping into her voice. 'He can't have his mobile on in court. I can take a message. He usually calls to pick up any messages if there's a recess at court.'

Ruth rolled her eyes heavenwards, sighing in exasperation. 'It's a family emergency,' she said, only barely managing to refrain from swearing at the gormless woman.

'Shall I get him to call you?' the secretary asked.

'Can you give me the number for the courthouse?' Ruth asked.

'Um... well, I suppose I could,' the secretary said dubiously. 'But...'

'Just give me the bloody number!' Ruth cried, running out of patience. After what seemed like an eternity – the gormless secretary had to look the number up on her computer screen and didn't seem able to perform even a simple task – she had the number, and dialled it, only to be told, by the annoying automated BT voice, that the number she had dialled had not been recognised. With a sigh of resignation, Ruth instead dialled Alex's mobile and left a frantic message, before dialling another familiar number.

The school secretary recognised Ruth's voice immediately, and would have launched into friendly conversation – asking how Nathan, Alex's younger brother, was getting on at university – had Ruth not hastily interrupted her.

'I need to speak to Jack – urgently,' she said. 'Can you get him for me?' Her husband had been head-teacher at the village primary school for almost twenty years, and the secretary, Margaret, had been there at least twice as long; when Ruth said it was urgent, Margaret took her at her word.

'He's supervising the cycle proficiency lessons,' Margaret said. 'I'll be as quick as I can – shall I get him to call you back, rather than you hanging on?'

'Tell him I'm at Luci and Alex's,' Ruth said. She paused, then ploughed on. 'Luci's gone missing. With the babies.'

'Oh, dear Lord!' Margaret cried. She shouted out to one of the other teachers, who must have been passing the office. 'Run and fetch Mr Rushden, Richard. You're faster on your feet than I am. Tell him Mrs Rushden's on the phone. Tell him it's about Luci, and to hurry!'

Though only minutes could have passed between Ruth hanging up the phone and Jack calling back, every minute seemed to stretch on for a lifetime. The phone in Ruth's hand only rang once before she hit the green button.

'What's happened? Margaret said that Luci's disappeared with the boys – I don't understand,' Jack said breathlessly.

'Ted rang. Walter died this morning. It hit Luci hard – it's the last thing she needed to hear this morning, when she's already depressed. I just went to make us a couple of mugs of sweet tea – for the shock – and when I came back from the kitchen, they were gone!' Ruth replied. 'Alex's in court, I can't get hold of him. And I don't want to leave the house in case they come back.'

'She's not taken the car?'

'No – Luci's on foot – she's taken the buggy.'

'Then I think I know where she'll have gone,' Jack said, sighing. 'Stay there – and put the kettle on. I'll go and find her and bring her back. I think we'll *all* be in need of a cup of tea.'

***

Jack parked his car on the grass verge outside the churchyard, hoping that he wasn't wrong in assuming where Luci would run to. It wasn't a wild hunch, after all – the churchyard was the place Luci often fled to in times of crisis. But if she wasn't there, then Jack had no idea where else to look.

The sky was blackened with angry-looking clouds that began to release heavy drops of rain as Jack pushed his way through the kissing-gate entrance to the churchyard. Within seconds, the few drops had mutated into a torrential downpour that soon soaked through Jack's shirt and trousers.

'Luci!' he yelled, breaking into a run as he headed towards the corner of the churchyard where his first wife and eldest son were both buried. At first, he didn't see Luci – he was looking for the buggy, hoping that Luci had had the good sense to put the rain-cover down to shelter the twins – but as he grew closer, he recognised Luci's prone form curled into the foetal position in the shadow of Luke's headstone. The buggy was nowhere in sight.

'Luci! Where are the boys? Where are Matty and Theo?' he demanded, crouching beside his daughter and touching her shoulder. She flinched.

'Safe,' she whispered, her teeth chattering.

'Safe where?' Jack asked.

'In the church. Safe, away from me. I asked God to look after them. I begged Him, because I keep killing people, *and I can't bear it anymore,*' Luci cried. 'You can go and get them. Take them home. Take them away from me. I can't be around them. I can't be around anyone. It's not safe to be near me. Tell... tell Alex I'm sorry. And Ruth. And... and when the boys are old enough, tell them that I didn't want to leave them, but I had to, to keep them safe.'

'I'm not going anywhere without you, too,' Jack said firmly. 'Come on, sweetheart. Let's get you out of the rain, before you catch...' He let the words trail away before he could finish the sentence.

'Before I catch my death of cold?' Luci suggested, sighing. 'Yes, please.'

Jack had enough experience of dealing with Luci to know it was pointless to try and use reason with her. Instead, he bent down and lifted her to her feet, holding her firm when she tried to resist. Matty and Theo were both wailing – most probably in fright, Jack thought – inside the church; Luci had parked the double buggy in front of the altar as if using the boys as an offering to God. Forcing Luci to sit down in the first pew, Jack went straight to his grandsons, pushing the buggy backwards and forwards to try and calm them down. He didn't want to pick them up when he was soaked to the skin from the rain. When the boys finally began to quieten, Jack fished in his pocket for his mobile phone and fired off a quick text message to Ruth; he didn't want to discuss Luci's state of mind in her hearing.

'As soon as the rain eases off, we'll make a run for it,' he said, sitting down next to his daughter. She didn't even look at him. Her gaze was directed straight at her feet. 'Luce?'

'Why does it keep happening, Dad?' she asked eventually, her voice cracked and broken. 'Why does death keep stalking me? Who's going to be next? Alex? Ruth? You? The boys? I can't stand it – the fear. I don't feel safe being around people, because I know that it's going to happen again. It always happens. Always.'

Jack sighed. He didn't like admitting it, but the truth was, he didn't know how to answer Luci when her mood was so low. Every word that left his lips was likely to be misconstrued, used to strengthen her conviction that death was a more promising option than life. He was glad of the distraction when his mobile rang and Alex's name flashed up on the display.

'You've found her? I just got off the phone with Mum. Is she all right? Are the boys all right?' Alex didn't bother with the trivialities of 'hello'.

'They're fine,' Jack said. 'The boys are fine.'

'And Luci? She's not...'

'No. Nothing like that,' Jack assured him, understanding the unspoken question.

'Where are you?'

'In the church,' Jack said, unwilling to say too much whilst Luci was looking at him.

'You found her at Luke's grave, didn't you?'

'Yes,' Jack said, sighing.

'Jesus. I should never have gone to work. The funny thing is, I was going to ring Ted and tell him not to call Luci if anything happened to Walter, but then I didn't have time, and it was probably too late, anyway,' Alex said regretfully. 'Will she talk to me, if you put her on?'

'Luce? It's Alex. He wants to talk to you,' Jack said softly, offering the phone to Luci. She took it, somewhat reluctantly.

'Sorry,' she said flatly.

''It doesn't matter. You're okay. The boys are okay. That's all that matters,' Alex assured her.

'No, not that. Sorry, for putting everyone in danger,' Luci amended. 'It's happening again, Alz. I wasn't crazy, before, when I thought it was me. It *was* me, all along.' Her voice broke and her shoulders started heaving with sobs she didn't even try to suppress. 'I'm sorry. I'm so sorry. I should never have let you love me. I should have made it stop then, instead of letting everyone lie to me.'

'Oh hell, Luce, it's not you. Of course it's not you,' Alex protested, but Luci had already thrust the phone back at Jack and was on her feet, stumbling blindly down the aisle towards the door.

'Luci!' Dropping his phone down onto the pew, Jack took off after his daughter, reasoning that the twins would be safe enough left in the buggy for just a few minutes. Luci had less than a minute's head start, and she'd left the heavy oak door standing open when she fled. Besides that, Jack suspected that she wouldn't be running very far at all.

He was right, of course, and he slowed his pace to a walk as soon as he saw Luci crouched on the wet ground next to Luke's grave. The rain had slowed to a light drizzle, although dark clouds still threatened ominously.

'Come on, sweetheart, this isn't going to solve anything, is it?' Jack was saying as he came up behind Luci. Then he realised what she was doing, and it felt as though his heart was breaking all over again. 'Oh, Luci,' he whispered. 'What are you *doing*?' Luci didn't so much as acknowledge his presence. She was sobbing as she tore at the wet earth with her bare hands, scrabbling frantically on the surface of Luke's grave. She fought violently as Jack hauled her to her feet, clods of earth still clinging to her fingernails.

'Please,' she begged. 'Please.'

Jack had to virtually carry her back into the church, and kept a firm arm around his shoulders as he retrieved his mobile phone.

'I'm so sorry, sweetheart,' he said softly, his voice cracking as he dialled a three digit number. 'Ambulance, please,' he said when the operator answered, because as much as it grieved him, he knew he, and Alex and Ruth, were powerless to give Luci the help she needed right now. And even though Dr Fielding had warned that there might be times like this, the actual act of phoning for an ambulance somehow still smacked of failure.

CHAPTER FIVE

'I'm sorry,' Luci said quietly. 'For putting you through all this again.'

Alex shook his head, grabbing hold of her hand and squeezing it tightly. 'You've nothing to be sorry about,' he retorted. 'You can't help being ill, Luce. Would you apologise for breaking your leg, or having a sore throat?'

'No,' Luci admitted, sighing heavily. 'But that's different. I wouldn't try to pretend to myself that I didn't have a broken leg or a sore throat, would I? And I wouldn't be putting you and Dad and Ruth – and the boys – through hell if I had a sore throat.' She swiped at the fresh tears on her cheeks with the back of her free hand. 'Dad cried when the ambulance came to bring me here. The only other times I've seen him cry have been when someone's died. That means me being like this, being in here, is as bad to him as me being dead.'

'He's worried about you. We all are. But it's temporary, baby. You're getting better. I said it was your meds that weren't right,' Alex said soothingly. 'I can see a big difference in you already. You haven't got that rabbit-in-the-headlights look in your eyes now. Remember what it said in that book – you've just got to remember that this will pass. It always does.'

'Yeah,' Luci said, sounding unconvinced. It was true that since she'd been admitted to the psychiatric hospital four days ago, the changes to her medications *had* begun to make a difference, but being back on the ward seemed like a massive step backwards, as if proving her old fear that she would never be able to function properly as a human being. It seemed like the slightest thing could set her back; she felt as though she was like a house of cards – one little knock and she'd come crashing down again.

Alex hesitated for a moment, his mouth half open as if he wasn't sure whether to speak or not. 'I was talking to Ted this morning. He feels bad for dropping such a bombshell on you the way he did.'

'I think I would have flipped anyway, no matter how he told me,' Luci sighed.

'He's arranged Walter's funeral for a week today. I think... well, he said that he was hoping that by then you'd be feeling well enough to go to the funeral,' Alex went on. 'You can say no, Luce. You don't have to feel obliged to go. I'd hate for it to be too much for you.'

'A week today?' Luci repeated uncertainly. 'I think I'd like to go. I didn't really know him, but he was still my grandfather.' The guilt she'd felt about his death was lessening, the more Alex had told her about Walter's declining health over the past few months. Rationally, she was almost able to see that he would probably have had another stroke and died regardless of whether she'd been to visit him. The fear that she was somehow cursed to lose everyone she loved was still there, though. That, she knew, was never going to be easy to shake. Every time her mood plunged, it seemed to creep back like an old, unwelcome but familiar, friend.

'There's no obligation, Luce. I've explained it all to Ted. He'll understand,' Alex said.

'I know. But I'd still like to go,' Luci said, more firmly this time. She locked eyes with Alex. 'I'd like to get out of here even more, though. I miss you. I miss the boys. I hate being stuck here.'

Alex smiled, leaning in to kiss her forehead. 'I miss you, too,' he said. 'And you must be feeling better if you want to come home.'

Luci nodded. 'I feel safer,' she said. 'In myself. I know that doesn't make much sense, but that's how it feels.'

'It makes perfect sense,' Alex said. 'We'll talk it over with Dr Fielding when we see her later, okay?'

Luci nodded again. 'Thank you,' she said, her voice cracking slightly. 'Thank you for being so bloody perfect and understanding. I sometimes wonder what I ever did right to deserve you, or if all this other stuff is to punish me for having you.'

Alex pulled her into a hug, holding her tightly against his chest. 'I love you, Luciana Rushden,' he murmured, close to her ear. 'Don't you ever forget it! I'm in this with you for the long haul. Whatever happens, we'll get through it. You're not being punished. It's tough. It's hell, sometimes, but you – we – are stronger than *it*, the Bipolar. Remember that, Luce. Hold on to it, hey.'

Luci nodded her head against his chest, letting the tears come again, because she'd had to learn, over the last couple of days, to stop being so frightened of her own emotions. It was okay to cry, she reasoned – so long as she knew she could stop.

***

'Dr Fielding's ready to see you now,' one of the nurses said, poking her head around the bedroom door. Alex gave Luci's hand a reassuring squeeze and led her, like a lamb to the slaughter, down the corridor after the nurse's retreating back.

'How are you feeling, Luci?' the doctor asked once Luci and Alex had sat down in the two armchairs opposite the one the doctor occupied. 'You look a little brighter.'

Brighter than she had when she'd been brought in? Luci sighed. She could hardly have felt worse, after all. She nodded. 'Better,' she mumbled, picking at one of the fingernails on her left hand. There was still soil engrained in her nails that she hadn't managed to clean out.

'How have you been sleeping? Any more nightmares?'

The first two nights she'd spent on the ward, Luci had woken up screaming each time she managed to drop off to sleep, her dreams tormented by images of her family as dead men walking, the flesh dripping off their faces grotesquely. It had been for that reason that Dr Fielding had decided to change her medication.

'No more nightmares,' Luci said. 'I slept better last night.'

'What about the panic attacks?'

Luci shrugged. 'Better,' she said, somewhat unconvincingly.

'I know you're anxious to get home, Luci, and I don't want you to have to spend any more time on the ward than you have to, but lying to me isn't going to help you in the long run,' Dr Fielding said, raising her eyebrows sharply. 'I'll ask again. What about the panic attacks?'

'About the same,' Luci said, sighing. The paralysing fear seemed to be stalking her, attacking unpredictably, when she wasn't expecting it; leaving her on edge, yet never entirely sure what she was so terrified about. The fear varied in intensity; at its worst, it would leave her fighting to draw air into her lungs, or sobbing uncontrollably; at other times it was just like a butterflies-in-the-stomach kind of uncertainty, just enough to leave her nerves frayed.

'I am concerned about the possibility of you becoming dependant on diazepam, but at the moment I think it's more imperative to give you some relief from the anxiety. I'll write up a higher dosage for you,' Dr Fielding said, frowning as she wrote something in the file open across her knees.

Luci wondered if she was supposed to say thank you. She didn't, just looked imploringly at Alex. He gave her hand another reassuring squeeze.

'Luce and I have been talking,' he began, and Luci recognised the authoritive tone to his voice. It was his lawyer-voice, the one he used for making his case in court. It always made her want to laugh, hearing him talk like that. 'It's Walter's funeral on Monday.' He shot Luci a look that told her not to contradict him – the funeral wasn't until Friday. 'We'd like to go to the funeral, to pay our last respects, but it's at half past ten in the morning, so we'd need to drive down to Derbyshire on Sunday and stay over with Ted. We were thinking that it would probably be best for Luci to have a day or so at home, to get back into the routine of things a bit before we leave.'

Dr Fielding smiled when Alex finished making his case. 'You want me to discharge Luci today, is that what you're saying, Alex?' she asked. 'I have to ask this – Luci, is that what you'd like, too?'

'I want to go home,' Luci said firmly.

'If I agree to discharge you today, Luci, you have to promise me that if you feel like you're not coping too well, or you're struggling, you'll contact me or the crisis team.'

'I will,' Luci promised. It would take a lot for her to admit it, but, if that was the only way she was going to get discharged, she was quite prepared to agree to it.

'I'm fairly confident that you're not likely to pose a risk to yourself now,' Dr Fielding went on. 'And sometimes, recovery happens more quickly away from the ward. My only concern is the effect your grandfather's funeral might have on you. Before I let you go, I think it would be a good idea for you and Alex to sit down with your CPN – Rebecca, isn't it? – and revisit the relapse prevention plan you made with her last year. I'll see if she's available to see you this afternoon, all right?'

Luci nodded again. If Dr Fielding had suggested that she go and dance naked in the garden, she would have done it just to be allowed to go home.

'And then, I'd like you to come and see me next Friday – a week today – just so I can see how you're getting on.'

'Uh, we were thinking of perhaps staying on at Ted's for a little while,' Alex interrupted, forgetting his lawyer-voice in his haste, 'rather than rushing straight home. I expect there will be a fair bit of sorting out to do. It would be rude of us not to offer to help Ted.'

Dr Fielding nodded in understanding. 'All right. How about a week on Tuesday?' she suggested.

'That'll be fine,' Alex said, giving Luci's hand another surreptitious squeeze. 'We'll be back by then.'

Dr Fielding stood up, offering her hand to first Alex and then Luci to shake. 'Take care of yourself, Luci,' she said, smiling as she held the door open for them. 'It's going to be a difficult few days. Try not to expect too much of yourself all at once. Remember what we talked about on Wednesday.'

'What was that?' Alex asked as he and Luci walked away from the office.

Luci chewed on her lip. 'Not being afraid of my emotions,' she said, sighing. 'I'm trying.'

Alex slipped his arm around her waist, pulling her close to him. 'I know you are,' he said. 'Don't look so worried. You're doing well. Remember what that doctor in Sheffield told you? Baby steps. It's all about taking baby steps.'

Luci smiled. 'Lilliputian steps,' she corrected, just as she had when she'd been released from the Sheffield psychiatric unit more than three years ago. Alex laughed, and the sound filled her with hope. She'd come a long way in three years, even if it didn't always seem like it.

CHAPTER SIX

The day of Walter's funeral seemed to come around too quickly, for Luci at least. She and Alex drove down on the Thursday, leaving the twins with Ruth and Jack. A funeral was no place for babies, though Luci hated leaving them so soon after her 'holiday' in the hospital.

'If I leave them much more, they'll start to wonder who I am,' she said fretfully on Friday morning after phoning Ruth – for the third time – to make sure Matty and Theo were okay. She hadn't expected to feel so bad about leaving them; she was half-wishing she hadn't said that she wanted to go to the funeral.

'They'll be fine. Stop worrying,' Alex said patiently, struggling to knot his tie. It amazed Luci sometimes how he'd never got the knack of it despite wearing a suit and tie to work every day. She batted his hands out of the way and knotted the tie, pulling it deliberately tight.

'I know they'll be fine. I know Ruth's more than capable of looking after them,' she said irritably. 'That doesn't stop me feeling bad about it.' She closed her eyes briefly. 'Sorry. I didn't mean to snap. I'm just a bit... on edge.'

'Valium?' Alex suggested.

'I don't want to fall asleep half way through the service,' Luci replied.

'Half a Valium, then,' Alex pressed. 'It'll help you calm down.'

Sighing, Luci agreed, already hating her dependence on prescription drugs just to get her through day-to-day life.

'It's not failure, Luce, to take a few pills,' Alex said, as if he could read her mind. 'It's not like you're snorting lines of cocaine or shooting up with smack.'

She smiled weakly. 'I know,' she murmured, swallowing the half-pill Alex offered her. 'It's the lesser of two evils – I know that, too.'

'Come on then – are you ready?' Alex asked, opening the door of the guest-room in Ted's rambling house.

'No,' Luci said honestly. She sighed. 'But as ready as I'll ever be.'

Ted was downstairs in the entrance lobby, looking dapper in a suit that he joked only came out for weddings, christenings and funerals. 'The hearse should be here any minute,' he said. He frowned slightly. 'Are you all right, Luci? You look very pale.'

'I'm okay,' Luci assured him, even though it wasn't entirely true. Her stomach was churning like it was full of somersaulting worms.

The hearse pulled up outside the cottage, and Luci felt for Alex's hand, gripping it tightly. He returned the pressure reassuringly. Following the old man's long-standing wishes, in a funeral plan made before the old man's dementia worsened, there was to be no funeral car, just the hearse; Ted was driving behind the hearse in his own car to the chapel some five miles away where Walter and his family had worshipped for many years. Ted had scowled when he'd departed that information, but he hadn't elaborated and neither Luci nor Alex wanted to press him on the matter.

'Will there be many people there, do you think?' Luci whispered to Alex as they climbed into the back of Ted's car.

'Uncle Walter *was* quite well respected in the community,' Ted said, overhearing the question. 'But that was some time ago.'

'Did you worship at the chapel, too, Ted?' Alex asked. 'And Elvina, did she?'

Ted snorted. 'Aye, until I was old enough to say no to all that nonsense,' he replied. 'And Elvina... well, she didn't have much choice, living under our grandmother's thumb as she did. I think it was all that nonsense about sin and evil that drove Elvina away, and who could blame her for not coming back?'

Alex glanced sidelong at Luci. There had been a time when all Luci could talk about was her mother and what had made Elvina leave home at sixteen and never again mention her family. But now, Luci was so tense that Ted's words barely seemed to brush her consciousness. She was sitting in the car like a tightly coiled spring, as if any moment she might make a break for it and flee.

The hearse stopped outside a non-descript stone building at the bottom of a steep hill in the small village. There were people gathered on the pavement outside, their heads bowed in respect. Most of them, Luci noticed, were fairly elderly – if not as old as Walter, then certainly older than Ted, who had recently turned seventy.

'Are they all here for Walter, or do they just come out for every funeral?' Alex hissed to Luci, making her smile and bite her lip so as not to laugh out loud.

'It's probably a day out for them,' she hissed back, covering her mouth with her hand. Alex slipped his arm around her waist as they got out of Ted's car, keeping her close to him. It was good to see her smile, but he knew that the next hour was going to be tough on her. The last funeral she'd attended had been Luke's; Alex didn't doubt that Walter's funeral service would bring all that back for Luci.

They followed respectfully behind the coffin, into the chapel. It was a dark and dingy building, its bare stone walls lending a chill to the air. The wooden pews were hard and unforgiving; as Luci sat down in between Ted and Alex in the front row, she glanced around the chapel, noticing that there was nothing at all welcoming about the place. If anything, it seemed to be deliberately *unwelcoming*. She shivered, and Alex tightened his arm around her.

'Okay?' he whispered.

'This place is *horrible*,' Luci whispered back.

'It is pretty grim,' Alex agreed.

Ted sighed. 'I would say it's more than grim,' he said. 'But Walter stayed faithful to his religion despite everything, and I thought it best to respect his final wishes.'

'Of course,' Alex murmured, nodding.

Footsteps rapped, almost impatiently, down the stone flags of the centre aisle, and a tall, dour-faced man, dressed entirely in black, stopped in front of Ted. His thin, bloodless lips were pressed into what Luci could only describe as a sneer, and there was coldness in his eyes that made her shiver.

'This is Walter's granddaughter and her fiancé, Pastor,' Ted said, keeping his head bowed low and not meeting the pastor's gaze.

'*What*?' The word was spat from the pastor's lips with an accompaniment of spittle.

'Elvina's daughter,' Ted explained.

The pastor swivelled his cold eyes towards Luci. 'Really?' he said, surprise in his voice. 'She sent her daughter rather than face judgement, I see.'

'Elvina died in 1993,' Alex snapped before Luci could speak. He felt her stiffen next to him.

'Without redeeming her soul, of course,' the pastor said, and his lips curved into a wolfish smile.

'Did you know my mother?' Luci asked tightly.

'Not personally. I was too young. But my uncle was pastor then, and of course, he preached often of the sinfulness that sadly pervaded our community,' the pastor replied, his eyes gleaming zealously. 'I can only assume you were not raised in the faith?'

'What faith?' Luci asked, a sharp edge to her voice.

'As I expected,' the pastor muttered, more to himself. 'My uncle was right. Her soul was damned from the start – a heathen.'

'Don't, it's not worth it,' Alex said quickly, pulling Luci back down onto the pew before she got to her feet. 'We're here for Walter, remember?'

The service was unlike anything Luci and Alex had ever encountered. By the end of the pastor's lengthy tirade about evil and sin and demons that walked amongst the faithful, Luci's jaw was aching from clenching her teeth, and her fingernails had left crescent-shaped indents in her palms. Walter's name was hardly mentioned, and no one else was invited to speak.

'Walter was a good and faithful man,' the pastor said finally, his voice full of fury. 'But his life was sadly tainted by evil. You may ask what a good and faithful man might have done to bring such evil into his life, and I tell you this: he was manipulated by a woman – a woman who pretended love for him, and blinded him with her wicked charm. But in the end, Walter triumphed over the evil, and he made great sacrifices to rid from his life those that were sinful.'

'He's talking about my mother,' Luci whispered to Alex. 'He's talking about Mum and Medora, isn't he?'

Alex nodded weakly, holding tightly onto Luci as she trembled with rage. The pastor concluded that Walter had passed all the tests that the Lord had placed in his path and would thus be allowed safe passage to heaven, where he would walk with the faithful of his family who had passed on before him. The pastor then invited the congregation to gather at the chapel burial ground at the other side of the narrow road running through the village, where Walter was to be interred beside his mother and father, sister and brother.

'I can't go,' Luci said as the congregation followed the pastor down the aisle towards the door. 'I can't listen to any more of that... nonsense.'

'It'll soon be over,' Alex said gently, hugging her close to him and kissing the top of her head. 'Five, ten minutes. For Walter's sake.'

Luci sighed. 'If that man says one more nasty thing about my mother, I'll push him in the grave after the coffin,' she warned.

'No,' Alex said firmly, 'you won't.'

The internment was the only really *normal* aspect of the whole funeral. Luci let her mind wander during the whole 'ashes to ashes, dust to dust' thing, and instead took the opportunity to take a good look at the people who had come to pay their final respects to

Legacy of Lies

Walter. She wondered how many of these people her mother had known, how many of them might be able to tell her stories about what Elvina had been like when she was a child. Because of all the secrecy, because Elvina had never talked about the past, Luci sometimes felt as though she didn't know anything at all about her mother. It was the bad stuff that she tended to remember – the drinking, and the way Elvina had committed suicide – but there had to be more to her mother than just that, surely? Trying not to make it obvious that she wasn't paying any attention to the internment, Luci craned her neck as someone cautiously approached the gathering – someone who hadn't been in the chapel, obviously. Luci frowned. It was a woman, possibly as old as Walter had been, judging by the way she walked, with a limping gait as if in a lot of pain. Luci wondered if this late arrival had been an old flame of her grandfather's, before he settled down and married her grandmother. A smile curved Luci's lips as she stared at the woman, recalling pictures of her grandmother, who had been, undoubtedly, quite a stunner. By contrast this stranger couldn't have looked more dowdy and manly if she'd tried, despite the fact that she was wearing a long black dress with white buttons all the way down the front, coupled with a coat that finished several inches above the dress. She wore thick-lensed, plastic-framed glasses and a bottle-green hat with the brim pulled down to touch the frame of her glasses. Although it was possible that the woman hadn't aged well, Luci could guess why Walter had chosen Medora to be his wife. The woman caught Luci staring, and her face blanched white as she gripped harder the walking stick she was leaning on. Her free hand crept to her lips in an exclamation of – what? Luci couldn't be sure whether it was surprise or dismay.

'Luci!' Alex hissed, digging his elbow sharply into her rips as Ted accepted a wooden box full of earth from the pastor. He dipped his hand into the box and threw a handful of soil into the grave, bowing his head respectfully.

'Goodbye, Uncle Walter,' he murmured, before handing the box on to Luci.

Luci accepted the box reluctantly, a shiver running down her spine. She remembered this part of the internment from her mother's funeral, the way she and Luke had backed away from the very idea of throwing clods of earth on top of their mother's coffin. But all eyes seemed to be focused on her now, and she couldn't just pass the box straight on to Alex under such close scrutiny. Half-closing her eyes and wrinkling her nose at the feel of the cloying dirt beneath her fingertips, Luci tossed a handful down onto the top of Walter's coffin and handed the box on to Alex.

'Ted,' she whispered urgently, and he glanced down at her, smiling faintly.

'All right, Luci?' he asked softly.

She nodded impatiently. 'I'm fine,' she said. 'But look – there's a woman just come over – do you know who she is? Why do you think she didn't come to the service?'

Ted turned his head, his gaze travelling over the mourners gathered at the graveside. He turned back to Luci with a puzzled expression on his face. 'Where?' he asked. 'I don't see anyone who wasn't at the chapel.'

'There!' Luci said sharply, turning around and pointing. Her finger faltered. The woman – whoever she was – had gone. 'She was there. Just there,' Luci muttered. 'I saw her.'

'What's wrong now?' Alex asked in a low voice.

'Luci thought she saw someone who wasn't at the service,' Ted replied.

'I didn't *think* I saw her – I *did* see her!' Luci snapped, elbowing aside the people standing behind her to break free of the gathering around the graveside, just to check that the woman hadn't slipped in amongst the crowd. But there was no sign of her. Luci ran to the edge of the burial ground, staring desperately up and down the street, a strange sensation of panic settling in her stomach. 'She was there,' she muttered savagely to herself. 'She was *there*.'

'Luce?' Alex touched her shoulder lightly, and she flinched. 'Come on, everyone's going to the village hall in a minute.'

'You think I was imagining her, don't you?' she said savagely.

'No...' Alex said quickly, but he couldn't hide the uncertainty in his voice.

'Just because I've got Bipolar, just because you and Ted didn't see her, you automatically think I'm hallucinating or something,' Luci snarled. 'She was there. She was real. And she looked... I don't know, *distressed* when she saw me looking. If she wasn't real, she wouldn't have looked at me like she'd seen a ghost, would she?'

Alex sighed. 'I don't think you were imagining her,' he said, more firmly this time. 'I just think you shouldn't get yourself wound up about it like this. She was probably just late, or maybe she was just passing and came over to see who was being buried.'

'Then why did she run away?' Luci demanded petulantly.

Alex sighed again. 'I don't know, Luce. Maybe she was embarrassed when she saw you looking at her.' He leaned forward and tucked Luci's hair behind her ears, smiling at her like he used to do when she was a child and he just wanted to pacify her. 'Does it really matter, huh? She's gone now, whoever she was. If she'd known Walter or anything, she would have stuck around. Let's just go to the reception, hey? I don't know about you, but I could do with a stiff drink after all that hell and damnation stuff.'

Luci swallowed down the sensation of panic that was still swirling up inside her. 'You'll have to make do with tea,' she said, sighing heavily. 'Ted said that this lot of Bible-bashers are all tee-total. They won't entertain alcohol.'

Alex smiled ruefully. 'Then the sooner we get it over with, the sooner we can adjourn to the pub,' he proclaimed, pulling a reluctant laugh from Luci's lips. He put his arm around her shoulders, and they followed the rest of the crowd across the street and into the village hall.

INTERLUDE

Whoever it was who said 'never go back' was a wise man, she thinks as she hurries away from the burial ground. She should not have come; she should have listened to her head and stayed away, instead of listening to her heart and returning to her childhood home.

'Take me home,' she says sharply, climbing into the back of the waiting car. Her driver glances shrewdly over his shoulder with a knowing smile, because after all, this is not the first time she has made trips that should never have been made. 'Never go back,' she repeats to herself, unable to resist the urge to glance back once more towards the burial ground. And once more, she sees the girl looking, frantic now, and an icy chill washes over her.

'Are you all right, Ma'am?' the driver asks as she lays her head back against the head-rest and presses the backs of her hands over her eyes.

'Of course,' she says irritably, the lie leaving her lips easily, as all the lies have always done. Once a life is built on lies, she thinks, her lips twisting bitterly, then each subsequent lie only becomes easier to tell, and the truth ever harder to recall. She cannot remember a time when lies have not been a part of her life; she was raised to lie, to mislead, and there are times when she wonders what her life might have been like without the deceit. She sighs. So many lies – lying even to the few she has truly loved. She tells herself, as she always has, that the truth would be too painful, that she has lied out of love, but she knows that lies only work when the truth is unknown, and she cannot lie to herself.

She is old now, and Walter's death has only served to remind her of her own mortality. It is why she came back, in truth, because death could be awaiting her around any shady corner. She came to see Walter lowered into the ground to satisfy herself that the truth can be buried with her when her time comes. She came expecting to see Walter's nephew and the members of the dreadful cult to which he belonged sending him on to heaven, and she would have been satisfied then. It is the girl that has resurrected the feeling of fear in her stomach. The girl with the fiery, familiar eyes, who can only mean trouble.

'She saw me,' she murmurs. 'No one was meant to see me.'

'What's that, Ma'am?' the driver asks. 'Is something wrong?'

Legacy of Lies

She shakes her head irritably. 'Nothing,' she snaps, but really, she means everything. She should not have come back. She should have been satisfied in her ignorance of the girl, because she knows now that the guilt will return to plague her, and the truth will haunt her, attacking her conscience until she weakens, as she weakened before, because she has never wanted, in her heart, to leave behind her such a legacy of lies.

CHAPTER SEVEN

'Mind if I join you?' Ted asked, not waiting for Luci to answer before he sat down on the Arber bench next to her. He handed her a steaming mug of coffee and put his own mug down on the floor between his feet. 'Are you all right, Luci? You've been very quiet these last couple of days.'

Luci shrugged, plucking a pink rosebud off the rambling rose climbing up the side of the Arber and crushing it between her fingers. 'I'm fine,' she said wearily, sick of answering the same question over and over again.

'Have you thought any more about what I said?' Ted asked.

Luci shrugged again. The evening following Walter's funeral, Ted had broached the subject of Walter's estate, of which Ted was executor. Because Walter hadn't known Luci even existed when he'd made his will, he'd left everything to Ted, naming his nephew as his sole heir. Ted, however, thought that the estate should go to Luci, as Walter's only grandchild. It wasn't as if Walter had been rolling in money – the estate mainly consisted of his house – Elvina's childhood home – a few thousand pounds in the bank and some stocks and shares from Walter's career in the banking industry.

'I want to sign everything over to you, Luci, as soon as everything's finalised,' Ted pressed. 'But we need to talk about what we're going to do about the house. If you want to sell it, I'd like to give the tenants at least a month or two's notice.' When Walter had moved, first into sheltered accommodation and then into the nursing home, Ted had opted to rent the house out rather than sell it outright. The same tenants had been occupying the house for the past four years – a family, Ted had told Luci, with two teenage children.

'He left it all to you, Ted,' Luci said. 'It's up to you what you do with it.'

'He was your grandfather, and if he'd known about you before he... deteriorated, he would have named you as the beneficiary, I'm sure of it,' Ted replied firmly. 'And what's more, I want you to have his estate. I'm certainly not in need of any money, Luci – I've been very fortunate in life.'

'And what, I haven't?' Luci said, a note of bitterness creeping into her voice. 'You think I deserve Walter's money because I'm living off Alex's wage and the £100 a week the DSS kindly pay me for being so fucked up I can't work, is that it?'

'That's not what I meant,' Ted said hastily.

'I know. I'm sorry,' Luci said, sighing. 'Ted, I just can't... think right now. I'm feeling a bit... I don't know, odd at the moment. All my thoughts are running round in my head with the rhythm of a steam train – clackety-clack, clackety-clack – and I can't concentrate.'

Ted frowned worriedly. 'Is that something you've experienced before?' he asked.

'Sometimes,' Luci admitted. 'It'll be fine. I'm seeing my shrink tomorrow. I'll see if she can give me something. But can we just... not talk about the whole Walter's estate thing until I'm a bit more... sorted?'

Ted nodded. 'All right,' he said. 'I won't say anything to the tenants, and we'll just leave things as they are for now, okay?'

Luci offered him a weak smile. 'Thanks, Ted,' she said, sighing heavily. She took a sip of her rapidly cooling coffee and stood up as Alex came down the garden towards them, his hands stuffed into the pockets of his jeans.

'I've put the bags in the car,' he said as Luci went to him and leaned her head against his broad chest. He slipped his arms around her, holding her close. 'You okay?' he asked, a frown in his voice.

'I don't know,' Luci murmured, her voice muffled by his shirt.

'Ready to go home?' Alex asked.

Luci nodded. 'I've missed the boys.' She'd missed them more than she thought was possible; missed them like they were an extension of her own body. She longed to breathe in their milky, baby smell; she even longed to hear them wailing in the early hours of the morning.

'Let's go then,' Alex said, exchanging a look with Ted over the top of Luci's head. The older man was frowning worriedly, and Alex couldn't help but share in his worry.

***

A week later, Ted was sitting out on the Arber bench, enjoying the last of the late-afternoon sunshine, when the gate at the side of the house squeaked open. He looked up sharply, knocking over his half-empty mug of coffee with his elbow and muttering a curse as the dark liquid crept slowly over his beige cotton trousers.

'Wash your mouth out with soap, boy,' a sharp voice admonished him. The voice was familiar, but Ted couldn't place it, and when he rounded the Arber, he didn't recognise the smartly-dressed old woman standing by the side gate.

'I'm sorry,' he said, frowning. 'Can I help you?'

The woman laughed. 'You always had such impeccable manners, Edward,' she said. 'Even as a boy. Your mother was very proud, and didn't she let everyone know about it. "Look at my boy," she used to say, "not wild like his heathen cousins".'

Ted's frown deepened. 'Should I know you?' he asked. 'I'm sorry, but I don't think...'

'And why should you know me?' the woman retorted. 'You were a boy in short trousers the last time I saw you.' She walked towards him, proffering a white-gloved hand. 'Violet, my dear. Your aunt Medora's sister. I've aged somewhat since the last time you saw me.'

'Violet, of course!' Ted said, shaking the old woman's hand warmly. 'Come inside, won't you? I'll make tea – or would you prefer coffee?' As he led Violet inside the house, he glanced back over his shoulder. 'You've come about Walter, haven't you? You saw the obituary? I'm sorry, I didn't think to try and contact you. It's been so long...'

'Tea's fine,' Violet said, sitting down at the kitchen table without waiting to be invited. She tugged off her white gloves, revealing careworn hands that were gnarled with arthritis. 'Yes, I came about Walter. Actually, I came on Friday, but I didn't think it prudent to stay.'

Ted paused in the process of pouring water from the kettle into the teapot. 'You came to the funeral?' he asked.

'I missed the service,' Violet said. 'My driver got lost – I sometimes question whether he would need a map to find his own backside. I arrived in time to see poor old Walter being put in the ground.'

'You were the person Luci saw!' Ted exclaimed. 'And to think Alex and I wondered if perhaps she was... imagining things.'

'The girl with the fiery eyes,' Violet said grimly. 'Yes, she saw me, and I saw her. Tell me, Edward, how did she come to find Walter? How did she come to be there, at his funeral?'

Ted smiled. 'That's a long story,' he said, pouring out two mugs of tea and passing one to Violet.

'I expect it is,' Violet said shrewdly. 'Spit it out, then.'

Legacy of Lies

'After my mother died, I put a notice in several newspapers appealing for Elvina to get in touch with me. Walter had just been diagnosed with dementia and I thought Elvina might want to see him. I heard nothing, at first, and then Luci got in touch. I first met her just over a year ago. Unfortunately, she didn't get much of a chance to get to know her grandfather. I think it's hit her hard, though she hasn't said as much. She's lost so much in her young life. I really feel for her.'

'You put a notice out for Elvina, and the *girl* got in touch with you?' Violet questioned, confusion in her voice.

Ted nodded. 'I'm sorry, Violet – I didn't make myself very clear, did I? Luci got in touch because her mother died some years ago.'

Violet paled visibly. 'Who told you that?' she asked sharply.

'Luci, of course. Elvina had a difficult time of it in the years before she died, unfortunately.'

'Oh!' Violet relaxed, taking a sip from her mug of tea. 'The girl – Luci – is Elvina's child?'

Ted's eyebrows arched sharply. 'Of course Luci is Elvina's daughter,' he said. 'How else could she be Walter's grandchild?'

Violet smiled thinly. 'Of course, of course,' she said. 'How foolish of me.' She shook her head, as if despairing of herself. 'Don't get old, Edward. Old age has little to recommend it. Arthritis, rheumatism and forgetful-ness. Sometimes it's a wonder I remember who I am and where I live.'

Ted gazed levelly at the old woman. She didn't strike him as being forgetful – in fact, he would have put money on her being as sharp as a button. He was confused, then, as to why she seemed surprised that Luci was Elvina's daughter. Was there something she knew that he didn't? Had Walter had a secret love-child that no one had talked about? He longed to ask Violet outright, but the manners his mother had instilled in him were too deeply ingrained. He managed a smile. 'I *am* getting old,' he said. 'Sixty this year.'

'That's not old,' Violet replied smartly. 'So Edward, tell me, what have you done with your life? You must have been about twelve the last time I saw you. But you went to Oxford University, didn't you?'

Ted nodded. 'I got a First in History,' he said, 'and I taught at a grammar school until I retired.'

'A wife, children?' Violet asked.

'Divorced,' Ted said. 'Caroline and I tried very hard, for the sake of the children, but it just didn't work in the end. I have a daughter – she lives in Australia with her husband and children. What about you, Violet? Do you have a big family, lots of grandchildren?'

'Me?' Violet smiled evasively. 'Oh no. I did marry, but too late for children. I have a step-son, but he's never married, although I believe he has got a child tucked away somewhere. Not that he'd tell me, of course.'

'You don't see eye to eye?' Ted asked.

'Something like that,' Violet said, glancing at her watch and draining her cup. She pulled her gloves on. 'Well, Edward, I won't outstay my welcome.'

'You're more than welcome to stay,' Ted replied. 'You've hardly been here five minutes.'

'When you get to my age, five minutes is a long time,' Violet replied, her smile not reaching her eyes, which were as cold and as hard as coals. 'I was passing and only called in on the off-chance of seeing you. I wasn't even sure you'd still be living here. You inherited your mother's house when she died, I presume?'

'Yes,' Ted confirmed distractedly. Passing? The last he'd known, Violet was living in Scotland. 'Are you living nearby, then, Violet, if you were just passing?'

The old woman looked momentarily thrown by the question. She glanced towards the door, as if seeking out an escape route. 'Not exactly nearby,' she said vaguely.

'Perhaps you could leave me your address and telephone number,' Ted suggested. 'In case Luci wants to contact you? I don't think Elvina told her much about the family – I'm sure Luci would be delighted to meet you.'

Violet hesitated. She made a show of rummaging her cavernous handbag but came out with nothing and held her palms upward as if in apology.

'I've got a pad and pen by the phone,' Ted offered. 'I'll go and get them.' He half expected Violet to have fled when he returned, but she was still waiting, although she looked like a cat on a hot tin roof. She scrawled down an address in Northumberland and a telephone number before handing the pad back to Ted.

'Of course, if her mother chose not to talk about the past, who am I to go against Elvina's wishes?' Violet said, her words forming a barely veiled warning not to encourage Luci to ask questions. 'It was lovely to see you again after all these years, Edward. Take care of yourself.'

'I'll pass your best wishes on to Luci, shall I?' Ted asked, still perturbed by Violet's odd reaction to her great-niece's presence at the funeral.

'Of course, of course,' Violet said quickly, moving towards the hallway and the front door. She didn't wait for Ted to open the door for her, but pulled it open herself, stepping out with surprising agility and pulling the door closed behind her. Through the small window at the side of the door, Ted watched her climb into the back of a waiting maroon Bentley; moments later, the driver drove away at speed – as if Violet was anxious to get away. Ted sighed, and returned to the kitchen. The pad with Violet's address and telephone number was lying on the table where he'd left it when he followed her to the door. He glanced at it again and then reached for the cordless phone. This was something he simply had to tell Luci – whether Violet wanted it or not.

CHAPTER EIGHT

When Ted called, Luci was only half awake, never mind that it was the middle of the afternoon, thanks to her new medication regimen. At the review meeting with Dr Fielding, the psychiatrist had readily agreed with Luci and Alex that the medication Luci was taking wasn't working well enough – and that a change was in order.

'Lithium doesn't work for everyone, unfortunately, or at least not always on its own,' Dr Fielding had said, somewhat ruefully. 'I'd like to try a different approach, if that's okay with you, Luci?'

Luci had shrugged, quite willing to agree to anything if it meant an escape from the depression. She had left Dr Fielding's office with a prescription for an anti-psychotic with a name that neither she nor Alex could properly pronounce – Quetiapine, otherwise known as Seroquel – that had been recently shown to be an effective treatment for Bipolar Disorder, and an increased dosage of her anti-depressant, Citalopram. She was still to take the Lithium – Dr Fielding preferred the idea of combination therapy than taking out the Lithium all together – but Dr Fielding had opted not to give her another prescription for Valium. There was too much of a risk of dependence, apparently, and Dr Fielding considered it more important that Luci learnt to manage the anxiety without too much medication as a crutch.

Dr Fielding didn't warn Luci and Alex the effect that Seroquel would have her. Even the starting dose of 25mg knocked her out for 12 hours solid and left her feeling like she was floating through life instead of living it.

'I can't look after the boys if I'm like this!' Luci wailed to Alex, threatening to throw the box of medication straight down the toilet.

'You can't look after the boys when you're paralysed with depression, either,' Alex pointed out. 'We need to give this a chance, Luci. Mum doesn't mind helping out with the boys. She loves it – you know she does. I just want to see you back on an even keel – that's all that matters to me. The sedation will pass once you get used to the medication – that's what it says on all the websites.'

'It's all right for you – you're not the one stuck feeling like you've been buried in cotton wool,' Luci grumbled, but she took the next dose at the right time, and resigned herself to sleeping incessantly until her body got used to the cocktail of chemicals she was pumping into it. Ruth would arrive at the house before Alex left for work, and stay until he came home again, seeing to the twins whilst Luci stumbled around in a fog. When Ted called, she picked up the phone automatically, but her brain was still lagging behind.

'Violet visited you?' Luci repeated, barely noticing the way her words slurred as they left her lips. Violet. The name was familiar, but in the fog, she couldn't place it.

'Medora's sister,' Ted prompted. 'Are you all right, Luci? You sound...'

'Drunk?' Luci suggested. 'No. I wish. Drunk would be preferable. New medication. They're trying to drug me into submission, I think.'

'Is it helping?'

'Stops me thinking – stops me being able to think, so that's probably a good thing,' Luci sighed. 'So... Violet visited you?'

'Quite out of the blue,' Ted affirmed. 'She was at the funeral. Violet was the woman you saw.'

'Definitely not hallucinating then. I was actually starting to wonder myself,' Luci admitted.

'No, and I'm sorry that I doubted you,' Ted apologised. 'The thing is, Luci, it was a very strange visit. I swear that she only came to see me to ask who you were, and she seemed relieved when I told her you were Elvina's daughter.'

'Huh?'

'She seemed to guess you were Walter's granddaughter, but not that you were Elvina's daughter. That struck me as odd.'

'Didn't she know that Isabella died?' Luci asked.

'I'm sure Walter would have told her,' Ted replied. 'Anyway, I persuaded her to leave me an address and telephone number if you wanted to get in touch with her.'

'Persuaded?'

'Yes. She was a little reluctant. In fact, I found the whole visit to be rather odd. I don't know whether I'm barking up the wrong tree entirely, but I get the feeling that Violet's hiding something – that she knows something that I – and therefore you – don't,' Ted said.

Any other time, Luci would have leapt on his words with eagerness, but her brain was still too befuddled for that. 'Ted, I'm really sorry, but can you give me a few days to try and force all this into my brain, and I'll call you back. Is that okay?'

'Of course,' Ted said warmly, and Luci could hear the smile in his voice. 'I just wanted to let you know right away. I'll let you go now. Take care of yourself, Luci. And give those two beautiful boys of yours a big hug from me.'

***

The depression had been slow to lift, but when it did, Luci felt as though she'd been finally released from a prison that had cast the whole world in shades of grey. It was a liberating feeling; even the simplest of things, like feeling the sun on her face or the grass beneath her feet, seemed somehow remarkable.

'You look a lot better,' Dr Fielding said warmly when Luci went in to the hospital for her monthly review meeting. 'It's nice to see you smiling again.'

'I feel fantastic,' Luci replied enthusiastically, lifting the boys out of their buggy and setting them down on the floor so they could demonstrate their newfound ability to crawl. Ruth had offered to look after them, and Alex had offered to come to the appointment with her, but Luci had refused both offers. She didn't need to be cosseted anymore. She found suffocating the way they still fussed over her like she was something fragile and liable to shatter into a million little pieces at any moment.

'How fantastic?' Dr Fielding asked. 'If you were to put a number on your mood right now – say on a scale of nought to ten – nought being the lowest you've ever felt and ten the highest – what would that number be?'

Luci regarded her psychiatrist shrewdly. 'Five,' she said, grinning. She wasn't stupid. She knew exactly what Dr Fielding was getting at.

'The danger with Bipolar Disorder, as I'm sure we've discussed before, is that aggressive treatment of depression can go on to trigger mania,' Dr Fielding said.

Luci rolled her eyes, bending down to pick up Theo's dummy, which he'd discarded in his eagerness to explore this exciting new environment. 'I know,' she said. 'But anything's better than being depressed.'

'Mania is equally as – if not more – dangerous as depression, Luci,' Dr Fielding cautioned. 'I think it might be advisable now to gradually reduce the Citalopram down to a lower dosage.'

Luci sighed. 'And what if that makes me depressed again?' she asked.

'Then we can increase it again,' Dr Fielding said smoothly. 'If you reduce the dosage by 10mg starting tonight, we'll see how that goes, all right?'

'All right,' Luci agreed, keeping her fingers crossed in her lap. The anti-depressant, she was convinced, was the only thing that was keeping her out of the pit of depression, and she had no intentions of reducing it and risking a plunge back into despair.

'How are you finding the Seroquel?' Dr Fielding asked.

'It's fine as long as I don't mind sleeping my life away,' Luci muttered. She hesitated. 'The morning dose is just no good. I can't look after the boys if I'm half asleep, so I'm taking it all at night.'

Dr Fielding frowned. 'Seroquel is better taken in divided doses,' she said.

'I don't care,' Luci retorted. 'Either I take it all at night or I don't take it at all,'

'You're not having any side effects from taking the whole dose at night?' Dr Fielding enquired.

'Not really,' Luci said. 'Nothing different from when I was taking it morning and night, anyway.'

'In that case, I suppose it won't do any harm taking it all in one dose,' Dr Fielding said, although she still didn't sound happy about the idea. 'It is helping with the anxiety, isn't it?'

Luci shrugged. 'I'm not anxious,' she said, 'so I guess it must be.'

'Shall we make another appointment for a month's time?' Dr Fielding suggested. 'Although if you think you need to see me before then, just ring the office. If I can't see you, one of my team will be able to.'

'That's fine,' Luci said distractedly, reaching down and grabbing Matty, who had crawled under Dr Fielding's desk and was happily untying the psychiatrist's bootlaces. She strapped him, as he protested loudly, back into the buggy and went to retrieve Theo, who had found a potted yucca plant with plenty of soil to play in. His hands were covered in soil, and some had found its way into his mouth, making him look at though he'd sprouted a black moustache. Luci bit back a snort of laughter, trying to reprimand him for the trail of soil on the carpet, but even Dr Fielding was smiling.

'He's going to be a handful, that one,' she said, writing down the next appointment on a card for Luci.

'They both are,' Luci replied. A note of sadness crept into her voice. 'Ruth says they remind her of me and Luke at the same age.

They even look like Luke. He would have loved them – but he'd have made a terrible uncle. He'd just have ended up leading them astray.' She shook her head, to rid herself of the image that popped into her mind of how different things might have been if Luke was still alive. 'I'll see you next month, then,' she said abruptly to the doctor, spinning the buggy around and pushing it out of the office before Dr Fielding could see the tears that were smarting her eyes.

***

'What did Dr Fielding have to say?' Alex asked late that evening when he finally returned from a case-meeting that had adjourned to the pub. The twins were asleep in the nursery, and Luci had gone to bed herself, having given up on the hope of Alex returning sober.

'Not much,' Luci said, shrugging. Alex sat down on the edge of the bed, leaning over to kiss Luci. She recoiled from him, pulling a face. 'You smell like a brewery!'

'Sorry,' Alex replied, not sounding at all sorry. 'But I'm not drunk.'

'Not much,' Luci muttered.

'No, really, I'm not,' Alex insisted. 'Come on, don't be like this. It's ages since I've been out at night!'

Luci smiled thinly. 'I know. I'm sorry.' She didn't sound sorry either. Alex suddenly shot to his feet and dashed into the en-suite bathroom. Luci grimaced at the sound of him being violently sick – and hoped he was aiming for the toilet bowl and not the floor. Alex never had been much good at handling heavy drinking sessions, especially not on an empty stomach, which Luci suspected had been the case tonight. She sighed heavily, glancing at the pills she'd already lined up on the bedside table ready to take. Because of the way Seroquel knocked her out, she'd come to rely on Alex to take care of the boys if they cried during the night – though they were sleeping longer, it certainly wasn't all through the night yet – but the likelihood tonight was that Alex would pass out into a drunken sleep. With the exception of the Citalopram, she swept the pills into the drawer and slammed it shut. The boys had to come first. They could hardly be left to cry because their parents were out cold.

'Ugh,' Alex moaned, stumbling back into the bedroom. 'Remind me never ever to drink again.'

'You never learn,' Luci retorted. 'You didn't eat before you went out, did you?'

'No time. Busy day,' Alex mumbled, kicking off his shoes and flopping down onto the bed.

'Get undressed,' Luci said, nudging him. 'You're not sleeping in your suit.'

Alex muttered something unintelligible before sitting up and starting to undress. It took him about five times longer than normal, and Luci ended up having to help him with the buttons on his shirt. Wearing just his boxer shorts, he collapsed back onto the bed again and grinned goofily up at Luci. 'I love you,' he said.

'I love you, too,' Luci said on a sigh.

'So what did the doc say?' Alex asked.

'That she wants me to reduce some of the meds now I'm feeling better,' Luci said, picking the Citalopram tablets up off the bedside table and swallowing them down with a glass of water.

Alex's only answer was a loud snore. Luci shook her head as she looked down at him. His mouth hung open and he was dribbling. 'Wonderful,' Luci muttered, sliding off the bed and throwing the duvet over Alex. She had no desire to share the bed with him snoring like a pig. Stopping by the airing cupboard on the landing, she pulled out a spare duvet and took it into the nursery. She curled up into the armchair in front of the window, nestling deep into the duvet. Sleep, however, was a million miles away, and after half an hour, she got up again, went downstairs and set about cleaning the kitchen. The twins woke around 3am, by which time Luci had cleaned most of the house. After feeding and changing the boys, and settling them back to sleep, she finally settled down to sleep herself.

It was a wonderful feeling waking up – just after six, when Theo loudly declared that it was time everyone was up – without the heavy, drugged feeling that she'd been waking up to since she'd started taking Seroquel. By the time Alex finally woke up and dragged himself into the shower, Luci had been up for over an hour and was playing with the boys in the living room.

'Have we got any hang-over stuff?' Alex asked, leaning against the door jamb. He looked dreadful, but Luci couldn't summon even an ounce of sympathy for him.

'Try the bathroom cupboard,' Luci said, returning her attention to the boys.

'I looked. I couldn't even find any paracetamol,' Alex moaned. 'I've got a banging headache.'

'You won't find any paracetamol in the bathroom cupboard. You hid all the paracetamol when you thought I might top myself,'

Luci replied. 'Don't ask me where you hid them, though. Funnily enough, you wouldn't tell me.'

Alex groaned. 'Shit. I'm supposed to be in court at ten. I can hardly even see straight.'

'Call in sick then,' Luci said unsympathetically.

'I can't. It's too obvious. I mean, they'll know exactly what's wrong with me,' Alex muttered.

'Alex, no one forced all the drink down your neck,' Luci snapped. 'Stop moaning like it's not your fault.'

Alex stared at her as though she'd grown an extra head. 'Do I have to pay extra for sympathy?' he asked in a wounded voice.

Luci couldn't help but smile at the expression on his face. 'Not if you deserve sympathy,' she replied. 'But you don't. So quit moaning and go to work. You can call at the shops on the way for some paracetamol or something.'

'You sound like my mother,' Alex grumbled.

'You sound like a petulant teenager,' Luci replied smartly. She lifted Matty up onto her lap and waved his chubby little arm in Alex's direction. 'Say "bye-bye Daddy",' she said in a sing-song voice. Alex shot her a filthy look and headed out of the house, making sure to slam the door on his way out.

***

There was no going back now for Luci. The decision to stop taking the Seroquel and Lithium seemed to make itself once she realised that she could be rid of the drugged feeling so easily. It didn't take much for Luci to convince herself that it was entirely possible that the Lithium – which she'd started taking as soon as the twins were born – had actually caused the deep depression, and therefore wasn't doing her any good at all. Besides that, it was a potentially toxic chemical – it was used in *batteries* for goodness' sake – and who in their right mind would willingly put toxic chemicals in their body? She was happy with the Citalopram – compared to the others, it was the equivalent of a cuddly toy – and carried on taking the high dose that Dr Fielding had prescribed at the height of the depression, just as a protection against the darkness returning.

It was more than a month after Ted's call that she finally remembered to call him back. The twins had just gone down for a nap, and Luci was in a flurry of activity; she held the phone in one hand and the iron in the other, inadvertently scorching one of Alex's crisp white shirts as she scrolled through the phone's memory for Ted's number.

'Hi, it's me,' she said the moment he answered, and went on immediately, not caring whether he knew who 'me' was or not: 'I've been thinking about what you said – well, I've been thinking about a lot of things, like the bathroom needing cleaning and buying a new car and getting Alex a new iPod because he's broken his, and toys for the boys – that rhymes – but what I called to tell you was that...' She paused momentarily, trying to recall why she *had* called. 'Oh yes, I called to tell you that I want to talk to Violet, because she sounds a bit weird to me, and I think I was right in the first place that Walter was hiding something and Violet knows about it, and I'm going to get to the bottom of whatever it is they're hiding because I think it might be important.'

There was silence from Ted's end of the phone line. 'Luci, are you all right?' he asked eventually – for Luci's racing mind, it felt like eternity, but was probably less than thirty seconds.

'I'm fine!' Luci said enthusiastically.

'It's just you sound a little – well, manic,' Ted replied.

'No, no. Just not depressed anymore,' Luci said quickly. 'So, can you give me Violet's number and address?'

'Have you got a pen?' Ted asked.

Luci laughed. 'Dozens,' she replied. 'Just not in my hand.' She grabbed the nearest pen she could find – a chisel-tipped permanent marker – and scrawled down the details Ted read out to her onto Alex's shirt – it was ruined already, so it didn't matter, she reasoned as an afterthought.

'Have you got all that?' Ted asked.

'Yep,' Luci said, squinting at the scrawl and wondering if she could read it. After a second, she decided she could. 'Definitely. I'll call her now. Bye!' She hung up without waiting for Ted's response. The iron was steaming away, and she impatiently switched it off at the wall – too busy to tackle the towering ironing basket now. She grinned to herself. If she left it long enough, Ruth would pop round, see the pile, and do the ironing for Luci. Now that, Luci thought, was a much better solution. She misdialled twice in her haste to speak to Violet, but finally the phone was ringing, and she held her breath in anticipation. The phone rang and rang, finally going through to BT's automated answering service.

'Auntie Violet? It's Luci, Elvina's daughter. Ted gave me your number, he said that you'd visited him. The thing is, my mother died without really telling me anything about the family and I'd love to get to know more about where I come from and I figured that you'd be the best person to ask because, well, you're the only relative left on my grandmother's side of the family, and I kind of know a lot about Walter already, so, anyway, will you call me back, please?' Pausing for breath, she rattled off the landline number and her mobile number and hung up. For ten minutes, she stared at the phone, willing Violet to call back, but the phone remained stoically silent. The twins, however, didn't share the sentiment, waking and wailing in unison to be released from the prison of their crib.

'I need another pair of arms,' she told them seriously. 'You're getting too heavy for me to carry you both. I can't wait until you can both walk. Me and Luke were walking at eleven months. How do you fancy trying that? Or earlier would be nice. In fact, if you had a go now, you could end up being the cleverest little boys in the whole universe.'

Matty and Theo regarded her with absolute trust in their eyes as Luci carried them downstairs and set them down on the play-rug in the living room. 'Bababababa,' Theo gurgled to his brother, and Matty replied instantly, 'Gugugugugu,' which, Luci thought, must mean something because Theo grabbed a rattle and thrust it at his twin. Luci sat on the edge of the sofa with her elbows resting on her knees and her chin resting on her upturned palms, just watching the boys playing happily. She could watch them all day, every day, forever.

***

Violet didn't call back that day, or the next, or the day after that. Luci bristled with impatience, but she knew from experience that a watched phone never rings, and so she threw herself into the million and one other things that breezed haphazardly through her mind.

She gave Violet a whole week to reply, and then, after Alex had gone off to work, loaded Theo and Matty into their car carriers and fastened them into the back of the car.

'We're going to visit your auntie Violet,' she told them, slipping a CD of nursery songs into the CD player. 'Maybe she doesn't know how to get her messages or something. It's probably better that we meet her in person, anyway.'

Legacy of Lies

It was a three hour drive to the address Violet had given Ted, but two hours was nothing in the grand scale of things, and Luci only had to make a couple of stops when the boys started crying and needed to be soothed. They passed a sign for the Holy Island of Lindesfarne and Luci made a mental note to visit there sometime. Maybe on the way back, she thought, depending on how long she was with Violet.

There was a car parked in the driveway of Violet's house, one of those compact little Smart-Car things that Luci always thought were more like toy cars. Not exactly the kind of car Luci expected her great aunt to have – but there was no accounting for people's tastes. Unfastening the two carriers from the back of the car, she walked up the driveway with a carrier hanging from each arm. She had to put the twins down on the ground to ring the doorbell, but picked them straight up again before they started to wail in protest. She could hear movement inside the house, but it seemed an age before there was the sound of a bolt being pulled back. Violet *was* old, though, so it was only understandable she'd be a bit slow on her feet.

'Can I help you?'

Luci opened her mouth automatically to answer but then stopped, the words she was about to say frozen on her lips. 'You're not Violet,' she said instead, because the young woman with a baby girl on her hip clearly wasn't Luci's great aunt.

'I'm sorry?' The woman's smile faltered.

'I'm looking for my great aunt, Violet. She said that she lived here. She gave me this address and said that's where she lived,' Luci replied.

'Sorry, there's no-one called Violet living here,' the woman replied. 'Maybe you wrote it down wrong? Or she gave you the wrong house number?'

'I didn't write it down wrong!' Luci retorted indignantly. 'No, I smell a rat. Ted said that she wasn't all that keen on leaving her details, I should have guessed she'd do something like this. I knew it! I knew they were keeping secrets. Secrets they don't want me to know. So many bloody secrets. Did you know, my whole life has been full of secrets? Everyone keeps secrets from me. What is it with me that everyone keeps secrets from me? Have I got a sign on my forehead? "Please keep secrets from me"?'

The young woman backed into the hallway and firmly closed the door, leaving Luci talking to the chipped red paint. She had a sudden thought and opened the letter-box. 'Did you buy this house off Violet? She's old. Really old. You'd probably remember her. Do you remember her?'

There was silence.

'Hey, I'm asking a sensible question here! *Do you remember Violet*?' Luci yelled.

'I'm going to call the police if you don't leave,' the woman retorted.

'Don't help me, then,' Luci snapped huffily, stalking back down the driveway and fastening the twins back into the car. 'I can't believe Violet lied to Ted like that,' she told them, pulling her mobile phone out of her pocket. Ted's number was engaged, putting her straight through to the answering service.

'Violet doesn't live where she said she did. I knew she was hiding something. They were all hiding something. Lies, lies and more lies. The whole bloody family lies – except you, of course, I don't think that you lie, Ted, of course. You're too honest.' She hung up and got into the car, drumming her fingers on the steering wheel. 'Shall we go to Lindesfarne, then, guys?' she asked, half-expecting the twins to answer. They were gurgling happily to each other, which Luci took as confirmation that visiting the Holy Island was a good idea.

The tide was in, cutting Lindesfarne off from the mainland until the tide went out again to reveal the causeway. Luci waited impatiently, feeling as though the island was mocking her. Staring across at the ruined castle, she felt sure that the tourists – just specks on the building from this distance away – were pointing and laughing at her. She vowed to give them a piece of her mind once the tide relented and actually let her across the causeway. Every minute dragged on for hours. Needing to pee, Luci left the boys in the car, locked it securely, and relieved herself behind a bush, not caring that she could easily be seen from the road. If anyone wanted to watch they were welcome to, the bloody perverts, she thought ruthlessly.

Finally, the tide revealed the whole of the causeway, and Luci led the way, with half a dozen cars following her, across to the island. It was only when she'd parked in the main car park and went to get the boys out of the back that she realised she hadn't thought to bring the buggy. She shrugged. It would be good exercise to carry the baby carriers around with her. She could do with building some muscle tone – and she did need to lose weight, it was no excuse saying that she'd just had twins when they were more than seven months old.

'This is fun, isn't it?' she asked the boys as she headed towards the castle. She toured it in minutes, earning a puzzled look from the man on the entry desk. She grinned broadly at him, but couldn't wave without risking dropping one of the carriers. The priory was visited similarly quickly; in fact, the whole visit to the island was conducted in whistle-stop fashion. Luci bought baby-food in one of the shops, because she'd forgotten to bring any and the twins were grizzling and fretful, and food seemed to be the one thing that was guaranteed to keep them quiet. She fed them, one at a time, sitting on a picnic bench, winded them and put them back in their carriers. She was just loading them back into the car – little over an hour since she'd driven over the causeway, when her mobile shrilled in her pocket.

'Where the hell are you? Mum just phoned to say you weren't at home and she was worried!' Alex said.

'Lindesfarne,' Luci replied, as if it was the most obvious answer in the world.

'*What*?'

'Lindesfarne. Are you going deaf?'

'What are you doing on Lindesfarne?' Alex asked. 'Are the boys with you?'

'No, I left them in the supermarket,' Luci retorted. 'Of course they're with me! We've been to visit Violet, except she gave Ted a false address and sent us on a wild goose chase, but it doesn't matter, because we've had a lovely day anyway.'

'You didn't think to call me and tell me where you were?' Alex asked.

'No,' Luci replied honestly. 'I forgot. Sorry. But we'll be coming home soon; we're just about to set off. And before you ask, yes, I've fed the boys, and I've changed their nappies and they are perfectly happy.' She held the phone out towards the twins. 'Tell Daddy how happy you are, boys!' They gurgled obligingly at the mention of their father.

'Promise me you'll drive carefully,' Alex was saying when Luci put the phone back to her ear.

'I always drive carefully!' Luci said indignantly.

'Of course you do,' Alex said dryly. 'Luce, I'm worried about you. You're talking a mile a minute and you sound really hyper.' He paused. 'Weren't you supposed to be seeing Dr Fielding today?'

'Was I?' Luci asked vaguely. 'Whoops. Will you call her and tell her I've got flu or something and reschedule?'

'If you promise to drive carefully, I will,' Alex replied.

'What are you, the happiness police?' Luci demanded. She sighed. 'Fine, I'll drive carefully. We'll be home soon.' She paused. 'I love you.'

'I love you, too,' Alex replied, but Luci detected a note of acquiescence in his voice. She hung up and tossed the phone onto the passenger seat.

'I don't think Daddy's very pleased with us,' she said to the boys, and laughed. 'Nothing new there, then.'

CHAPTER NINE

'Luce, I think you really need to calm down a bit,' Alex said, slipping his arms around Luci's shoulders as she tapped frantically away at her laptop. 'You're manic, and that's really not good. Do you want me to come with you to see Dr Fielding this afternoon?'

Luci shrugged him off. 'I'm not manic,' she protested. 'You're just that used to me being depressed that you've forgotten what I'm like when I'm not depressed. And I can manage to talk to Dr Fielding without your supervision.'

'You *are* manic,' Alex insisted. 'You've got that look in your eye. I can always tell. You can't fool me, not anymore.'

Luci laughed. 'You mean the fire in my eyes?' she asked mischievously, causing Alex to sigh heavily.

'Yes,' he replied. 'Look, why don't you take the boys round to Mum's for a bit – she's moaning that it's ages since the two of you had a chat over coffee.'

'Why don't you say what you really mean?' Luci asked. 'Because I'm not stupid. I'm far from stupid. Far, far, far from stupid. What you mean is that you think I need supervising, which I don't, by the way, but you think that if you wrap it up and put a pretty bow on the parcel I won't know what you're thinking. But it's written all over your face, Alz, and I know *you* too well, you can't hide anything from me. I don't need supervising. I'm fine. I'm better than fine, I'm wonderful.'

'You are worrying me, Luce. I'm not happy about leaving you on your own with the boys all day,' Alex replied. 'It's not that I don't trust you or anything, but when you're like this, you're not exactly thinking clearly.'

'I'm thinking perfectly clearly,' Luci retorted. 'All my thoughts are travelling in straight, perpendicular lines, and it's very ordered and organised, and they're not even overlapping. If you cut my brain in half you'd be able to see for yourself how pretty it is.'

'Maybe I could work from home today,' Alex mused, running his fingers through his hair.

'And be under my feet all day, driving me crazy? I don't think so,' Luci shot back. 'Go to work. I do not need babysitting.'

'That *is* a matter of opinion,' Alex sighed. 'I'll tell Mum you're going to be in all day if she wants to pop round, all right?'

'If it gets you off my back, then yes, fine,' Luci snapped. 'God, it's like having the happiness police on my back the whole time.'

Alex smiled thinly. 'It's only because we care about you,' he said, bending to kiss her. She turned her head away impatiently, waiting until he'd left the house before letting out a muted scream of frustration. The twins looked at her in alarm, but, used to their mother's oddities, soon returned their attention to the toys scattered around in their playpen. Luci turned back to her computer screen, resuming her thus fruitless search for Violet's real address. She'd discovered that Violet had married – late in life – and had tried typing her great-aunt's name into several electoral roll and directory enquiries websites, but it seemed as though Violet had somehow managed to completely disappear. There was no trace of her – not even on the electoral roll going back to 2002.

'Why would she want to make sure that no one could find her?' Luci asked the boys, who didn't even look at her. Plastic rattles were far more interesting to them. Luci sighed with frustration. There was nothing more she could do now – with no hope of tracking Violet down, Luci had to resign herself to the fact that once again she'd hit a brick wall in her quest to uncover the secrets that she was certain Walter – and now Violet – had been keeping. 'Bugger it,' she muttered, deciding on impulse to take the boys to the nearby play park, just to get out of the house and spend some of the restless energy that was pulsating through her whole body.

There was a message waiting on the answering machine when Luci returned from the park with Matty and Theo both fast asleep in their buggy. Expecting it to be Alex or Ruth calling to check up on her, Luci was tempted to delete the message without even listening to it – but she hit the play button on the off-chance that it was something more important than the smothering concern of her family.

'Luci, it's Ted. I've got some news I thought you should know. The tenants in Walter's house have had a bit of a family emergency and have had to give notice to quit the house. They've paid the rent up until the end of the month, but they've moved out already. The thing is, I put a lot of Walter's things up in the attic when he moved into sheltered accommodation, and I wondered if you might like to help me sort through it. He was a bit of a hoarder – there are boxes of paperwork and all sorts – and there might even be an address for Violet – I don't know if they kept in touch, but it's entirely possible. Anyway, give me a call back, will you?'

Luci grinned inanely at the answering machine, her pulse quickening with excitement. She snatched up the phone and punched in Ted's number. 'I'm on my way,' she said the moment he answered.

'Luci?'

'Of course,' Luci replied impatiently. 'I'll have to bring the boys with me, but it's okay if we stay, isn't it?'

'You're coming today?' Ted asked in bewilderment.

'Of course – there's no time like the present,' Luci retorted. 'Walter's paperwork might be the key to all the secrets – I can't believe you never told me about it before!'

'Is Alex coming with you?' Ted asked.

'Oh no, definitely not,' Luci replied. 'He's at work, and anyway, I need to get away from him before he smothers me completely. It's like living in Colditz – everything I do is monitored and noted, and if I laugh, I'm manic, and if I cry I'm depressed, which is crazy, because everybody laughs and cries, though, admittedly, probably not at the same time, which I do sometimes.' She paused for breath. 'I'm just going to pack and get the boys ready, but I should be with you in a couple of hours. We could make a start on the stuff in the attic this afternoon!' Without waiting for Ted's response, Luci hung up and tossed the phone down onto the dresser. Leaving the boys sleeping contentedly in their buggy, she ran upstairs, dragged a suitcase out from under the bed, and started throwing clothes haphazardly into it. She tossed a couple of bottles of shampoo and a box of Tampax into her vanity case along with her make-up bag and fastened the vanity case up, turning her attention then to all the paraphernalia that had to accompany the twins on holidays. Considering how small they were, their luggage amounted to much more than Luci's. Making several trips up and down stairs and out to the car, it was half an hour before Luci was ready to leave, and then, after putting the boys into their car carriers, she had to struggle to fit the buggy into the already full boot. It took a lot of manoeuvring, but finally they were ready for the off. As an afterthought, she called Alex's office, knowing full well that he'd be having coffee with the rest of the partners, and left a somewhat gabbled and bewildering message with his secretary, who was, by now, quite used to Luci's rambling messages. 'At least Daddy can't say that we didn't tell him where we were going,' Luci commented to the boys, who were gurgling happily and seemingly feeding off their mother's excitable mood.

***

'I think we should have some lunch before we go over to the house,' Ted suggested sagely after he'd helped Luci carry all the luggage up to his spare bedroom. After Luci had called, he'd had to go up into his own attic to fetch down the cot that had been used for his daughter and grandchildren when they were babies. It was still in good condition, though some of the paint had chipped – not that Ted thought for a minute that Luci would notice something like that. He *was* concerned about her. Her rapid speech, the way her sentences ran into one another, and the way she flitted from thought to thought without any apparent connection were sure signs that all was not well, but Ted felt helpless to do anything more than keep a watchful eye on Luci. He didn't want to risk raising his concerns in case she took flight with the twins. It was far better to know where she was – and Ted could easily call Alex if he felt things were getting out of hand. They weren't, yet – at least Ted didn't think so. Going through the dozens of boxes in the attic of Walter's house might help Luci to calm down, anyway.

'But I want to get started. I haven't got time for lunch,' Luci protested petulantly.

'I'll make us something,' Ted insisted. 'Do you like omelettes?'

'Only if it doesn't take long to make and eat them,' Luci replied, sighing.

'It won't take long,' Ted promised, smiling indulgently at Luci. The more he got to know Luci, the more she reminded him of Isabella, who was always such a livewire. Isabella had always been Ted's favourite; although he got on well with Elvina, too, there was something about Izzy that was almost enchanting.

It was another hour before Ted drove Luci over to the house that had been her mother's childhood home, by which time Luci was fairly brimming over with anticipation. Leaving the twins asleep in their buggy in the hallway, Ted led the way up the stairs and stopped in front of a door at the head of the stairs which had a padlocked bolt across it.

'When Walter moved, I just carted everything up into the attic room – which used to be your mother and Isabella's room, by the way – and put a lock on the door so the tenants couldn't go poking around up there,' Ted explained, pulling a bunch of keys from his pocket and selecting the correct one to open the padlock. It was a fiddly lock and Luci hopped from foot to foot in impatience, anxious to explore her mother's room and the treasures that it might hold. She felt certain, suddenly, that she was just moments away from discovering Walter's secrets.

'Why did Mum and Isabella have an attic room?' she asked whilst Ted still struggled with the padlock. 'It's a three bedroom house!'

Ted glanced sideways at Luci as the padlock released with a satisfying click. 'That's an interesting question,' he said.

'So answer it, then!'

'The girls each had a bedroom of their own up until Medora's death, and then Grandmother Georgina moved in to help Walter take care of them – they were still only eight at the time, of course – and it was decided that since the girls would have to share the room, it would be better to have a bedroom made up in the attic to give them more room.'

'Who decided?' Luci demanded. 'Let me guess – Georgina?'

Ted nodded, smiling ruefully. 'Of course. She could be a very domineering woman. When she made her mind up about something, that was the end of it. There was never any arguing with her. She was always right, always knew better than everyone else, no matter what the situation was.'

'She sounds horrible. I can't imagine how awful it must have been for Mum and Isabella having to live under her rule. It's no wonder really that Mum never talked about her past.' Luci said, bounding up the wooden staircase after Ted. He switched the light on at the top of the stairs – a single bare bulb hung from the rafters.

The attic room was almost the length and breadth of the house, with just one corner boxed off where, Luci presumed, the boiler and water tanks were housed. The walls were painted a pale cream, and the floorboards were bare. A fitted three-door wardrobe occupied one corner.

'Was it carpeted? When Mum and Isabella slept in here?' Luci asked, frowning.

Ted shook his head. 'No. Grandmother Georgina didn't believe in such luxuries, although Elvina and Izzy made a couple of rag rugs as they got older to make the room a little more homely.'

'Witch,' Luci muttered, her gaze travelling over the cardboard boxes that were stacked in rather unstable-looking towers.

Ted followed her gaze. 'By the time Walter moved into sheltered accommodation, his study was overflowing with books and filing cabinets,' he explained. 'I'm afraid it's going to take us quite some time to sort it all out!'

'That,' Luci said, laughing, 'could possibly be the understatement of the year!'

There were boxes full of bank statements that dated right back before Walter married Medora, receipts, insurance certificates, gas and electric bills and all manner of letters. Luci's attention span wasn't long enough to give any of them more than a cursory glance although she was determined that at some point – once her mind slowed down a little, perhaps – she would go through the bank statements and letters in case there were any secrets lurking there. There were at least a dozen boxes of books, which Luci lifted out one by one to gaze at the titles, trying to gain some measure of the man her grandfather had been before he lost his marbles. He had been a serious man, she gathered from the amount of classics – mainly Charles Dickens, Henry James and William Shakespeare – that Walter had collected. He had been an intellectual man, too, reading works by Charles Darwin and Albert Einstein – books that Luci couldn't understand for the life of her.

'Shall we take a break?' Ted suggested, and Luci looked up, blinking as if emerging from a dream. She was surprised when she looked at her watch and realised that a good couple of hours had passed, and she'd lost the feeling in her legs from kneeling down for too long.

'Sure,' Luci said, standing up and hopping around the room as pins and needles shot up from her feet all the way up her legs. 'I could use a coffee, to wash down all the dust I've inhaled from these boxes.'

Ted had brought a spare kettle, mugs, coffee and milk with him, and he and Luci sat around the table in the kitchen, until their peace was disturbed by Theo and Matty when the babies woke to find themselves in a strange place.

'I should have thought to bring the baby monitor – we could put them down to sleep in one of the bedrooms and have the monitor in the attic with us so we'd hear when they woke up,' Luci mused. She sprung to her feet. 'Can you look after them while I go and buy a new baby monitor? Can I take your car? I won't be long. Half an hour, tops.' She dashed out, snatching the car keys off the kitchen counter, before Ted could even find the words to reply.

***

Legacy of Lies

Luci returned, an hour later, not just with a brand new baby monitor but with a dozen bulging carrier bags filled with an eclectic mixture of clothes for herself and the twins and enough food to fill the pantry of her mother's childhood home.

'I've had an idea,' she said breathlessly, dumping the carrier bags on the kitchen table and throwing herself down into one of the chairs. The twins were happily crawling around on the kitchen floor, in their element at having a new environment to explore.

'Oh yes?' Ted said, putting a mug of coffee in front of Luci.

'Well, I was thinking, whilst I was out, that it's going to be an awful waste of petrol coming here and going back to your house every day, and seeing as the house is standing empty, *and* there's a whole *mountain* of paperwork of Walter's to get through, it makes much more sense for me to stay here with the boys. I can get much more done that way, and it'll save so much time.'

'I'll still be using petrol to come over here to help,' Ted pointed out.

Luci waved her hand dismissively. 'Oh, I can manage – you must have a million things you'd rather be doing than wading through fifty years of bank statements,' she said, grinning. 'He was my grandfather – that makes it my responsibility, I reckon.'

'Luci, I really don't mind,' Ted said.

Luci cocked her head on one side and looked at him through narrowed eyes. 'Don't you start,' she said shrewdly. 'I am perfectly capable of taking care of myself and the boys. I don't need bloody well babysitting.'

Ted sighed. 'It's not that I think you need babysitting,' he said. 'I just thought that with there being so much of Walter's things to go through, it would be quicker with two of us.'

Luci snorted dismissively. 'Don't be ridiculous,' she said, entirely unaware of how rude and arrogant she sounded. 'You'd only slow me down. Do you know how frustrating it is watching you take a whole hour over a box when I could do ten in that time?'

Ted smiled thinly. 'What about the boys?' he asked. 'Where are they going to sleep?'

'Aha!' Luci crowed. 'You see, I think of everything! I bought a Moses basket from Mothercare – it's in the car, I'll go and fetch it.' Jumping to her feet, she dashed back outside and returned moments later carrying a large blue Moses basket. 'I know it's not all that big, but it's the biggest they had, and the boys like to curl up together anyway, and at least they'll be nice and cosy.' She paused for breath, her eyes shining brightly with excitement. 'Do you know which bedroom was Mum's before your grandma exiled her to the attic? I think the boys should sleep in there. Did you know that babies have a much better connection with the spirits than adults do? Maybe they'll be able to sense Mum. I'd like them to get to know her. I know she wasn't perfect, but she's still their grandma.'

'Luci...' Ted began tentatively, alarmed by the speed at which she was talking, and how overly animated she seemed.

'What?' Luci retorted. There was a challenge in her eyes as if she was defying him to question her judgment. Ted felt a shiver of apprehension as he looked at her. He was beginning to wish that he hadn't called Luci in the first place. She was obviously manic – and Ted was ashamed to admit that he didn't really know how to deal with her.

'Elvina's room was the one right at the top of the stairs,' Ted said weakly. 'There's an adjoining door through into the next room – that was Isabella's.'

'Perfect,' Luci said, already heading towards the stairs. 'Can you keep an eye on them while I get the room ready? Won't take me more than five minutes.'

After returning Theo to the kitchen after he started commando crawling after his mother, Ted sat down at the kitchen table and took his mobile phone out of his trouser pocket. The number he needed was the first one in the phone's memory. He kept one eye on the stairs as he dialled the number. Alex picked up before the third ring.

'Ted! Is Luci with you? I got a garbled message, and I've been trying to call her all afternoon, but she hasn't been answering,' Alex said, sounding harassed.

'She's with me – and the boys,' Ted assured him. 'But...'

'Does she seem manic to you?' Alex asked. 'I thought she was, but she won't listen to me when she's like this. It's like talking to a brick wall – Luci knows best and she won't take the damnedest bit of notice of anyone else.'

'I am concerned about her,' Ted said, relieved to hear that he wasn't the only one who struggled in the face of Luci's manic mind. 'I'm afraid it's my fault she's here. I called to tell her that the tenants in Walter's house had moved out and there was a lot of paperwork up in the attic – and she insisted on coming straight here.'

'Don't worry about it. If it hadn't been you, it would have been something else. At least I know she's safe,' Alex replied. 'She's staying with you, right?'

'She was,' Ted said. 'Until about ten minutes ago. Now she's decided that she and the boys should stay here at Walter's house.'

'*Why?*'

'So she can get more done, she says. There are boxes and boxes of paperwork up in the attic – I was happy to help, but Luci won't hear of it. She wants to do it all herself.'

Alex sighed heavily. 'Can you stay with her, Ted? I know it's a lot to ask, but I've got a massive case in court this week, and I really can't get down to you until the weekend.'

'Will Luci agree to me staying, do you think?' Ted asked, already knowing that the answer was 'no', regardless of what Alex thought.

'No, probably not,' Alex conceded. 'Bloody hell. Of all the times for this to happen.' He was silent for a moment. 'You said something about boxes in the attic, right? So, who's looking after the boys whilst she's up there?'

'She's bought a baby monitor,' Ted said.

'But it would be much better if there was someone there to look after them, so Luci can get on with whatever it is she's gone fanatical over now,' Alex cut in. 'That's how you need to put it to Luci – but whatever you do, don't mention me or she'll never agree.'

'Right! Yes, yes, I see what you mean,' Ted said. He heard footsteps crossing the room above. 'She's coming down – I'd better go.'

'I'll keep trying to call her. She'll answer eventually – she always does,' Alex said, hanging up – seconds before Luci came crashing down the stairs like an overexcited toddler.

'I thought I heard you talking to someone,' she said, frowning.

'Just the boys,' Ted said, hoping that his smile was convincing enough. 'Theo was investigating whether he could make it up the stairs on his own.'

Luci laughed, bending down to scoop the little boy up into her arms. 'Is that right, little man?' she asked, kissing the top of his head. 'I've told them both – the sooner they start walking and talking, the better,' she added seriously to Ted.

'You'll regret saying that once they do start walking and talking,' Ted replied – from experience. He hesitated. 'I was thinking whilst you were upstairs. I know you've got the baby monitor now, but these two little lads seem to like their freedom. Why don't I stay here too to take care of them whilst you tackle everything up in the attic?'

Luci set Theo back down on the floor. He immediately started crawling towards the stairs, and Matty soon followed suit. Luci sat back on her haunches and watched them for a moment, before looking up at Ted. 'You're right,' she said, nodding. 'It's not fair to keep them cooped up. But do you mind? They can be little horrors!'

Ted smiled, hoping that he didn't look too relieved. 'Of course I don't mind,' he said quickly. 'I've had plenty of practice – I spent nearly a year in Australia helping Toria with the girls when Richard was ill.'

Luci nodded. 'I remember – I gave up hoping you'd ever get in touch when your neighbour said you were away visiting your daughter. I thought you must have emigrated!'

'That's settled, then,' Ted said brightly. 'I'll nip home and grab a few things, and then get the bedrooms made up.'

Luci grinned. 'You're quite excited about having a little holiday, aren't you, Ted?' she teased.

Ted shrugged, laughing along with her. 'It's a change of four walls,' he said. 'I won't be long.'

'Don't be – I can't wait to get back up into that attic and find out what secrets Walter was keeping from us all,' Luci replied, disappearing into the hall to retrieve her wayward sons.

CHAPTER TEN

By the time Ted convinced Luci to stop for lunch the next day, she was fast giving up hope of finding anything of interest amongst Walter's papers. She had started with the bank statements – which dated back to long before her mother had been born, before even Walter had married Medora. Her grandfather had kept every single statement, every cheque book stub, and every receipt for everything he had ever purchased. The odds of finding anything remotely attention-grabbing were getting longer with each batch of paper Luci lifted out of the boxes. Walter had to be the most anally-retentive, squeaky-clean man in existence. The monthly cheques to a man named Tyrell piqued Luci's interest at first – until Ted quashed the faint whiff of a scandal. Tyrell was just the pastor of the church Walter had belonged to. Membership of the church had been on a tithe basis – 25% of Walter's salary was paid to the church every month.

'25%?' Luci repeated incredulously. 'What the hell sort of church was that?'

'Your mother called it a cult – and I'm afraid I'd be inclined to agree with her,' Ted replied, setting a plate of bacon sandwiches down in front of Luci. 'Pastor Tyrell's grand-father set it up back in 1888. They called it the Church of the Glorious and Great God.'

'The *what*?' Luci spluttered.

Ted smiled. 'I know,' he said. 'I had to worship at the church for eighteen years – until I escaped away to Oxford University. I was the laughing stock at school. Pastor Tyrell was known for miles around for being a zealot and a tyrant – but he had the people in this community hanging on to every word that left his lips – and Grandmother was his fiercest supporter.'

'Is that why Mum ran away? To get away from all that?' Luci asked.

'I can't say for certain,' Ted said hesitantly. 'I was living away in Oxford when all that happened. I can only go on what my mother told me – and what I heard later.'

'What do you mean, what you heard later?' Luci asked. Ted had been very evasive the first time she'd asked what he knew about why her mother had cut herself off from the rest of the family, and she'd never thought to ask him again.

'It might just have been idle gossip – I'm afraid I was never brave enough to ask my mother outright,' Ted hedged. 'Although I do know that some of Pastor Tyrell's practices were somewhat *controversial*.'

'*Ted*,' Luci said in exasperation. 'Just spit it out – don't keep me guessing.'

'There was a rumour that I heard when I came home for Christmas,' Ted said, still reluctant to reveal his secret. Luci glowered at him. 'I can't say whether it's true or not – but I heard mention of some kind of ceremony that Elvina was involved in, after Isabella had died.'

'What sort of ceremony?' Luci asked suspiciously.

'A... cleansing ceremony,' Ted said reluctantly.

'What's that when it's at home?' Luci asked.

'A ceremony to cleanse a person of evil,' Ted replied.

Luci narrowed her eyes suspiciously. 'You mean like an exorcism?'

Ted sighed. 'I suppose you might call it that,' he agreed, looking very uncomfortable.

'They *exorcised* my mother, and you wondered why she didn't want to have anything to do with her father again?' Luci muttered incredulously. 'Good God. I didn't think those sort of things still happened!'

'It's possible that Isabella was made to go through the same ceremony,' Ted admitted.

'What kind of nutcase was this Tyrell bloke?' Luci demanded.

'He was very dedicated to his religion. Grandmother was, too,' Ted said.

'That isn't a religion,' Luci snapped. 'It's a bloody cult – and a crazy one at that. There's no wonder Mum was messed up.'

'I have heard it called that,' Ted said. 'Although around here the community is still strongly connected to the church.'

'Do they still exorcise people?' Luci asked. 'I'd better be careful or they'll be dragging me off into their little chapel to rid me of evil!'

'I don't think the current pastor is quite so extreme in his beliefs,' Ted replied. 'Although I have as little to do with the whole thing as I possibly can.'

'I think I can understand now why Mum never talked about her childhood. You wouldn't want to if you'd been through hell. You'd just want to pretend it never happened,' Luci said, finishing her sandwiches and pushing back her chair. She was half way upstairs when a sudden thought struck her and she came clattering back down again. 'You said that Isabella had been through the same ceremony. Why would they do that if she had TB? Surely they didn't think that TB was caused by evil spirits.'

'I know,' Ted agreed. 'It never made sense what people said.'

'Why, what did they say?'

'The funny thing about it was that the village doctor – he was an outsider, didn't believe in the church and didn't get involved – was never consulted about Izzy's health,' Ted said. 'I only found that out by chance when I had to see him for something the Christmas after Izzy died. He'd heard that she'd died, of course, but knew nothing about her having TB.'

'I smell a rat,' Luci said succinctly. 'What with the way Walter went nuts when he saw me and everything – I knew something wasn't right about it all.' She cocked her head and stared directly at Ted. 'Did she really have TB, or was there another reason she had to be sent away?'

Ted shrugged. 'I only know what I was told,' he admitted.

'Who told you?'

'Mother, of course.'

'You didn't speak to Elvina?'

'Walter wasn't on the telephone. I had letters from Elvina, but we didn't have a chance to speak.'

'Not even at Isabella's funeral?'

Ted shook his head. 'There wasn't a funeral – not here, at least. She was buried at the sanatorium where she died.'

'That's weird, isn't it?' Luci asked. 'You'd think Walter would have wanted his daughter buried at home, so the family could pay their last respects. Did he and Mum go to the funeral at the sanatorium?'

Ted shook his head again. 'No. I did find that odd, but I suppose it might have been difficult. It was a long way to travel just for a day.'

'Where was the sanatorium?' Luci asked.

'In Scotland, I think,' Ted replied.

Luci's eyebrows arched sharply. 'Did Walter have some kind of weird obsession with Scotland?' she demanded. 'He sent his wife there – to die, and he sent his daughter there – to die. Freaky. Did he want them to be as far away from him as possible or something?'

'No, no, of course not,' Ted said quickly. 'I think it was because Violet was a nurse up in Scotland – she had contacts. I suppose it made sense for Walter to ask for her help and advice.'

'Yeah, and I don't think it's a coincidence that *she's* as elusive as the scarlet bloody pimpernel,' Luci muttered. She squared her shoulders. 'Somewhere in that mountain of paper, there must be some kind of clue to what the hell was going on in Walter's head – and I'm damn sure I'm going to find out what it was that he was hiding!'

***

An hour later, Luci came clattering down the stairs from the attic with a bundle of receipts in her hands. She'd found them right at the bottom of a box of bank statements, half hidden beneath one of the sealing flaps.

'Who were the Sisters of Mercy and Deliverance?' she demanded of Ted. He was sitting on the floor of the living room with the twins, building towers of wooden blocks for them to immediately knock down. It was their favourite game.

'I've heard the name,' Ted said, frowning. 'But I can't remember where.'

'Well Walter started paying them five hundred pounds a year since 1968,' Luci said jubilantly. 'It went up to a thousand in 1980, and up to two thousand in 1998. Stopped in 2003, of course, when you started handling his affairs.'

'I don't understand,' Ted said, sounding bewildered. 'I can't think why he'd be paying that kind of money to anyone. He was comfortably well off, but certainly not rich – and it's an awful lot of money to be paying as a charitable donation.'

'Think, Ted – where have you heard the name?' Luci asked sharply. 'There's no address – just the receipts with the name on. A Sister Margaret signed the receipts for the first twenty years, then a Sister Anne after that – but they're probably the two most common names in the bloody English language.'

Ted shook his head. 'I don't know who they are, Luci, I'm sorry. The name rings a bell, but I could have heard it anywhere – on television, or read it in a newspaper.'

'Walter never mentioned it?'

'Not that I can recall – and I think I would have remembered if he had – it's not exactly a common name. I presume it's a nunnery of some kind.'

'I could probably find them on the internet,' Luci mused, brightening. She bent down to drop a kiss on Matty and Theo's foreheads. 'Mummy's just popping out,' she told them. 'You be good for Uncle Ted.'

'Where are you going?' Ted asked.

'To buy a laptop and a thingy to use mobile broadband,' Luci replied, as if it was obvious. 'How else am I going to find out what the hell Walter was up to?' Before Ted could say another word, Luci dashed out of the front door, came charging back for the car keys, and then was gone again, the wheels of Ted's car squealing as she accelerated hard off the driveway.

***

'I don't get it,' Luci muttered, frowning at Ted over the top of her new laptop. 'I can't find any mention of the "Sisters of Mercy and Deliverance" *anywhere*. It's like they don't exist!'

Ted smiled. 'Just because they're not on the internet doesn't mean that they don't exist. I'm sure that there are plenty of people who've missed out on the technological revolution.'

Luci scowled. 'Well how am I going to find them, then?' she demanded. 'You'd think they'd at least have a listing in Directory Enquiries – but there's nothing.'

'If it was a very private nunnery, I suppose they wouldn't want to have a listing in the Directory,' Ted suggested. 'And anyone can be ex-directory if they want to, can't they?'

'I suppose so,' Luci grumbled, slamming the lid of the laptop closed. 'Bugger. I guess that means I've got to go back to trawling through Walter's bloody boxes. I really thought we were on to something with this. Damnit!'

'I'll try and think of where I might have heard the name,' Ted offered.

'What's the point?' Luci muttered. 'We're still not going to find out where they are.' Sighing heavily with resignation, she headed back up the stairs, despondency beginning to set in. Walter had secrets – she was certain of it. They were just too damn well hidden.

***

When Alex arrived on Friday night, having driven down to Derbyshire straight from work, the welcome he got from Luci was far from warm. It wasn't even lukewarm.

'What are you doing here?' she demanded, coming down from the attic when she heard him and Ted talking downstairs. 'Checking up on me?'

'I thought we could spend the weekend together,' Alex said, smiling as he moved in for a kiss. 'I was lonely at home on my own. I missed you and the boys.'

Luci gazed suspiciously at him. 'You sure you're not just checking up on me?'

Alex put his hands on her shoulders and stared right into her eyes. 'I promise,' he said seriously. 'How are you getting on with all Walter's stuff?'

'I'm not,' Luci groaned. 'Every time I think I've found something, it turns out to be nothing – or a complete dead end. Like the bloody Sisters of Mercy and Deliverance!'

'I remember the name from somewhere, but I can't place where,' Ted chipped in.

'Something Walter was involved in, then?' Alex asked.

'Something suspicious,' Luci said darkly. 'He was sending them money – lots of it – for years.'

'You're as tense as a coiled spring,' Alex said, slipping behind Luci to massage her shoulders. 'Are you going to take a break from all that stuff while we have a takeaway or something?'

Luci sighed. 'I suppose so. I'm beginning to understand how a hamster feels. I've been going through all those boxes, and getting nowhere – just like a hamster running round and round on a bloody wheel! Most of what Walter kept is just junk – but I've got to look at it all just in case there's something in there that might give me some clues to whatever it was he was up to.'

'I'll help,' Alex offered. 'It'll be quicker with two of us. And before you say anything, I'll be just as careful as you are – I promise!'

'All right,' Luci said grudgingly.

'You look tired,' Alex said softly whilst Ted went to fetch the takeaway menu he and Luci had been using for the past few days.

'I'm fine,' Luci said irritably.

'Have you been sleeping?'

'Of course I have,' Luci lied. 'I've told you – I'm *fine*.'

'Okay, okay, I was just asking!' Alex held his hands up in defence. 'I worry about you, you know that.'

'I'll be better once I get to the bottom of what Walter was keeping secret,' Luci conceded. 'I'm just a bit edgy, that's all. I know the answer's up there – there's just so many bloody boxes to go through. And you can guarantee it'll be in the last box that I open.'

Alex smiled. 'So why don't we start opening some of the boxes you were going to do last?' he suggested.

Luci looked up at him in surprise. 'Why didn't I think of that?' she asked.

'Because you've been living and breathing those boxes for days, and you've got too close to it,' Alex said. 'Come on, let's order dinner – I'm starving!'

***

'Why do you have to always be right?' Luci asked Alex when the first box that he opened – after spending a couple of hours rearranging the neat stacks of boxes to get to the ones at the very back of the attic room – revealed bundles of envelopes tied together with black ribbon and leather bound ledgers filled with Walter's pedantically neat handwriting.

'It was just a hunch,' Alex said dismissively.

'A hunch that could have saved me days of searching through crap!' Luci retorted, falling on the booty like it was the crown jewels Alex had unveiled. 'You can take the ledgers – they look boring! I'll do the letters.'

'Thanks,' Alex said drily. 'Shall we take them downstairs? – the light's better down there.'

Luci shrugged. 'I'm okay here. You go down if you want to.' She didn't mention that she liked being up in the attic because she felt closer to her mother up there – Alex would only laugh at her for being sentimental.

Alex sat down cross-legged on the floor. 'If you're happy up here, I might as well stay too,' he said, cracking open the first of the ledgers. A cloud of dust rose up. 'I think that says it all,' he muttered, wafting his hand in front of his face.

'Get looking,' Luci said mock-sternly. 'You never know what secrets Walter might have concealed in there.'

'Yeah,' Alex said sarcastically. 'Let's just hope the moths didn't get to them first!'

Luci rolled her eyes. 'Get on with it!' she commanded, and sat down under the window – the only other completely clear space in the room. She struggled for a moment untying the knot of the ribbon around the envelopes, and then they tumbled into her lap, revealing the neat – and familiar – writing on the front of each. Four of the five envelopes were addressed to Walter, but there was one that had been addressed to Georgina Warburton, too.

'They're all from Violet,' she said in surprise. 'I recognise her writing from the letters she wrote to Medora – you know, the ones that Mum kept.'

'The same Violet who sent you off on a wild goose chase?' Alex asked wryly.

'I told you there was something weird about it all,' Luci retorted, opening the first envelope and tugging the paper out. The letter was dated 1968. 'Why would she be writing to Walter? This was *years* after Medora died.'

'Maybe she wanted to keep in touch for Elvina – and Isabella's – sake,' Alex suggested.

'Why leave it until then?' Luci demanded.

'How do you know that was the first?' Alex asked.

'Because Walter was meticulous in everything else, so it figures that he would be with these, too,' Luci said, but she opened each envelope one after the other, to prove that Walter had stored them all in date order, before she started reading them.

Violet wasn't one to mince her words, Luci soon discovered. The first letter began with a polite thanks for Walter's letter – Luci wished Walter had kept copies of the letters *he'd* sent – and then cut straight to the chase.

'With regard to your enquiry,' Violet had written, *'I understand completely the difficulty of the situation you find yourself in. I am sure you are more than aware of my feelings about the dreadful **cult** you dragged my sister into, but nonetheless, for my dear niece's sake, I am sure that something could be arranged to remedy the situation. It would be preferable not to involve anyone else in the matter – you will appreciate the need for discretion. The least outside involvement, the better for all concerned, particularly as – I assume – you wish to keep the matter private. I would advise action before the delicate matter becomes too obvious.'*

'What the hell?' Luci muttered, reading the letter again before passing it over to Alex. 'Does she have to be so bloody cryptic?'

'This was something to do with either your mother or Isabella,' Alex said, frowning. 'What did Isabella die from?'

'TB,' Luci replied.

'Are you sure?'

'That's what Ted said.'

'Could he have been wrong?'

'How should I know?' Luci demanded. 'Why, what are you getting at?'

'What would have been a difficult situation and a delicate matter that could become too obvious?' Alex prompted. Luci looked blankly at him. 'I think Isabella was pregnant,' Alex went on.

'But why would Ted think she died of TB?' Luci asked.

'It was 1968, Luce. Teenage pregnancy was really frowned on back then – and with what you've told me about this church thing that Walter was involved in...'

'Maybe,' Luci said dubiously, picking up the next letter. It was just as cryptic, but towards the end, Violet asked for an '*expected date – as accurate as you can be without medical intervention*'. Luci looked up at Alex. 'All right, smart arse,' she muttered. 'You're probably right.'

Alex grinned. 'At least you've got something interesting to read,' he replied. 'This is worse than reading law statues. Did you know that Walter wrote down every single payment he made for *anything*. Including *milk*.'

Luci laughed distractedly, already reading the third letter. She looked up again, shocked. 'The nunnery,' she said. 'The Sisters of Mercy and Deliverance. *That's* where they sent Isabella – not to a sanatorium to recover. They sent her to a *nunnery*.'

'To give birth?' Alex asked.

'Presumably. It doesn't say as much,' Luci said. 'God, how awful. And she must have died giving birth, on her own. It's barbaric. What kind of parent would *do* that to their own child? No wonder Mum ran away. She must have known that Izzy was pregnant. And that explains why she was so screwed up. Her twin died – on her own – and Mum could have been there, it wasn't like Izzy was infectious, like Walter told everyone.' Luci screwed her eyes closed, shuddering. 'Just thinking about Luke dying on his own makes me feel sick. What must Mum have felt like? *That's* why she never talked about having a twin. It must have been eating away at her all those years.' Luci let the letter slip from her hands. 'I'm glad he's dead,' she said viciously. 'I'm glad I didn't find this out before he died, because, God help me, I would have gone round to that nursing home and strangled him myself!'

'No, you wouldn't,' Alex said sensibly.

'I would,' Luci insisted, her eyes flashing with anger. 'He was *evil*, him and his mother. I told you what Ted said – that they exorcised Izzy before they sent her away! You can't tell me that's not perverted!'

'It's... not nice,' Alex said weakly.

'Not *nice*?' Luci repeated scornfully. 'Not nice is pushing in front of an old lady in the supermarket. Not nice is not telling someone they've dropped a twenty-pence piece on the floor. What *they* did was pure evil – and they dared to claim that Isabella was possessed!'

'You don't know that what Ted said is true,' Alex pointed out. 'It was only a rumour that he heard.'

Luci picked up the remaining two letters, and read the first. 'It wasn't a rumour,' she said, the triumph in her voice tempered by fury. She dropped one letter into her lap and brandished the one she'd just read in her hand, waving it towards Alex. 'Georgina was a monster. I'm descended from evil!'

Alex took the letter from her hand, the frown lines on his forehead deepening as he read aloud:

'*I understand from your letter,*' Violet had written to Georgina, '*that you are concerned for Isabella's spiritual welfare. I will not pretend to share your extremist beliefs, but I can, unreservedly, assure you that the Sisters of Mercy and Deliverance are devout in their Christian faith and ensure that all the young women in their care receive a very strict regimen of religious instruction. Many of these young women have been tempted by evil ways, and the Sisters are extremely experienced in returning the girls to a more righteous path.*

'*If Isabella is, as you say, possessed by evil spirits, then I am certain that the Sisters will take steps to alleviate her suffering and return Godliness to her heart. Of course I understand your concerns regarding my sister's legacy to the child, but, again, the Sisters have much experience in these matters, and have helped many young women to overcome states of extreme immorality.*'

'Immorality?' Alex repeated, handing the letter back to Luci. 'Surely she's not equating your grandmother having bipolar with immorality? Didn't Violet work in a psychiatric hospital?'

'So Ted said,' Luci said grimly, now reading the final letter. The colour drained suddenly from her face and she rocketed to her feet. 'No!' she cried. 'Surely to God he wouldn't do *that*?'

'What?' Alex demanded, but Luci didn't answer him. She was already charging frantically back down the attic stairs.

'What kind of monster was that man?' she shrieked at Ted, who was in the kitchen making a pot of tea.

Ted turned around and stared at Luci. 'What do you mean?'

'She was never coming back!' Luci yelled. 'Even if she hadn't died, she was never coming back. Listen to this. Just listen!' Her voice shook with the force of emotion as she read from Violet's final letter to Walter, written soon after Isabella went to the convent.

'I'm sure you'll be glad to hear that Isabella has settled in well with the Sisters of Mercy and Deliverance. I was surprised to receive the letter that you sent with my niece, however, as this is a most unusual situation. It is usual for the girls to return to their families after their illnesses have passed, but, nonetheless, I have spoken with the Sisters on your behalf and they have kindly agreed that Isabella may indeed join their order in accordance with your wishes. The Reverend Mother, Sister Catherine, shall be writing to you personally to discuss Isabella's future with the Sisters as soon as the other matter is dealt with.'

'I don't understand,' Ted said in bewilderment.

'Isabella didn't have TB,' Luci snapped. 'She didn't go to a sanatorium, and she certainly didn't die of consumption! It was all lies – lies your grandmother and Walter concocted to protect their honour. She was pregnant! Isabella was pregnant and they sent her away to a convent to give birth, and even if she hadn't died, she wasn't going to be allowed to come home!'

'Calm down, Luce,' Alex said softly. He'd come downstairs in time to hear Luci read the letter, and as she shook with fury, he slipped his arm around her shoulders and drew her close to him.

She shook him furiously off. 'No, I won't calm down!' she yelled. 'What the hell kind of people were they?' She rounded on Ted. 'Why didn't you tell me? Were you so ashamed of them that you couldn't tell me what they were really like? You let me feel guilty for upsetting Walter and then him dying, and I needn't have gone through that, because he was callous enough that he could send his own daughter away to die all on her own in a convent full of people wanting to rid her of evil!'

'I didn't know, Luci,' Ted said sincerely. 'Honestly, I didn't. I truly believed that Isabella went away to a sanatorium to recover from TB, and died there.'

'Your mother must have known,' Luci snapped.

'If she did, then she kept it a secret from me,' Ted replied.

'Ted's as shocked as we are, Luce,' Alex said.

'If he wasn't dead, I'd kill him – Walter, I mean,' Luci muttered savagely, pushing past Alex out of the kitchen. She stormed through to the sitting room, where the twins were sleeping in their buggy – Ted had taken them earlier to the local park – and grabbed the handles of the buggy, swinging it around and almost running straight into Alex.

'Where are you going?' Alex asked, looking alarmed.

'Out,' Luci snapped.

'I can see that – but where?' Alex replied, following her to the front door. 'I think you need to calm down before you go anywhere.'

'I'm going to do what Mum should have done instead of running away,' Luci snarled. 'I'm going to go to the police and have that evil apology of a church shut down before they destroy anybody else's lives!'

Alex caught hold of the buggy, forcibly holding Luci back. 'No, you're not,' he said severely. 'You've no evidence that those practices are still going on – you'd be accused of wasting police time – and I don't want to have to represent you in court!'

'What am I supposed to do? Let them get away with what they did to Mum and Isabella?' Luci demanded.

'There's nothing we can do now,' Alex pointed out.

'But they're evil. Look what the pastor said to me at Walter's funeral!' Luci protested.

'There's still nothing we can do.'

Luci's shoulders slumped. 'There must be someone we can complain to,' she said petulantly. 'The Church of England? The Archbishop of Canterbury? The Pope?'

'From what I understand, it's an independent church – not governed by anyone,' Alex said.

'So they get to carry on poisoning people's minds, knowing that no one can stop them?' Luci asked incredulously.

'We don't know that's what's happening now,' Alex said.

'I do,' Luci muttered darkly. 'I knew there was something wrong at Walter's funeral. I could sense the evil – I just didn't know what it was!' She took control of the buggy again. 'I need to get out of here. My head's going to explode if I don't go out.'

'We'll take the boys for a walk then,' Alex said.

'I'd rather go on my own,' Luci said.

'Not a chance,' Alex replied smartly.

'Don't you trust me?'

'Right now – no,' Alex said firmly. 'There's no knowing what you might do once my back's turned.'

Luci allowed herself a secret smile. Alex would have to go back to York on Sunday night, ready for work on Monday. It wasn't long to wait. If he was right and the police wouldn't get involved, then she would have to take matters into her own hands.

CHAPTER ELEVEN

'You've found Walter's big secret – I'm sure Ted's more than capable of getting rid of the rest of the stuff up in the attic,' Alex said, trying – and failing – to convince Luci to return home with him on Sunday evening.

'I promised Ted I'd help,' Luci lied, smiling. 'I can't just abandon him now – we've made one hell of a mess up there.'

'We could come back next weekend,' Alex suggested.

'It makes more sense for me to stay here and get it all done,' Luci replied, winding her arms around his neck. 'What's the matter – don't you trust me to be a good girl?'

Alex looked straight into her eyes. 'In a word – no!' he said.

'I promise I'll be good,' Luci said in a wheedling tone of voice.

'If I thought you meant it, I might not be worried,' Alex said wryly.

'I do mean it,' Luci said innocently. 'What trouble can I possibly get up to just throwing boxes of old papers out?'

'None,' I suppose,' Alex said, sighing. 'You're still a bit manic, though. *That's* what worries me.'

'I am not manic,' Luci protested. 'I'm sleeping and everything – just like a normal person.'

'You were awake at four this morning. I heard you get up,' Alex retorted.

'Only to check on the boys. I'm not used to them sleeping for so long without waking us up,' Luci replied. It was almost true. She *had* been concerned that the twins were so quiet – but she'd been lying awake, pretending to be asleep, for hours, so as not to arouse Alex's suspicions. 'Alex, I'll be fine! Besides, Ted's here to keep an eye on me if you really can't trust me!'

'How much longer do you think it's going to take you?' Alex asked, sighing again in resignation. 'I'll miss you and the boys. The house is empty without you.'

Luci shrugged. 'A couple of days – no more than that, I promise. I'll be home on Wednesday – Thursday at the latest.'

'You'd better be – or I'll come straight out here to fetch you back,' Alex warned. He wasn't joking, Luci knew that.

'I'll be back on Wednesday,' Luci promised. 'Call me when you get back, so I know you've got home safely, okay?' She reached up to kiss him, before giving him a gentle shove towards the door.

Legacy of Lies

'You'd better go. I don't want you driving in the dark – you've left it late enough leaving as it is!'

Reluctantly, Alex picked up his overnight bag and put it over his shoulder. 'Wednesday,' he said darkly. 'Or I'll come and fetch you.'

***

After just a couple of hours sleep, Luci was wide awake again – and with Alex gone, she didn't have to lie there staring at the ceiling. Grinning, she got up, went into the twins' room to check they were still sleeping peacefully, and then went straight up into the attic. Alex had suggested that she take a break from sorting through the boxes, so Sunday had been an entirely attic-free day. Stupidly, Luci had actually missed it. Her anger at what Walter had done had faded somewhat, leaving her thinking a little more clearly. She'd been thinking about what she'd discovered all day – and the more she thought about it, the more she was certain there was something else that Walter had been hiding. She remembered how he'd rummaged through her mother's box, looking for something. That something wouldn't have been the letters. There had to be something else that had got him so agitated.

She started with the boxes in the same stack as the one she and Alex had discovered the letters. She found letters that Medora had written to Walter whilst he was away doing National Service soon after their marriage, and letters that Walter had written in return – but after reading a few, Luci dumped the whole lot back in the box and moved on to the next box. This one was filled with bundles of type-written sheets of paper – tied with the same black ribbon that Walter had obviously been inordinately fond of using. For a moment, Luci thought she might have found something of interest – but it turned out that Walter had considered himself to be a bit of a Charles Dickens or Henry James, and had churned out dozens of Dickensian short stories over his lifetime – none of which he seemed to have done anything with. The next two boxes contained more of the same – and Luci found herself wondering how Walter had found the time for so much writing, and whether anyone else had ever seen the stories that he'd written. She made a mental note to ask Ted over breakfast.

She almost missed the bundle of envelopes half-hidden beneath one of the bottom flaps of the third box of Walter's manuscripts. It was the black ribbon that caught her eye as she was dumping the stories back into their box; tucking the sheaves of paper under her arm, she tugged the envelopes free, and then tossed Walter's stories carelessly back into their box. She sat down on the floor, eagerly tugging at the ribbon to free the envelopes.

The first thing she noticed was that none of the envelopes had been opened. The second was that they were all addressed to her mother.

'What the hell...' she muttered, stretching her legs out and leaning back against the wooden panel that divided off one corner of the attic where, Luci presumed, the boiler and water tank were housed. As her elbow came to rest against the panel, Luci felt something give, and found herself toppling back as part of the panel folded in on itself – revealing not a boiler or water tank, but a small, dark space, just big enough for Luci to crawl into.

The space was pitch dark – there was no way for light to get in – but as Luci squinted in the darkness, she realised that it wasn't an *empty* space. There were things – she couldn't make out what – on the walls, and something like an old storage trunk in one corner. Luci crawled hastily back out and went crashing down the stairs in search of a flashlight. Of course, it was sod's law that there wasn't a flashlight to be found anywhere in the house, nor in Ted's car, nor in her own car.

'Why is it,' Luci asked the empty kitchen, 'that when you really need something, you can't find it? If I *didn't* need a torch, there'd be *dozens* lying around!'

Patience was certainly not one of Luci's virtues. She roamed the house restlessly until the twins finally woke up just before 6am, and then, as soon as they were fed, changed and dressed, she loaded them into their car carriers for a trip to the nearest 24-hour opening supermarket. The supermarket, Luci reasoned, was bound to sell flashlights – and if they didn't, then there was something seriously wrong with the world.

An hour later, she was back with not one but six torches – and enough batteries last a month. She wasn't taking any chances – not when she was on the verge of uncovering the contents of the space that even Ted didn't know about. Not wanting to wait until Ted was awake, she took the twins in their carriers up into the attic with her, and gave them a couple of rattles to keep them amused whilst she investigated the hidden space.

Crawling back inside with one torch in her mouth and another in the back pocket of her jeans, Luci saw immediately that she'd inadvertently stumbled upon something intriguing. There were photographs covering the walls in the space; rocking back on her heels, Luci took the torch out of her mouth and shone it over the photos, sucking her breath in sharply. She'd always thought it odd that her mother had kept no photographs from her childhood – but now she understood why. The photographs were all here – in what must have been Elvina and Isabella's hiding place – the only place, Luci presumed, that was safe from their grandmother's repressive manipulation. She recognised Medora, and her mother – and the mirror image of her mother, Isabella. The photographs showed a happy young family, enjoying seaside holidays and other kinds of outings. Walter must have taken the photographs, because he didn't feature in any of them. But the happy scenes halted abruptly when Elvina and Isabella were eight, and the remaining few photos showed the two girls as they grew older, looking decidedly more serious and, Luci realised with a jolt, unhappy as time went on.

The longer Luci stared at the photographs, the more certain she became that this place had been made into a shrine by her mother and Isabella – a shrine to a happy childhood that had given way to an unhappy adolescence. There was no wonder her mother had never talked about her childhood. There had been evil in this house, Luci was certain of it.

Finally tearing her attention away from the photographs, Luci turned towards the trunk tucked away in the corner. It looked old – older than her mother at the very least. She guessed that it had probably been Medora's – that would explain why it was hidden away up here, anyway. But it opened easily enough – as if Izzy and Elvina had opened it often after their mother's death. Kneeling in front of the trunk, Luci shone the torch inside, disappointed that there wasn't much inside. There were a few stray photographs from the mid-sixties, when Izzy and Elvina were in their mid-teens, a couple of cardigans that Luci figured might have been Medora's, and – Luci brightened when she saw it – a small notebook that looked suspiciously like a diary. Seizing her prize, Luci crawled back out of the hiding space, tossing the torch down onto the floor. The twins gurgled enquiringly at her, but Luci was far too interested in what she'd found. Cracking the notebook open, she grinned when she read the neat writing on the fly-page. *'This diary belongs to Isabella Edith Warburton – Keep out, or else!'*

'This is more like it, boys,' Luci murmured, settling back to read her aunt's diary.

ISABELLA'S DIARY

15TH JULY 1967

Anne Frank called her diary 'Kitty', and wrote as if she was writing to a real person, but even though that sounds like a sensible idea, I would feel too foolish to do so myself. A diary is not a person – and of that, I am glad, because there are things that I would like to write here that I couldn't even bring myself to confess to my own **twin***.*

Today is our fifteenth birthday – this journal is a gift from Elvie, almost identical to the one I have given her, but for the colour of the leather that binds it together. On swopping gifts, we each made a solemn promise not to read the other's private thoughts. I don't like to keep secrets from my sister – we have always told each other everything – but I suppose it is a mark of growing up that we no longer share everything with each other.

16TH JULY 1967

*Turning fifteen should be a liberation. Other girls are leaving school and getting jobs – **and** they are treated like adults – but not us! Elvie is too placid and too meek to complain about the way we are still made to feel like children when we are young people on the cusp of adulthood. It's odd this feeling that Elvie and I are somehow slipping apart. Is it that I am – like Grandmother says – too wilful and defiant? Or is it just that Elvie has become quieter and more introverted as I have become emboldened? I don't want us to grow apart! We have always been so alike – like two peas in a pod, Mum used to say, laughing because she could hardly tell us apart.*

*I miss Mum more now than I did even when she was newly dead. She would have stood up against Father and Grandmother – Father who would have us remain children forever, and Grandmother who never ceases to remind us how privileged we are to have a nice, comfortable home and a grammar school education. Oh, but I don't feel privileged! I want to be free – free to do as I please and not be tied to my desk every night with endless hours of homework. I didn't ever ask to be clever – oh, no! Elvie and I both tried our very hardest **not** to pass our Eleven Plus – and not only to spite Grandmother.*

The girls we knew at primary school ignore us now in the street – and even though I know that in part that's because of Grandmother and the Church, those girls who were once our friends and equals now look at us and point and sneer. Sometimes I hear them laughing as we board the bus – they call us snobs and stuck up, and hiss that we think ourselves too clever to mix with the likes of them. They would never listen – much less believe me – if I tried to tell them how much I envy their simple lives.

I feel now as though I really do understand how a caged bird feels – and I pity the poor canary that Grandmother keeps.

22ND JULY 1967

Father has confined me to our room and even Elvie is not allowed to share my solitude. He knows that is the worst possible punishment he can inflict on me, and he has to be seen to be taking a firm hand to me – to please Grandmother, who denounced me as evil in front of the whole chapel. As he sent me up to the attic, Father whispered that of course he knew that I wasn't evil – but I had to be made to realise the error of my ways. He told me too that I must apologise to Grandmother. I would sooner spend the rest of my days locked in the attic than apologise to her – but for Elvie's sake, I will – even though I will not mean a single word of my apology. I am not sorry for what I did. I only wish that I could set myself and Elvie free the way that I set Grandmother's canary free.

29TH AUGUST 1967

I am, I know a terrible correspondent! More than a month has passed since I last wrote – so much for my intention (and it was a sincere intention, I promise) to write every day – or at least every other day. I meant to write – honestly, I did – but oh! so much has happened this month that I have scarcely had the time to catch my breath, much less write!

But where to start! Firstly, on the very first day of the school summer holidays, Grandmother tripped in the Chapel and fell, breaking both her arm and her ankle – which has rendered her bedridden since.

Freedom *– oh, such **freedom** – the like of which Elvie and I have not known for almost seven whole years. Not, I'm afraid, that Elvie has used her freedom as productively as I have. But that's not really fair. She's used her freedom productively in a very different way to me. She writes obsessively – over the last month, she has filled two whole notebooks with her stories, and is well into a third notebook. She writes beautifully – I enjoy reading her stories almost as much as I enjoy reading Jane Eyre and Wuthering Heights – and I envy* *her for being able to sit for hours by the brook at Padley Gorge (if the weather is fit) and return home with two or three stories written. I haven't the patience myself. I used to enjoy writing, but now my brain skips about like a rabbit in spring, and I cannot possibly bear to sit still for so long! Instead, I have been using my freedom to do all the things that Grandmother would forbid me to do, if she knew that I was even thinking of doing them. Sometimes, I've convinced Elvie to take a break from her writing and join me – but the last time she came out with me, she grew so wide eyed and shocked, and has refused ever since to join me on my adventures! I'm afraid that Grandmother has beaten the spirit out of my twin – both figuratively and literally, that even when Grandmother is unable to stop us, Elvie is too afraid to defy her too openly. It is almost as though when Elvie lost her spirit, I absorbed it, so that now I have more than enough for both of us!*

*I think, dearest Diary, that I am in love! In love with life, first and foremost, but literally in love, also. His name is Ricky, he's nineteen, and he rides a Triumph motorcycle that I love almost as much as I love **him**! Elvie knows about him, of course, and she has met him once, but she was terrified when he took her around the block on his Triumph, and she begged me later not to make her go again. She warned me, too, to be careful – but what can I possibly have to be careful about? Ricky loves me, and I love him – and there is nothing – **nothing** – that I could ever have to worry about when I am with him. He wants us to marry as soon as I'm sixteen – he's promised that we will run away to Gretna Green, and there will be nothing in the world that anyone – not even Elvie – can do to stop us! I don't like keeping secrets from my twin – but if I told her, I know that she would tell Father, and he would confine me to our room until I'm sixty five!*

Today, we had our picture taken together – one of Ricky's gang – I didn't mention that he's the leader of a motorcycle gang, did I? Well, anyway, he is, and one of his mates, Phil, got his hands on a Polaroid camera and took a photo of Ricky and me together, and Ricky's got his copy in his wallet, and I'm going to paste my copy in here, because it's the only place that I know is totally secret. We were kissing when Phil took the Polaroid. You can see how much we're in love. I feel like we're destined to be together. I think if Mum could see us, she at least would be happy for us.

She, I'm sure, would understand how constrained I feel by Father and Grandmother. She would understand why I need so much to escape!

*I didn't go out looking for love, honest I didn't. I only went out looking for a bit of adventure and excitement – but I found so, so much more! I like to think that it was fate that brought Ricky and I together. Kismet. There's really no other explanation for why I decided to walk into **that** cafe on **that** day. Me and Elvie were usually too scared to go in there on our own – because of the things that we'd heard about it – but Elvie wasn't there, and I was feeling brave that day. I bumped (literally) into Ricky on my way in. He caught hold of me as I stumbled, and when I looked up at him to say thank you, my stomach did a somersault when our eyes locked. I could hardly speak when he asked to buy me a drink, but I soon got over my shyness. By the time I had to leave to catch the train home, I knew I was in love with Ricky. He took me to the station on his Triumph – and the ride was so exhilarating I never wanted it to end. We've met every day since then – we can hardly bear to be apart, and I dread to think how we will cope when the new school term* *starts next week and I have to go back to being a stupid school girl again. I'm a woman in love and I will have to pretend to be a child! Ricky is a student – he's studying philosophy at Sheffield University – but he says that he hardly has to be there, and wants me to bunk school. I know that Elvie won't approve, but I can't imagine getting through a whole five days without seeing him. I'll do it. I'll bunk school, and he'll pick me up at the bottom of the hill, and we'll go riding around the moors together, until it's time for me to go back to catch the bus home. I can't wait. I really, really can't wait. It will be the first time we've truly been alone since we met!*

8TH SEPTEMBER 1967

Today, dear Diary, I became a Woman! I am no longer a child – for all that I may still be treated as one!!

*It was raining when Ricky picked me up at the bottom of the hill – so we couldn't go riding over the moors like we had been doing on other days. I know I shouldn't have agreed when he suggested that we go back to his student digs – but I'm tired of always being a good girl – and I **wanted** to be with him. He didn't force me. He said we could stop at any time – but I didn't want to stop. It is such a **liberating** feeling – but I'm almost afraid to tell Elvina. I know she won't understand. She doesn't know what it's like to be in love. She keeps telling me to be careful – when there's nothing at all for me to be careful about. Ricky loves me – he would **never** do anything to hurt me. It's not wrong to be in love, or to be lovers, even if Father and Grandmother would think that it is. I know that Father loved Mum, though – he loved her enough to go against Grandmother's wishes to marry her – but he's been so long without her now that he's forgotten – or Grandmother's brainwashed it out of him.*

I will tell Elvina, I will. But just not yet. I don't want her to put a damper on my happiness.

16TH OCTOBER 1967

I knew Elvina wouldn't understand. Her face when I told her! Ricky says that she is only jealous, and that I shouldn't take it to heart, but I hate the way things are between Elvina and me now. She looks at me as if she doesn't know me, and she refuses to make excuses for me when I bunk off school to be with Ricky. This last week, she has barely spoken to me. She won't even let me copy her homework. Miss Rawling, our form tutor has spoken to Elvina about me – but Elvina won't tell me what she said.

Legacy of Lies

I feel so lonely. Even when I'm with Ricky, it still feels as though there's a hole somewhere inside me. Ricky doesn't understand – how can he understand when he's never been a twin? But Elvie and me have always been like two halves of a whole, but now there's this big gaping gap where Elvie should be, and even Ricky can't fill it. I would never have done it if I'd known this was what was going to happen – and now it's done, it's too late. I can't go back. But it feels like I can't go forward, either. I'm stuck, and I think that even Ricky doesn't love me as much as I love him, because he keeps losing his temper with me because I won't go to his digs when there's no one else there. He says that I'm being silly – that doing it again isn't going to make things between me and Elvie any worse than they already are, but... oh, I don't know how to explain it!

Something's changed. Something's changed inside of me, I think, because, well, because nothing's the same as it was. It's like there's something stopping me from being happy – and just a few weeks ago, I was so, so happy, I felt like the whole world was mine for the taking and I could do anything. I had so much energy, and I felt so exhilarated all the time, but now I feel sort of numb, like there's a dark cloud hanging over me, and I just want things to go back to being how they were! I keep wanting to cry, and not just because of Elvina. Today, when I was with Ricky, I burst into tears for no reason at all, and Ricky just looked at me as though he thought I was mad.

I'm so scared that I am going mad, because nothing makes sense like it should – and Mum used to cry for no reason, too, and Grandmother has always warned me and Elvina that we'll end up turning out like Mum if we don't give ourselves over to God like good girls! I'm not a good girl, I know I'm not, and I don't want to be like Grandmother – but I don't think I want to be like Mum, either. Or, not like Mum when she cried all the time, or... or when she got so ill that she had to be taken away.

I miss Elvie so much, even though she's asleep just across the room. It's worse than her not being here at all!!

22ND NOVEMBER 1967

Oh God, oh God, oh God! This can't be happening. It just can't be happening!

25TH NOVEMBER 1967

I keep hoping that I'll wake up and realise that this is just a nightmare – but deep down I know that it's real, and it's happening. I've missed two periods. I've always been so regular – both Elvie and I have. I'm not stupid. I know what it means, even though I've been trying to make excuses ever since October, when I thought I was just late. But my last period was at the beginning of September, and now it's almost the end of November, and I can't pretend any more that this isn't happening. Oh God. Ricky promised me that he'd been careful. He swore to me that I wouldn't get pregnant, but there's no other explanation!

Grandmother will kill me – if Father doesn't kill me first. And I can hardly face telling Elvie, though I know I'll have to tell her soon. I need to tell someone. I can't do this by myself. Tomorrow, I'll have to tell Ricky. He'll stand by me, I'm sure he will – not that that will matter to Father, or Grandmother.

26TH NOVEMBER 1967

God must hate me. He must hate me so much; why else would he be punishing me like this? Why, God, why do you hate me?

30TH NOVEMBER 1967

I want to die. I want to die so much. I remember Mum saying that once, saying it over and over and over again, and Elvie and me were crying because we didn't understand. But I understand now. I understand how she felt because that's exactly how I feel now. What other alternative is there? What else can I do but die?

I told Ricky. I agreed to go back to his digs, and then, when he tried to kiss me, I just told him, and I tried to smile and pretend that it was okay, that I wanted to have his baby, and for us to be a family – but I needn't have tried to pretend. I thought he loved me. I thought that he might be worried at first – with him being a student and all – but he wasn't worried. He looked at me like I was something disgusting that he'd stepped in. He looked at me like that for what felt like all eternity, and then he pushed me away from him – hard – and his face changed, like he'd been possessed or something. His eyes – oh, God, his eyes were so cold, it was like they were daggers of ice!

*'Oh no,' he snarled. He was so angry. 'Oh no you don't! You're not pinning **that** on me.'*

Legacy of Lies

'What do you mean?' I asked him, and he laughed like I'd said something funny.

'You little hussy,' he sneered. 'Did you think I didn't know you'd drop your knickers for any Tom, Dick or Harry?'

I couldn't believe that he'd think that of me – but he wasn't finished.

'No one will believe it's mine,' he said. 'Not when I've finished telling them how you begged me to make you a woman and then went around screwing every bloke that so much as glanced in your direction. You were gagging for it, like a bitch on heat!'

I started crying then, but Ricky just slapped me, hard, across the face. 'Get out,' he hissed, 'and if you so much as try and blame me, I'll make sure everyone knows what a hussy you really are!'

It was raining when I ran out onto the street, and I only had my school blazer on, but I couldn't even care about how wet I was getting. I was crying so hard I could hardly see, and I just stood on the kerb, as the traffic whizzed by, and I thought about stepping out into the road, because then it would all be over, and I wouldn't have to worry about anything anymore. But I couldn't do it. Every time I tried to step out, it was like my body refused to obey the commands I was giving it, and I was just stood there, on the kerb, for so long. I remember people stopping to ask if I was all right, but I couldn't answer them. I don't know how long I stood there, but suddenly, Mr Major from the post office was standing next to me – he'd got out of his car when he recognised me – and he made me get into the car and took me home with him – to his house, I mean – so that I could dry off before I went home. He knew I couldn't go home as I was – because everyone in the village knows how strict Grandmother is, and how angry she would be with me. He didn't ask me what was wrong – or if he did, I didn't hear him – but I couldn't have answered anyway. There were no words to describe how I felt – how stupid, how frightened, how betrayed I felt.

When I did go home, I pretended to Grandmother that I was ill, and went straight to bed. I couldn't face Elvie. I couldn't even bear to look at my own reflection in the mirror. But Elvie knew that something was wrong. She knew me too well, and the next day, she was like a dog with a bone until I finally told her the truth – all of it. She tried to tell me that everything would be okay, that we would work something out together, and she told me that Ricky wasn't worth the ground he trod on, but even as she said it, I knew she was only trying to make me feel better. There was no answer. There is no answer. I'm having Ricky's baby, and he doesn't want to know. I'm having a baby and someday soon Father and Grandmother are going to find out, and all hell is going to break loose.

There is only one answer. From the moment I realised I was pregnant, there has only ever been one answer. If I die, the baby dies, and then it will all just be over. It's all I can think of. It's the only thought that fills my head. It's like a drum beat in my mind. Die, die, die, die, die. A drum beat calling to me, every second of the day.

11TH FEBRUARY 1968

They know. Father and Grandmother know, and all I can think is that it is some kind of miracle that Elvie and I were able to keep it from them for so long.

I can feel the baby moving inside me now, and when I look in the mirror, it is obvious that I am pregnant. I cannot bear to see myself now; I have to dress and undress in the dark. I hate the thing that is growing inside me. I hate it because it signifies everything that is wrong in my life. Nine months seems an eternity. I want to be rid of it.

Grandmother has forbidden me to go to school now; I must not even leave the house, lest someone from Chapel see me and realise the shameful truth. I don't care. I have no desire to go out and be shamed by what I am. Grandmother said that I am a foolish girl and that I am being made to pay for my mother's sins, but I know that the sins are my own, not Mum's.

Father has said nothing. He just looked at me with sadness in his eyes, and I knew that he was disappointed in me. I never wanted to make him sad. I never wanted him to be disappointed in me. I think of those months in the summer, when I met Ricky and went wild, as my months of madness, and now I am being made to pay for them with my misery. The weight of my own sadness sometimes feels as though it is going to crush me, and I wish often that it would. I don't have the courage to take my own life, but I would be happy if it was taken from me.

21ST MARCH 1968

I know now why Grandmother hated Mum so, and why she looks upon Elvie and I with such trepidation. She is worried that the madness will pass down to us – as it was passed down to Mum. I wish Father could have told us the truth, and not left us to find it out in this way – although I don't suppose he thought we **would** ever find out. I wonder if he even knows about the book – though surely he would not have left it here for us to find it if he did.

Since I am not allowed out of the house, this attic room has almost become my prison, and the days seem so long whilst Elvie is at school. The neighbours and the Chapel community think that I am ill, and send their prayers, which would make me laugh were I not so weighed down with despair.

It was by accident that I found the book, really. Elvie and I had known about the false wall in the corner for years, and it was there that we had hidden the photographs of Mum that we'd salvaged before Grandmother had chance to burn them. As old as I am, I still feel closer to Mum sitting there amongst the photographs, and looking through the diaries she wrote when she was younger even than Elvie and I. Since my imprisonment, I often spend hours in the cubby hole – I've even fallen asleep in there – but it was only yesterday that I found the loose floorboard and prised it up. It was only a small hole – but big enough to hide a leather-bound notebook filled with tiny, precise handwriting.

It took me three or four hours to read it all, and when I was done, I was crying harder even than I cried when Mum died, and all I could think was how she must have felt when she read it – because no one other than Mum could have hidden it there – and how she must have felt when she realised that the madness that had infected her mother and aunt had infected **her**.

Elvie found me sitting sobbing in the cubby hole, and I made her read it before I could confess my own new fears – that I too was infected. Elvie held me and tried to tell me that it was not so, that I wasn't like Mum at all – but we both knew that her words were nothing more than barefaced lies. We put the book back – and made a pact not to speak of it again – but I am sure that every word is etched in my mind, and I shall never forget. Never.

6TH APRIL 1968

Today, Grandmother dropped a bombshell that has left both Elvie and I reeling with the shock of it. I can't stop shaking. I'm to go away, Grandmother says, to a home for unmarried mothers, until the baby is born. I'm ashamed to say that I cried when Grandmother broke the news, because I don't want to go away, I really, really don't! Grandmother says, though, that I must – I can't *stay here to give birth, because everyone would know, no matter how hard we tried to hide it.*

The baby is going to be adopted – Auntie Violet has arranged it. She helps lots of girls who get pregnant, Father says, and visits the home for unmarried women frequently. It's run by nuns, and Grandmother says that it will be the best place for me to go to cleanse my soul. The pastor has been to see me every day this week. He has always frightened me, talking of hellfire and damnation, but now he is worse than ever. He insists I must repent my sins and banish the devil from my soul; like Grandmother, he thinks that both Elvie and I were born with evil in our hearts because of Mum, but I won't do what he says, I won't!

28ᵀᴴ APRIL 1968

*I thought that nothing could be worse than having to carry a child I don't want. I was wrong. Pastor Tyrell is like a man possessed. He came today and screamed at me when I would not repent. He screamed and screamed, like the devil was within him, and then he dragged me down the stairs, where Grandmother, Father and Aunt Louisa were waiting. I thought he was going to kill me, honestly I did. But what he did was worse, so, so, so much worse. I fear I will never feel warm again. I fear I will never stop shaking. They said that the evil must be cleansed from me before I went away. They said that I could not allow the devil to accompany me to a place of God. And then they exorcised me. I have never been more afraid than I was today. Not afraid of the evil they say is inside me – afraid of them, of the madness that drives **them**. And there is more to come, I am sure of it. Grandmother says that the Sisters of Mercy and Deliverance are devout, and have been warned of the dark shadow of evil that stalks me. I am so frightened, and I can't even tell Elvina what has happened. Grandmother has forbidden it, and I am too frightened of what she is capable of to defy her. I don't want her to hurt Elvie. If I can do nothing else, then I surely must be able to protect my sister!*

CHAPTER TWELVE

'Luci, are you up here already?' Ted asked as he came up the attic stairs. 'It's only eight o'clock.'

Putting Isabella's diary down, Luci swiped self-consciously at the tears trickling down her cheeks. Izzy's plight had struck a raw nerve, and the thought of what her aunt had endured was sickening.

'I couldn't sleep,' she said, unable to keep the tremor of emotion out of her voice.

'Are you okay? Have you been crying?' Ted asked, frowning.

Luci shrugged. 'I'm fine,' she said weakly. She lifted the diary and held it out to Ted. 'Izzy's diary. I found it – back there, in a cubby hole in the wall. Did you know about it?'

Ted crossed the room to take the diary. 'I had no idea,' he said, flicking through the pages. 'Why don't you come downstairs for some breakfast? You don't look so good, Luce.'

Luci shook her head. 'I'm fine,' she repeated. 'You could take the boys down, though. There's something Izzy said in her diary. Something she found. You know how Walter got really agitated when I showed him that box that Mum had – the one that was Medora's – and he was looking for something else? I think Izzy found it – the thing that he was looking for. It was hidden here all the time!'

'Come downstairs first,' Ted suggested. 'Just to have a break from all this.'

'I don't need a break!' Luci snapped irritably.

'I think you do,' Ted said firmly. 'I've just made fresh pot of coffee.'

'Let me guess, you're under orders from Alex,' Luci said, sighing heavily. 'One coffee, and then I'm coming back to find it – whatever *it* is!'

***

After being bullied by Ted into drinking a couple of mugs of coffee and eating a slice of toast, Luci finally escaped back to the attic to look for the book that Izzy had written about. She could hardly bear to think about how awful those last few months must have been for Izzy – cooped up inside with her grandmother and that crazy pastor telling her that she was evil. It was enough to send anyone mad – but what was troubling Luci more than anything else was the realisation that her aunt's months of recklessness that had led to her pregnancy had been frighteningly similar to Luci's own months of madness that had led to Charlie's conception. Izzy had been ill – and instead of getting help, she'd been told she was evil. And – even worse – she must have *died* thinking that she was evil. The very thought of it made Luci want to curl up in a ball and sob her heart out – but instead she retrieved her torch and crawled back into the cubby hole.

Thanks to Izzy's description of where she'd found the book, it took less than ten minutes for Luci to find the loose floorboard and prise it up, breaking a couple of fingernails in the process. With the torch in her mouth, she eagerly opened the book, marvelling at the neat, precise writing inside. Oddly, it reminded her of Luke's writing – the only part of him that could ever have been described as neat. The fly-leaf of the notebook – which was filled almost to its capacity – bore the intriguing words '*A Testament of Truth*' in neat block capitals. Dropping the torch, Luci tucked the book under her arm and crawled back out into the attic. At first, she thought about settling down to read there and then, but reconsidered when she looked at the number of pages. It would take hours to read it all – and the attic was hardly the most comfortable place to sit and read. Instead, she went down the attic stairs, into her bedroom and wedged the door firmly shut. She didn't want to be disturbed whilst she discovered what exactly the 'testament of truth' *was* – and why it had upset Izzy so much.

Legacy of Lies

A TESTAMENT OF TRUTH
NOVEMBER 1930

They came for her in the night: three, big strong men who held her firm whilst she kicked and struggled and screamed. She raged at them for dragging her from her bed, and then, when they carried her, still screaming, down the stairs, she raged that she couldn't go out in the street in her nightdress – which Father later said was the only sane thing she'd said for weeks.

'Where are they taking Mother?' Austin, my brother, asked when Father came upstairs to shoo the lot of us back to bed.

'Go to bed,' Father said, in the tone of voice that we knew meant that we were not to ask questions of him now. 'You have school in the morning, all of you.' This was true, for even though I had left school two years previously, I had returned to the infant school as an assistant to the teacher, such was my great love of learning.

Violet's eyes were wide as she clutched at my hand and sucked furiously on her thumb, because at five years old she was still much too young to understand the horror of what was happening. Although Father frowned in disapproval, I picked Violet up and carried her into our bedroom, tucking her up in her bed before going into the room next door to see that Austin and Harold had gone to their beds, also. Soft snores soon filled the house, but sleep would not come easily to me. As the eldest child, at sixteen, I was more than a little aware of the suffering Mother had endured, and her screams echoed in the quietness of my mind. I knew where the men were taking her. I knew, and my heart went cold at the very thought of it.

In the room next door, the baby began crying – loud, angry wails that set my teeth on edge. I waited – for Father to lift her from the crib and carry her downstairs like he had on many nights since the baby – my sister Medora – was born. But this night – the night all our lives changed irrevocably, as melodramatic as that sounds – the baby kept on crying, and the stairs didn't creak under Father's foot-falls. I crept from my bed, careful not to wake Violet and the boys, and tentatively pushed open the door to our parents' bedroom. The room was in darkness, but Father sat, silhouetted in the window – the curtains were still wide open, letting in light from the gas-lamps out in the street – with his head held in his hands.

'Father?'

He acted as though he could not hear me, as though entirely unaware of my being there. Still the baby cried, until I crossed the room to her crib and lifted her out. Her napkin was soaked, and she sucked upon my finger as if ravenous. With my finger in her mouth, she could not cry, however, and I took advantage of the sudden silence to speak to Father again. Again, he did not raise his head, nor even seem aware that Medora was no longer wailing. I carried the baby downstairs to change her napkin and to warm one of the bottles of milk always kept ready since Mother had been unable to feed my sister. Her milk had dried up during the early weeks when she refused to leave her bed – refused even to hold Medora in her arms. I felt the tears start in my eyes and blinked them away furiously; I was too old for tears. With Mother gone – for in truth she had been gone to us for some time before the night when she was actually taken away – I was the woman of the house, and responsible for caring for my father and siblings.

***

I wanted to begin my story with that night, for it was that night that proved to be the moment when everything changed irrevocably, but I think, now that I have begun, that I might better have started the story before that night, back in the years when I was still a child and learned much of what I write now from eavesdropping words that I should not have been privy to hear. Even now, many years on from when these events took place, I do not think that Father knows exactly how much I heard in my childhood eavesdropping. The truth is simple: he would like to forget, and pretend that none of these things happened. He would like, instead, to believe the lies that he has spun to us all. I think perhaps that he does believe it. Why, he even makes a show of leaving flowers on the small memorial slab he had placed in the churchyard when we came here, as if she were really dead, as he has always had us believe. He would happily die leaving a legacy of lies behind him, and yet there is something that compels me, as much as I love him and want to be a good and dutiful daughter, to write down the words that he would never have me speak – as my legacy of truth, as it were.

And so, I must step back through time from the point at which I began this tale, to the beginning – or the beginning for me: the day whence I first stumbled upon a truth that cracked the protective

Legacy of Lies

casing of lies that my parents had, until then, enveloped myself and my siblings in.

February 1924

It was, I recall, the evening before my tenth birthday when I learned some of the shocking secrets that haunted my mother's eyes. Far too excited about the promised birthday tea-party to sleep, I crept down the stairs, ever careful to miss the third step from the bottom which had a terrible squeak that would surely give me away, and sidled silently into the tiny cloakroom off the narrow hallway. Quite by accident the year before, I had discovered that the mouse-hole in the skirting board allowed even the softest spoken words in the sitting room behind the cloakroom wall to be clearly heard. Crouched amid boots and shoes, with my head resting on the softness of Father's winter coat, I listened to my mother and father talking, hoping, in my childish way, that they might give mention to my birthday gifts. I was hoping for a bicycle, but feared I was to be disappointed, as where could Father possibly conceal a bicycle out of sight? My parents, however, had far graver matters to discuss than their daughter's birthday.

'I will not have her here!' Father said, his voice sharp and loud. 'I will not have her corrupting the children's minds with her nonsense!'

'She is my sister, Maurice!' Mother cried in response, a fretful edge to her voice. 'She is my sister, and I promised my mother I would take care of her.'

Sister? I frowned. I was all but ten years old and yet I had never once heard mention of Mother having a sister. Brothers, yes – my uncles were older than Mother and visited, with their own children, no more than once a year.

'She does not belong with us, Edith,' Father said firmly. 'You know where she belongs.'

'No!' Mother's cry was almost a scream. 'I will not have her sent to one of those places, Maurice!'

One of what places? I wondered, because I was innocent then of the dark secrets that lurked in our family, which had long been hidden out of a sense of shame. My heart was beating furiously with the childish thrill that always came from eavesdropping secrets not meant for young ears.

'We cannot care for her here,' Father said. 'Use reason, Edith. She is a danger to herself and to the children.'

'We do not know that!' Mother protested. 'We cannot know that.'

Legacy of Lies

'*She is going the way of your grandmother and your aunt, Edith, you cannot deny it. The signs are there,*' Father said, and his voice was unnaturally grim.

'*She needs our help, Maurice,*' Mother said. Her voice was choked, and after a moment I heard her sobbing. I smothered a gasp of shock with my hand. I had never heard my mother cry before; she was not given to displays of emotion, and discouraged them in us children, also.

'*There is only one thing that we can do to help her, Edith,*' Father replied. '*I will speak to Dr McKenzie tomorrow. He has an unusual fondness for Alice. He will see that she is... given the appropriate care.*'

'*You have not seen inside one of those places, Maurice,*' Mother sobbed. '*You have not seen what damage those places do to people.*'

'*Edith, my dear, it is not the asylums that damage their inmates; they are damaged already. It is why they must be kept apart from society,*' Father said. I could almost hear him smiling, which struck me as odd given Mother's distress. '*If there was not a need for asylums to keep the insane away from the populace, there would be no asylums.*'

'*Alice is not insane. She is not. She is my sister – I would know if she was insane.*'

'*Your loyalty to your sister is admirable, Edith, but misguided,*' Father insisted. '*You forget that she has been known to introduce herself to strangers as the Virgin Mary. If that is not insanity, then I am sure I do not know what is.*'

What happened next always sticks in my mind as the very moment that my safe and innocent childhood shattered into something altogether more... unstable. My mother's sobbing reached a crescendo, and then there was the unmistakable sound of flesh hitting flesh – hard. I had never known my father to strike anyone, least of all my mother, but surely that was what had happened, for Mother's sobbing stopped, the door was flung open, and then, down the hall, the door to Father's study slammed closed. I found myself shaking, tears of fear slipping silently down my cheeks. I did not understand yet what I had overheard – the words *asylum* and *insane* were not ones in my vocabulary. Over the months and years to come, however, I would come to have an uncomfortably close understanding of those dreadful words.

***

129

The next morning, Father had already gone to his office – he was an accountant – by the time I had helped Austin and Harold, who were four and six years younger than me, to dress and led them downstairs to breakfast. Mother's eyes were red-rimmed; I had heard her sobbing in the bedroom when I had finally dared to creep back upstairs to bed long after the grandfather clock in the hallway had struck the witching hour.

'Where's Father?' Austin, always an inquisitive child, asked, lifting a spoon of lumpy porridge to his mouth.

'He had to leave early for work,' Mother replied, her voice husky.

I stirred my own porridge uneasily. I was not hungry; not even sure that I could force the grey-looking sludge through my lips and down my throat. Sleep had been a long time coming – which was not unusual for a child on the eve of its birthday, except for the fact that it was not excitement that had kept me awake. Perhaps it was as well that I had lost all interest in the fact that it was my birthday, because it appeared that Mother had forgotten. Certainly, there were no presents laid out in front of my place at the table, as there had been every other year that I could remember.

'Hurry up and eat your breakfasts,' Mother said suddenly. 'We need to go out.'

'Where?' Austin asked, his mouth full.

'Out,' Mother replied sharply.

'Is it a surprise for Lilly's birthday?' Austin asked.

Mother froze. After a moment, she raised her hands to her lips and gasped, 'Oh, Lillian!' She hurried from the room and returned a few moments later with a small stack of parcels in her arms. She must have retrieved them from the very cupboard I'd been hiding in the night before. 'I completely forgot, my darling,' she apologised, kissing my forehead tenderly. 'Happy Birthday.'

I unwrapped my gifts quickly, because behind her suddenly smiling face, Mother still seemed anxious and on edge. 'Thank you, Mother,' I said, for although there was obviously no bicycle amongst my gifts, I was perfectly happy with the books and dresses instead.

'Can you help your brothers into their coats and boots, Lillian?' Mother asked the moment the breakfast things were cleared away. She seemed anxious and nervous; she flinched even when a pigeon landed on the roof and hooted down the chimney.

'Where are we going, Mother?' I ventured to ask.

Legacy of Lies

She touched my shoulder briefly. 'To visit your Auntie Alice,' she said, and it was all I could do not to look up at her in shock. I remembered only just in time that I was not supposed to even know that I had an Auntie Alice.

'Who's Auntie Alice?' I asked innocently, the calmness of my voice not betraying the sudden churning of my stomach. I had never known Mother defy Father's wishes over anything, but surely that was what she was doing now.

'My sister,' Mother replied shortly. 'Hurry up now, Lilly, or we shall miss the tram.'

'The tram, the tram!' Harold chanted happily as he shoved his feet into his boots and held out each foot for me to lace up for him. Austin hopped impatiently from foot to foot, equally excited about the prospect of a tram ride, for we almost invariably walked the short distance into the town centre from home, and tram journeys were a very rare treat indeed.

In fact, our journey involved not one tram, but two, taking us deep into a part of the town that we'd never before visited. The houses were built in tightly-packed, back-to-back rows, and no trees lined the streets as they did at home. The children who played on the pavement edge had thin, pinched faces, and their clothes were, whilst not ragged as such, certainly well-worn and patched in places. I could not help the feeling of unease as we alighted the tram at the end of one of those streets, and the children regarded us like a pack of hungry wolves.

'Hold hands with your brothers, Lilly,' Mother said, striding purposefully ahead of us down the street. Gripping Austin and Harold's hands firmly, I followed quickly, so that the boys had to run at my sides to keep up with the pace that Mother was setting.

As we passed house after identical house, I noticed that the bricks, doors and windows were often coated in a thin layer of soot, and although some doorsteps were spotlessly clean, others bore the hallmarks of neglect. The net curtains at some windows were yellow and stained, whilst other windows were bare, allowing me to glance inside the strange little houses with undisguised curiosity. Staring in through one window, I was shocked to find myself locking gazes with an old man sitting, in vest and underpants, on a chair that had one caved-in arm. I jumped back from the window, feeling my cheeks flush with the heat of embarrassment. I expected a frown of disapproval from Mother, but she appeared not to have even noticed.

She stopped abruptly outside one of the houses and – to my amazement – reached her hand through the letterbox, fumbled around for a moment, and then drew out a key on a long grubby string. The key turned easily in the lock, and then Mother was ushering us, ahead of her, inside the house.

'Where are we?' Austin asked in a loud whisper.

'Shush!' Mother snapped. 'Alice? Alice, where are you?' Stepping past us in the narrow hallway, Mother pushed open the first door on the left, which opened up into a small, musty-smelling sitting room. The curtains were tightly drawn so that the room was still in darkness, but Mother walked in without a moment's hesitation, as if she was familiar with the house.

'Oh, Alice,' Mother said, crouching down in one corner of the room. Curiosity got the better of me and I crept closer, further intrigued when I was able to make out the silhouette of a person cowering in the corner. Surely that could not possibly be my mother's sister Alice?

'They'll get in!' the creature in the corner cried. 'Lock the door! Lock the door! They'll get in!'

Mother sighed. 'Lilly, will you go and lock the door, please?' she called, and I scuttled out into the hallway to turn the key in the lock. By the time I re-entered the sitting room, with Austin and Harold clutching at my hands in nervousness, Mother had coaxed Alice out of the corner and onto the tatty sofa.

'Who are you?' Austin asked bluntly.

'Austin Molineux! Where are your manners?' Mother shrieked at him, and he shrank back against me, unused to the sharpness of Mother's voice. We stood there by the door, afraid to move closer, whilst Mother moved around, drawing the curtains and picking up piles of dirty crockery from the floor. With the light flooding in through the curtains, the sheer filthiness of the room became apparent. The smell of unwashed bodies was strong – not quite overwhelming, but still very unpleasant – and I could not help but feel anxious to leave.

'Are they there?' Alice kept asking. 'They must not see me. You won't let them see me, will you Edie?'

'Who are they?' Austin hissed to me, but I had no answer for him and shook my head at him to warn him to be quiet.

'I cannot leave you here on your own, Alice,' Mother said, sitting down next to the pitiful creature that seemed to be her sister, despite the improbability of it. 'You cannot take care of yourself.'

Legacy of Lies

Alice sat up sharply, her expression one of a wild animal cornered by a predator. 'I won't go out, I won't!' she shrieked. 'They will come for me! It isn't safe!'

'Hush now, Alice. Have I not told you a dozen times over, I will not let anyone hurt you?' Mother said patiently, in the same tone of voice she often used when reassuring Austin and Harold. She glanced up at the three of us standing silently watching. 'Children, we are going to stay here with your Auntie Alice until she is feeling better,' she said, her expression dark.

I thought about the argument I had overheard the night before, of Father's insistence that we were not to be corrupted by Alice, and I couldn't help but be shocked that Mother would so openly defy his wishes. I had always understood that Father was the head of the household, and that Mother was as much under his hegemony as we were. She had never before defied him, at least not in front of us children.

'Where will we sleep?' Harold asked, his voice small and frightened. 'Is Father coming?'

Mother sighed. 'No, Father is not coming,' she said. 'He is busy and cannot come.'

I tried to hide my shock at such a blatant lie, but my face must have betrayed me, for Mother glowered sternly at me. 'Lilly, take your brothers upstairs and show them the bedroom you will all be sharing.' She paused, considering. 'The door on the right of the landing.'

The boys gripped my hands firmly as I led them up the steep staircase with its threadbare, faded carpet. 'I don't like it here,' Harold whispered. 'It smells funny.'

The house did smell – as if it had been closed up for a very long time – and it was a far cry from the home we were used to, which Mother always kept spotlessly clean. I could hardly imagine anyone being happy to live here – which, to my childish mind, I thought might explain Auntie Alice's obvious distress.

'Stop whining, Harold,' I said, because that is what Mother would have said to him.

The landing at the top of the stairs was little more than a square with two doors leading off it – one on the right and one on the left. There was a small window in the roof which let in precious little light – barely enough to illuminate the landing. I tentatively pushed open the door on the right; it resisted at first and then swung slowly open, revealing a room that was completely in darkness. At first, I thought that the curtains were drawn, as they had been downstairs, but after a moment of squinting, when my eyes began to adjust to the darkness, I realised that instead the windows – and the walls also – had been completely covered by newspaper clippings. There must have been hundreds of them, all of varying sizes and lengths. Shaking my head in bewilderment, I stepped back out of the room, tugging the boys back down the stairs after me.

'Mother, we cannot sleep in there!' I announced, standing in the doorway of the sitting room. 'There is no bed, and the walls and windows are covered with newspaper.'

'Of course there is a bed,' Mother protested. Her eyes narrowed and she regarded me with what I could only describe as suspicion. 'Do not try my patience, Lillian,' she warned. 'I know that there is a bed, for I slept in it every night until I was eighteen and married your father.'

'You lived... here?' I asked, shocked by the very thought of it. I could not imagine for one second that my mother – such a proud gentlewoman – had grown up here in this cramped and damp house.

'I am not ashamed of where I came from, Lillian,' Mother snapped. 'It did not matter to your father when he met me, and it will never matter to me.' She regarded me with sad eyes. 'Do not look at me like that, Lillian. Snobbery is not a virtue, and it does not become you.' Pushing past me, she started up the stairs, and I hastened after her, with the boys at my heels like eager puppies, none of us wanting to be left in the company of that strange creature that was our aunt.

'Oh!' Mother's voice held a note of absolute dismay when she saw the state of the bedroom. She hurried back down the stairs, with the three of us children trailing again after her like she was the Pied Piper of Hamlyn.

'Oh, Alice, what have you done?' Mother asked her sister, a tremulous quaver in her voice. Alice merely stared blankly at her. 'Upstairs. The newspapers,' Mother prompted.

A strange, strangled sound left Alice's lips, and she shook her head repeatedly. 'They were watching me,' she moaned. 'Watching me, always. Everywhere. Their eyes were everywhere. I had to stop them. I had to stop them looking.' Her eyes were wide and fearful; her anxious fingers plucked again and again at the ragged hem of her dress. 'I didn't know what to do, but then the words started calling to me, telling me what I must do. They told me how I could be safe, Edie. They made me safe again!' She jumped to her feet with sudden eagerness and grasped Mother's hands. 'Let me show you!'

She all but ran up the stairs, the soles of her bare feet as dirty as her hands. I could not help but think of all the times Mother commanded us children to wash our hands, the baths that we had no less than twice a week, and the ewers of water that were carried up to our bedrooms each night that we might go to bed clean and fresh. I could never imagine Mother being dirty, making Alice's state all the more astonishing, because, of course, I did not know then what ailed my aunt.

In the bedroom, Alice flitted from wall to wall, stubby fingers pointing excitedly as she babbled what seemed to me to be a stream of nonsense about the significance of the clippings that covered the walls and window. There may have been logic to her reasoning, but it was, I learned later, too skewed by her diseased mind to make any sense to my ten-year-old self. I thought then of her as a rambling mad-woman, a little like the woman we saw sometimes in the park who talked only to pigeons, not knowing the truth that lay at the heart of the thought.

Mother smiled tensely as she listened to Alice, and then she went and put her arms around her sister's shoulders. 'Hush now, Alice,' she said soothingly. 'Everything is all right. You have nothing to fear now. I told you I would take care of you. Now you have me to look after you, you do not need these newspapers to protect you, do you? Shall we take them down, and have a bit of a tidy up, and then, perhaps we could go together to buy some food for dinner.'

Alice blinked uncertainly, but nodded eventually, and a heavy sigh left Mother's trembling lips. She composed herself quickly, however, and turned to me. 'You must help me, Lilly,' she said. 'We have a lot to do.'

***

We stayed little more than a few hours in the end, although Mother did not plan it that way. Together, she and I, with the boys trying to help in their own little ways, stripped the newspaper clippings from the second bedroom, and moved on to Alice's own room – which Mother told me had been her parents' bedroom before they died. At first, Alice merely watched proceedings like they were completely unconnected to her, but there came a moment when it was as if some kind of switch flipped in her mind. She gazed at the bare walls in horror, and then she began to scream, a sound so piercing that I could not help but cower and cover my ears. I screamed myself when Alice flew at Mother and started hitting and biting and scratching her, still screaming like a banshee.

I panicked; having never witnessed any violence in my short life, I was consumed by the fear that Alice might kill Mother, and I put my own selfish fears of being left alone before all else. I ran out of the house and onto the street, my own hysterical screams bouncing off the cobbles of the road like stones skimming the surface of a stream.

'Help! Help! Somebody, please help us!' I cried, beating my fists on random doors as I ran in a frantic frenzy. 'She's going to kill her, she's going to kill her!'

My cries acted as a bucket of ice-water on the inhabitants of the neighbouring houses, and the old and sick and unemployed seemed to pour from their front doors like hungry wolves descending on the faintest whiff of excitement. A burly man grabbed me by my shoulders and held me firm as he told me to calm down and explain myself. The words choked in my throat, tumbling in a garbled stream from my lips, and I drew in great gulps of air to calm myself enough to tell the stunned spectators that my aunt was trying to murder my mother.

I did not see what happened next – a kindly woman, with white hair, glasses and hands that were caked in flour, ushered me inside the house next door to Alice's, and although I tried to tell her that I had left Harold and Austin alone in the house, she would not let me leave. The boys saw it all, and I fear that it scarred them both forever.

The walls of the neighbouring house were thin, and I could not help but hear the sound of Alice screaming still, and Mother's voice, thin and frightened, begging her sister to calm down. It was too late, however, for any hope of Alice calming. She continued to scream, and wail and moan even when deep male voices could be heard from the bedroom.

I did not see the men in white coats come to take Alice away, but Austin described to me the strange contraption that they fitted her into to stop her flailing and hitting out with her hands. Strapped into a chair, effectively paralysed by what I later learned was a straight-jacket, she was carried from the house, put into the back of a waiting ambulance, and taken away. It was the last time we saw her.

Legacy of Lies

That day – my birthday of all days – came to signify the beginning of the end of my safe family unit.

***

'She didn't mean to hurt me. She meant no harm. She was frightened, just frightened! You cannot keep her locked away just for being frightened.' Mother kept saying, over and over again, unable to forgive herself for the part she played in Alice's commitment to the asylum. I took to hiding each night in the cloakroom so that I might hear what she and Father said to one another. Even at a young age, I was astute enough to know that all was not well in their relationship; they barely managed to be civil to one another in front of us children, and I knew that Father now slept on the leather couch in his study most nights instead of the bed in his and Mother's bedroom

'She is a danger to herself and to others,' Father snapped. 'What if she had turned on one of the children? She needs to be kept away from society – heaven knows your father tried hard enough to do that before he passed on.'

'She would never have hurt the children!' Mother protested.

'As she would never have hurt you,' Father snarled. 'It is for the best, Edith. She will be cared for, and you will be able to rest knowing that she cannot come to any harm.'

'I promised I would not allow them to take her,' Mother whimpered.

'That was a promise you could never keep,' Father said 'There is madness in your family, Edith. Had I known...' He sighed. 'Alas, no one thought to tell me, and so we must now bear the consequences. I pray each night that you have not brought with you into our family a legacy of insanity. I wish for my children to be strong and steadfast, not individuals crippled by their own weak minds. You should pray also that they be spared.'

Weeks passed; Mother grew quieter and quieter, but Alice's name was never mentioned in front of us children again. It was as if she had never existed. We knew, of course, that she had been taken away, but there was never any explanation for why – and certainly neither Mother and Father ever sat us down to tell us what it was that ailed our aunt, although I was certain that they knew.

There was one day, a little more than a month after that horrible day when Alice was carted away, when Mother was not waiting at the gates for us at the end of school, as she always was. She wasn't at home, either, when I led Austin and Harold by the hand up the garden path, and the door was locked. We sat for what felt like hours, shivering as we huddled together on the doorstep, sighing deep sighs of relief when finally we saw Mother hurrying down the street, breathless and flushed from running.

'The tram did not come,' she said, gathering us in her arms and hugging us fiercely, as if she was afraid, suddenly, to let us go. 'I meant to be home before school finished, but...' Her words trailed away to nothing, and I pinched Austin's arm to stop him asking her to finish the sentence. I could feel the dampness of tears on Mother's cheeks, and it took little deducting to guess where she had been. That night, I crept down to the cloakroom as always, but heard nothing more than the deafening silence that often stretched between Mother and Father now. She did not tell him that she had been to visit Alice – and I made certain that the boys did not mention Mother's absence from the school gates to Father. If Mother wished to keep her own counsel, then the very least we could do was honour it.

I could hardly help but notice the change in Mother after Alice was committed. It was as if a great shadow of sadness had passed over her and would not leave. Where she had before always been ready to smile and laugh, now it seemed as though her smiles were thin and her laughter forced. Often, she would sit and stare into the fire as if the flames held the answers to her troubles – even though I was certain she must know that the only person who held the answers to her troubles was Father, and he did not care for them. Once a week – and only once – he would sleep in the bedroom with Mother; the other nights he would stay in his study with the door firmly shut, and although I knew little then of the things that happened between married couples, I knew that this strange new arrangement was not right somehow. The tension in the air between them was palpable – sometimes it seemed as though I could reach out and touch the wall of ice they had built up with frosty stares. And although I had yet to learn anything of 'the birds and the bees', I was certain that babies only came when married men and women loved each other – and so I was more than a little shocked when Mother's girth began expanding again, and she wearily announced to Austin, Harold and I that we were to have another brother or sister.

Legacy of Lies

The baby screamed constantly, it seemed to me. It was screaming when I led Austin and Harold by the hand to the school, and it was screaming still when we returned in the afternoon. Mother seemed at a loss as to what to do with it, and Father was no help – he had barely even glanced once into the crib since the baby – who remained nameless for three whole weeks – fought its way into the world. Mother could not even feed it; perhaps it sensed her apathy, for it refused to suckle, and feeding bottles and special milk had to be bought at Dr McKenzie's insistence.

'What are you going to call her?' the jovial doctor asked when he called in – on his way home, he said, though I knew it was not on his way at all – one evening shortly before Father returned from work.

Mother looked at him blankly, so the doctor turned his attention to me, hovering, as always, in the doorway like an inquisitive butterfly.

'What do you think, eh, Lilly? Don't you think your little sister needs a name?' he asked.

I nodded my head slowly, sucking on my bottom lip.

'She's a pretty little thing, isn't she?' the doctor prompted. 'I think she needs a pretty name to match. Can you think of one?'

I considered that for a moment. 'Violet,' I said finally.

Dr McKenzie smiled. 'A very pretty name, I'm sure,' he said nodding. 'What made you think of it?'

I offered him a shy smile. 'Well, when she cries a lot, she sort of goes a funny purple colour that's a bit like violets, so...' I let the sentence trail away, suddenly certain that he would think me foolish.

'It suits her just fine, don't you think, Edith?' the doctor said, still smiling.

'Yes,' Mother replied, but I wasn't entirely sure whether she even knew what she was agreeing to. Her eyes looked almost glazed, as if she wasn't wholly in the room with us. It was an expression she often seemed to wear now; sometimes I caught Father staring at her with a saddened look in his eyes, but mostly he seemed indifferent to Mother's increasingly odd ways. He was hardly ever home, working increasingly long hours as if he had no desire to be with his family anymore.

Because Mother seemed somehow unable to rouse herself enough to care for baby Violet, it fell to me to look after my sister, because, of course, there was no one else. It was, I suppose, fortunate that the baby was born just weeks before school broke up for the long summer holiday; I often find myself wondering what might have happened had the baby been born earlier, when I was not there to look after her.

I did not go back to school immediately the new term started in September, for Mother wept the night before the term started and begged me not to leave her alone with the fretful child. Father sent a note with Austin, explaining my absence; it was not until I returned to school in November, when Mother had recovered from her melancholy state sufficiently to care for Violet herself, that I learnt that Father had lied in his note, telling my teacher instead that I was suffering from Scarlet Fever. That Father could tell such a blatant, bare-faced lie stunned me, and made me realise, fully, the extent of the shame he must have felt for his wife's incapacity to do her wifely and motherly duties.

To say that Mother made a full recovery from her melancholy would be quite an exaggeration, but after a while, life seemed to settle itself into a predictable pattern. There would be spells of time when Mother would seem to be back to her jovial, happy self, and I could not help but hope each time that the safe, secure normality of my early childhood had returned for good. Each time, I was disappointed, and those periods grew increasingly few and far between, punctuated by increasingly lengthy spells of melancholy. It was as if someone had perched Mother on one end of a see-saw and was bouncing her up and down – in and out of despair – as if for fun. I came to grieve for the Mother I had lost, because somehow I couldn't love her the same as I had before. She had changed, irrevocably, and she was as distant to me now as the sea was to the beach head at Morecombe.

Austin, Harold and I soon learned that we could easily tell whether Mother was likely to be happy or sad when we returned from school, simply by checking to see whether the curtains were drawn back and the windows open or not. If the curtains were drawn and the windows were open, we would often hear Mother singing in the kitchen as she baked or cleaned; if the curtains and windows were closed, then we were likely to find Mother shut up in her bedroom with Violet clutched tightly in her arms and tears dribbling down her cheeks. With predictable childish selfishness, we longed to see the curtains drawn back, and dreaded the days when they were not.

This became our life: the household ruled by the peaks and troughs of Mother's moods whilst Father kept himself hidden away from it all, as if by not acknowledging how desperate the situation sometimes was, he could pretend that all was as well as it had been before Alice's committal. Sometimes it seemed as though only I was aware of the extent of the changes in Mother. Austin and Harold were young enough still to be able to give themselves over completely to a game of soldiers or marbles and not notice the way Mother was slowly unravelling before us. It fell to me, as the oldest child, to somehow hold the family together. I took to doing the chores that Mother neglected to do when she was prone with despair – the simple things that I had always taken for granted just didn't seem to get done if I didn't take the initiative myself. Saturday became washday, because my weekdays were consumed by school and the smaller chores that took less time to do. Once a week, I cleaned the steps outside the front door, and black-leaded the range just as I had once sat and watched Mother do. Come bedtime, I would be more than glad to crawl, exhausted into bed, and morning always, without fail, came too soon.

FEBRUARY 1930

If Violet's conception had been a surprise, Medora's was even more shocking, and when Mother broke the news to the boys and I, I am afraid to say that I stood for a long time with my mouth hanging open, before I recklessly allowed my lips to form the words of my thoughts.

'How? How can you be having another baby?' I asked, too shocked to worry about politeness. 'You and Father...' I stopped mid-sentence, my cheeks flaming red with shame. I wasn't even supposed to know 'the facts of life'. It just happened that Betty Carr, my closest friend, had three older brothers who had nearly broke their necks to tell their little sister about 'the birds and the bees' – in graphic detail, and she had been generous enough to sell this important knowledge to her friends for sixpence. I had thought it to be the best sixpence ever spent, but that was some years before, and since then I had begun to find my own rapidly developing body to be a source of much embarrassment, particularly when I attracted the attention of boys older than myself – attention which I certainly neither encouraged nor desired – well, not much, at least. Knowing the facts of life, and about the intimacy required to conceive a child, I was confused. The way Mother and Father lived now, I could hardly imagine them being intimate enough for Mother to be carrying another baby.

Mother looked frankly at me, her eyebrows raised and her lips pursed into a moue of surprise. 'Ah,' she said after a moment, that single word acknowledging the fact that I was no longer basked in the innocence of childhood.

'When?' Austin asked. 'When's the baby coming?'

'In a few months' time,' Mother replied, smiling, as she often did, at his bluntness.

'It had better be a boy,' Austin said, scowling somewhat. 'We don't want another stinking girl!' He made no attempt to hide the fact that he did not like Violet; he teased and tormented her mercilessly, and called her a cry-baby when he succeeded in making her cry. As much as I disliked admitting it, my brother seemed to be growing into a bully rather than into a considerate young man. He was wilful and stubborn, and seemed to listen to no one but himself. With no other role model – for Father took little interest in his sons – it concerned me that Harold was going to turn out the same.

Legacy of Lies

'Can we go now?' Harold asked, his voice a plaintive whine that grated on my nerves. Mother nodded and smiled at both boys, as if unaware of their rudeness. I wondered often whether it was that she did not care whether they had manners or not, or whether she was merely afraid of their tempers, which could be foul at times.

When they had gone, their footsteps pounding on the staircase as they went up to their bedroom, Mother folded her hands in her lap and looked at me. 'Your father has his needs,' she said. 'And if I did not satisfy them, he would only look elsewhere.'

I looked down, embarrassed by her frankness.

'I had thought that I would be the one to explain such matters to you,' Mother continued. 'How long have you known?'

'Some time,' I said vaguely, feeling uncomfortable.

'Who told you?'

'Betty. She heard it from her brothers,' I replied. I hesitated. 'Mother, is it true that once a boy has kissed a girl, they have to get married and... and have babies?'

Mother laughed. 'Oh, Lilly!' she said, making me feel small and childish. 'You should know better than to be taken in by Betty's brothers' teasing.'

'But they swore to Betty it was the truth,' I protested.

'Several boys kissed me before I met your father and fell in love,' Mother replied, hugging me briefly. 'I forget that you are growing up fast, Lilly. Have you been kissed – is that what has made you look so pensive these last days?'

I thought it impossible to feel any more embarrassed than I did then. 'Robbie kissed me,' I admitted.

'Betty's brother Robbie?' Mother asked. I nodded. 'And did you like it?'

I hesitated. 'Only a little bit,' I said finally. 'But I do not want to marry him!'

'Of course you don't,' Mother replied. 'For one thing, you are much too young. I think I shall have to have words with Mrs Carr and tell her what scoundrels she has for sons.' She said it with a hint of laughter in her voice that made me bristle with indignation. My pride did not take kindly to being laughed at.

I stood up. 'May I be excused now, Mother?' I asked sharply. 'I have some lessons to mark before school tomorrow.'

Mother was still smiling. 'You are a funny little thing, Lilly,' she said. 'All prickly and spiky, and pretty and clever, like a little *hedgehog.' Her smile became wistful. 'So like my Alice, once upon a time.'*

Her words left a cold, empty feeling in my stomach, knowing as I did where Alice still languished, in the asylum which Mother visited nearly every week. I could neither see nor want to see any similarities between myself and my aunt – but my opinion was tempered by the Alice I had seen, not the Alice that she had once been. I'm afraid I feared the madness, just as I felt sure that Father feared it, too.

Legacy of Lies

The baby, another girl, who Mother mysteriously named Medora, was born in the evening of the last day of July, amidst much screaming from Mother and sobbing from Violet, who, in her childish innocence, was convinced that the midwife in attendance was in some way torturing Mother. Nothing I could say or do could reassure the child, even though Violet was closer to me than she was Mother, being that often I was charged more with her care than Mother was. Mother had become more excitable and easily distracted as her pregnancy progressed, sometimes completely forgetting about Violet – indeed, forgetting all of us, but we three older children were much less dependent on Mother's care. Perhaps the strangest moment had been on the last day of the school term, when Austin, Harold and I had returned home to find Mother and Violet happily engaged in decorating the house for Christmas. We three stopped, bemused, on the threshold of the kitchen, staring at the gay decorations festooning the walls. Seeing us, Violet came skipping out of the sitting room with a bundle of tinsel in her arms, which she immediately thrust at Austin.

'Can't reach the top of the tree,' she said. 'You do it!'

'What tree?' Austin demanded, refusing to accept the tinsel.

'Come and see!' Violet said, unperturbed, as she always was, by Austin's coldness towards her. She led the way through into the sitting room, where the fir tree that had, until that day, stood in the middle of the front lawn, was standing in a bucket full of sand. Gaudy baubles hung from its branches and tinsel was draped haphazardly around the tree. Mother was sitting in her usual chair, with her swollen feet propped up on a padded footstool, wearing a delighted grin on her face.

'Happy Christmas!' she cried, holding out her arms as if to invite us for a hug.

'It's not Christmas,' Harold said, regarding Mother suspiciously.

'We're having an early Christmas,' Mother replied, laughing. 'There's a turkey in the oven and all the trimmings!'

Austin looked at me. 'Has she gone mad?' he hissed. 'Like Alice?'

I had never paused to wonder whether he remembered what had happened to our Auntie Alice – but clearly he did, and I'm afraid at that moment, I shared his concern that Mother had been in some way infected by Alice's madness. I shook my head quickly to hush him, however, because Violet was looking up at him in adoration, and hanging off his every word as always. 'Help her put the tinsel up, Austin,' I said, as sternly as I could manage.

'It's not Christmas!' Austin muttered, but he took one look at the expression on my face and immediately stopped protesting. He even managed a smile for Violet's sake, which was shocking in itself.

I stationed myself in the kitchen, ostensibly to keep an eye on dinner, but actually my intention was to intercept Father when he returned from work, so as to warn him of the early festivities. I imagined he would be less than pleased to see what Mother had done. His reaction, however, when I stepped out into the garden and told him the news the moment he came through the gate, was far from what I had expected. Instead of being angry at Mother's strange behaviour, he seemed saddened instead; there was moistness to his eyes that could even have been tears. He surprised me further when, instead of demanding that the decorations be taken down at once, he allowed them to remain, and allowed Mother to continue in her festive charade. In the months that followed, I could hardly help wondering if he had somehow sensed the turbulence that was yet to come.

Medora's birth was a difficult one; Mother laboured for almost a day and a half, and when Medora was finally eased from the womb with forceps, the umbilical cord was taut around her neck and for minutes – minutes during which Mother wailed like a banshee – there was no lusty cry from the baby. When finally that first cry came, it was weak, like the mewling cry of a tiny kitten, not at all like the indignant wail I remembered from when Violet was born. I left Violet in Austin's reluctant care and crept up to the bedroom, fearful that all was not well. The midwife frowned disapprovingly at me, but Mother beckoned me in as she tried to encourage the tiny child to suckle at her breast.

'It's a girl,' Mother said in a voice that was hoarse from screaming. 'She's to be called Medora.'

Fool that I was, I was encouraged by the fact that Mother had named the baby immediately, since Violet had remained nameless for so long. I felt certain that Mother was not going to suffer as she had after Violet's birth, and I smiled broadly, like a fool, before going downstairs again to report to Father that he had another daughter.

Legacy of Lies

'And your mother? Is she well?' Father asked tightly, replacing on the bookcase a slim volume he had been studying.

'Perfectly well,' I said, completely unaware of how violently those words would return to haunt me.

'Then let us pray that the trouble of the past is done with,' Father said, for the first time speaking to me as if I was an adult and not a child. It did not occur to me that there was no one else to whom he could speak about Mother. I allowed myself instead to swell with pride that my father regarded me now as adult enough to speak with me on his own level.

'I think that it is,' I said sagely, feeling that his comment required some answer. 'Mother looks happy, and the baby seems well, if a little small.'

'Go up and tell your mother I shall leave her to rest tonight and meet my new daughter in the morrow,' Father said, already reaching for another volume from the bookcase. He paused. 'Perhaps you should stay with her tonight, and help with the baby. Your mother will be tired, and will not want that interfering midwife to stay.'

I went gladly back upstairs, feeling terribly important when I told the midwife that she would not be needed any more, that I would take care of Mother in her stead. I received a grateful smile from Mother in return. This, I reassured myself repeatedly, was not at all like it had been when Violet was born. All would be well. I felt certain that this time Mother was not going to sink deep into melancholy.

***

For the first few days, it seemed as though my certainty of Mother's good health was well founded. The change was sudden and unexpected, catching each of us entirely unawares. It seemed that one day Mother was well, caring for Medora, rocking her in her arms and singing gentle lullabies, and the next she had plunged deep into such melancholy that we had never before seen. She would not leave her bed, nor would she speak, nor even show any recognition when we spoke to her. It was as if she had shut herself down, and stayed alive only because her body kept on breathing. She drank a little water, but only when she was alone, as if she did not want anyone to witness her giving sustenance to her body – not that water could keep her alive indefinitely. I took to leaving food along with water when I left her alone, but the food always went untouched.

The fact that Father refused to call the doctor only added to the worry that kept me awake at night. He forbade us to mention to the neighbours Mother's melancholic state, and it seemed to me that he was in some kind of denial – as if he thought that by pretending Mother was well, he could make her well. I was still only a child on the cusp of adulthood but even I knew that his denial could do no good.

Thankfully, Medora took well to a bottle, placid creature that she was, and sucked greedily at the mixture of evaporated milk and water that was the most readily available substitute for Mother's milk. I cared for her during the day, as well as keeping house and keeping Violet and the boys in check. To my surprise, Father insisted that I must sleep at night – although worry kept me awake – and it was he, unless he slept too deeply, who soothed, fed and changed Medora throughout the night. Sometimes I would catch him gazing down at her, when he thought I was not looking, with such fierce love in his eyes that I had never before seen. Perhaps it was because he knew, even then, that she was going to grow up without a mother, and would need his love – or perhaps he had looked upon each of us children in the same way, but I had merely never noticed.

Medora was five weeks old before Mother seemed to come back to herself, raised herself up out of bed and attempted to resume daily life as if naught had been amiss in those long weeks of melancholy. She laughed again, and the house would be filled with the smell of baking when we children returned from school. Her breast-milk had dried up, but she seemed not to mind bottle feeding her baby, and I foolishly allowed myself to believe that the worst was over, and all would be well again.

***

Even with the benefit of hindsight, I could not honestly say what it was that made me return home from school that lunchtime, instead of eating in the dining hall with the children. If I believed in such nonsense, I might have said it was a sixth sense, but thankfully I was always too sensible to be taken in by such notions. An instinct, perhaps, or the niggling feeling that something had not been right that morning when I left with Violet and the boys for school.

Legacy of Lies

Whatever it was that drove me home, there is a part of me that wishes that it hadn't, for what I returned home to will haunt my mind until the very end of my days.

It was a Thursday, and Thursdays had always been wash-day throughout my life, so I thought nothing wrong when I came in through the kitchen door and saw the washing tub brimming with water. It could have been any other washing day – but for the madness that had suddenly infected Mother's mind. She was standing over the tub, staring down into the water, with Medora lying placidly in her arms. Her face was a grief-ravaged mask; her eyes blood-shot and red-rimmed. Steam rose from the water, which was, oddly, I thought, devoid of any soap. Mother seemed to be in an almost trance-like state, oblivious of my presence until I tentatively spoke her name. Then, she raised her head to look – not at me, but more like through me. A strange smile twisted her lips.

'You!' she shrieked, startling both myself and Medora, who started to wail in fright. Mother's voice rose even above the baby's shrill cries. 'What have you done with her? What have you done with my baby? Where is she? Where have you taken her?'

I stepped forward quickly as Mother suddenly dangled Medora over the washing tub, so the baby's tiny feet almost touched the steaming water. As I tried to grab my sister from Mother's arms, Mother danced nimbly out of reach, still dangling Medora threateningly over the tub.

'No!' she shrieked. 'You're not having the changeling 'til you tell me where my baby is.'

My guts twisted painfully with fear for my sister's safety. Mother had lost her mind; there could be no other explanation. 'Mother, please,' I begged, as calmly as I could manage. My voice shook dreadfully, however, and Mother seemed not to even register my words.

'You can't fool me,' she spat. 'Shape-shifter! Pretending to be my Lilly, when Lilly is at school. Tell me where my baby is, or I'll drown the changeling!' She lowered Medora so that the water touched her tiny toes and she wailed louder. 'Where is she? What have you done with my baby?'

Perhaps I was wrong to do as I did, but I knew that if I did not do something, then Mother would surely drown her own baby. I ran screaming out into the yard – screaming at the very top of my lungs for someone to help me. I'm ashamed to admit that I screamed too that Mother had lost her mind, and who knows how many of the neighbours heard my cries. From that moment, everything happened so quickly that, in my terrified state, I was hardly able to comprehend what was happening. It was Mr Armstrong from next door who plucked the screaming baby from Mother's arms as she was about to drop her into the water, and after thrusting Medora into Mrs Armstrong's waiting arms, he proceeded to wrestle Mother to the ground and sit on her whilst she shrieked. Ashamedly, I merely stood by and watched, shaking so hard that my teeth seemed to be rattling in my head.

'That monster took my baby, she took my baby and swapped it for the changeling. She thought I wouldn't notice, but I know my own baby. It smells different, you see. Smell it. Smell the changeling. You can smell the rot, the decay!' Mother yelled, struggling against Mr Armstrong's superior strength. 'That's not my baby. That's not my baby. She took it. The monster took my baby, and now she's pretending to be my Lilly!'

'Come on, deary,' Mrs Armstrong said to me, giving me a gentle push towards the kitchen door. 'Come on next door with me, and help me get your little sister nice and dry and warm.'

I allowed myself to be led away, too shocked to move of my own accord; too disturbed by Mother's words to be able to speak. I said nothing as Mrs Armstrong dispatched her eldest son Billy, who'd been laid off from his job only the week before, to fetch Father from the office. I knew, of course, that a point of no return had been reached, but I could not find my own voice to give sound to the horror that was churning through my mind. Indeed, I remained mute as Mrs Armstrong stripped Medora of the wet clothing and went to the cupboard beside the fireplace and produced baby clothes that she had, inexplicably, saved from when her three children were infants – more than ten years since.

'Here, drink this,' Mrs Armstrong said once Medora was settled in a drawer in front of the fire, pressing a mug of sweet tea into my hands. 'For the shock, lovey. You're as white as a sheet.'

My hands shook as I lifted the mug to my lips and took a sip of the scalding hot liquid. 'She was going to drown her,' I whispered, finally finding my voice as the sugar seeped through my veins.

'I know, lovey,' Mrs Armstrong said, putting her hands on top of mine. 'But she's not herself. Surely, she's not herself. Your poor mother would never harm a hair on any of her babies' heads in her right mind.'

Legacy of Lies

Far from being soothing, her words left a cold chill in the pit of my stomach, as they confirmed my worst fears. Mother's past melancholy was nothing compared to this new madness. This was madness like that which I had seen in Alice – and that frightened me.

Billy soon returned with Father, but with one sharp look, Father forbade me to return home. 'Take care of your sister,' he said, shrugging off his coat as he went inside our house. Shortly, Mr Armstrong came back, bearing the scars of his battle to restrain and calm Mother from her hysteria. There were deep scratches on his forearms, some still welling blood, and marks on his face where Mother had raked her fingernails down his cheeks. I felt my own cheeks flame with mortification, and could not bring myself to meet his eyes.

It seemed an eternity before Father came to fetch Medora and me. His face was pale and drawn; he looked wearied beyond words, but still managed to thank Mr and Mrs Armstrong for their help and hospitality. He said nothing until I had settled Medora into her crib in the kitchen, and then he sank down into the chair in front of the fire.

'Your mother's sleeping,' he said on a heavy sigh. 'She exhausted herself ranting.' He levelled a look at me. 'What happened, Lilly? What on earth happened?'

I had no answer for him. I could only tell him what I had come home to find, and when I had finished, he was holding his head in his hands in horror. It was a long time, or at least it seemed so, before he lifted his head from his hands and looked directly at me.

'What am I to do, Lilly?' he asked in a voice that was cracked and broken and so unlike his usual authoritive tone that I stared at him for a long moment as if a stranger had stalked in and stolen his place in our family.

In the end, of course, there was little choice in what he could do. Mother's state of mind was not improved when she woke after sundown, and although the doctor when he came was able to give her something to calm her, I knew that when he and Father disappeared into Father's study to talk that our lives would never be the same again. When the men came, some hours later, to take her away, I'm afraid that I was neither surprised, nor sorry, for she had become a danger to herself and to us, and after what she had tried to do to Medora that day, I knew, as surely as I knew my own name, that the point of no return had been reached.

***

'Where has Mother gone?' Austin asked the moment Father departed for work at the usual time, as though nothing was wrong.

I swallowed hard against the lump in my throat and tried, in vain, to summon a smile. 'To hospital,' I said – and felt no guilt, for it was the truth, after all. The asylums were supposed to be called mental hospitals now, though most people still referred to them by their age-old name.

'When's she coming back?' Harold asked, with his mouth full of porridge.

I sighed. 'I don't know.'

Austin narrowed his eyes at me. 'Is she coming back?' When I didn't answer straight away, he shook his head and pushed back his chair. 'She's not coming back, is she?'

'I don't know, Austin!' I snapped.

'They took her away like they took Auntie Alice away – and she never came back,' Austin retorted.

'Who's Auntie Alice?' Violet asked, her voice distorted by the thumb that was almost constantly in her mouth.

'No one,' I said, shooting a warning look at Austin. He knew better than to talk about such things in front of Violet – his trouble was that he didn't think before he opened his mouth. 'Go and get ready for school, boys, please. No arguments. Not this morning.'

Violet, thankfully, was in a placid mood, and allowed me to buckle her feet into her shoes and button up her duffle-coat, leaving me a precious few moments to write a quick note to Mrs Morrissey, the infant school teacher who I assisted. Father had not actually said anything, but of course the house and the baby needed taking care of, and as the eldest daughter, it would be expected of me to take on the responsibility of the woman of the house. I tried very hard not to mind, but the truth is that I never did stop regretting the way I had to give up my hopes of one day teaching a class of pupils of my own.

We settled into a routine over the coming days. I took over Mother's responsibilities, and even Austin accepted my authority without question. Father did not even mention Mother's name, as if by not speaking of her, he could avoid awkward questions. He left me to take care of the house and children, and carried on as he always had, spending the evenings in his study, with a stern warning to the boys that he didn't want them to disturb him with their rowdy games.

A week after Mother was taken away, I walked Violet and the boys to school as usual, and then, instead of going home to deal with the housework, I climbed aboard a tram, with Medora in the wicker carrying basket that Mother had used for all of us children when we were babies, and travelled across town to a building I knew only by its reputation. The asylum – the term mental hospital did little to soften the blow of those words. It looked a pretty, unassuming place – it could have been a local lord's country house, or perhaps a rest home for men who had been wounded in the war. To look at the building, you would not have imagined the horrors that went on within the walls.

Beyond the heavy wrought iron carriage gates, which were always open during daylight hours, there was a long driveway leading to the front of the Georgian brick building. The drive seemed indeterminably long as I trudged through piles of damp leaves towards the front door; the heavy winds of the last few days had stripped the trees lining the driveway of their leaves. The damp air lay heavy across my shoulders and I shivered – though it might well have been fear and not cold that caused me to tremble so.

Standing on the stone steps beneath the imposing front door, I reached for the bell and rang it, just once, hearing from within heavy footsteps approaching. The door swung suddenly inwards, with a creak and a groan, to reveal a man only a little taller than myself, wizened with age, and wearing a black frock coat and a red cravat.

'What is your business, miss, please?' he asked, in a voice that seemed to rumble from deep within him. I took a step back, swallowing hard. I tried to speak, but found that my voice had deserted me. The man repeated his question with a touch of impatience.

'I... I've come to see my mother,' I stammered, finally. 'She was... brought here last week.'

The man shook his head slowly, as if the movement took tremendous effort. 'No visitors for a month,' he said, already beginning to close the door again. 'Come back in three weeks. Visitors are allowed on Wednesdays and Sundays.' The door was closed in my face before I could gather my wits enough to ask why.

The journey home seemed to take at least twice as long as the journey to the hospital had taken, as my mind was weighed heavy with the thought of Mother being kept in the hospital without any hope of visitors. I could not imagine what it might be like inside, for the door man had opened the door only wide enough to stand in the gap, giving me no chance to see what lay beyond. Somehow, though, I could not imagine it being a cheerful, happy place.

I said nothing about my unsuccessful visit to Father or my brothers. I suspected that Father would not be happy about me going, and I did not want him to forbid me to return. So long as he did not say openly that I was not to go, I felt no guilt in wanting to visit my own mother.

Three weeks does not sound like a great length of time, but those weeks dragged dreadfully. If they dragged for me, when I was occupied with housework, cooking and caring for the children, then I could hardly imagine what they must have been like for Mother.

I could not, of course, visit on a Sunday, and so it was on the Wednesday, a little more than four weeks after Mother's admission to the hospital, when I made the return journey, after lunch. Medora was fretful. She was teething and had been awake and crying for much of the night, which meant in turn that I had had little sleep myself. My stomach was knotted with apprehension – imagine that! Nervous about visiting my own mother. It was not the person, but the place that made me nervous however.

The same man opened the door to me, and intoned the same question, in the same tone of voice. I wondered if he ever tired of making the same greeting to every visitor who came knocking at the door.

'I'm here to see my mother,' I said, keeping my voice steady this time.

'Her name?'

'Edith Molineux.'

He took a step back, allowing me in through the door. I found myself in a draughty, entrance room, tiled with alternating black and white tiles like a giant chessboard. The walls were painted dark chocolate brown, and the windows were high up so they afforded little light. Combined, these features made the room both dark and gloomy.

'Wait here,' the man said, jerking his head towards a row of stiff-backed wooden chairs lined up against the opposite wall. He walked stiffly across to a bell pull next to a closed door opposite the front door. I sat down as the bell jangled – obviously intended to alert some member of staff.

Legacy of Lies

Presently, a woman dressed in a nurse's uniform appeared through the door, and the door man muttered my mother's name to her. She shot me a look of surprise and then approached me. 'You're here to visit Mrs Molineux, I understand?'

I nodded. 'My mother,' I said. 'She was... admitted...'

The nurse waved her hand dismissively. 'Yes, yes, I know when she was admitted. I was led to believe, however, that Mrs Molineux was not to expect visitors. The family was leaving the area, I was told.'

I stared at her. 'No. Who told you that?'

The nurse smiled – rather vindictively, I thought. 'Mr Molineux himself,' she replied. She scowled at Medora, in her basket at my feet, and shook her head. 'You cannot bring a child here, girl. I suggest that if you wish to make a visit to your mother, you leave your child at home.'

'She's not my child. She's my sister!' I protested.

'That is of no concern to me. Whoever's child she is, you cannot bring her into the visiting room.' The nurse looked pointedly towards the door. 'Good day to you, Miss Molineux.'

Once again, I found myself standing on the doorstep with the door firmly closed in my face. Tears of frustration pricked at the corners of my eyes, but I blinked them furiously away, refusing to give the nurse the satisfaction of making me cry. I began trudging back down the driveway, dejection making my shoulders slump.

'Excuse me?' Footsteps came hurrying up the driveway after me; I stopped and turned to find a young flush-faced nurse, not much older than myself hastening to catch up with me. 'I'm sorry,' she said apologetically. 'Only I heard Sister sending you packing, and I wanted to make sure you were all right. She can be very blunt, and... cruel, sometimes.' She bit her lip. 'Not – not to the patients, of course,' she added hurriedly.

'I understand what you mean,' I said.

'I'm just coming off duty,' the young nurse said with a tentative smile. 'I could... I could look after the baby, if you'd like, so you could visit your mother.'

I could hardly refuse such a kind offer – not that the thought of refusing actually crossed my mind. 'She's a bit fretful,' I apologised.

The nurse laughed. 'Aren't all babies?' she said. 'I have five brothers and two sisters. I know all about babies.' She took the basket off me and smiled down at Medora, who immediately quietened. 'I'll take you in through the kitchens and get one of the other nurses to take you to the visitor's room. Sister won't approve, but she doesn't have to know everything.'

The kitchens smelt of broiling meat and were as hot as hell. The nurse, who told me to call her Bess, led me quickly through, and called after a girl who was about to disappear around the corner. 'Lizzie, can you take Miss Molineux to the visitor's room? Sister wouldn't let her in because of the baby. She's here to see her mother.'

'Mrs Molineux? But...' Lizzie glanced from me to Bess and then looked down at her feet. 'Sister won't like it, Bess. I don't want no trouble.'

'Sister won't even know,' Bess cajoled. Medora started to cry, and Bess immediately offered the baby her finger to suck. 'Please, Lizzie. What if it was your mother in here?'

Lizzie sighed. 'Come this way,' she said to me, already moving off.

I glanced back at Bess. She smiled encouragingly. 'I'll wait in the grounds for you,' she said, turning back towards the kitchens. Lizzie shot me a look of impatience, and I hurried after her down the long, stone-flagged corridor.

I cannot rightly say exactly what I imagined I would find in the visitor's room, but the best I can say is that the reality was far from what I might have imagined it would be. Lizzie left me sitting on another hard wooden chair, whilst she went to make Mother 'fit for visitors'. Her words alarmed me somewhat, implying as they did that for the rest of the time, Mother was not fit for visitors.

I was not the only visitor there, of course. I found that it was very easy to distinguish visitors from the patients they were visiting, seeing as the patients – all women in this visiting room – were all dressed identically, in dresses of a sort of cotton tweed in washed-out shades of charcoal, grey, pink and fawn. Their shoes, too, were identical, slipper type things with a strap and button that would be of little use outside. I felt conspicuous, sitting stiffly in my chair in the corner of the room, with a dozen pairs of eyes gazing upon me with undisguised curiosity.

It seemed an age before Lizzie returned with Mother, and for a moment, I simply sat there staring at the strange woman who bore my mother's face. She did not give any sign of recognition and Lizzie had to prompt her to sit down. Her eyes were glazed, as if she was in some kind of stupor, and she sat rigid, looking not at me but at some point past my left shoulder.

'Mother?'

She did not respond to the name, and I looked to Lizzie for some kind of explanation 'What is wrong with her?' I asked.

Lizzie pursed her lips and shook her head at me, as if the answer should have been obvious. 'She has lost her reason,' she said, with not the slightest compassion. 'The doctor prescribes paraldehyde and sodium amytal to calm her agitation.' She cast her gaze around the room, forcing me to acknowledge that most of the patients sat in similar states of stupor.

I found myself fighting back tears as I reached out and took Mother's hands in mine. As I did so, I noticed the scabs of dried blood on her fingers, where it looked as though she had been gnawing at her skin with her teeth. There were faded rings of bruising around her wrists, also, and clumps of hair missing from her scalp.

'Mother, it's me, Lilly,' I said, a catch in my voice. 'I wanted to come and see you. I would have come sooner, but they said I couldn't come for a month. I've brought Medora, too, but I wasn't allowed to bring her in.'

At the mention of Medora's name, some of the glassiness lifted from Mother's eyes and she looked sharply up at me.

'Medora?' she repeated, in a voice that did not sound like hers. She shook her head vigorously. 'No. NO! They took my baby. The monsters took my baby and swapped it for a changeling, and thought I wouldn't know, but I know, I know what they did, they can't fool me. My baby is gone. Gone.' She slapped my hands away from her and grabbed my face with both hands, squeezing and tugging at my skin with her ragged fingernails. 'You are one of them, too,' she hissed, spitting at me. 'I can see the rotting flesh beneath the mask. You might be able to fool the rest, but you can't fool me. It is in your eyes, too. There is evil in your eyes!' Letting go of my face, she shoved me hard enough to make me tumble off the chair. 'There is a monster in here. You let a monster in here!' she shrieked, over and over again, whilst frantically tearing clumps of her hair from her scalp.

The two nurses on duty in the room hastened across to help Lizzie to restrain Mother. One removed a small glass vial from the pocket of her smock, and whilst Lizzie and the other nurse held Mother firm, she poured a foul-smelling green liquid down

Mother's throat. The nurse then opened the door to the visiting room and rang three times a bell fixed to the wall of the corridor. I sat in a kind of stupor myself whilst Mother slipped back into her previous vacant, staring state, and merely watched when two male orderlies came with a basket chair on wheels to take Mother back to her ward.

'Sister will be bound to find out now,' Lizzie grumbled as she hurried me out of the room and back towards the kitchens. 'She will be furious. Upsetting the patient like that!'

'Mother was never like this before,' I said weakly. 'The madness came on so suddenly. I thought... I thought she might be recovered of it now.'

Lizzie gave a sigh that could, I thought, have been out of exasperation. She made no answer, nor offered any words of comfort, and when she let me outside through the kitchen door, she turned back inside without a single word.

I found Bess sitting on a wrought iron bench in the gardens, with Medora perched prettily on her knee. My face must have given away my distress, for Bess immediately replaced the baby in her basket and clasped hold of my hands in comfort.

'The first visit is always so difficult,' she said kindly. 'Was it so very awful?'

'She is no better than the day they took her away,' I said, sniffing miserably.

Bess smiled sympathetically. 'I was so shocked on my first day here,' she said. 'It wasn't a bit like I had expected it to be. I am used to it now, of course, but some patients can shock me still.'

'Will she ever get better?' I asked.

'Some patients get better suddenly and are allowed home. Others... others have to stay,' Bess said, somewhat reluctantly.

I thought suddenly of Alice, who had been taken away six years before and never again mentioned. I hesitated a moment before asking Bess directly. 'My aunt – Mother's sister Alice – was brought here some years ago. Father would not have her name spoken in the house after that. Is she... is she still here?'

Bess looked pityingly at me. 'Alice Carr?' she asked, and I nodded, because I knew that Carr was my mother's name before she married Father. Bess gave my hands a squeeze. 'I'm afraid Alice died four months ago. Somehow she managed to convince an orderly to open a window in the ward, and then she jumped from the open window. It was in one of the upstairs wards.'

Legacy of Lies

Four months ago, I thought, was around the time when Mother plunged into melancholy. That, at least, I could understand. It was the strange belief that Medora was not her child that confounded me. 'Do you know what is wrong with Mother?' I asked tentatively.

Bess hesitated. 'The doctor believes her to be suffering from one of the psychoses,' she said. 'From the quick changes in her state, he suspects manic-depressive psychosis, although her particular delusional beliefs are more commonly found in the schizophrenic type of psychosis.'

None of the words meant anything to me, and I did not want to ask for an explanation, because, to be quite frank, I was not sure that I actually wanted to know what the strange words meant. I tried to form my lips into a smile as I bent down to pick up Medora's basket, but my lips trembled rebelliously.

'I must go,' I murmured, keeping my gaze directed down towards my feet. 'My brothers and sister will be home from school soon.' I heard Bess call out a farewell as I hurried away down the driveway, but I could not bring myself to look back towards the building that had, I could not help but feel, stolen my mother away from me.

***

I waited until Austin, Harold and Violet had gone to bed before I knocked lightly on Father's study door and waited for him to invite me in. He looked at me over the top of his wire-rimmed spectacles, but didn't ask me to sit down; nor did he put down the newspaper he had been reading.

'I went to see Mother today,' I began hesitantly.

Father put his newspaper down. 'You did what?' he demanded, his voice rising sharply.

'I went to visit Mother,' I repeated. 'You did not tell me that I could not,' I added bravely.

Father glowered at me. 'Then I am telling you now!' he snapped. 'Your mother is not well enough to receive visitors.'

'The Sister said that you had told her we were leaving the area, and Mother was not to expect any visitors, not that she couldn't have any,' I said.

'Who do you believe, Lillian? A nurse or your father?' Father asked grimly.

'You, of course, Father,' I replied meekly.

'I am glad to hear it,' Father said. He sighed. 'Was it a successful visit?'

I shook my head miserably. 'She denied again that Medora was hers,' I said. 'She talked of monsters – said that I was a monster, too.'

'You should not have gone there, Lillian,' Father said, as if Mother's behaviour towards me was some kind of punishment for me visiting the hospital. 'You must not go again. The madness has her in its grip. I fear it will not let her go.'

'Like Alice, you mean?' I asked without thinking.

Father's eyes narrowed as he gazed stonily at me. 'What did your mother tell you about Alice?' he demanded.

'Only that she was ill and had to go away,' I said, because that was what Mother had told us. 'To the mental hospital.'

Father grunted. 'You children saw too much. Your mother should not have subjected you to that. It was immoral of her, and foolish.' He sighed again. 'But yes, I fear that your mother is afflicted as Alice was.'

His use of the past tense suggested that he knew that Alice had taken her own life, but I was not foolish enough to admit that I knew also. 'Then she won't be coming back?' I asked.

'You ask too many questions, Lillian. It is one thing to have an inquisitive mind, but quite another to allow that inquisitiveness to become bothersome,' Father replied, picking his newspaper up again and disappearing behind it. He did not need to tell me I was dismissed. I backed out of the study and closed the door behind me.

***

Usually, Father had left for work by the time I had chivvied Austin and Harold into their school clothes and got Violet washed and dressed, but the morning after I made my visit to Mother, he was still sitting at the kitchen table when we came downstairs.

'Sit down, children,' he said gravely. 'There is something I have to tell you.'

We glanced at each other before sitting down; Violet, sensing that something was amiss, jabbed her thumb firmly in her mouth and insisted on sitting on my knee.

'You all know that your mother has been ill in hospital for some weeks now,' Father began. His gaze was fixed on me, as if daring me to contradict him. 'I am afraid I have some rather bad news. Your mother passed away last night.'

He was lying. I knew that much just from looking at him, but I could not accuse him of such in front of my siblings. Austin and Harold were both looking at me, their faces blanched white with the shock of Father's blunt announcement. Even Austin, always ready with a question, had nothing to say.

'There is something else, I should tell you,' Father went on, as if he had just announced nothing more serious than a bad weather forecast. 'We will be leaving this house and moving to a village just outside Sheffield.'

At last, Austin found his voice. 'Why?' he asked, as bluntly as Father had delivered the news about Mother.

Father frowned. 'Because I have been promoted to the Sheffield office,' he said curtly. Austin opened his mouth to speak again, but Father held his hand up to silence him. 'Enough! We will be moving at the end of next week. I shall expect you boys to pack your own things in the trunks I will bring down from the attic, and you, Lillian, can be responsible for your own things as well as your sisters' things. I shall send a note to the school explaining the situation.'

Father would say no more on the matter, and so, the following Friday, our belongings and furniture were loaded into the back of a removal van, and we left our childhood home – and, of course, our mother – for good.

Our new home was nestled in the midst of a sleepy village in the Derbyshire peak district, and Father soon established himself as a pillar of the little community, offering his accounting services to the local businesses at discount rates. He played the part of a widower and father well, going so far as to lay a memorial stone in the churchyard to Mother's memory. I felt like a hypocrite each time I led my siblings to lay flowers on the stone on her birthday and at Christmas, knowing as I did the level of Father's lies.

I kept my silence, however, for the sake of the children, not out of any sense of duty to Father. He lost his right to my respect when he forced from me a promise not to break my silence. I long thought it best to maintain the lie: that the truth would, perhaps, be harder to bear – for surely it was for me. I break it now, however, as I await my own swift end.

Death has come too soon for me; I feel a girl still, at only twenty-six years old, but the doctors tell me I have but months to *live. My* girls, *my beautiful Violet and Medora, are still children yet – too young to bear the truth – and the boys away at war – and so I leave this tale to the keeping of one whom I trust, to give to my girls when they are old enough to hear this, my testament of truth.*

CHAPTER THIRTEEN

Generations of tears stained the pages of Lilly's 'Testament of Truth', Luci thought, swiping at her cheeks as her own tears dripped down onto the cover of the notebook. Whoever said that the truth never hurts was lying. The truth *did* hurt, like a poison-tipped knife stabbing at her heart. Madness flowed through her veins, generations of madness, stretching back almost a century – and who *knew* how much further back in time it went. Great wracking sobs shook Luci's shoulders as she lay back, curled her knees up to her chest and tried – in vain – to block the vivid images her great aunt's writing had conjured up in her mind.

'I'm going to make some lunch, Luci – are you coming down?' Ted's voice drifted up the stairs, but Luci remained prone on the bed, her tears soaking into the bed-spread. 'Luci?' Ted's voice came again, followed by an indignant wail from one of the twins, objecting to being woken by Ted's shouts.

Luci sat up sharply, her heart suddenly pounding violently. Her babies' cries were like hot needles penetrating her skull. 'Oh God,' she whispered brokenly. 'Oh *God*, what have I *done?*' Her legs wobbled traitorously, as if reluctant to hold her up, as she stumbled across the room and yanked the door open. She met Ted on the landing, on his way up to see to the twins.

'Whatever's the matter?' he asked, the moment he saw her grief-ravaged face.

There were no words to answer him. Luci shrugged off the hand he put on her arm and pushed past him into the twins' bedroom. Both babies were awake now and kicking furiously in their Moses Basket. Dropping to her knees in front of the Moses Basket, Luci stretched out her hands to touch their cheeks, bursting into tears at the way they gazed trustingly up at her.

'I'm sorry,' she whispered. 'I'm so, so sorry!' A memory flared in the back of her mind, of her mother uttering the same words to her and Luke when they were small. 'But *she knew*,' Luci wailed. 'All along, she knew. She'd read it – she'd read it all, and she knew about the madness, and she still did it – she still had us!' She bent closer to Matty and Theo, her tears dripping down into their downy hair. 'I promise you – I promise you with all my heart, that I didn't know. I didn't know anything about the madness until it was too late – I swear to you I didn't. Not until today. Not until today.'

'Luci!' Ted said sharply, seizing hold of her shoulders and wrenching her away from the twins. 'Luci, stop it! You're frightening them!'

Luci slowly swivelled her head to look at him, her vision blurred by a sheet of tears. His voice seemed to be coming from a long way away, like it was echoing back at her. 'Frightening them?' she repeated numbly.

'You're upsetting them,' Ted pointed out more gently. 'Why don't you go downstairs whilst I settle the boys down again?'

'I just wanted them to know that I'm sorry,' Luci whispered.

'Go on downstairs,' Ted prompted. 'I'll be down in a minute – and then you can tell me what's wrong.'

Luci looked from him to the twins. They had no idea what she'd done to them, no idea the legacy that she had passed onto them. Bile rushed up into her throat and she lurched from the room and across into the bathroom, hanging her head over the porcelain bowl until the nausea had passed. She heard Ted murmuring soothing words to Matty and Theo – a sharp contrast to her own hysteria – and felt fresh tears of despair start trickling down her face. She turned and stumbled blindly down the stairs.

***

When Ted came downstairs after settling the twins back to sleep, he found Luci sitting at the kitchen table, holding her head in her hands. She was shaking, her teeth chattering, and when she lifted her head to look at him, there was such grief and despair on her face that Ted felt his stomach knot with apprehension.

'They used to sterilise them,' she said, her voice barely audible.

'What?'

'They used to sterilise women who came from families with a history of madness,' Luci said. 'I remember reading that – at school maybe – and thinking how awful it must be to come from a family of madwomen. I didn't think it would be me. I never thought that. Why would I?' She hugged her arms around herself, swallowing back tears. 'She should have told me! She should have bloody told me. Never mind telling me she was sorry and then topping herself. She should have warned me. If I'd have known, I could have saved them. I could have stopped it from happening again!'

Ted pulled out the chair next to Luci and sat down, sliding his arm around her shoulders. 'Luci, love, you need to calm down and tell me what's wrong. You're not making much sense.'

'I'm sorry,' Luci whispered, gulping. 'It's just... it's just the thought of what I've done to them. And – and to Charlie. If I'd have known... Oh, God, how am I going to tell Hannah and Mike?'

Ted stood up, grabbed a glass from the draining board and filled it with water. 'Come on, drink this, and just calm yourself down. You're going to make yourself ill.'

Luci sipped at the water, and gradually her sobs reduced to sniffles. She slumped forward, holding her head with both hands as if it pained her.

'That's better,' Ted said gently. 'Now what's all this about? What have you got yourself so worked up about?'

'Izzy found it,' Luci said, her voice muffled. 'This book – a handwritten notebook called "A Testament of Truth". It must have been so awful for her, finding it like that, when she had nobody but Elvina, and she was going to be sent away.'

'What about this book?' Ted cut in as Luci's voice started to tremble with the threat of tears.

'It was written by Medora's sister,' Luci said, her voice still trembling a little.

'Violet?'

'No. Another sister. She died – when Medora and Violet were still young,' Luci replied. She swallowed hard before giving Ted a summary of Lilly's wretched tale. The words kept sticking in her throat, and Ted had to keep refilling her glass with water. 'She – Lilly – wanted to warn her sisters about the madness, to try and stop it happening all over again, but it didn't work, did it? It's still there – the madness that just keeps on being passed down!'

Ted covered Luci's hands with his own and squeezed them reassuringly. 'I think it depends on how you look at it,' he said. 'What you've just told me, Luci, just seems to capture all the old negative attitudes about mental illness.'

'But that's how it was then!' Luci snapped. 'That's how they treated mad people. Mad people like me!' Her voice quivered. 'That's why Mum was so frightened, Ted. That's why when she looked into my eyes and saw the madness that day – that's why... that's why she went... went and threw herself in front of a train! She couldn't bear it. She couldn't bear to see it happen to me like she saw it happen to her mother, and like she knew it happened to her grandmother, and her great aunt, and God knows how many other relatives stretching back into history! She couldn't bear it, Ted, and I don't blame her, I don't blame her one little bit! But she should have told me. She should have warned me properly, not some silly cryptic words that didn't mean anything to me. "The fire's in your eyes", she said. That's all. "The fire's in your eyes, and it's dangerous", she told me, and she was trying, she was trying to warn me, but I didn't know, I couldn't know, not from that. It meant nothing to me – a joke, that's all, a stupid joke, but who's laughing now, huh? Who's fucking laughing now? The joke's on me! She could have bloody told me what she meant. She could have told me, and then I could have stopped it.'

'Luci, stop it!' Ted said sharply.

'No!' Luci shrieked back at him, standing up and pushing her chair back so hard that it clattered noisily to the floor. 'I won't stop it, because it's all true. She knew it all – every word of it – and she did nothing. She got pregnant, knowing what she was doing, knowing that the madness flowed in her blood, and she gave birth, and she raised us, all the time knowing what she'd done, knowing the fate she'd sealed for us, knowing all the bloody time that she could have infected us. She had no excuse. She knew.' Pacing around the kitchen, Luci tore her fingers through her hair, gasping with the force of the emotion that was tearing through her. 'All the time, she knew, and she did nothing, NOTHING! She had the chance to warn me, but no, oh no, she couldn't do that, could she? She didn't even warn Dad, didn't let him know her dirty little secret. She knew what she came from, and she fooled him, fooled him into thinking she was a poor orphan, never telling him anything about her family – because she was too ashamed of where she came from!'

'Luci, please,' Ted begged. 'Calm down!'

'She could have stopped it, Ted. All it took was the contraceptive pill or a condom, and she could have stopped it! But no, she was too selfish for that. She would have had to tell Dad why, then, wouldn't she, and she couldn't do that. She was too selfish to tell him – *and just look what she's done!* Look at me, Ted! She knew she could pass the madness on – she knew she *had* passed it on, and she couldn't even stick around long enough to warn me properly! She preferred to die, so she didn't have to see it again!' Luci leaned against the kitchen counter, her heart pounding so hard, it echoed like a frantic drum beat in her ears. 'She didn't even try to stop having babies after me and Luke. She kept on getting pregnant – but maybe God had a conscience after all, because they kept on dying before they were born, all those babies with the mad genes. I should have died too. I cheated death – did you know that? It should have been me who died, not Luke, but I'm paying for it now, aren't I? – I'm bloody paying for it now!'

Ted stood up, rubbing his hands over the stubble on his cheeks. Sidestepping Luci, he reached for his mobile phone, sitting on the top of the fridge freezer. He'd already started dialling when Luci rounded on him.

'What are you doing?' she demanded. 'Can't you even be bothered to listen to me?'

'I'm calling Alex,' Ted said.

'And what, Alex can wave a magic wand and make everything all right again, can he?' Luci shrieked. 'The damage is done, Ted. Mum did it when she didn't take any heed of Lilly's story. It can't be stopped now. Too late. I'm infected. I'm infectious – just like Izzy was. Did you know that, Ted? Did you know that your precious cousin was mad, too? That's why she was sent away, because they knew she was mad, and they didn't want to be associated with it!'

'Alex, can you call me, please. It's urgent. It's Luci. I don't know what to do. She's hysterical, and I can't get her to calm down,' Ted said, sounding desperate as he left a message on Alex's voicemail.

'Of course I'm hysterical,' Luci snarled. 'That's what they used to call madness in women, did you know that? Hysteria. It's my mad genes coming out.'

A wail from the baby monitor punctuated the brief silence as Luci paused to get her breath and gulp down another glass of water. She turned automatically towards the stairs, but Ted put a hand out to stop her. 'Let me see to them, please,' he said. 'You'll only upset them when you're so wound up. They can sense it. It's not good for them.'

Luci stood back, letting him go to the foot of the stairs. 'Of course I'm not good for them,' she said, some of the anger seeping out of her voice. 'Of course I'm not. That's my mother's legacy to me. She had the chance to leave a legacy of truth – like Lilly did – but no, she had to go for the easy option, the coward's option – a legacy of *lies*.'

Ted's phone rang whilst he was upstairs – he seemed to be a long time, as if he didn't want to come back down and face Luci again – and Luci hesitated a moment before snatching it up and answering it.

'Ted, it's me – what's going on?' Alex asked, sounding out of breath.

'Something terrible's happened,' Luci snapped. 'I've infected the boys. I'm infected, like Izzy was and Medora was, and Edith was, and Alice was. You should call Mike, too – Charlie's infected, and there's no stopping it – tell him that – tell him that there's no stopping it – it can't be stopped – well it can, but it's too late, because she didn't warn me, she didn't give me the chance to stop it, because she decided not to stop it, and maybe she felt guilty, maybe that was why she jumped in front of the train, or maybe it was because she couldn't bear to see it again, couldn't bear to see what she'd done – willingly – she did it willingly, Alex, she knew and she still did it.'

'Slow down, Luce! What's wrong, what is it? Has something happened to the boys? Is Ted there? Can I talk to him?' Alex said, and the rush of questions left Luci momentarily confused.

'No,' she said, because it seemed to answer all his questions. Nothing had happened to the boys – not yet, it was far too early to tell if the madness had passed on to them, after all – and Ted wasn't there, so Alex couldn't talk to him.

'No what?' Alex asked.

'I feel sick,' Luci replied, dropping the phone down onto the table and lurching towards the sink. Her retching brought up the water she'd gulped down so frantically, and left her feeling dizzy and disorientated.

'Luci! Luci!' Alex's disembodied voice sounded frantic as Luci slumped at the table and picked the phone up again.

'Why did she do this to me, Alex?' Luci sobbed into the phone. 'Why? She could have stopped it. Why did she have to do it?'

'I've no idea what you're talking about,' Alex said gently. 'Listen to me. Listen, okay? I don't know what's happened, but you're not making a scrap of sense, and I'm really worried about you. I'm on my way down to the car park – I'm going to come and get you – but I need to talk to Ted, okay? Can you get Ted to come to the phone, or call me back, or something?'

'He's with the boys,' Luci choked out through her tears.

'Can you shout him down?'

Luci put the phone down and stumbled – like she was drunk – to the hallway. 'Ted? Ted, Alex wants to talk to you.' Stumbling back to the table, she slumped back down and picked the phone up again. 'I shouted,' she said. 'Oh, God, Alex, I feel like I'm going mad – not like before – really mad, really, really mad. My brain won't stop. It's churning and churning and churning, like a washing machine stuck on a fast spin, and all these thoughts, all these horrible, horrible thoughts keep going round and round and round, and it feels like my head's going to explode. I just want it to stop. Please, I just want it to stop.'

'Where are you?' Alex asked softly.

'Kitchen.'

'Why don't you go into the living room and lie down on the sofa?' Alex suggested. He paused. 'Luci, do you feel safe? You're not... you're not thinking of *doing* anything?'

'I don't know,' Luci said in a small voice.

'Is Ted coming down, Luce? Did he hear you?'

As Luci staggered out of the kitchen, Ted appeared at the top of the stairs. 'He's coming,' Luci said, going into the living room and sitting on the end of the sofa, too agitated to lie down. Ted followed her into the room and Luci wordlessly handed him the phone.

'Alex?' Ted said, watching with some alarm as Luci lurched to her feet and started pacing around the room with her hands pressed to her head.

'What the hell is going on? She was fine when I left last night!'

'She found Isabella's diary, and a notebook belonging to one of Medora's sisters,' Ted explained. 'Medora's mother apparently had manic depression, too, and Luci's got herself worked up into a terrible state about the "madness" – as she's started calling it – being genetic.'

'What's she doing now? I told her to lie down.'

'Pacing – pacing like she's possessed. It's as if she can't stop.'

'She can't,' Alex said grimly. 'Ted, listen – if you go up into Luci's room, and have a look in the bedside chest, there should be some packets of medication. Look for a box that says Seroquel on it. See if you can get her to take one. That should help her calm down a bit. Just until I get there.'

'And if it doesn't?' Ted asked. 'Should I call...'

'No!' Alex interrupted sharply. 'Just sit tight. I'll be there as soon as I can. I'm on my way to the station now. I don't want to risk getting snarled up in traffic. I'll get a taxi from Sheffield station – I should be with you in an hour and a half.'

Ted found himself listening to dead air, and disconnected the call. 'Alex is coming,' he said to Luci, who looked up at him with haunted eyes. 'Do you think you could sit down for a minute, whilst I go upstairs and get you something to help you calm down?'

Luci nodded numbly. 'Okay,' she mumbled, perching on the edge of a chair.

'I'll only be a minute,' Ted promised, taking the stairs two at a time. He yanked open the top drawer of the bedside chest and found the box that Alex had described. The box said '200mg' on the side, which sounded like a pretty hefty dose, but Ted popped one round white pill out of the foil and hurried back downstairs – glad to see Luci perched exactly where he'd left her. 'I'll get you a glass of water,' he offered, but Luci shook her head. She took the pill and placed it in the centre of her palm, staring suspiciously at it for a moment before swallowing it dry.

'It takes a while to work,' she said, her voice sounding small and frightened. 'Ted, you won't laugh at me, will you?'

'Of course not.'

'If I lie down, will you sit on me? I need... I need to feel contained. Please. I just need to feel contained.'

Ted frowned at the odd request, but he could tell by the expression on Luci's face that she was serious. He forced his lips into a smile. 'Of course I will,' he said, feeling helpless. The sooner Alex was there to take charge of the situation, the better.

CHAPTER FOURTEEN

After so long off meds, the 200mg of Seroquel had the effect of a horse tranquilizer on Luci. She wasn't asleep – but she couldn't keep her eyes open. She felt as though she was buried under a mountain of cotton wool – but as the anti-psychotic began to do its job, her thoughts at least slowed to a more reasonable pace – even if it did seem as though her brain had got stuck on a loop.

When the doorbell rang, Ted eased himself gently up, and Luci forced one eye open to look at him.

'It'll be Alex,' Ted said soothingly. 'I'll just go and let him in, okay?'

Luci tried to nod, but her head felt too heavy. What seemed like only seconds later, Alex was kneeling down in front of her and holding her hands between his.

'Oh, God, Luce,' he murmured, shaking his head. 'I *knew* I shouldn't have left you. I *knew* I should have made you come home with me.'

'I had to find out,' Luci tried to say, but the words slurred together in an unintelligible string, making her sound as though she was completely drunk – or stupid.

Alex looked sharply up at Ted. 'How much Seroquel did you give her?' he asked.

'Just one, like you said. I thought 200mg sounded a lot, but...' Ted said defensively.

'200mg doesn't normally have this effect,' Alex muttered. He narrowed his eyes. 'Unless... Luci, did you stop taking it? Did you stop the Seroquel?'

'Mmm,' Luci murmured, because there seemed no point in denying it.

'Jesus! When? How long have you been off it?' Alex demanded, but Luci was incapable of giving him a sensible answer.

Alex sighed. 'Ted, would you do me a favour and go and throw Luci's stuff into the bag she brought? I'll see to the boys' stuff.' He held Luci's face in his hands, making her look at him. 'Don't move a muscle,' he said firmly. 'I'll only be a few minutes, okay?'

Luci nodded, just glad to not have to struggle to keep her eyes open any longer. It might have been minutes or hours before Alex and Ted came back downstairs. The twins were protesting loudly at being disturbed. The sound of their cries seemed to fill all the empty space in Luci's head, and she closed her eyes against the noise.

'I'll go and put them in the car first,' Alex said. 'Keys?'

'Kitchen,' Luci mumbled. It took a supreme effort to stand up; her body felt like it was weighted down with several tonnes of ballast, but with Ted's support she did at least make it out to the car. She collapsed down into the passenger seat and closed her eyes again. Ted gently closed the door for her.

'Will she be all right?' he asked anxiously as Alex straightened up from fastening Matty and Theo into the back of the car.

Alex sighed. 'She will be,' he said guardedly. 'It's just a blip. I should be used to these episodes by now – but I appreciate it must have been a shock for you, to see her like that.'

'To be honest, I feel responsible for Luci getting so distressed in the first place. If I hadn't...'

'It's not your fault,' Alex said firmly. 'I used to do that, drive myself to distraction thinking of all the things I could have done differently, but it's pointless. Luci stopped her meds, Ted. *That's* why she's so distressed – because she can't think logically whilst she's in the middle of an episode. Something would have triggered it regardless.' There was resignation in Alex's voice, born out of the growing sense of helplessness where Luci was concerned. He felt as though no matter what he did to try and support her, there was always something that went wrong. How *could* he help her – when she wouldn't help herself?

'You will let me know how she is, won't you?' Ted asked as Alex climbed into the driver's seat.

'Of course,' Alex promised. 'Thanks for looking after her, Ted. I dread to think what might have happened if you hadn't been there.'

'It's no trouble, really,' Ted said, stepping back as Alex gunned the engine.

'I'll give you a call tonight, or tomorrow,' Alex called out of the open window, pulling off the drive. He wasn't a reckless driver – but he wanted to get onto the motorway before the rush-hour traffic snarled up the roads. The sooner he got Luci home, the better.

***

By the time Alex finally pulled into their drive – having managed to get stuck in every possible snarl-up on the motorway, much to his growing frustration – the worst of the sedation had begun to wear off, and Luci was at least able to keep her eyes open and string words together into intelligible sentences.

'Are you angry with me?' she asked. 'You are, aren't you? I can tell – you've got that look on your face again.

'I'm not angry with you,' Alex said flatly.

'Don't lie. You shouldn't lie. You're setting a bad example for your sons.'

'And you're not?' Alex shot back. He grimaced. 'I didn't mean that. I'm sorry.'

'You did mean it. Don't lie anymore. You're right, of course. I'm a terrible mother. But I would never have *been* a mother if I'd been properly warned, and then I wouldn't be inflicting myself on them, or risking infecting them with madness.'

'Luce, slow down, will you?' Alex said quietly.

'It's not me, it's my brain,' Luci retorted. 'I hate this! I bloody fucking hate it!'

'Then why did you stop taking your meds?' Alex ground out.

'Because I couldn't look after the boys when I was drugged up to the eyeballs!' Luci yelled back at him. 'I was like a bloody zombie – not that you'd have noticed, working all the hours God sends, just so you didn't have to be anywhere near me!'

'You know that's not true.'

'I don't care if it's true – that's how it bloody well felt!' Suddenly, Luci found herself sobbing bitterly, her shoulders shuddering. Alex leaned across the gear stick and gathered her into his arms.

'I'm sorry,' he said, his mouth close to her ear. 'I didn't know. You didn't say anything. I wish you'd talk to me instead of trying to fly solo all the time.'

'I feel like someone's put my head in a blender,' Luci said. 'I don't know whether I'm manic, or depressed, or both, or what the hell is going on in my head, Alex. It's freaking me out!'

'It's probably a mixed episode,' Alex said knowledgably, his certainty born out of all the books on bipolar he'd devoured in the wake of Luci's diagnosis. 'Let's get the boys inside, and then you can go upstairs and lie down, whilst I call Dr Fielding's office and see if we can get anyone to come out.'

'No!' Luci protested, pulling away from his embrace. 'No way. You know what they'll say – you know what they'll do.'

'Not necessarily,' Alex said soothingly. 'There's the Crisis Team. They try to keep people *out* of hospital, Luce.'

'They'll take one look at me and have me locked up again,' Luci wailed, tears hovering on the edge of her eyelids. 'Please, Alex, please don't do that to me again. I can't stand it. I can't go back in there again!'

Alex tore his fingers through his hair, feeling as though he was being tugged in two directions at once. Luci needed help – help he wasn't psychiatrically qualified to give – but the last thing he wanted was her blaming him for her being hospitalised again. She needed to be able to trust him – and having her sectioned – because she surely wouldn't agree to a voluntary admission – was hardly going to build trust.

'All right,' he said finally. 'I won't call Dr Fielding. But you have to go back on the meds, Luci. I can't help you if you won't help yourself.'

Luci nodded, swallowing back the tears. 'Is there any Valium left?' she asked weakly. 'That helps. It's the only thing that helps.'

'I think so,' Alex replied, unbuckling Luci's seat belt for her. 'Maybe a few days' worth.' He opened the car door and got out; after a moment's hesitation, Luci followed suit, opening the rear door at her side of the car to release Matty's carrier from the seat belt. Alex watched her as she walked up the path at the side of the house. God only knew whether he was doing the right thing in not calling in the professionals.

CHAPTER FIFTEEN

Alex sighed with relief as he watched Luci sitting on the floor with the twins, building a tower of brightly coloured wooden blocks for the boys to gleefully knock down as soon as she was finished.

'Feeling any better?' he asked. Luci had seemed calmer since they'd come home and she'd swallowed a couple of Valium.

'I'm not sure *better* is the right word,' Luci replied, forcing a smile. 'More grounded, maybe.'

'Grounded enough to talk me through what the hell happened this morning?' Alex asked.

'Not in front of the boys,' Luci said quickly.

'Luce, they're only seven and a half months old. They're not going to understand a word you say,' Alex pointed out. 'I need to understand what freaked you out.'

'You should have brought the book then,' Luci said. 'I don't want to talk about it, Alex. I don't want to even think about it right now. Please don't make me. If you really want to know, call Ted – I gave him the potted version.'

'I'd rather hear it from you,' Alex pressed.

Luci swallowed hard. 'Why are you doing this to me?' she demanded.

'Because I need to know what you're thinking, I need to know *your* interpretation of the book, not Ted's. I need to stop you pulling the shutters down on me, because that's what I'm really afraid of right now.'

'When the boys have gone to bed,' Luci haggled. 'I think I've upset them enough for one day.'

Alex sighed, glancing at the clock above the mantel piece. It wouldn't be long before the twins were in bed – and Luci was right, it wasn't fair to upset them. 'All right. Shall I order us a takeaway for later?' he asked, reaching for his laptop.

'Knock yourself out,' Luci said, returning her attention to the building of another wooden block tower as if the wooden blocks were far more important than her earlier hysterics. Alex watched her for a moment before logging onto the internet. He knew her too well to be completely fooled.

***

Predictably, Luci took rather longer than was necessary over bathing the twins and putting them to bed, so that by the time she finally came back downstairs, the pizza Alex had ordered was starting to go cold in the box.

'They settle okay?' Alex asked. Luci had forcefully refused his offer to help with the boys, insisting that he read over his case-notes for court the following morning instead.

'Fine. They're probably glad to be back in their nursery,' Luci said, avoiding meeting Alex's gaze.

'I don't think they care where they sleep,' Alex replied, cupping Luci's chin and forcing her head up. 'You promised to tell me as soon as they were in bed.'

'Can't I eat first?'

'You can eat and talk at the same time,' Alex pointed out.

'It's rude to talk with your mouth full,' Luci shot back. '*My* mother did teach me some manners – what about yours?' As soon as the words left her lips, Luci winced, as if they caused her physical pain.

'Talk to me,' Alex begged. 'Don't you dare shut down on me now.' He could almost see in Luci's eyes what was happening – as if the depression that relentlessly followed a manic or hypomanic episode was something tangible to the eye. He knew the signs too well. This morning she'd been hysterical – in the grip of what the doctors called dysphoric mania – but now she was almost monosyllabic.

'Isabella left a diary,' Luci said quietly. 'Hidden in the attic. I thought that was bad enough, what she went through – what my grandfather and his mother did to her – but she wrote about something that she found, too, a notebook that her aunt – Medora's sister – had left as her legacy. I found it. I was determined to read it – but... but God, Alex, I wish I hadn't. It freaked me out so much. It must have freaked Izzy and Mum out, too. There's part of me that almost understands why she didn't tell me, maybe she just didn't want to think about it, maybe she tried to forget all about it – but she should have told me. She should have warned me, not left me to find out like this.'

'Tell me what it said, this notebook,' Alex prompted gently. 'I want to know it all.'

Luci gazed at him for a long moment, and then she started to talk, whispering as if by lowering her voice she could somehow soften the blow.

She was sobbing by the time she finished, her words becoming lost in hiccupping sobs as Alex held her tight in his arms, wanting to protect her but not knowing how. When he'd talked to her on the phone that morning, he'd assumed that she was merely blowing everything out of proportion – which she was, to an extent – but there was also an element of truth to her hysteria.

'She should have warned us,' he said softly, rubbing Luci's back soothingly. 'Or at least told Jack the truth. But I don't think for a minute that we shouldn't have had the twins. The odds are higher, but it's not a dead cert – and even if they did get bipolar, Luce, it's not the end of the world. We live with it. They'll grow up with it. They'll know better than you did how to live with it.'

'I'm not fit to be a mother,' Luci said pitifully.

'Of course you are!' Alex protested.

'Half the time I'm not,' Luci insisted.

'Not if you keep taking your meds.'

'I can't look after them if I'm half-asleep,' Luci snapped. 'It's a catch-22 situation, Alex, and...' Her words trailed away on a choked sob.

'Listen to me,' Alex said, using his thumbs to smooth away her tears. 'You're a brilliant mum, and once we get your meds sorted out, everything will sort itself out.'

'You live on cloud cuckoo land,' Luci choked out.

'No,' Alex said firmly.

'If you'd have known about the legacy, would you have wanted to... to...' Luci couldn't finish the sentence, but Alex knew what she meant.

'Never. Not in a million years. I love them to bits, Luci – just like I love you to bits. I wouldn't swop you – or them – for *anything*,' Alex said, hugging Luci tightly. 'I mean it, Luce. Bipolar makes you *you*.. It's part of what I love about you.'

'But what about all the *trouble* it causes?' Luci sobbed. 'Look what happened to my great grandmother – locked up in an asylum for the rest of her life because she tried to drown her own baby. What if that happens to me, Alex? What if I try to harm the boys?'

'You wouldn't,' Alex said instantly. 'We'll get the meds thing sorted out – that's the first thing we need to do – and then things will settle back to normal. You were doing really well up until all that with Walter and him dying.'

Luci managed a weak smile. 'I don't think it was all Walter's fault,' she said softly.

'He was a trigger,' Alex countered. 'A trigger that caused this whole roller-coaster effect.'

'There's always going to be triggers,' Luci said, sighing.

'And we'll learn how to handle them better,' Alex said instantly.

'You make it sound so simple,' Luci said. 'I wish it was. I wish I could believe you that it could be that easy. But I can't, Alex. I can't believe it when I know how easily it can all go wrong.' She pulled away from his embrace and stood up, swiping at the tears on her cheeks.

'Luce...' Alex began.

'Don't try and lie to me, Alz. You can't protect me from myself. When are you going to learn that?' Luci said. 'I need to sleep – I feel like I haven't slept in a week – which, actually, I probably haven't. I don't want to talk about this anymore. It's making my head ache.'

'Don't shut me out, Luci,' Alex begged.

'I'm not shutting you out. I'm just going to bed, that's all,' Luci said, heading for the stairs.

Alex had no choice but to let her go. Nonetheless, he couldn't help but think that her going to bed so suddenly was *exactly* the same as shutting him out. With a heavy sigh, he reached for his laptop. There were some things he needed to look up. Sometimes the best way to help Luci was with cold, hard facts.

CHAPTER SIXTEEN

'Are you sure you'll be all right?' Alex asked anxiously as he hovered in the hallway with his briefcase in his hand. 'I'll come home straight after court. If it wasn't for this damn case, I'd...'

'Alex, go,' Luci said wearily. 'I'll be fine.'

'You promise to ring and make an appointment with Dr Fielding to discuss our options with your meds?'

'Yes,' Luci ground out between her teeth. 'Just go, or you'll be late!'

'You'll call Mum if you need anything?'

'Yes! Alex, for God's sake, anyone would think you don't trust me,' Luci said, exasperated. She gave him a gentle shove towards the door. 'I can look after myself and the boys for a few hours!'

He went, reluctantly, and Luci closed the door behind him, leaning back against it and letting her breath hiss out between her teeth. She'd woken in the night to find Alex propped up on one elbow just staring at her, worry etched deep in the furrow on his forehead. Luci knew he had every right to worry after the crisis yesterday, but all the same, he could, all too easily, make her feel like she was being smothered.

As the morning wore on, however, Luci began to wonder if Alex was right not to want to leave her on her own. She was fine whilst she was playing with the boys, her attention entirely focused on them, but once they went down for a nap mid-morning, Luci was left alone with her own thoughts – and as much as she didn't want to think about everything she'd learned over the past twenty-four hours, she couldn't *stop* the thoughts revolving around in her head. She sat on the sofa with her head in her hands, Lilly's words flowing through her synapses like poison.

After ten minutes, she'd had enough. She couldn't bear to think about the legacy that her mother had left her, about the corrupted DNA that she, too, might have passed on to her children. She knew it was bad parenting when she went upstairs and woke Matty and Theo – but she needed them to distract herself from her own vicious thoughts. She couldn't after all, she reasoned bitterly, be any worse a parent than her mother had been. As soon as the boys were old enough to understand, she was going to tell them the truth – not shirk her responsibilities like her mother had.

***

It was gone three in the afternoon when Alex finally made it home, fraught after a disastrous day in court. He'd lost the case he'd been working on for over three months – much to the client's open disgust. After being sworn at on the steps of the court – in front of reporters – he was more than glad than to get home. He found Luci and the twins in the living room, and stood in the doorway for several minutes, trying not to laugh at the scene in front of him. The boys' toy railway was set up in the middle of the floor; Matty and Theo were sat in the circle on the inside of the tracks, sucking on rusks and looking totally disinterested whilst Luci was busy manning the railway.

'I always knew you bought that train set for yourself and not the boys,' Alex said, startling Luci. She looked up at him, smiling, but the smile didn't reach her eyes, which looked troubled.

'Distraction,' she said. 'They might not be interested, but it takes my mind off... everything else.'

Alex knelt down next to her, snaking his arm around her shoulders. 'You've been okay?' he asked.

'So long as I keep myself distracted,' Luci said, her voice wobbling a little.

'Did you call Dr Fielding?'

'The secretary's calling me back when she's consulted Dr Fielding's diary,' Luci replied. 'She asked if it was an emergency. I said that it wasn't.'

'Luce...'

'It *isn't* an emergency, Alex. I'm okay. It's just a bit of a blip.'

'We need to get your meds sorted,' Alex protested. He stood up. 'I'll give them a call.' To his surprise, Luci didn't try to stop him. Instead, as he went in search of the cordless phone, she returned her attention to the train set – but not before he realised that her eyes were glistening with tears. She seemed more fragile than ever – and Alex hated feeling so helpless in the face of it.

After just a few minutes on the phone he'd negotiated an appointment for Luci the following afternoon – with the court case over he'd at least be able to take the time off to go with her. 'She doesn't like admitting when she's not coping very well,' he told the receptionist quietly. 'It's not exactly an emergency, but all the same...' The woman had understood, squeezing Luci into the psychiatrist's busy schedule. Dropping the phone back into its cradle, Alex turned back towards the living room, coming to an abrupt halt in the doorway.

Legacy of Lies

The wooden tracks of the train set were scattered across the floor, the wooden train and its carriages overturned nearby. In the midst of the carnage, Luci was sitting with both boys in her arms, her shoulders shuddering as she sobbed over them. Stepping over the toys, Alex gently extracted the bewildered babies from Luci's arms.

'I'm sorry,' she sobbed, making an obvious effort to stop crying. 'I've been trying so hard to hold it together, and I just flipped. It was so *stupid.* The train fell over, and I just *flipped.*'

'Shush,' Alex said gently. 'It's okay. You don't have to explain, not to me.'

'Not to you,' Luci said quietly, her voice thick and choked. 'But I will have to explain to them, one day, why their mummy isn't like other mummies, and I'll have to tell them that maybe – just maybe – their mummy passed the madness on to them, too, and then they'll know – they'll know that if it happens to them, too, it'll all be my fault!'

Alex set the boys down, letting them crawl around whilst he lifted Luci up off the floor and led her over to the sofa. She buried her face against his chest, so he could feel her tears soaking through the thin cotton of his shirt.

'You've got to stop thinking like that, Luce,' he said softly. 'It's not your fault you've got this illness – and it won't be your fault if the boys get it. What are the statistics – one in a hundred for bipolar?'

'It's genetic, Alex. My family history is riddled with it,' Luci sobbed. 'The genetic link increases the risk.'

'Genetics is a lottery,' Alex said. 'I was looking it up last night, after you'd gone to bed. They've done studies. Even with identical twins, that have *exactly* the same DNA, there's dozens of cases where one twin develops bipolar and the other doesn't. Your mum didn't have it when Isabella did; Luke didn't have it. The whole genetic link thing doesn't make sense when you look at it like that. If twins have the same DNA, how do you explain that one gets it and one doesn't?'

'It'll be bad enough if one of them gets it, Alex. I'd still feel guilty. I'd still feel *responsible.*'

'Luce, you can't go on thinking like this. You're going to drive yourself crazy,' Alex protested, rubbing her back soothingly.

'Like I'm not already?' Luci said, lifting her head to look at him.

'You know what I mean.'

'I wish I could stop thinking it, Alz. I wish I could stop the thoughts spinning round in my head, but they won't stop.'

'You've got to challenge them, Luci, like you learnt when you had that course of Cognitive Behavioural Therapy,' Alex said firmly. 'I'll print some of the worksheets out – I think I've still got the files the therapist sent us.'

'It's a whole lot easier to challenge irrational thoughts than it is ones that you've got written back-up for,' Luci said weakly. She pulled away from Alex's embrace. 'I'd better see what the dynamic duo are getting up to whilst their mother's been having *another* meltdown.' She disappeared into the hallway, and seconds later Alex heard her groan.

'What's wrong?' he asked, dashing out of the room.

Luci poked her head out of the downstairs toilet. 'I'm not sure now whether I should worry more about them taking after me or taking after their father and uncle. Do you remember that day when you and Luke unravelled loads of toilet rolls and stuffed them down the toilet? It seems like *that's* genetic, too.' She paused. 'On a more positive note, they seem to have learned how to stand up on their own, too.'

Alex tried hard not to laugh. 'At least it was only toilet roll,' he said. 'They could have got at my briefcase.'

'Give them time,' Luci said, smiling weakly. 'They haven't figured out buckles yet.'

The phone rang suddenly, making them both jump. As Alex went to answer it, he smiled as he heard Luci muttering, 'Typical, leave *me* to do all the cleaning up. That's what I'm here for, I suppose.'

'Leave it for a minute – I'll come and help as soon as I've answered the phone,' he yelled over his shoulder.

'Or you could let the machine pick it up,' Luci retorted, backing out of the toilet with a baby in each arm. 'I'll have to take them up and change them first, anyway. They stink.'

'Both of them?' It never ceased to amaze Alex that his sons somehow managed to synchronise even their bowel movements.

'Oh yes,' Luci said, wrinkling her nose as she headed upstairs.

Alex reached the phone just as the answering machine intercepted the call. Not bothering to intervene, he left the machine to do its job whilst he went to do his – undoing whatever damage the twins had managed to do in the short time they'd had to wreak their mischief. He had visions of having to call out a plumber – but he managed to clear out the thick wads of toilet roll by forcing himself not to think about what his fingertips might be brushing against as he shoved his arm, up to his elbow, into the u-bend.

He was trying to figure out how to transport the sodden mountain of Andrex into the kitchen bin when Luci reappeared, minus the boys, in the doorway.

'I just played back the message on the machine,' she said, her voice like a tightly strung bow.

'Who was it?' Alex asked.

'Ruth,' Luci replied. 'Is nothing in my life sacred, Alex? Do you have to tell her *everything*?'

'I didn't tell her everything,' Alex protested, grabbing the towel off the rail by the tiny sink and piling the toilet roll mountain onto that. 'Just the edited highlights, so she and Jack knew about what happened at Ted's – and about the notebook, that's all.'

'Well she sounded well weird on the answering machine,' Luci muttered. 'You should listen to it – I'll clear this up.'

Alex went straight to the machine, hit the button and leaned against the wall as the robotic voice announced that there was one saved message.

'Luci – are you there, sweetheart? If you are, can you pick up? I need to talk to you. Alex told us about what happened yesterday – about what you found at your grandfather's house. Alex said you were very angry with your mother – and of course I understand why, sweetheart, of course you're angry, but I think – I think that there's something you should know. No – you *need* to know it. I know your mother and I weren't on the best of terms when she died, but I still thought of her as my best friend, and if I'd known about the letters, if I'd known that your father had ignored her dying wish, I would have done something about it. He had no right – and if he'd shared what he knew with me *before it was too late*, things would have been so different! I'm sorry, I'm rambling, sweetheart. There's so much I need to say to you, but I can't say it all to a machine! If you're there Luci, please pick up!'

The message ended and the robotic voice cut in with 'end of messages'.

'I've never heard Ruth talk like that before,' Luci commented, edging past Alex and into the kitchen. 'She sounded as though she was a bit drunk.'

'She sounded confused,' Alex said. 'I'm going to give her a call and ask her what the hell's going on.'

Luci shook her head as she emptied the soggy toilet roll into the bin. 'Why waste time? We should just go over there.'

'All right – but I'll just give her a quick ring, tell her we're coming over, all right?'

'Okay,' Luci said tensely. 'I'll go and put the boys in the car – grab the nappy bag and a couple of bottles out of the fridge on your way out, will you?'

'Baby food, too?' Alex asked.

'Mention that word to your mother and she'll spontaneously combust,' Luci said. 'You should know she doesn't believe in the stuff. She'll make something for them – she'll insist.'

'Is baby food in the same evil league as microwave meals, then?' Alex asked, laughing.

Luci paused to consider that for a second. 'No,' she said. 'Actually, I think it's worse.'

***

'Dad, has Ruth been drinking?' Luci asked her father the moment he opened the front door to let them in. 'She left the strangest message on the answering machine.'

'I know – I heard her leaving it,' Jack sighed. 'But, no, she's not been drinking. We've been... having a bit of a row, that's all, and she got herself worked up into a right state.'

'And do you blame me, Jack? Do you really blame me, after what you told me?' Ruth demanded, appearing at the foot of the stairs behind him. 'After what you did.'

'What did you do?' Luci demanded to know, still standing on the front doorstep. Alex nudged her from behind.

'Let's go inside – or else the neighbours will have a field day!'

Luci followed her father and step-mother down the hallway and into the living room, sitting down on the edge of the sofa whilst Alex released the twins from their carriers and went back to fix up the temporary baby gate to stop them escaping from the living room and wreaking havoc again.

'What's all this about?' Luci asked, looking from her father to her step-mother. Ruth was glowering at Jack.

'I think you should tell her what you told me,' Ruth said tersely.

'For goodness' sake, Ruth, do you have to make such a melodrama out of this? I told you – it wouldn't have made any difference. The letters didn't make any sense. Elvina was incapable of talking sense.'

'Let Luci be the judge of that,' Ruth snapped.

'Don't you think she's been through enough?' Jack demanded.

'I am still in the room,' Luci cut in. 'Will one of you please tell me what this is all about? What letters? What do you mean that Mum was incapable of talking sense?'

'Ask your father,' Ruth said stonily. 'I just want you to know, Luci, that I had no part in it – he told me none of it until this morning – *this morning*, for God's sake, he didn't even think to say anything when you were so ill before they boys were born!'

'Because her letter didn't make sense!' Jack snarled. 'It was like a dot-to-dot puzzle without any connections between the dots. Only in the context of what Alex told you did it start to make any sense! How could I tell you anything when I didn't understand it myself?'

'Dad, will you please stop rowing with Ruth and tell me what the hell is going on?' Luci demanded.

'Before your mother... before she died,' Jack began tentatively.

'I'm not a child, Dad. Why don't you say it like it is? Before she killed herself,' Luci cut in.

'She left a note,' Jack went on.

'I know. I came in after you found it, remember?' Luci muttered.

'Of course I remember! I remember every awful second of that day!' Jack cried. 'I was angry – with her, for what she'd done; with myself, for driving her to it. I read her note, I read it over and over again after the police had gone and I'd identified the body. It didn't make any sense, and in my anger, I dismissed what she said in the note as just drunken ramblings, and I suppose I thought that in some way, by not doing as she asked me to do, I was punishing her for what she'd done. I didn't ever think that it wasn't her that I was punishing. I thought that I was protecting you, Luci, I honestly, honestly did. I thought I was doing the right thing. It never crossed my mind that it would end up being you I was punishing.'

'You're the one not making any sense,' Luci said tightly.

'I kept it – the note. All these years, I've kept it, hidden away, God only knows why,' Jack said. He picked an envelope up off the small table at the side of his chair and held it by the edges, as if he was afraid that it would burn him. He held it out towards Luci. 'Read it. Ruth thinks it makes sense – but, I still can't see it. Without the benefit of hindsight, it makes no sense at all! How could I have been expected to understand *then,* when everything I knew about Elvina was based on lies?'

Luci's fingers were trembling as she pulled out the flimsy notepaper. The sight of her mother's familiar handwriting brought tears to her eyes, and she closed them tightly for a moment, wondering if she could bear to face any more of the past. Alex squeezed her shoulders gently.

'Do you want me to...?' he asked, and she felt herself nod, relinquishing her hold on the notepaper so that he could read it aloud for her.

'*I was raised to believe that suicide was a dreadful sin, for which there could be no forgiveness,*' he read. '*But I was raised to believe that many things were sinful – so many so that I'm certain that my soul was damned long before today.*

'*I don't ask you for forgiveness, Jack. I don't expect even for you to understand why I must do this. You will think me selfish for ending my life and abandoning my children. You will think me a coward for not facing up to the hardships of life. I can't blame you for thinking in such a way. I am guilty of both selfishness and cowardice – but not only for what I am about to do.*

'*My selfishness began more than twelve years ago; my cowardice soon after. I am guilty, too, of the sin of lying to you. There are things I should have shared with you – truths that you were entitled to know, but the truth has always frightened me, and it was far easier to lie. I told myself that I was protecting you and the children, to make the bitter taste of the lies sweeter in my mouth.*

'*I lied because I am a mother, and it is my duty to protect my children – but I have come to realise that all the lies in the world cannot save them. They should not have been born. I vowed never to have children, before I met you, but then I watched Alex growing from a baby into a little man, and my resolve weakened. I wanted the unconditional love of a child, and I became selfish because of it.*

'*Oh, Jack, how I prayed that they would not be punished for my selfishness! Punish me, instead, I begged of Him, but now I realise that to punish them is to punish me also, and I cannot bear it. The guilt has weighed upon my shoulders so long now that I simply cannot bear it. I have failed as a mother; failed time and time again. Each time I reach for the bottle, I am reminded of my failure, but I need something to numb the guilt of what my selfishness might have wrought.*

Legacy of Lies

'No, not might. Not might at all, because today I have seen that my punishment is complete. If your affair, Jack, had not strengthened my resolve to do what I must, then the realisation of what I have done surely has. I am sorry. I am more sorry than I can ever express in words, for what I have done is unforgiveable. I knew of the risks. I knew the danger, as surely as my mother knew, but I continued all the same. I prayed it would not happen, but the truth is there in her eyes, in my poor baby's eyes and I cannot bear to see it happen again. I cannot bear to be faced with what I have done.

'The fire is there in her eyes, Jack, and I have seen it enough to be sure. The fire is the one sure sign of what I have done, and I beg of you to keep her safe. Protect her from herself, Jack. Protect our daughter from what I have done to her. It will change her, the fire will change her, and it can't be stopped.

'I wanted to be the one to tell her, to hold her as I explained the truth, but she is too young, and I cannot bear to see the fire take hold of her. I ask only this of you, Jack, that when she is old enough to bear the truth, perhaps two or three years from now, you will give to her – and to Luke – the letters that I have written them. I want it to be my own words that tell them the gravity of what I have done. You'll find the letters in the bottom drawer of your desk, beneath our marriage certificate.

'Our marriage has been over for some time, and I do not expect you to grieve for me. You will be angry with me, I know, but I beg you to give me my final wish – that you will give the letters to Luci and Luke when they are ready, so that they can be prepared.'

'You bastard!' Luci yelled, rocketing to her feet the moment Alex stopped speaking. 'She *did* try to warn me, she *did* feel bad about it – and you wouldn't even allow Mum her dying wish!' Her fists flailed, catching Jack on his chest and shoulders before Alex jumped up and restrained her. 'You could have saved me from all those years of... craziness. We would have known. We would have been looking for it. Didn't you ever wonder what she meant? Didn't you ever stop to think what she meant about the fire? Didn't you wonder why I needed to be protected from myself?'

'It sounded so farfetched,' Jack said weakly. 'As if she was just trying to justify taking her own life. Self-pity, that's what I thought it was – and drunkenness. I didn't think it was worth putting you through any more pain. She was dead, we'd moved on with our lives, and I didn't want to go raking up the past. You and Luke were doing well at school, there didn't seem to be any problems. As I said, with hindsight, of course I wish I'd taken more heed – but I couldn't have made sense of it from what the letter said.'

'And when the problems started you just closed your eyes to them, and didn't stop to wonder whether that was what she meant?' Luci snapped.

'With hindsight...'

'Fuck hindsight,' Luci snarled. 'Were there letters, like she said?'

Jack sighed. 'I thought I was doing the right thing, Luci. I thought I was protecting you – you *and* Luke. Nothing that she said in the letters made sense – just like her note to me didn't make sense. It would only have upset you to read them. I thought it was better to leave your mother's drunken ramblings in the past.'

'You read them?' Luci choked out. 'And then what?'

'And then I burnt them,' Jack admitted. 'I wanted for us all to be able to move on, Luci. I wanted to put an end to all the nonsense.'

'It wasn't nonsense! And you had *no right!* She was trying to warn me. Everything could have been different – *everything*.'

'She wrote in riddles, Luci. She danced around what she must have been trying to say, as if she couldn't even bring herself to write it. I remember the words she used. She said that the fire was a legacy – a legacy that she should never have passed on. We couldn't have known anything from that, Luci. Sweetheart, look at me. She *tried* to warn you – to warn *us* – but she couldn't even put it into words. Looking back – I'm, well, I'm not sure whether she might have been ill herself.'

'She *tried* though,' Luci whispered, wrapping the words around herself like a comforter. 'She did *try*, even if she killed herself because of me.'

'It wasn't because of *you* – it was because she couldn't live with *herself*,' Jack protested.

'I think I know how she felt.'

'You don't mean that,' Alex said sharply, interrupting the intensity between father and daughter.

'If anything happened to them – to my babies – I'd be devastated, but if I knew I was *responsible* for it, then...' Luci shook her head, the tears running freely down her cheeks. 'I hate her for it – I hate her for not having the guts to look me in the face and tell me – but at the same time, I understand why she chose to die instead.'

Jack hesitated. 'I suppose I might have felt the same,' he said finally. 'To know what she did – and live with it – must have been a burden. Not that I agree that it's some kind of curse that she's passed on to you – it's an illness and it's treatable, and it's not as bad as your mother must have thought it was. She'd had a bad experience – and there *was* a lot more prejudice then...'

'If she was so afraid of passing it on, then why did she have us?' Luci demanded harshly, cutting her father's floundering words off. 'There were condoms in 1980. There was the pill. And why did she keep getting pregnant if she was so frightened?'

'Luci, sweetheart, I can't pretend even to be able to guess what your mother was thinking...'

'*Did* she want us – or did you pressurise her?' Luci demanded.

'She wanted you,' Jack said fiercely. 'We *both* wanted you! We were both overjoyed when she found out she was pregnant.'

'And then she started feeling guilty,' Luci muttered. 'But why keep on getting pregnant? *Why*? *It doesn't make any sense!*' Coldness crept over her suddenly, and she felt sick. 'All those miscarriages, Dad. What if they weren't...?'

Jack blanched white. 'No,' he said firmly. 'She was devastated every time it happened.'

'Because she knew what she'd done! She carried me and Luke nearly to full term without any problems, and we were twins, but all of a sudden she couldn't carry single babies to full term without miscarrying. It doesn't make any sense!'

With a muted cry, Ruth suddenly fled from the room, her hand pressed over her mouth. Luci didn't hesitate in following her step-mother, finding Ruth doubled over the kitchen sink, retching.

'You knew the miscarriages weren't an accident, didn't you?' Luci asked softly. 'You were her best friend. She confided in you, didn't she?'

Ruth's face was a mask of misery when she straightened. 'She didn't tell me why,' she whispered.

'Jesus Christ – and you had the gall to turn on me because I couldn't make sense of a drunken suicide note!' Jack snarled from behind Luci. 'Did you help her? Did you help her get rid of my babies?'

'Of course not!' Ruth cried, horrified by the very suggestion. 'She confided in me, that's all. She got hysterical every time she became pregnant, and she never told me why. I thought it was because of the difficult labour she'd had with Luci and Luke – she gave me no reason to think anything else. She begged me never to let you find out – and I kept my word. It wasn't the same as ignoring her dying wish, Jack. It wasn't the same as destroying letters that she left for her children. I was her friend. She talked to me, that's all. I did no harm.'

'Neither did I,' Jack said softly.

'Yes you did!' Luci snapped at him. 'You could have told me the truth. You could have given me the letter Mum left for me.'

'I'm sorry, sweetheart. I thought I was doing what was best for you and Luke,' Jack said, sounding suddenly weary.

'Being sorry doesn't make it better, Dad,' Luci yelled. 'You could have saved me going through hell. We'd have had some idea, however vague, and we might have seen it happening, and realised what she meant, and I'd have been on meds before everything got so stupidly out of hand.' She stopped as a sudden thought blasted through her brain. 'Luke might even still have been alive.' Her words ended on a sob and she whirled around, crashing into Alex, who wrapped his arms tightly around her. She buried her face in his shirt, her shoulders heaving.

'I think I should take her home,' Alex said coldly to his step-father. 'She's been through enough these last couple of days as it is.'

'Do you want to leave the boys here, to give you and Luci some time on your own?' Ruth asked quietly.

Alex hesitated. 'Luce? What do you think?'

She shook her head violently. 'I'm not letting them out of my sight,' she sobbed. 'I'm certainly not leaving them anywhere near *him*.'

'Luci, please, don't be like this. It wasn't my fault that your mother wasn't able to articulate what she needed to tell you.'

'Stop making excuses, Jack. You're really not helping,' Alex snapped. 'I'm with Luci and Mum on this one. You should have given us the chance to at least try to figure out what Elvina meant, instead of destroying the letters and keeping the note to yourself.' He gave Luci's shoulders a gentle squeeze. 'Let's get the boys into the car and go home,' he said softly.

Luci broke away from him without a word and pushed past her father. He tried to catch her arm, but she shook him angrily off. Still saying nothing, she stalked into the living room, closely followed by Alex. She said nothing as she fastened Theo in his carrier, and carried him out to the car, and she kicked the door shut in Jack's face as he tried to come after her with the word sorry hanging off his lips. She didn't want to hear any more of his apologies. The only apology she wanted to hear was from her mother – and Jack had destroyed Elvina's final chance of that.

CHAPTER SEVENTEEN

'I felt sure I'd discussed with you the dangers of stopping Lithium suddenly, Luci,' Dr Fielding said after Alex had explained to the psychiatrist what had happened. 'It can cause what we call rebound mania – which can be much worse than an ordinary episode of mania.'

'There's nothing *ordinary* about mania,' Luci muttered, her gaze focused on her feet.

'It sounds to me like you've been experiencing a mixed episode,' Dr Fielding went on as if Luci hadn't spoken. 'Are you still experiencing the racing, negative thoughts?'

'I'm nearly out of Valium. Alex has been rationing it. So yeah, I'm still *experiencing* the washing machine effect,' Luci snapped.

'Are you managing to sleep?' Dr Fielding asked.

'No,' Alex answered, when Luci remained silent. 'She won't take any Seroquel – she reckons she can't look after the boys *and* take it – so she's hardly sleeping at all.'

'I've got more than just myself to think about!' Luci snapped. 'It's about priorities – and the boys are more important than me.'

Dr Fielding frowned. 'How much Valium have you been...?'

'Not enough,' Luci cut in bitterly.

'How would you feel about changing the Seroquel for another anti-psychotic?' Dr Fielding asked, scribbling something down in Luci's file.

'I'm not psychotic,' Luci muttered.

'I'm sure we've had this conversation before, Luci,' Dr Fielding said, sighing. 'Because you *have* been psychotic – on several occasions – it is advisable to take an anti-psychotic to prevent future episodes.'

'Do you want to end up like your grandmother and great-grandmother?' Alex asked bluntly, the harshness of his words making Luci gasp.

'That was below the belt!' she snapped, even though she knew he was right. She sighed heavily. 'If there's an anti-psychotic that won't make me feel like a zombie, I'll take it,' she conceded.

Some of the tension in the room lifted; Dr Fielding even cracked a smile. 'There's a relatively new anti-psychotic that I'd like you to try,' the psychiatrist said. 'It's called aripiprazole.'

'Ari-what?' Luci cut in.

'Aripiprazole,' Dr Fielding said, her smile widening. 'It is a bit of a mouthful – and its trade name, Abilify, isn't much better. But I've had some very positive result with patients when I've switched them to Abilify. It's much less sedating than other anti-psychotics. Are you willing to give it a try?'

'I'll *try* it,' Luci emphasised.

'I'll write you up a prescription,' Dr Fielding said, searching around on her desk for the green pad. 'I'd like you to start off with a dose of 10mg for the first five days, and then increase it to 15mg after that, okay?'

Compared to the doses of Seroquel she'd been expected to take – between 200mg and 400mg at a time – 15mg seemed a tiny dose. Luci nodded in reluctant agreement.

'And we need to get your Lithium levels back up to a therapeutic dose. I'd like you to start back on 800mg and go for a blood test in a week, all right?' the psychiatrist went on. 'Have you got enough, or shall I write you up some more?'

'I've got enough,' Luci admitted in a small voice, thinking of the boxes stuffed under the bed in the very darkest corner. 'But I need some more Valium.'

'Valium is very addictive, Luci. I'd much rather you learnt to manage feelings of anxiety than rely on benzodiazepines,' Dr Fielding said. 'Besides which, the Abilify should help to calm things down. I'll see you again in a fortnight – we can discuss how you're getting on then.'

Valium, Luci was certain, was the only thing stopping her from going completely insane. She gritted her teeth, knowing it was futile trying to argue. 'Thanks,' she muttered, accepting the prescription that Dr Fielding tore off and thrust at her.

***

'How long do you think Ruth's going to stay?' Luci asked Alex as they walked back to the car park. Ruth had turned up late the night before, asking if she could stay in the spare room. It was a drastic move, leaving Jack to look after Zack, Zoe and Danny – but Luci didn't blame her step-mother for it – not after Jack had accused his wife of helping Elvina to miscarry all those years ago.

'Until Jack comes to apologise,' Alex said with a grimace. 'Which, knowing how stubborn your father is, could be *days*. On the plus side, that does mean we get free babysitting services on tap. I thought we might go out for dinner and catch a movie – do something *normal* after everything you've been through this week.'

'I don't deserve you,' Luci said quietly. 'You're always there for me, always wanting the best for me, and half the time, I just throw it back in your face.'

'Don't be daft,' Alex said, slinging his arm around her shoulders. 'I love you just as you are. You might be a royal pain in the arse sometimes – but I wouldn't have it any other way.'

'You would. You'd rather I wasn't always swinging from happy to sad; you'd rather I didn't keep stop taking my meds; you'd rather I didn't keep getting obsessed about things,' Luci protested.

Alex laughed. 'Okay, so I wish you wouldn't stop taking your meds – but the other stuff – it makes you who you are, Luce. That's what I fell in love with – the wild, obsessive, flamboyant Luci – and nothing's changed.'

'That's why I keep stopping the meds,' Luci said in a small voice. 'I'm frightened that the illness makes me who I am, and the meds will take that away, and you won't want me anymore. Where do I draw the line, Alz? Where does Luci stop and the illness start – or are they too closely entwined that if you take the illness away, there'll be nothing left.'

'Oh, Luce!' Alex pulled her into a hug, kissing her forehead tenderly. 'I would *never* leave you, no matter *what* happened. And the meds aren't going to take the illness away, just help us to manage it – you daft thing!'

Luci buried her face against his shoulder, so he wouldn't see the tears swimming in her eyes. 'This is *exactly* why I don't deserve you,' she whispered.

'Stop it!' Alex commanded. 'If you say that one more time, I *will* leave you.'

Luci let out a shuddering breath. 'All right, I won't say it,' she said, leaving the rest of the sentence unspoken: *but you can't stop me thinking it.*

***

Although it *was* nice to have an extra pair of hands to help with the twins, after Ruth had been staying for five days, Luci was beginning to wish her father wasn't quite *so* stubborn. Zack and Zoe missed their mother so much that they had moved in, too – leaving Luci feeling like an impostor in her own home. She took to retreating to the privacy of the master bedroom every time the boys went down for a nap – just for a bit of peace and quiet. The twins' cot had been moved into the master bedroom, to make way for the inflatable bed that Zack and Zoe were sleeping on – meaning that whilst the boys were napping, no one was likely to burst in on Luci's peace.

'I'm a bloody exile in my own house,' she fumed to Alex when he called – to say he'd be late home – a week into Ruth, Zack and Zoe's stay. 'Will you have a word with Dad – tell him to stop being a prat and apologise.'

Alex hesitated. 'I can't,' he admitted. 'He left a message on my mobile, asking me to tell Mum he was taking Danny on a father-son bonding holiday.'

'*What*?' Luci squeaked. 'When? Where?'

'He said they were setting off at lunchtime, and they'd be back on Sunday night.'

'So Ruth and the kids can go home?' Luci said hopefully.

'If I tell her, she'll probably start divorce proceedings,' Alex said glumly.

'So – we don't tell her? *Alex*! She's going to find out if she calls Danny.'

'He's a smart kid – he won't let on,' Alex said. 'He's nearly fourteen – he knows the score.'

'And whilst all this subterfuge is going on, I'm having live like a bloody refugee!'

'You don't *have* to,' Alex pointed out.

'I do if I value my sanity,' Luci retorted. 'It's like a mad-house!'

'It's not *that* bad,' Alex protested.

'You're out all bloody day – what would you know?' Luci exploded. 'Send Dad a message. Tell him that when he gets back, he'd better get over here and apologise! *I'm* the one who needs a holiday, not him.'

Alex laughed. 'I'll send him a text,' he promised. 'I'd better go – can't keep my client waiting any longer. Shall I grab us a pizza on my way home?'

'And hurt your mother's feelings?' Luci said sarcastically. 'Heaven forbid! She'd busy making a steak and kidney pie as we speak!'

Alex was chuckling as he hung up, leaving Luci glowering at her mobile. 'It's not bloody funny,' she muttered. 'I don't even *like* steak and kidney pie!' As if in response, Theo woke up and started kicking his legs, waking his brother in the process.

The twins' naps were getting shorter and shorter, Luci was sure of it – either that or time went twice as quickly when she tried to snatch time on her own. With a sigh, she lifted Theo up out of the cot, changed his nappy, and set him down on the floor before repeating the process with Matty.

It wasn't fair to keep the boys penned up in the bedroom when their toys and play-mats were downstairs – and Zack and Zoe *did* seem to enjoy playing with their nephews. Sighing again, Luci picked Matty and Theo up – realising with a jolt that she wouldn't be able to carry both of them for much longer. They were growing fast – only the other week the health visitor had commented that they were both the weight of nine-month old babies. As Luci carried them downstairs, Theo grabbed a fistful of her hair and yanked, making Luci yell out. The twins gurgled as if it was hilariously funny.

'I'm not laughing,' Luci told them irritably.

'They're going to run you ragged once they start walking,' Ruth said, appearing, like a spectre, in the kitchen doorway, her hands swathed in a layer of flour.

'Thanks. I can't wait,' Luci muttered, heading for the living room, where Zack and Zoe were sprawled out in front of the TV. Ruth followed in her wake, much to Luci's surprise.

'Can you two watch Matty and Theo for a minute whilst I have a word with Luci?' Ruth asked Zack and Zoe, startling Luci even further. After depositing the twins on the floor, Luci turned to face her step-mother, her brain whirring with anxious thoughts as to what Ruth wanted to talk about. Was Ruth already thinking of making her separation from Jack permanent? Luci tried not to let the horror that thought provoked show on her face.

In the kitchen, Ruth wiped her hands and opened one of the drawers, pulling out a bundle of envelopes.

'I was looking for a whisk – and I found these,' she said. 'Letters – addressed to your mother.'

Luci glanced down, recognising the envelopes she'd found in the attic at Walter's house – the ones she'd instantly forgotten about the moment she'd discovered the cubby hole that had been Izzy and Elvina's hiding place.

'How did they get into one of the kitchen drawers?' she wondered. 'I'd forgotten about them – I don't even remember bringing them down from the attic!' She *did* vaguely remember stuffing the envelopes into her pocket before investigating the cubby hole, though. Alex must have found them after he brought her home and hidden them out of sight. 'Arsehole,' she muttered, taking the bundle from Ruth.

'What are letters to your mother doing hidden in a drawer?' Ruth asked.

'Ask your son. It's his idea of breaking an obsession, I presume,' Luci snapped, backing towards the stairs.

'Where are you going?' Ruth asked.

'To read them,' Luci replied, her tone of voice suggesting that it was a stupid question. She took the stairs two at a time, and closed the bedroom door firmly behind her.

The envelopes were still sealed, but the gum had long since dried up and cracked open easily when Luci stuck her fingernail under the flap of the first envelope. There was a single sheet of notepaper inside. Luci pulled the sheet out without looking it, and moved onto the next envelope, noticing as she did so that Walter had meticulously arranged them in order of postmark – all five of them.

The envelopes had all been addressed in neat block capitals, but the moment Luci unfolded the first sheet of notepaper and recognised the handwriting, she felt her stomach lurch. With shaking hands, she fumbled for the envelope, staring at the postmark and then at the date at the top of the letter.

Izzy didn't die.

The words spun around in Luci's mind, making her dizzy with disbelief. The first letter was dated August 1968 – more than a month after Izzy's supposed death. She'd written to Elvina, never knowing that her sister – believing her to be dead – had already fled. Tears welled up in Luci's eyes as she forced herself to read the letters.

Convent of the Sisters of Mercy and Deliverance,
Near Cairncarrock,
Scottish Borders

4th August 1968

Dear Elvie,

I am having to smuggle this letter out of the convent, because the Sisters do not want me to have contact with the outside world. They say that my soul is in peril, and have me kneel on the stone floor of the private chapel for no less than six hours a day to pray for deliverance from evil.

Please help me, please, I'm begging you! I am not evil, you know that I am not. Save me from this hell. Grandmother promised that I would come home as soon as the baby was born, but her words were nothing more than lies, and I am trapped here, a prisoner, with no way of escaping. I'm so scared that I will go mad if I stay here! I need you, Elvie, I need you so much. I can't bear living like this. Death would be better than this. Please save me. Please! Don't try to reply to me here – the Sisters will punish me if they know I have smuggled letters out.

Please come for me. Please come, Elvie. Please come and save me! I need you. I shall go mad if you don't come!

With all my love, until you come for me,
Izzy.

Convent of the Sisters of Mercy and Deliverance,
Near Cairncarrock,
Scottish Borders

7ᵗʰ September 1968

Elvie!

This place is horrible. The Sisters look upon me as if I am evil, and many of them will not walk past me without crossing themselves and muttering prayers. Why do they think this of me? I am only human – my only sin has been to make a mistake, and I know it was a big one, but I am not evil – I'm not!

Will you come and save me, Elvie? Please. I know Father and Grandmother will never let me come home, but we could run away somewhere together – we are not children now. There must be some way that you can get to me! Tell me that you will come. Say it to yourself, and I know that I will hear it – I will hear it in my heart, and I will know that you are coming to save me. Say it, Elvie, please say it. I will go mad if I am kept here much longer, and I cannot escape by myself!

I love you, Elvie, and I need you.

Always and forever,

Izzy.

> *Convent of the Sisters of Mercy and Deliverance,*
> *Near Cairncarrock,*
> *Scottish Borders*

> 3rd *November 1968*

Where are you Elvie? Why haven't you come? You have to save me. I cannot live like this without losing my mind.

Please come. Please save me, I beg of you!

My love always,

Izzy.

> *Convent of the Sisters of Mercy and Deliverance,*
> *Near Cairncarrock,*
> *Scottish Borders*

> 8th *January 1969*

The madness is within me, Elvie. I cannot hide from it any longer. The madness is within me, and it tells me, again and again that I must die, that I am evil to the core and must be punished for my sins in hell.

The Sisters tell me that I cannot die. They tell me that my punishment is the madness, but nothing makes sense. Who is right, Elvie?

Why won't you come? I need you to come. I'm so scared. I need you. I need you so much. Why have you abandoned me, too? Are you punishing me, too? Please don't punish me. Please, please save me, I beg of you! You are my only hope – and the hope that I have of seeing you is the only thing that I have to cling on to. I don't want to die here all alone. I need you, Elvie. Only you can save me! Please don't leave me here – without you to save me, the madness only

grows stronger and stronger, and if you do not come, it will consume me, I know it will!
My love, forever and always,
Izzy.

Convent of the Sisters of Mercy and Deliverance,
Near Cairncarrock,
Scottish Borders

4th February 1969

I know now that the Sisters are right. I am being punished by God for my sins – and He is keeping you from me, also. I miss you, Elvie, I miss you so much, but I know now that you cannot come to save me. I cannot be saved. Nothing can save me, because this is God's will, and I must submit to the fate that He has sealed for me. I wish only that He had allowed me to see you one last time, to say 'goodbye' at least, and to tell you this: that I wish I could have been more like you, and not allowed myself to be tempted so badly by the Devil. I wish that I had listened to you when you warned me that I was walking on thin ice, and not laughed in your face when you were only worried for my soul. I love you, Elvie. I have always loved you, even when I have been cruel and spiteful to you. Believe me that it was the Devil acting through me that made me be so cruel.

Be good, Elvie. God is punishing me for being bad, and so you **must***, you really, really **must** be good, for my sake if nothing else. Do not give yourself the same fate as me. I must end my days paying penance for my sins – but you are **free**, Elvie!*

I will always think of you. The thought of you is all that keeps the madness at bay. I will always think of you with love in my heart.
Forever,
Izzy.

Luci let the last letter slip from her hands, hugging her arms around herself in an attempt to stop herself shaking. Was there no end to the horror of what her grandfather had done? He'd let everyone believe that his daughter was dead, when all the time he had known. He'd known Izzy was alive – *that* was what the payments to the convent had been for. Even after his mother died, he'd left Izzy there, when he could have saved her. Worse still was the thought of what Izzy had been made to believe. The despair in her final letters was heart-breaking. All Izzy's hope had gone, leaving her with no choice but to believe the awful lies the Sisters of Mercy and Deliverance were feeding her. Luci lurched up from the bed, clasping her hand over her mouth as nausea swelled up from her stomach.

Emerging from the bathroom several minutes later, Luci stumbled back to the bedroom and picked the letters up again. What would her mother have done if she'd known her twin was still alive? What would she have done if she'd actually received one of Izzy's heart-wrenching letters? Luci didn't have to think too hard to know the answer. If it had been Luke – if there had been some way that she could have saved him – she would have gone to the ends of the earth if she'd had to.

The address at the top of the letters was a bit vague – Luci had no idea where the hell Cairncarrock was for a kick off – but it was enough of a signpost to point her in the right direction.

'I'm going to find her, Mum,' Luci said to the empty room, wishing her mother could hear her. 'I'm going to find her and explain to her why you didn't save her, and then, if it's not too late, *I'm* going to save her!'

Gathering the letters up and stuffing them in one of the bedside drawers, Luci went back into the bathroom, splashed water on her face to get rid of the tear stains, and then clattered down the stairs, grabbing her shoulder bag off the banister at the bottom of the stairs.

'Alex just called,' she said to Ruth, who was still slaving over the steak and kidney pudding in the kitchen. 'There's something wrong with the car, and he wants me to pick him up. You don't mind watching the boys, do you?' She couldn't take the twins with her, after all – and they loved Ruth to bits. It wasn't as if she was leaving them with a complete stranger, she reminded her nagging conscience.

'Of course not,' Ruth said. 'Is it the alternator that's gone again?'

Luci shrugged, forcing a smile. She was too good at lying – that surely wasn't a good thing. 'He didn't say. But then, I wouldn't know one end of a car from the other, so it wouldn't make much difference if he did. I won't be long.' It seemed somehow fittingly ironic that lies had left Izzy stranded in a convent – but it was taking more lies to get her out.

CHAPTER EIGHTEEN

The traffic on the A1, as Luci drove north towards Scotland, was horrendous. If she managed fifteen minutes without the cars in front of her grinding to a halt, she thought herself lucky. With no postcode to tap into the sat-nav, she had to make do with the road map she'd bought at the Tesco Petrol Station on her way out of the city, and she had no idea how long the journey was *supposed* to take – not that it mattered: with the traffic as it was, she'd be lucky if she even made it across the Scottish border before it got dark.

The traffic ground to a halt again just before Morpeth; it was already nearly 9pm, and the light was beginning to fade. Yanking on the handbrake, Luci snatched up the road map and reconsidered her route. She'd been planning to take the A1 straight up to Berwick-upon-Tweed – but that was another 50 miles or so away, and Luci didn't relish spending all night sitting in traffic jams. Frowning at the map – map reading had never been at the top of her skills list – she plotted an alternate route that would take her off the A1 and up the A697 to Coldstream – within 20 miles of Cairncarrock. Her mobile started ringing – *again* – as she finally made the turn off the A1, but she ignored it – like she'd ignored it every time it rang.

'Sorry, Alz,' she murmured, turning the car stereo up, 'but I can't afford to waste time listening to you yelling at me.'

An hour and a half later, she finally made it into Scotland, crossing the River Tweed into Coldstream. The road had been quiet, but the journey had still seemed to take forever, and Luci had begun to wish she'd stayed on the A1 – at least in a traffic jam, the darkness wouldn't have been quite so eerie. There was no way she was carrying on the 20 miles to Cairncarrock – the map indicated that the village was literally in the middle of nowhere, on a road that had neither a name nor a number. She'd have to find a hotel or B&B to stay in instead – Izzy had waited 40 years to be rescued – another day was hardly going to matter to her.

***

Luci was back on the road before 8 o'clock the next morning; the hotel room came with an inclusive breakfast, but there seemed little point in sitting down to something she wouldn't be able to eat anyway. She'd barely slept all night – and when she had, her dreams had been punctuated by images of the horrors that Izzy must have endured over the past 40 years. As she drove out of Coldstream, her eyes felt gritty with tiredness, and her concentration was shot to hell – twice she took the wrong turning and had to turn back, meaning the 20 mile journey ended up taking well over an hour. Finally, though, she drove over a narrow humpback bridge fording a gushing brook and passed a stone marker with the name 'Cairncarrock' chiselled into it.

She pulled up outside the village shop-cum-post-office and ventured inside, aware of the curtains twitching in the stone cottages opposite the shop. She could well imagine that the tiny village didn't get many tourists passing through – it was certainly hard enough to find!

A man, who looked like he'd walked straight out of a Victorian novel, emerged from the back of the shop as Luci approached the counter. His smile seemed genuine enough – though Luci suspected that was just in anticipation of a sale. Hastily, Luci glanced at the glass jars of old-fashioned sweets arranged in neat rows behind the counter.

'Um, can I have a quarter of cola cubes, and a quarter of rhubarb and custards, please?' she asked, wistfully remembering how she, Luke and Alex would ride their bikes to the next village to buy sweets by the quarter when they were kids. 'And... um... these.' Luci scanned the shelves for something more expensive than a couple of bags of sweets and picked up an extravagantly priced box of chocolates.

'Just passing through, are you?' the man politely enquired as he jabbed buttons on the cash register.

'Sort of,' Luci said, taking a deep breath. 'Actually, I'm looking for somewhere - only I can't seem to find it on any maps. It's a convent – the Convent of the Sisters of Mercy and Deliverance.'

The shop-keeper looked up sharply. 'You won't find that place on any map,' he said. 'What would you be wanting it for?'

'I'm looking for someone. My aunt,' Luci said, stopping short of telling a complete stranger the whole sorry story. 'Do you know where it is?'

'Aye, I know where it is, but you won't be welcome, lass. They don't like visitors – don't let any folks inside the place. Not since...' He stopped and shook his head.

'Not since what?' Luci asked.

'There was a bit of a scandal back in the early 90s – lassies saying about the Sisters stealing their babbies – but it were soon hushed up, and they stopped folk goin' up there sharpish. They closed up the gates, and if it weren't that one of the nuns be seen cycling out for groceries, you'd think the place were abandoned.'

'Can you tell me how to get there?' Luci asked anxiously, a shiver of apprehension slithering down her spine.

'Aye, I can – for all the good that it'll do you!' the man said.

'I have to try,' Luci said desperately. 'My aunt - she was sent there when she was pregnant – my grandfather paid for her to be kept there. She sent letters to my mum, begging to be saved, but my mum never got them, and...'

The shopkeeper put his hand on top of Luci's. 'Alright, lass, don't go upsetting yourself now,' he said kindly, and Luci realised that her cheeks were damp with tears.

'Sorry,' Luci murmured, swiping at the tears in embarrassment. 'It's just that I've only just found out – my grandfather told everyone that Isabella had died –and I don't want it to be too late!'

'I hope it's not, lass,' the shopkeeper said, sounding as though he meant it. Reaching for a notepad, he drew a map with the directions to the convent, which was situated at the end of an isolated road three miles west of the village. 'You want to watch out for the potholes,' he added. 'That road was made for carriages not cars.'

Thanking him for his kindness, Luci returned to the car and pulled back onto the road, driving much too fast for the sleepy country roads in her haste to discover Izzy's fate.

***

The convent looked as though it had once been a massive manor house. The sprawling building was surrounded by walls covered in climbing ivy, and the one entrance gate was firmly chained and padlocked closed. A rusty bell hung to the left of the gate. Luci rang it – several times – but no one came to answer it. It was like the shopkeeper had said: the convent didn't welcome visitors. She craned her neck to look up at the windows, but they were all firmly shuttered. If she didn't know otherwise, she'd think the whole place was abandoned and derelict.

Sighing, Luci went back to her car and slumped into the driver's seat, resting her forehead on the steering wheel. Izzy was inside the convent, Luci was sure of it – but short of trying to scale the wall and break in, she was stumped. With another heavy sigh, Luci closed her aching eyes, allowing herself to doze.

She woke with a start at the sound of the gates creaking open. Sitting up sharply, she scrubbed at her gritty eyes and fumbled for the door handle as one of the Sisters pushed a rickety-looking bicycle through the gates. She was already re-locking the gates by the time Luci had climbed out of the car.

'Excuse me,' Luci said, making the woman jump. 'Is this the Convent of the Sisters of Mercy and Deliverance? I'm looking for someone - my aunt...'

The woman turned to face Luci, her face blanching suddenly white. 'Isabella,' she breathed, covering her mouth with her hands as a veil of confusion slipped across her face.

'Yes!' Luci said eagerly. 'She's still here, isn't she? I found letters, and...'

The woman seemed to shake herself. 'I'm sorry,' she said, 'but this is a closed community. You should not be here.'

'I just want to see my aunt - *please*,' Luci begged.

'You should not be here,' the woman said, glancing anxiously towards the convent. 'If I am seen talking to you...' Her words trailed away as she mounted the bicycle and began peddling quickly away.

'Wait! Please!' Luci yelled after her, but the nun kept peddling frantically –almost as if she was afraid of something. Luci jumped back into the car and started driving – slowly this time – down the pothole infested lane after the fleeing nun. She powered down her window as she drew level with the woman.

'My aunt was sent here in 1968,' Luci yelled through the open window. 'She was kept here against her will. She sent letters to my mother, begging to be saved – but my mother never got them. Izzy's spent 40 years thinking my mother abandoned her – I need her to know the truth!'

The woman stopped peddling. 'I can't be seen talking to you,' she said fearfully. Her voice was trembling. 'I want to help you, but if they knew I was talking to you... We are forbidden to speak to anyone about the convent – because of what happened.'

'Were you sent here, too, like Izzy?' Luci asked.

The nun hesitated. 'There's a car park by the lake,' she said, 'five miles from here. Wait there. I'll come. No one will see me there. No one will know me there.' She started peddling quickly away again, and this time Luci allowed her a head start.

Luci's mind was reeling. What was the nun so frightened of? What kind of people *were* the Sisters of Mercy and Deliverance if they could instil such fear in members of their own community?

***

The car park by the lake was deserted – not surprisingly, since the fishing pier had all but collapsed into the water and the wooden building that might once have been a café was boarded up and derelict. Parking up, Luci turned off the engine and settled down to wait - hoping that the nun's fear wouldn't get the better of her desire to help.

The minutes dragged by like hours. Luci started tapping her fingers against the steering wheel. Finally, after what felt like an eternity, she saw the nun on her bicycle weave her way, somewhat unsteadily, into the car park. Luci reached across and popped open the passenger side door, so the woman could get in. After a little hesitation, the nun climbed in.

'I've not been inside a car since 1967,' she said nervously, turning sideways to face Luci. 'My name is Frances. When I was a girl, my friends would call me Frankie, but it is more than forty years since anyone called me that!'

'Which do you prefer?' Luci asked.

'Oh, Frankie, but the Sisters would think it vulgar,' Frankie said with a girlish giggle.

'I'm Luci,' Luci said. 'Thank you for this, Frankie.'

'You look like her – like Isabella,' Frankie said. 'Are you – are you Elvina's daughter? Isabella talked a lot about Elvina at first. She was going to take me with her, when Elvina came to get her – but Elvina never came.'

The sadness in Frankie's voice brought tears to Luci's eyes. 'It wasn't Mum's fault. She didn't even know Izzy was still alive!' she explained. 'If she'd have known, she would have come. That's why I'm here now – to explain to Izzy.'

'I came here in 1967,' Frankie ventured. 'I was thirteen. My uncle... made me pregnant, and my parents were so ashamed, they arranged for me to come here. I was supposed to go home once the baby was born, but then my mother died and my father said that he couldn't have me home, so the Sisters agreed to take me in and have me join the order once I was eighteen,' Frankie ventured, without any prompting. 'When Isabella came, she didn't know she was going to have to stay, either. She thought she'd be going home afterwards, like the other girls, but then the woman came and told her that she could never go home. It was odd – I remember it so well – because Isabella looked at the woman and spat at her, and she said something so strange – perhaps that's why I remember it. She said: "If Mum knew what you were doing, she'd hate you, but not as much as *I* hate you!"'

'Who was the woman?' Luci asked, though she already had a good idea, recalling the letters from Violet that she'd found in the attic.

'She was the one who met us girls at the station and drove us to the convent, and then she would arrange for the babies to be adopted afterwards,' Frankie said. 'I asked Isabella if she knew the woman – before she was sent here, I mean – but Isabella didn't give me a proper answer. She just said "not anymore," and when I asked her what she meant by that, she wouldn't tell me. She always kept out of the way when the woman came, after that. We all did, because it was because of her that we were there. We all hated her – but not as much as Isabella!'

'Violet,' Luci muttered. 'I think the woman was Violet – Isabella's aunt.' She paused. 'How many girls ended up not going home, Frankie?'

Frankie looked down at her lap. 'Not many. Three or four besides Isabella and me. Most of the girls went home to their families. But...' She stopped, as if unsure about continuing.

'But what?' Luci prompted.

'But there were some – later on, perhaps two or three years later – that couldn't go home – their families didn't want them – but the Sisters wouldn't let them stay.'

Probably because their families wouldn't pay for their keep, Luci thought bitterly, recalling the regular payments Walter had been making.

'What happened to them?' she asked.

'I don't know. The woman came with two men – the first time I'd seen men in the convent – and took them away. We weren't allowed to keep in contact with any of the girls after they left, so I don't know where they went or what happened to them,' Frankie said. 'The Reverend Mother said we should not ask questions. She would only say that the girls had new families. Isabella shouted at the Reverend Mother – but the Reverend Mother just made Isabella pay penance for her outspokenness.'

Frankie might have been woefully innocent about the outside world – but Luci wasn't. She didn't want to *think* about what Violet had been mixed up in – but she was fairly certain that it was neither moral nor legal. Not that she could tell Frankie that. She did some quick calculations. If Frankie was 13 in 1967, that made her 54 now – but it was almost as if she'd stayed mentally a teenager, untouched by the aging process that her body had gone through.

'But Isabella's still at the convent?' Luci asked, returning the conversation to her own agenda.

Frankie nodded. 'Oh, yes. She hasn't been out, not since the accident.'

'What accident?' Luci's heart started to pound erratically.

'It must have been about... oh, 15 years ago,' Frankie said.

Fifteen years ago – the year Elvina committed suicide, Luci reckoned, holding her breath.

'I'm not supposed to know what happened. The Reverend Mother said that I must never speak of it,' Frankie went on. 'There was such a lot of blood. An awful, awful lot of blood, and they had to take Isabella to the hospital – to replace some of the blood that she lost. It was quite frightening – she looked so white, so bloodless, when they carried her out.'

'Did she hurt herself, Frankie?' Luci asked, feeling sick.

'Yes,' Frankie said quietly. 'She... she cut herself, with a knife she took from the kitchen. I only know because I found her. No one else knows. The Reverend Mother said that it was an accident, that she hurt herself by accident – but I know that she meant to do it. I know she was so very sad, and she told me that she didn't want to be alive anymore.'

'What made her so sad?' Luci asked.

'She said that she felt empty,' Frankie said with a frown.

'When was it that she had the accident, Frankie, can you remember?'

Frankie pondered for a moment. 'February,' she said finally. 'I remember, because it had been snowing. February 1993.'

'She felt it,' Luci whispered, covering her mouth with her hands. 'Even so far away, she felt it.'

'Felt what?' Frankie asked innocently.

'My mother died in February 1993,' Luci said. 'And Izzy must have felt it – felt the loss of her twin, even though they'd been apart for so long.'

Frankie stared at her as if she was mad – but Luci knew exactly what Izzy must have felt. She'd felt the severing of a connection when Luke died – it had felt as though a part of her had died, too. For Izzy, isolated from her family out here in the middle of nowhere, it must have been so much worse.

'In the letters – the ones Izzy sent to my mother – she said that the Sisters told her that she was being punished,' Luci said, gazing intently at Frankie. 'Is that what they're like? Are they all hellfire and brimstones?'

Frankie broke eye-contact and stared down at her hands, folded tightly in her lap. 'God punishes us for our sins,' she said softly. 'That is what the Sisters believe – that the trials we face in life are God's way of punishing us for our many sins. We are punished for vanity, for greed, for our carnal desires. The Sisters of Mercy and Deliverance aim to walk a more Godly path, so that we might please Him and not face His wrath when we reach the Gates of Paradise.'

The poor woman had been brainwashed, Luci realised. She'd been brainwashed to believe in a vengeful God – and if she had, then it was likely that Izzy had suffered the same fate.

'I need to see Izzy,' Luci said decisively. 'I have to let her know that Mum didn't just abandon her!'

Frankie shook her head woefully. 'You can't,' she said. 'Nobody but the Sisters are allowed inside the convent. And even if they were, you still couldn't see Isabella. She has been in solitary – I mean, she took vows of solitude after the accident. She doesn't see anyone.'

'No one?' Luci echoed disbelievingly.

'No one but the Reverend Mother, who administers to her spiritual needs,' Frankie confirmed. She hesitated. 'And…me. The Reverend Mother would punish me if she knew, but Isabella is my friend, and I can't bear the thought of her always being so alone. I have to sneak up to see her after dark.'

'For fifteen years?' It seemed inconceivable that anyone could spend fifteen years almost entirely on their own.

Frankie nodded. 'The Reverend Mother counselled that it was the best for Isabella's spiritual welfare. I think it is because she is frightened Isabella will try to hurt herself again.'

'Who is this Reverend Mother?' Luci asked, already feeling the strong desire to strangle the woman, whoever she was.

'She was the Reverend Mother of the Sisters when I came to them,' Frankie said. 'She's always been at the convent. I think she was born there, before the war. She was chosen to be the Reverend Mother when she was still quite young, because of her piety and dedication to the Lord.'

Her words sounded like a propaganda speech; Luci resisted the urge to roll her eyes. It wasn't Frankie's fault that she'd been brainwashed to believe such nonsense.

'Frankie, I really appreciate you talking to me like this,' Luci said, choosing her words carefully. 'But I need to you help me some more. I need you to get me into the convent, so I can talk to Izzy.'

Frankie's eyes widened. 'You can't!' she gasped. 'I told you – no one is allowed inside the convent. We are a closed community.'

'If you don't help me, I'll have to go to the police and tell them that my aunt is being held at the convent in solitary confinement – against her will. They'll have to investigate, and then there will be police crawling all over the convent, delving into all the shady things that have been going on there over the years.' Luci didn't like having to resort to emotional blackmail, but she was determined to get inside the convent – whatever it took.

'But...' Frankie faltered.

'Please,' Luci said imploringly. 'I have to see Izzy. There are things you don't understand. When Izzy got pregnant, it was because she wasn't well – mentally, I mean. She shouldn't even be there at the convent – she should never have been there. If my mother had got the letters, she would have saved Izzy – and I owe it to my mother to try.'

Frankie wrung her hands anxiously. 'Will you take Isabella away?' she asked.

'If she'll come with me,' Luci said, aware that after forty years, her aunt might well be frightened of leaving the convent.

'The Reverend Mother will punish me when she finds out that I helped you,' Frankie said worriedly.

'Would *you* like to leave, Frankie?' Luci asked.

The woman worried her lip between her teeth. 'I've nowhere to go,' she fretted. 'The convent's been my home for most of my life.'

'If you came with me and Izzy, the social services would be able to find you somewhere to live,' Luci said, not entirely sure if that was true or not. At that point, she would have said *anything* to get inside the convent.

'Would you really help me?' Frankie asked, as if the idea of someone helping *her* was entirely alien to her.

'Of course,' Luci said, meaning it.

'If you go round the side of the walls, you come to some woods,' Frankie said. 'Follow the wall through the woods, and there's an old door in the wall. It only opens from the inside – I don't think anyone else has ever used it, but I used to, a long time ago, when I used to think about running away. Come when it's dark, and I'll open the door. Everyone will be asleep then, even the Reverend Mother.'

Luci gripped Frankie's hands tightly. 'Thank you,' she said fiercely. 'Thank you so much!'

Frankie blushed. 'Isabella is my friend,' she said simply. 'She would have helped me, if she could. Now I'm helping her.' With that, she opened the car door and climbed out, slamming the door closed before Luci could say another word.

CHAPTER NINETEEN

It was eerie returning to the convent after dark. It was all Luci could do not to scream when an owl swooped down from the trees at her as she climbed out of the car at the edge of the woods. There were no lights shining from within the convent, thanks to the shutters – and with no houses for miles the darkness was complete. Luci had grown up in a city, where even in the middle of the night, the darkness was punctuated by street-lights. Here, there was nothing, and it was freaking her out.

She kept close to the wall as she stumbled through the woods, tripping and falling several times over tree roots it was impossible to see. The wall seemed to stretch on for an eternity; in the darkness, Luci almost missed the wooden door that fitted snugly into the brickwork. The paint was peeling, the wood was stripped bare in places with neglect, and there was no handle on the outside at all.

'Frankie?' Luci hissed. 'Frankie, are you there?'

The door gave a loud creak before slowly beginning to open. As soon as the gap was wide enough, Luci squeezed through, finding Frankie standing on the other side looking positively terrified.

'You'll have to take your shoes off before we go inside,' Frankie whispered, gesturing towards her own slipper-clad feet. 'It's all bare stone and wood floors.'

'Okay,' Luci whispered, bending down to unlace her boots so she'd be able to slip out of them easily at the door.

'Isabella's room is on the top floor,' Frankie whispered, leading the way to a side door at the back of the convent. 'We'll have to use the servant's stairs. It's the only way to get to the room. Watch for the fifth stair from the bottom – it creaks.'

Luci nodded, feeling suddenly sick with anticipation. She tried not to give attention to the anxious thoughts rattling round in her head: what if Izzy didn't *want* to be rescued now? What if she was caught effectively breaking into a convent in the middle of the night? She followed Frankie inside, waiting whilst the older woman closed the door quietly behind them.

'It's this way,' Frankie whispered, leading the way down a dark, narrow corridor with wood panelled walls. The stairs were equally narrow, and uncarpeted. Luci trod carefully, stepping over the fifth stair from the bottom and almost losing her balance. Her heart was pounding so loudly, she felt sure that everyone in the sleeping convent would be able to hear. At the top of the stairs, Frankie turned into another narrow corridor; the ceiling was so low it brushed the top of Luci's head so that she had to duck down to avoid showering herself in crumbling plaster. There was a strong smell of damp; Luci reached out to touch the wall, grimacing when her fingertips came back wet.

'How many people live here?' she asked Frankie in a whisper.

'Twenty,' Frankie whispered back.

'How many bedrooms?'

'Fifteen, not counting the Reverend Mother's rooms,' Frankie replied. 'Some of the Sisters share.'

'But nobody else sleeps up here?' Luci asked, although it was obvious that they didn't.

'Just Isabella,' Frankie confirmed.

Luci gritted her teeth in anger. The conditions up here weren't fit for animals, let alone a human being – and it was clear that Izzy was being treated *like* an animal by the Reverend Mother.

Frankie stopped outside the door at the end of the corridor. There was no key in the lock, but Frankie stooped and retrieved a long, rusty iron key from within a space between the skirting board and the wall. Her hand tremble as she turned the key and twisted the handle carefully until the latch released with a tell-tale click. 'Isabella?' Frankie called out softly, fumbling around for the light switch, which activated a bare bulb hanging from the low ceiling. A narrow bed was placed up against one wall, where the eaves of the roof started sloping down – but the bed was empty.

'It's me, Isabella,' Frankie said quietly. 'Frances.'

'Where is she?' Luci hissed, stepping into the room behind Frankie and casting her gaze around. Her breath caught in her throat as she realised that the shape huddling under a bedspread in the corner of the room was her aunt. A pair of frightened eyes peeked out from the top of the bedspread, and then slowly the bedspread lowered, revealing a woman that was still – despite the intervening fifteen years – the very image of Elvina. For Luci, it was like coming face to face with her mother all over again – and for Isabella, Luci's resemblance to her mother was obviously strong enough to overcome the older woman's fear.

'*Elvie?*' Isabella breathed, fixing her gaze on Luci, her fear forgotten. 'You came! I *knew* you'd come!'

Luci swallowed hard against the lump that rose in her throat. All these years, Izzy had been trapped here, just waiting for her twin to come and rescue her. Even after forty years, she'd never truly given up hope.

'I'm Luci,' she said softly. 'Elvina was my mum.'

'But she sent you? She sent you here to get me?' Izzy was on her feet now, her eyes wide with wonderment.

Luci hesitated. How could she possibly even begin to explain the situation that had led her here? Elvina *would* have sent her – if she'd still been alive to do so – but there was no easy way to break *that* news to Izzy. 'Sort of,' she said weakly.

Izzy grabbed hold of Luci's hands and held them tightly as the tears started dribbling down her cheeks. 'I've been waiting so long,' she whispered. 'So, so long.'

'I know,' Luci whispered, feeling her own eyes welling up with tears. 'It must have been horrible.'

'Horrible?' Izzy echoed on a sob. 'Oh, it was worse than horrible!'

'I'm sorry,' Luci choked out, feeling guilty even though it wasn't her fault that Izzy had been left here. 'Mum never got your letters – she never knew. Walter told her – he told her that you'd *died*.'

'I tried,' Izzy said earnestly. 'I really, really tried, but *they* wouldn't let me.'

'I came as soon as I found out that you were here,' Luci said, fighting back a tide of emotion. 'I know it's forty years too late, but I came as soon as I possibly could.' Carefully, she turned Izzy's hands to reveal the scars criss-crossing her aunt's wrists. 'Izzy…'

'Elvie used to call me that. Nobody's called me that since I came here,' Izzy sobbed pitifully. 'Say it again. I like hearing it. It makes me feel like she's here with me.'

'Izzy, you know, don't you?' Luci whispered.

Isabella lifted her head to stare into Luci's eyes. 'Don't say it,' she begged. 'Please don't say it.'

Luci swallowed hard. 'My mum died,' she said, because she had to say it now, before she lost the courage. 'She died fifteen years ago. But you knew that, didn't you?'

Izzy rocked her head up and down in a nod, pulling her hands away to cover her ears. 'No,' she whispered. 'No, don't say it, please don't say it. I wanted to be wrong! *I wanted to be* **wrong**!'

'I'm sorry,' Luci said, feeling awful for breaking her aunt's heart. 'But I thought you should know.'

Isabella's sobs intensified, reaching a crescendo that had Frankie grasping her shoulders in panic. 'Shhh!' Frankie cried. 'They'll hear us! The Reverend Mother will hear us!''

Izzy wrenched herself free. 'Let her hear,' she spat, sudden anger flashing in her eyes. 'Let her come up here and see that I was right! I said Elvie would come for me – and, and…' She stopped to draw in a deep breath, seeming to grow in both strength and stature as she turned back to Luci. 'And she did – she came, in you. She's in you – I can feel it – I can see it. I can see her in your eyes, I can feel her in your touch. She's here. She came – and I *want* the witch to know it!' She was shouting now, shouting as if she didn't care who heard her.

'If the Reverend Mother hears us, she'll *never* let us leave!' Frankie wailed in desperation.

'Leave?' Izzy repeated in confusion. 'Leave here? Now?'

Frankie nodded. 'That's why Luci *came*,' she said anxiously. 'To *rescue* us. That's what you wanted, isn't it?'

Izzy nodded uncertainly. 'I begged her. I begged her to come for me. But I thought she was never coming. I thought I'd be here forever.'

'Not if I have anything to do with it,' Luci muttered grimly. 'And Frankie's right. We'll have to hurry. You need to get dressed, Izzy. Quickly.'

'Dressed. Yes,' Izzy said, as if the word was alien to her.

Luci quickly scanned the room, snatching up a shapeless, sack-like dress, identical to the one that Frankie was wearing. 'Here – put this on,' she said, thrusting it at her aunt. After a moment's hesitation, Izzy pulled the dress on over the top of her nightgown. 'Have you got coats?' Luci asked Frankie. 'It's cold out.'

'We'd have to go to the cloakroom. That's near the Reverend Mother's rooms,' Frankie said worriedly.

Luci shook her head. 'Forget it,' she said, grasping Izzy's hands. 'We have to be quiet, Izzy, or we won't be able to leave.'

'I won't let her stop us,' Izzy said defiantly, her eyes flashing again with fire. Luci's stomach did a back-flip, realising that *this* was what her mother had feared – the wild, emotion-charged recklessness that seemed to surge through Isabella like an electric current. For the briefest moment, she wondered if Alex felt the same anxiety when looking into *her* eyes as she felt now looking into Izzy's.

'Just be *quiet*,' Luci said firmly. 'Please.'

'You sound like her, too,' Izzy said.

'Shhh!' Frankie hissed, leading the way back down the corridor. Luci made Izzy go in front of her, so her aunt was sandwiched between her and Frankie. Thankfully, Izzy remained silent all the way down the stairs, and along the narrow corridor to the side door, but instead of following Frankie outside, she stopped, looking suddenly frantic.

'No! I promised them!' she cried, making no sense whatsoever.

'Shhh!' Luci whispered, glancing anxiously back over her shoulder and listening for any sign of movement in the convent.

'I can't go without them,' Izzy said, lowering her voice to a stage whisper. 'I promised the girls.'

'We can't go back for anyone else!' Luci protested.

'No, no!' Izzy said impatiently, shaking her head. 'Not people – the files. I know where they are. I know what they did – and I know where to get the proof. We can't go without it!'

'We have to go, now!' Frankie said desperately, but Luci hesitated.

'Where?' she asked Izzy.

'In the office,' Izzy whispered. 'This way!'

'We *can't*,' Frankie wailed.

Luci thought about Violet, the other girls that Frankie had mentioned, and the ones who had been taken away by Violet and her henchmen. Izzy was right – if there was proof about what had been happening here at the Convent of the Sisters of Mercy and Deliverance – then they couldn't leave without it.

'Show me,' Luci whispered to her aunt. 'But we'll have to be quick – and quiet.'

Isabella set off down another corridor almost at a run, leaving Luci hurrying in her wake. At the end of the corridor there was a stout door with a brass plaque reading "Office" screwed into the top panel. Izzy turned the handle, and Luci breathed a sigh of relief when the door immediately yielded to the pressure: it wasn't locked.

'No one would dare come in here without the Reverend Mother's permission, so why should she keep it locked?' Izzy said with a devilish grin. 'Not when she thinks she's got me safely confined to the attic – just like Grandmother.' She tiptoed across the room, not bothering to switch on the light – much to Luci's relief – and carefully slid open the bottom drawer of the filing cabinet that stood in one corner. Peering over her aunt's shoulder, Luci stared at the buff-coloured cardboard file folders that filled the drawer to capacity.

'We need a bag or something,' Luci said as Izzy started lifting the thin folders out and shoving them into Luci's arms.

'Look in the cupboard by the door,' Izzy whispered. 'Our dear Reverend Mother can't bear to throw *anything* away.'

Putting the stack of files on the floor, Luci padded across the room and opened the tall-boy cupboard that Izzy had pointed to. It was full of satchels – the type that girls would have used in the 1950s and 1960s.

'Mine was red,' Izzy hissed. 'Can you see it?'

Luci rooted through the pile of satchels, trying to guess how many there were in the cupboard – at least twenty-five, she reckoned. That meant twenty-five girls who didn't go back to their families – and the Reverend Mother had kept their belongings like trophies. After a few minutes, Luci found the red leather satchel and pulled it free of the rest. Unbuckling it, she lifted the flap to start putting the folders – which Izzy was still pulling out of the filing cabinet – inside. Something fluttered free, drifting to the floor near Luci's foot. She stooped to pick it up, hesitating when she recognised her mother's handwriting on the back of the square of photographic paper. 'United we stand, united we fall,' Elvina had written, and Luci felt her breath catch in her throat as she turned it over. The Polaroid picture showed Elvina and Isabella together, their arms wrapped around each other, laughing as they gazed into each other's eyes. They looked so happy, so carefree. Tears suddenly rained down Luci's cheeks as if the photograph had broken a dam inside her. As Izzy turned around with a final bundle of files, Luci thrust the photograph at her, busying herself with forcing the folders into the satchel in an attempt to hide her tears.

'I thought the witch would have burned this,' Izzy said, with a note of wonderment in her voice. 'She obviously didn't find it.' Bending down to help Luci with the files, she slipped the photo into the front pocket of the satchel, only then noticing Luci's distress. 'What's the matter?'

Luci shook her head. 'Nothing,' she choked out. 'Ignore me. I'm fine, really.' She was surprised when Izzy put her arms around her and started rubbing her back gently – exactly like Elvina used to do whenever Luci was upset.

'Shhh,' Izzy whispered. 'Don't cry. It's all going to be all right now you've come for me.'

'Mum should have been here,' Luci sobbed.

'She *is* here,' Izzy said firmly. 'I told you that. She's here in you.' Giving Luci a tight hug, she pulled back and bent back over the satchel, allowing Luci a moment to try to pull herself together. The creaking of a floorboard above their heads made them both freeze and exchange an anxious glance.

'We'd better hurry,' Luci said, her voice still thick with tears. Izzy nodded, fumbling with the buckles of the satchel before passing it to Luci.

'One second. Just one second,' Izzy said, flinging open the door to another cupboard on the opposite side of the room. This one was filled with bundles of clothes tied together with ribbon. Izzy snatched one of the bundles up and tucked it under her arm, leaving the cupboard door swinging open as she lead the way back out of the office and towards the side door where Frankie would be waiting.

Frankie wasn't waiting. She wasn't by the door, or in the corridor, and she wasn't anywhere outside that Luci could see, either.

'Frankie?' Luci hissed. 'Frankie, we're ready. Where are you?'

There was no answer. Luci called out again, but still Frankie made no reply.

'She's frightened,' Izzy said. 'She's too frightened of the world to go back. She never wanted it as much as me.'

'But she asked me to help her get out,' Luci protested.

'She goes out every day and always comes back,' Izzy said. 'I watch her from my window. The Reverend Mother would never let me out like that – *never*. She only lets Frances out because she knows that Frances will always come back. All those chances Frances has had. Day after day after day. All those wasted chances! She'll never leave. She'll always be trapped here – but she could accept that. I never could, Luci. Never. Never could I accept that I might have to stay here forever. I never gave up hope, not really. There was always a little part of me that knew that one day – *one* day – somebody would come and save me!'

Luci felt guilty leaving Frankie behind, when the poor woman had risked so much to help her and Izzy, but it would be worse, she thought, to try to *make* Frankie leave the place that must have been a kind of sanctuary for her.

'Are *you* frightened?' she asked her aunt softly.

Izzy laughed. 'Only of having to stay,' she replied, already beginning to pick her way – barefoot – across the undergrowth towards their door to freedom.

CHAPTER TWENTY

'It's like losing forty years of my life,' Izzy said as Luci drove down the narrow country lanes back towards civilization. 'The world's passed me by.' She picked up a CD case and stared at it. 'I don't even know what this is!'

Luci smiled. 'It's a CD – a new-fangled type of record, I suppose you'd call it,' she explained.

'But it hasn't got any grooves! How do you play it?' Izzy asked, taking the CD out of its case and turning it over in her hands.

Luci took the CD out of Izzy's hand and slotted it into the CD player. 'Things have moved on a bit,' she said.

'That's Elvis!' Izzy squeaked. 'God, I used to *love* Elvis. Is this his latest album?'

'Not exactly,' Luci said. 'He died in 1977.'

'Really?' Izzy asked. 'I've missed so much, haven't I? It was like being in prison. We weren't even allowed to read newspapers. There were no outside influences in the convent at all. The only book the Reverend Mother would permit was the Bible. Grandmother would have loved it. She would have liked the whole world to be like the convent. Everything other than the Bible, she thought was evil.'

'He should have protected you,' Luci said softly.

'Who? Father?' Izzy laughed. 'He was more frightened of her than we were. If Mum hadn't died – if he hadn't had *her* put away, too – things would have been different. But after that, Grandmother ruled. And I made her angry, all the time, even when I was trying to be good. Elvie was better at being good than I was. That's why Grandmother hated me more than she hated Elvie, except when Elvie used to try and protect me. She did that a lot, even though I used to make Elvie really mad with me sometimes. She used to say that I was just like Mum – like that was a bad thing. Maybe she was right though. Maybe if I'd tried harder...'

'It wasn't your fault,' Luci cut in. 'You couldn't have stopped being yourself. '

Izzy turned to look at Luci. 'You're talking about the madness, aren't you? The thing that killed Mum?'

'It's got a name,' Luci said. 'Manic depression – bipolar.'

'I remember hearing Dad talk about it with Grandmother, but I was just a child. The words didn't mean anything,' Izzy said. 'They still don't mean anything. They're just words.'

'It's like living by extremes,' Luci said. 'Extremely happy, extremely sad. And extremely happy and extremely sad both at the same time.'

'Yes!' Izzy said, pouncing on the description of a mixed episode. 'Extremely happy and extremely sad at the same time. *That* means something.'

'I know,' Luci murmured.

'The Reverend Mother didn't believe in illness – just sin, and punishment for sin,' Izzy said. 'Everything came down to sin, and God's punishment for evil ways. I almost believed it. She almost made me believe in what she was telling me. But I read the Bible. I read it over and over again, and I couldn't find anywhere where it said that. I stopped listening to her then.' She shook her head. 'I knew I was being punished – but not by God. By her – and by Father and Grandmother.'

'They were evil,' Luci said, sighing. 'I know what they did to you. I read your diary. I know it was private, and that I shouldn't have read it, but...'

'I try not to think about what they did to me,' Izzy said quietly. 'I try to push it from my mind. The only thing that kept me going was the hope that Elvie got away. And she must have done – if she had you. Was she happy? I wanted her to be happy – to live a full life for me.'

Luci's vision blurred with tears, and she pulled into the side of the road. 'Oh, yes, Mum got away,' she said, her voice trembling.

'Tell me she was happy,' Izzy begged.

Luci shook her head. 'I can't lie to you,' she whispered.

'But I wanted her to be happy!'

'I don't think she could be. Not in her heart. She thought you were dead, Izzy – and I know what it feels like to lose a twin. That emptiness, that void. I don't think she ever got over it. She tried to be happy – for me and Luke – but I think the sadness was always there.'

'You had a brother – a twin?' Izzy asked. 'And he died?'

Luci nodded. 'Ten years ago,' she said. 'Almost exactly ten years ago.' In a week's time, it would be the tenth anniversary of Luke's death.

Izzy covered Luci's hands with her own. 'I'm sorry,' she said with a heartfelt sigh.

'It's okay. I got over it a long time ago.'

'No you didn't,' Izzy said simply. 'How did he die?'

'An accident,' Luci said.

'And Elvie? Was her death an accident, too?'

'No,' Luci said flatly.

'Tell me, Luci, please. I'd like to know. I knew she was dead – I felt something inside me break – but I tried to tell myself that I was wrong, that she was too young to have died. Because she *was* too young. We were only forty-one fifteen years ago,' Izzy said.

Luci lifted her head so that she could look at her aunt. 'She killed herself. My dad had been having an affair, she thought that you were dead, and so she must have decided that she didn't want to be alive anymore.'

'How old were you?' Izzy asked, a catch in her voice.

'Twelve, just turned.'

'She shouldn't have left you like that. You were too young,' Izzy said, with a touch of anger in her tone. 'She was selfish. She had *children*. She had something to live for!'

Luci shook her head. 'The guilt was too much. She could see it in me – the fire, the madness – and she couldn't bear it. I don't blame her. She was unhappy, she couldn't take anymore. She did it because she couldn't see any other way.'

'But there's *always* hope,' Izzy said fiercely. 'I know that I tried to die, too – but I didn't have what Elvie had. I *had* lost everything – and she still had so much! And even though I tried to die, I lived and that made me think that it was God's way of reminding me that I should be grateful to be alive, even though I didn't seem to have a lot to be grateful for. I had to find something to hold on to. I had to keep holding on to the hope that one day something would happen to set me free again.'

Luci shrugged. 'Maybe Mum wasn't as strong as you,' she said. 'Maybe it was just that she couldn't bear to look at me anymore.' Swiping furiously at the tears on her cheeks, she turned the car stereo up and threw the car back into gear, accelerating back onto the road much too fast.

'But you're beautiful!' Izzy protested, raising her voice to be heard over Elvis.

'I don't want to talk about this anymore,' Luci snapped. 'It hurts too much.'

'I'm sure it wasn't because of you that Elvie... did what she did,' Izzy said. 'She must have loved you so very much. She always wanted babies – she loved looking after other people's children.'

'But not her own,' Luci muttered. 'No, that's not fair. She did love us. She was good with us, until she started falling apart. She just couldn't live with herself, Izzy, that's what it amounted to. I *know* she felt guilty for having me and Luke when she knew about the family history of madness. Maybe she felt guilty for being alive when she thought you were dead. There's no knowing what the hell was going on in her mind – but what I do know is that she made the decision to die *after* she realised that I had "fire" in my eyes.'

'She used to say that about Mum – and me,' Izzy said. 'But *that's* no excuse to kill herself. The Elvie I knew would never have done something like that. The Elvie I knew would have protected you, and taken care of you – like she used to take care of *me!*'

'She must have changed,' Luci said flatly. 'Please, Izzy. I can't talk about this anymore. I'm tired. I've hardly slept in two days. And I'm sick to death of crying over my bloody mother!'

'I'm sorry,' Izzy said, sounding as if she meant it. 'I just can't believe that Elvie would end up like that. It doesn't sound like my sister at all!'

Luci rubbed at her aching eyes, swallowing hard against the hard lump of emotion in her throat. 'She must have changed,' she repeated, sighing. For the first time, she realised that this must be how Alex felt when she started being all obsessive over something. It was dreadfully wearing. She yawned, wondering whether she should try and find somewhere for her and Izzy to stay for what was left of the night. She immediately dismissed the idea. Stopping at a hotel would only give Izzy more time to ask more questions. It was better to keep going – in the hope that Izzy might not keep going on quite so much if she thought that Luci had to concentrate on driving.

'All right – we won't talk about Elvie anymore,' Izzy said, giving Luci's knee a comforting pat. 'Tell me about you, instead.'

Luci sighed. It was going to be a long night.

***

After so long driving on dark – and empty – minor roads, the head- and tail-lights of other cars when Luci pulled out onto the A1 were positively dazzling. Blinking rapidly, she took her foot off the accelerator and took a deep breath in a futile attempt to stave off the fatigue that was weighing her down.

'Where are we?' Izzy asked, breaking a silence that had lasted at least two minutes.

'We've just left Berwick-upon-Tweed,' Luci said wearily.

'How much further have we got to go?'

Luci tried to shape her lips into a smile. 'Only about another 150 miles,' she said.

'How long's that going to take us?' Izzy asked.

'Hopefully not as long as it took me driving up here,' Luci replied. 'Maybe three hours or so.'

'I remember the day Violet drove me to the convent,' Izzy said. 'We kept having to stop so I could go to the toilet – because of the baby pressing on my bladder, you know. The journey seemed to take forever.'

'You must have been frightened.'

'Not so much then – because I thought I was coming home after the baby was born,' Izzy said. 'I didn't know then what my grandmother and Violet had been plotting. I didn't know that Violet regularly "helped" girls like me. She was my mother's sister. I trusted her. I couldn't have got it much more wrong, could I?'

'How could you have known?' Luci pointed out.

'I should have realised. I *knew* that Grandmother was evil. I was too trusting,' Izzy said bitterly.

'You were only fifteen – you couldn't have possibly guessed what they were plotting!' Luci protested, taking her gaze off the road to try to reassure her aunt with a smile. 'It's easy with hindsight – Alex is always getting at me for saying "I should have" – and there's been an awful lot of "I should have" moments in my life.'

'Everything would have been different, though,' Izzy said sadly. 'Elvie wouldn't have had to be so sad, and...' Her words disappeared into a sound that was somewhere between a scream and a sob as she grabbed frantically at Luci's arm.

It felt as though everything was happening in slow motion. Luci swivelled her gaze forward again and slammed her foot down on the brake – the words *I only took my eyes off the road for a second* flashing like bullets through her brain. She wrenched the wheel hard left to try and avoid the articulated lorry that had skewed, at a crazy angle, across the carriageway in front of her, but it was already too late for evasive action. The last thing Luci heard before she lost consciousness was Izzy screaming out for God to save them, and the sickening sound of metal tearing and glass shattering.

CHAPTER TWENTY-ONE

Phone-calls in the middle of the night can never bear good news. Alex snatched the phone up on the second ring, fear shrinking his voice to a croak as he tried to say 'hello'. He hadn't been asleep; since Luci's sudden disappearance, he'd been trying desperately to reach her, sitting by the phone in the vain hope that she would call him to let him know, at the very least, that she was okay.

'Alex Freeman?' a woman's voice asked, and Alex recognised the calm professionalism of someone used to delivering bad news.

'Yes?' he asked, offering a silent prayer to a God he didn't even believe in.

'I'm calling from the Wansbeck General Hospital. There's been an accident involving Luciana Rushden. You're listed as an emergency contact?'

They were the words nobody ever wanted to hear. The room spun as Alex struggled against a rising tide of panic. 'Is she...?' *Please, God, let her be all right. Please let her be alive.*

'The doctors are with her now,' the woman said, with the same calmness in her voice – as if she was telling him that it might rain later. 'She was involved in a serious road traffic accident. Her condition is critical, but...'

'She's alive,' Alex cut in. 'She's alive, that's all that matters.' He could breathe again knowing that however badly injured Luci was, she was *alive*. 'I'm sorry, which hospital did you say?'

'Wansbeck,' the woman replied.

'Which is where?'

'I can give you directions, if that helps?' the woman offered. Without waiting for Alex to reply, she reeled off instructions on how to find the hospital.

'Will you tell her I'm coming?' Alex asked, his voice breaking. It would take him at least a couple of hours to get there, and the thought of Luci lying, frightened and hurt, alone in the hospital waiting for him made his heart ache.

'She's not conscious,' the woman said. 'But the moment she wakes up, I'll tell her.'

Alex disconnected the call, dropping the phone down onto the chair arm as he buried his head in his hands.

The living room light suddenly flickered to life and Alex lifted his head sharply.

'Was that Luci?' Ruth asked anxiously from the doorway.

Alex shook his head. 'Hospital near Morpeth,' he croaked. 'Luci's been in an accident. I have to go to her, Mum. If she wakes up and I'm not there...' He got shakily to his feet. 'Shit, I shouldn't be sitting here *talking*...'

'You're not driving in this state!' Ruth snapped. 'You've not slept...'

'I've got to go to her!' Alex yelled. 'She needs me.'

'Then you'll call a taxi, but you are *not* driving, Alexander,' Ruth said firmly. 'What use are you to Luci if *you* have an accident?'

'They said she was in a critical condition,' Alex whispered, his shoulders heaving. 'I can't lose her, Mum. I *can't*!'

'Luci's a fighter – you know that,' Ruth said gently. 'Pass me the phone – I'll call you a taxi. Why don't you run upstairs and put a few things in a bag for Luci? Some pyjamas and a few clothes, maybe?'

'I don't want her to wake up without me being there,' Alex said weakly.

'I'll tell them to hurry,' Ruth promised, hugging her eldest son tightly. 'She'll be fine, Alex. She's stronger than she looks.'

Alex stumbled blindly towards the stairs, unable to take any comfort from his mother's words. He couldn't stop thinking that Luke, too, had been strong, a fighter – and he'd still died.

***

The journey took a little over two hours, but for Alex, sitting in the back of the taxi, with nothing to do but think, it seemed infinitely longer. Twice, he called the hospital from his mobile to ask how Luci was. The first time, the receptionist told him that Luci's condition was stabilising. The second time he rang, he was told that Luci had been rushed up to Theatre for emergency surgery.

The Accident and Emergency department was quiet, just a few people sitting waiting to be seen, when Alex ran frantically up to the reception desk. 'I'm Alex Freeman,' he barked at the receptionist. 'Where is she? Where's Luci?'

'Why don't you come and have a seat in the relatives' room?' the receptionist suggested. 'I'll get one of the doctors to come and talk to you.'

'Oh, God, *no*,' Alex moaned, shaking his head.

'Miss Rushden's still in surgery,' the receptionist said quickly.

'*Still?*' Alex echoed weakly.

'Come this way. I'll get one of the doctors to talk to you,' the receptionist repeated, leading Alex to a small room and closing the door for privacy. There were several plush-covered seats, but Alex couldn't sit down. He paced the room like a caged animal, until finally the door opened again and a young, female doctor slipped in.

'Mr Freeman? I'm Dr Ealing. I'm a member of the trauma team that's been treating Miss Rushden.'

'Luci,' Alex said automatically. 'She hates being called Miss Rushden.'

'Luci, then,' Dr Ealing said with a tense smile. 'Luci was in an RTA involving four cars and a lorry about four hours ago. She had to be cut from the vehicle and she was airlifted here. I'm afraid the woman travelling with her died at the scene – but there was no identification on the woman, and...'

'I'm not interested in any other bloody women!' Alex snapped. 'I'm only interested in Luci.'

'You don't know who she was travelling with?'

'No – and I don't bloody care, either!' Alex yelled.

'Okay – that's fine,' Dr Ealing said quickly. 'Luci's up in surgery at the moment – I'm sure you've been told that already. She's sustained a lot of injuries, but, thankfully, most of them are just broken bones that will easily mend – her right femur and tibia, her collar-bone, her right shoulder and elbow, and several ribs.'

'Then why's she in surgery?'

'There are some internal injuries, too,' Dr Ealing explained. 'Luci started haemorrhaging, and she was taken immediately up to Theatre. We'll know more when she's out of surgery. Someone will come and fetch you the moment she comes down, all right?'

'How long will that be?' Alex demanded.

'It shouldn't be much longer,' Dr Ealing said evasively. 'Would you like a cup of tea?'

'No,' Alex said shortly. Tea was the last thing he wanted. He didn't subscribe to the theory that a cup of tea could solve every problem. A cup of tea wasn't going to mend Luci's broken bones, or undo whatever internal damage had been done. As the doctor let herself out of the room, Alex sat down and tore his fingers through his hair, glancing at his watch. It was just after 6am. It didn't even cross his mind to wonder why Luci had been driving in the middle of the night.

***

Floating in that strange place between unconsciousness and consciousness, Luci could hear her name being spoken, and she could feel pain piercing the cotton-wool feeling that enveloped her. A voice was urging her to wake up, but Luci found herself fighting against it. She didn't want to wake up. Images flashed ruthlessly through her brain, disjointed memories of the brief moments of consciousness. There was blood, lots of blood, blue flashing lights, sparks flying as something cut through metal horrifically close to her head. Luci writhed, as if she could physically escape from her own mind.

'No,' she moaned. 'Make it stop. Make it stop!'

'Luci? Luce, can you hear me?'

Alex's voice. Alex was here.

'I'm here, baby,' Alex said, his fingers curling tightly around hers. 'It's okay, I'm here. You're safe. You can open your eyes now. Come on, baby. Come on, you can do it.'

The pull towards consciousness was too strong to fight. Luci's eyes flickered open and then closed again immediately. 'The light's too bright,' she moaned.

'The light's hurting her eyes,' Alex snapped, and Luci realised that there was someone else in the room. After a moment, Alex squeezed her hand again. 'It's okay now. The nurse has fixed the light,' he said gently.

Luci opened her eyes again, struggling to focus on Alex's face. 'Where am I?' she asked, her voice sounding weak to her own ears.

'Hospital. There was an accident. Do you remember?'

Luci tried to shake her head, but pain smashed through her whole body at the movement and she let out a cry that was half sob, half groan.

'You've got to stay still,' Alex said gently. 'You hurt yourself pretty bad, baby.'

'I don't want to remember,' Luci whispered pitifully.

Alex stroked her hair back off her forehead. 'I know,' he said soothingly. 'I know.'

Luci cast her gaze around the room. 'Where's Luke? He was here. I saw him. He was here with me!'

'Oh, God!' The words seemed to choke from Alex's lips and he bowed his head.

'He held my hand, and told me it was going to be okay,' Luci murmured. 'He said he was going to look after me. I wasn't scared anymore, then.'

'I nearly lost you,' Alex whispered, stroking her cheek.

'It hurts so much,' Luci moaned. 'When Luke was here, it didn't hurt.'

Alex looked up at the nurse who was hovering nearby. 'Can't you give her something?' he demanded harshly. The nurse murmured something about speaking to the doctor and left the room. 'I wish I could take the pain away for you,' Alex whispered.

'I only took my eyes off the road for a minute,' Luci mumbled. 'A minute. And then it was too late.'

'Shhh,' Alex soothed. 'You don't have to explain. It was a bad accident. It wasn't your fault.'

Luci felt a heavy tiredness creeping over her, as if the very act of being awake was draining her body of energy. 'I'm so tired,' she tried to say, but the words piled up in her mouth and came out as an unintelligible mumble. With a sigh, she gave in and let her eyes close again, falling thankfully back into nothingness.

***

The next time she woke, it wasn't so much of a struggle, and she came to consciousness without feeling as though she'd left part of herself back in the fog. She flicked her tongue over her parched lips and cast her gaze slowly and carefully around the room. Alex was asleep in the chair at the side of the bed, and she was wired up to some kind of machine that kept emitting rather reassuring beeps. Almost all of the right side of her body seemed to be either in plaster of heavily bandaged, and there was pain when she breathed. The only part of her body that didn't seem to hurt was her head.

'Alz?' she murmured, the words thick in her parched throat. He woke with a start, sitting bolt upright with a smile.

'You're awake!' he said, sounding as though it was the best news he'd heard in weeks. 'Properly awake!'

'Can I have some water?' she asked, gulping down the ice-cold liquid when Alex lifted the glass to her lips.

'How do you feel?' Alex asked, folding her fingers in his.

'Don't ask,' Luci replied, trying to shape her lips into a smile.

'Do you remember what happened?'

'I was talking to Izzy, and then...' Luci stopped. 'Oh, God! Izzy – is she all right? Have you seen her?'

Alex looked bemused. 'Izzy, as in Isabella?' he asked. 'Your mother's sister?'

'How many other Izzys do you know?' Luci asked irritably.

'Can we back up a minute?' Alex suggested. 'Isabella was with you? Is that where you went – to the convent?'

It took Luci a moment to remember that Alex knew nothing about what had happened in the past 48 hours. 'I'm sorry. I should have told you, but I knew you'd be angry and try to stop me,' she said. 'I went to the convent, to get Izzy out of there. We were driving back, just talking, and then the lorry must have jack-knifed or something, and it was too late, I couldn't stop...' She closed her eyes briefly as the disjointed images of the accident flashed again through her brain. 'Can you find out – about Izzy? Please, Alex, I need to know if she's okay!'

Alex squeezed her fingers tightly. 'I had no idea she was with you,' he said, his voice trembling. 'When they said – all I was bothered about was you.'

'I tried to swerve the car so she wouldn't get hurt,' Luci said, trying to ignore the suddenly anguished expression on Alex's face. 'I took the brunt of the impact, didn't I?'

'Luce...' Alex drew in a deep breath. 'The doctor told me that there was someone else in the car with you. A woman.'

'Izzy,' Luci said impatiently.

'Luce, she died. She died at the scene. There were other cars involved. I talked to one of the firemen. Another car hit yours after you crashed, and then another two cars hit that.'

Luci shook her head against the pillow. 'No. No, you're lying. You're lying to me!' Her voice rose to a high-pitched wail as Alex gripped her fingers harder.

'I'm so sorry, baby,' Alex whispered. 'I'm so, so, sorry, but it's true. I would never lie to you – never!'

Luci pulled her fingers free, directing her gaze up at the ceiling. 'What did I ever do wrong?' she whispered, but it wasn't Alex she was talking to. 'What was it, God? Why do you hate me so much?'

'Oh, Luce!' Alex cried, trying hard to comfort her.

'She waited forty years to be rescued. Forty bloody years,' Luci said brokenly. 'Forty years, and then I kill her.'

'No! Luci, you didn't kill her. The accident wasn't you fault,' Alex protested.

'I want to be on my own,' Luci whispered.

'I'm not leaving you.'

'Please,' Luci begged. 'I just want to be on my own. Please, Alex. I just need a minute, that's all.'

Alex stood up reluctantly. 'I'll go and get a coffee,' he said. 'Just a couple of minutes – I'm not leaving you for any longer.'

Luci squeezed her eyes tightly closed, waiting for the click that came when Alex closed the door after him. Only then did she allow the tears to come and the sobs to shake her broken body, every shuddering sob sending waves of nauseating pain through her body. When Alex came back, she was still sobbing, and he climbed onto the edge of the bed to hold her as best he could without hurting her more.

'It's not fair,' Luci sobbed. 'I just wanted to save her. I wanted to help her. Why does everything I touch go wrong? Why does it always have to be like this?'

'It wasn't your fault,' Alex said gently. 'You didn't cause the accident.'

'But if I hadn't tried to save her, she wouldn't be dead!' Luci wailed.

'But if you hadn't tried to save her, she would never have known that she had a family out there that wanted to help her,' Alex countered. 'You can't blame yourself for what happened, Luce. It was an *accident*.' He stroked her hair gently and then mopped her tears with a tissue plucked from the box beside the bed. 'Calm down now, hey? You're not doing yourself any good getting so worked up.'

Luci looked up into his eyes. It was no coincidence that he'd used the exact same words her mother used to use to calm her down as a child – the words that Izzy, too, might have used. Luci drew in a shuddering breath, struggling to control the sobs. The pain was making her feel sick and her vision go hazy.

'That's better,' Alex said softly, smoothing a few stray tears away with his thumbs.

Luci tried to offer him a watery smile – but failed. 'I feel like I've woken up in the middle of a nightmare. If I go to sleep, will I wake up and it'll all be over?'

Alex shook his head sadly. 'I wish I could take all the pain away,' he said, a catch in his voice.

'I don't mean the pain,' Luci murmured.

'I know,' Alex said. 'I didn't mean the *physical* pain, either.'

Luci angled her head against the soft contour of his chest. 'Just hold me,' she whispered. 'If you're holding me, I can't fall apart.'

***

The combination of pain and heavy doses of morphine meant that Luci was sleeping the first couple of times the surgeon who had operated on her came down to talk to her and Alex, so it was more than 36 hours after the operation before he finally managed to find her awake.

'Don't look so grim,' Luci said in an attempt to be cheerful when the dour-faced man, who introduced himself as Mr Kelsey, pulled a chair up to the side of her bed. 'Trust me, there's nothing you can tell me that's any worse than what's already happened.'

'The impact of your accident caused some internal bleeding,' the surgeon said gravely.

'Alex told me,' Luci said.

'We had to operate quickly when you started haemorrhaging,' Mr Kelsey went on.

'Alex told me that, too,' Luci added.

'I'm afraid that because your spleen had been ruptured, we had to remove it,' Mr Kelsey. 'Of course, many people live very full lives without their spleens, so it's nothing really to worry about.'

'Why are you talking to me like I'm five years old?' Luci asked wearily.

'Unfortunately, the spleen wasn't the source of the haemorrhage,' the surgeon said, ignoring Luci's barbed question. 'Miss Rushden, I'm terribly sorry, but I'm afraid you lost the baby, and we had to remove your uterus because...'

Luci held up her hand to stop the man from continuing. 'I don't understand,' she said weakly. 'I think... I think you've got me mixed up with someone else!'

'No, no – I performed the operation myself.'

'*What baby*?' Luci shrieked.

'You didn't know...? Oh! I'm sorry. I'm so very sorry,' the surgeon said, running his hand over his bald head.

'I didn't know,' Luci whispered, gazing, panic-stricken, at Alex. 'I didn't know!'

'It's all right,' Alex murmured, grasping hold of her hand. He glanced at the surgeon before tentatively asking, 'How many weeks?'

'Six or seven,' the surgeon said, tugging at the collar of his shirt.

'I can't mourn it if I didn't know, I can't mourn it if I didn't know,' Luci started muttering over and over to herself like a mantra. Nausea was swirling in her stomach; a dizzy feeling started creeping over her. In the midst of the horror that was taking over her body, her brain finally latched on to the other piece of news that the surgeon had delivered. 'I'm going to be sick,' she choked out as bile rushed up into her throat. She retched into the kidney shaped bowl Alex thrust under her chin, but spat up nothing but thin strings of bile.

Alex glared at the surgeon. 'Can you give us a minute?' he snapped, and the man shot to his feet and left the room as if glad to have a reason to go. 'Look at me,' Alex said softly to Luci as she started gasping for air. 'Luci, look at me! You've got cracked ribs – I'm sorry, baby, but you really can't afford to have a panic attack now. You could puncture a lung! You've got to breathe – come on, breathe with me.'

Luci raised panic stricken eyes to his, fighting to bring her breathing back under control as she folded her left arm over her stomach. How, she wondered, could she have been pregnant and not known? How could she have *lost* the baby and her womb and *not known*?

'Luce, say something,' Alex begged. 'Talk to me. Don't shut down on me now.'

'It would have been too small for them to know whether it was a girl or a boy,' Luci whispered. 'Wouldn't it?'

'Yeah,' Alex said, talking hold of her hand again.

'We can't even give it a name.'

'We could give it a unisex name,' Alex suggested.

Luci rocked her head from side to side. 'No. There's no point.' She couldn't even cry; it was as if she'd already exhausted her reservoirs of tears and there was nothing left to give. She looked up at Alex again, swallowing hard. 'I'm sorry,' she said simply.

'What *for*?' Alex exploded.

'For everything,' Luci explained, and then she closed her eyes and refused to open them again, no matter how much Alex pleaded with her.

***

'How's Luci?' Ruth asked when Alex called with an update that evening.

'The lights are on but nobody's home,' Alex said. 'She won't talk to me. She won't say a word. She's either staring at the ceiling, sleeping, or pretending to be asleep. And now the bloody doctors want to call down a psychiatric evaluation team. Like I can't already tell them what's wrong with her! She's just lost her aunt, her baby, and her womb, and they can't understand why she's like this?'

'Sweetheart, shouting isn't going to help,' Ruth pointed out gently. 'Luci just needs some time. Have you asked about when she'll be able to come home?'

'If the psych team get hold of her, it could be weeks,' Alex snarled.

'Don't exaggerate.'

Alex sighed. 'I don't know. They won't give me a straight answer. One of the doctors said a few days, but the nurse thinks maybe a week or more before she could make the journey.'

'Do you think she'd talk to me, if I got Mike and Hannah to have the children?' Ruth asked.

'I don't know, Mum,' Alex said wearily. 'I just don't know what I can do to help!'

'Be there for her. Make sure she *knows* that you're there. But you need to get some rest, too, Alex. You sound exhausted.'

'That's because I *am* exhausted,' Alex replied. 'I should get back to her. I don't like leaving her on her own.' He disconnected the call and went back into Luci's hospital room. She was still staring up at the ceiling, exactly the same as she had been when he popped out to make the call.

'Mum sends her love,' he said. 'She's going to get Mike and Hannah to look after the boys and come up and see you.'

Luci turned her head away from him, still saying nothing.

'Luce, please don't do this,' Alex begged. He reached for her hand, but she snatched it away. He sighed. 'It was my baby, too!'

Slowly, Luci turned her head back to look at him. 'I know,' she said, the first words she'd spoken in hours. 'But you can go off and make more. *I can't!*'

'I wouldn't – I would never... Jesus, Luci! I love you! I don't care about having more babies – all I care about is *you!*' Alex gasped.

'You say that now, but what about later, when all your friends are having more kids, and the twins are growing up, and you start getting broody? You won't want me then, you'll won't a *proper* woman, who can give you children, and who isn't crazy, and...' The words disappeared in a sob as Luci's shoulders started to heave.

'Never,' Alex breathed, close to Luci's ear as he tried to console her. 'Never in a million years.'

Luci pushed him away. 'It's best if you just go,' she said, the words choking her. 'A clean break and all that. It's okay. I understand. You don't have to stay. I know what's happening. I understand it all. This is just God's way of making sure – making sure I don't have any more babies. He's made it quite clear.'

'Don't be ridiculous! You don't even believe in God, not really!' Alex protested.

'And *that's* why He's had to do this!' Luci snapped.

'You're talking nonsense.'

'I want you to go, now, please,' Luci said. 'If you don't go, I'll call the nurse and get her to call for security. I don't want you here, Alex.' She stuck her left index finger in her mouth and used her teeth to pull of her engagement ring, pushing it into Alex's hand. 'Just go!'

'You don't mean that,' Alex cried. Luci reached for the call button, and Alex stood up, holding his hands out in surrender. 'Don't do this, Luce,' he begged.

'Just go, please,' Luci said coldly. She was sobbing before he'd even reached the door, but he kept on walking. He didn't want to force her to follow through on her threat – not when she was already breaking her heart. He closed the door behind him and stumbled blindly down the corridor to the visitor's waiting room, waiting all of thirty seconds before fishing out his mobile and calling his mother in desperation.

CHAPTER TWENTY-TWO

'I know you're not asleep,' Ruth said, sitting down in the chair at the side of Luci's bed.

Luci opened her eyes. 'Did Alex send for you?' she muttered.

'He's in pieces out there, Luci. I've never seen him so distraught,' Ruth said.

'It's for the best,' Luci said woodenly.

'No. I don't believe that – and I know you don't either!' Ruth insisted.

'It's better to end it now, not wait until he finds someone else to give him what he wants like Dad did with you,' Luci whispered, tears dribbling down her cheeks. 'I saw it happen, remember?'

'What happened between your father and I wasn't anything to do with Elvina not being able to have any more children!' Ruth cried.

'Maybe not directly, but...' Luci tried to shift position and winced.

'No buts, Luci,' Ruth said firmly. 'Sweetheart, I know you're hurting. I know that what you're going through is devastating – but punishing Alex and punishing yourself isn't going to make it better!'

'I *know* that!' Luci sobbed. 'But you don't get it! I'm trying to *protect* him -protect him from *me*. I'm not punishing myself – I'm *being* punished, by God, for all the sin, all the...the badness in my blood. When God sends down His next lightning bolt, I don't want it to hit Alex by mistake. He's innocent – why should *he* be punished because of me?'

'Isn't that the kind of cruel nonsense that your great-grandmother would have been spouting?' Ruth asked. 'I thought you didn't believe in it? I thought that was what made you so angry that you decided to go and find Isabella? I don't understand why you'd want to set her free, only to go and lock yourself in exactly the same kind of mental prison!'

Luci's eyes widened, making it obvious that she hadn't thought about it in that light. 'It feels like I'm being punished,' she said weakly. 'Isn't there a difference between thinking it myself and being made to think it like Izzy was?'

Ruth shook her head. 'Luci, you've been through such a lot of trauma in your life, but until you started finding out about your great-grandmother and what she subjected your mother and aunt to, you never once spoke about being punished for being sinful. Those aren't your thoughts, sweetie. You're just projecting them as your own.'

'But it *fits,'* Luci whimpered. 'All the bad things – Mum, Luke, Ben, and now Izzy – if I'm not been punished, then...' Luci broke off as the door opened and one of the nurses came in. From out in the corridor, there came the sound of a baby crying lustily. Luci stared at Ruth. 'That's Theo!' she cried.

Ruth nodded. She'd had to bring the babies – she'd set off from York as soon as it was light. 'Are you going to try and tell me that they're some kind of punishment, too?' she asked. 'You've got two beautiful, healthy babies and a fiancé who loves you more than life itself! How can you possibly think that they are God's way of punishing you?'

'They're not! Of course I don't think that!'

'So God's selective, is He? One minute he's punishing you for your bad blood – the next he's rewarding you?'

'No!' Luci moaned, screwing her eyes up as if in pain. 'I don't know... You're just trying to confuse me!'

'No,' Ruth countered. 'I'm trying to make you realise that your thinking's flawed. Luci, you're not being *punished.* Terrible things happen in life, but I do not believe that that's a form of punishment! Terrible things happen to good people – it's never about good and bad, or sinfulness, or any of the other outlandishly stupid things your great-grandmother might have believed in.' She took hold of Luci's hand. 'Sweetheart, I think you're already hurting enough without making yourself feel any worse.'

'I don't know how else to make sense of it,' Luci whispered.

'Sometimes things happen that you *can't* make sense of,' Ruth said. 'Like me falling in love with my best friend's husband. Stop *trying* to make sense of what's happened, Luci. It's terrible – and I'll admit that I can't even begin to *imagine* how you must be feeling – but there is no *sensible* explanation that can even begin to make sense of it. You know that. Deep down, you don't really believe all that silliness.'

Luci clung desperately to Ruth's hand. 'With Luke, there was someone else to blame,' she said, her voice shaking. 'With Ben – it was his own decision, like with Mum. But this – with this, there's no one else to blame, Ruth, only me, and I can't stand it! I feel like my head's going to explode. It's like there's a drum beating in my head, over and over again, with someone shouting "it's all your fault, it's all your fault!", and there's no escaping from it. All right –

I'm not being punished, you're right, I don't believe all that stuff, but – but if it's not God punishing me, then that means it's just me – I can't even share the blame with *God*! How can I look Alex in the eye knowing that I killed our baby, killed Izzy, and killed every chance of us ever having another baby?'

'What about the lorry driver?' Ruth asked.

'I wasn't looking at the road. If I'd braked sooner, if I'd taken evasive action, if I'd...'

'And what about the cars that hit you from behind?'

'Don't try and make me feel better!' Luci sobbed.

'I'm not,' Ruth said. 'I'm trying to make you see that you weren't the only one involved in the accident. The road was wet. The lorry driver hadn't taken the proper amount of time off driving because he was anxious to get home to his family – didn't Alex tell you that he came to apologise whilst you were still unconscious? From what I understand of it, the lorry jack-knifed across the entire carriageway. Even with the best driving skills in the world, you couldn't have avoided hitting it!'

'But I still *feel* responsible! And even if Alex says otherwise, he can't not be thinking it, too!' Luci snapped. 'Look at Dad – look how he felt when he found out about Mum making sure she didn't have any more kids, when he found out that the miscarriages weren't really miscarriages!'

'There is a big, *big* difference between deliberately losing a baby and having an accident that causes a miscarriage, Luci,' Ruth said sharply. 'And your father's reaction last week was more down to him feeling angry that I knew and never told him. We've talked about it. He came home with his tail between his legs when you went missing.'

Luci sighed. 'I can't stop myself thinking it, Ruth. I know what you're trying to say, but it still comes down to me. If I hadn't taken off like that looking for Izzy, if I'd booked into a hotel instead of driving through the night when I knew I hadn't slept for days... If I hadn't done all those things...'

'What if I hadn't fallen in love with Jack, what if Elvina hadn't found out, what if, what if – Luci, we could all drive ourselves insane wondering what might have been! The fact is, you did not go out with the deliberate intention to crash the car and lose the baby, did you?'

'Of course not! I didn't even know I was pregnant!' Luci snapped, pulling her hand free of Ruth's and resting it over her stomach as if trying to belatedly protect the tiny life that had been growing inside her.

'So what happened is not your fault, and Alex certainly – *certainly* – doesn't think that it is, any more than I do, or your dad does!' Ruth said. She rubbed her hands over her face. 'We could go around in circles like this all day, Luce, or you could at least try to accept what I've been trying to tell you. What do you think?'

'I don't *know*,' Luci whispered brokenly. 'I can't turn my brain off, Ruth. I can't stop *thinking*.'

'You can try and change what you're thinking. You could think about getting better and coming home. You could think about Matty and Theo out there, who've missed their mum like mad,' Ruth said gently. 'They need you to look after them, and to do that you're going to have to be strong, and stop dwelling on all the things that have gone wrong. Look at how your mum ended up because she was consumed by all those bad thoughts and guilt. You don't want to end up like her, do you? You want to be a better mum to your boys than she was to you and Luke, don't you?'

Luci drew in a deep shuddering breath. 'Of course I don't want to be like her! Of course I want to be better than that. I don't want to let them down, or let them think that I don't love them!'

'Then you have to stop torturing yourself – or you *will* end up going down the same path your mum ended up on,' Ruth said. She knew her words sounded harsh, but she knew, too, that Luci needed to hear them. 'You're stronger than her, Luci. You always have been.' She plucked a wad of tissues from the box and handed them to Luci. 'Dry your tears, sweetheart. You don't want Matty and Theo to see you so upset, do you?'

'I can't see them yet – look at me!' Luci protested.

'They need you,' Ruth said. 'Forget yourself – forget self-pity – you've got to think about *them*. I'll send Alex in with them, all right?'

'Will you tell him that I'm sorry?'

Ruth shook her head. 'No. You need to tell him that yourself, love.' She stood up and walked across the room, pausing by the door. 'No more nonsense. You've got to be strong.'

Out in the corridor, Alex was pacing up and down with the twins in their double buggy. There were deep purple smudges under his red-rimmed eyes, and his skin was the colour of putty.

'How is she?' he demanded.

'Why don't you go and ask her?' Ruth suggested with a wan smile. She felt drained by the emotionally charged conversation. 'You two need to talk. Be gentle with her, Alex. She needs to know that you're not going to hold her responsible – and she needs one hell of a lot of reassurance. I don't think I've ever seen her so shattered – not even after losing Luke.'

***

Alex seemed unnaturally nervous when he pushed the buggy into the room. Luci could hardly blame him for being wary, but before she had a chance to speak, there were two delighted squawks from the buggy.

'Mamamama!' This from Theo as he waved his chubby arms out to Luci.

'He said Mama!' Luci gasped.

Alex smiled. 'He's missed you – they both have; only Matty hasn't quite got his lips round it yet. He can manage Mmmm – which is nearly there.' He tried to keep the tremor out of his voice, but he couldn't manage it. 'Luce...'

'Let me go first, please?' Luci begged. Alex nodded, sitting down and pushing the buggy back and forth with his foot.

'When... when I said... what I said last night, it wasn't – it wasn't because I didn't want you. It wasn't because I don't love you – it was because I *do* love you! I was trying... trying to protect you. I thought it would be the best way. I wasn't trying to hurt you or push you away, or...' She stopped, drawing in a deep breath and blinked hard to clear the tears from her eyes. 'I love you and the boys so much, but I thought – I really thought – that if the bad stuff keeps happening because of me, then the only way to keep you safe was for me to stay away from you. I don't want anything to happen to you. I couldn't bear it!'

'But the accident wasn't your fault!' Alex cut in.

'I know. That's what Ruth's been trying to tell me. And I know – I know in my heart that she's right, but my head's having a hard time catching up.'

Alex sat back and gazed into Luci's eyes for what felt like an eternity, and then he felt in his pocket and pulled out the engagement ring Luci had taken off the night before. 'Can I put this back?' he asked softly – and the gesture said more than a hundred thousand words could have done. He slipped the ring back over

Luci's knuckle and kissed her hand before folding both his hands over hers. 'We will get through this,' he said softly. 'Whatever it takes, we'll get through it.' He gave Luci a watery smile. 'Can your head get a hold on *that*?'

Luci nodded. 'It'll have to,' she said, at the same moment that Matty screwed up his little face in concentration and said, 'Mmmmmammma!' Somehow, he made it sound almost like an exasperated admonishment. Theo, not to be left out, immediately joined in, and the tension broke. Alex lifted the boys out of their buggy and set them carefully down – Matty in the crook of Luci's good arm, and Theo just below his brother. Over the top of the babies' heads, Luci smiled at Alex.

'I think my brain's finally getting the message,' she murmured. Everything that mattered was right there in front of her. In that moment, she realised that she couldn't keep basing her happiness on ifs, buts and maybes. It was that mentality – and that alone – that had destroyed her mother. She couldn't let that happen again.

EPILOGUE
22ND MARCH 2009

It had been a logistical nightmare trying to arrange the wedding for Mothering Sunday – but somehow Alex had pulled it off. Sitting in the back of a horse-drawn carriage with her father, Matty and Theo, Luci was still finding it hard to believe that it was really happening. She was wearing a dress that Alex had bought for her – despite her protestations that there was no sense in spending so much money on a dress that she'd wear only once – and the twins were dressed in the cutest little pageboy outfits that Luci had ever seen. They looked more like their father every day.

'You're shaking,' Jack said with a smile. 'Surely you're not worried that Alex is going to do a runner on you now?'

Luci laughed. 'I'm more worried about falling flat on my face,' she said, but that wasn't really what was making her shake. The Sunday newspapers had been delivered just before the carriage arrived to take them to the church, and Luci's stomach was still doing back-flips after seeing the headlines on most of the front pages.

"Caring Convent Exposed as Evil Baby-Trafficking Ring" was just one of the colourful variations on the same theme.

'Did I do the right thing?' Luci asked her father suddenly.

'In agreeing to marry Alex?' Jack asked, puzzled. 'Of course!'

'No. In going to the papers.'

Jack felt for Luci's hand and gave it a squeeze. 'I'm sure every one of those girls will thank you for it,' he said firmly.

Luci let out the breath she'd been holding. 'I hope so,' she said. 'I hope that it's what Izzy would have wanted me to do.'

'I'm sure she would,' Jack said, sitting up straighter as the church came into sight. He tugged at his tie and then busied himself checking the boys' outfits, too. When he looked up at Luci, his eyes were bright with tears. 'I'm so very proud of you, Luciana,' he said thickly.

'Don't you dare set me off crying,' Luci warned. 'It took Ruth an hour to do my make-up because I kept blubbing! I am not getting married with mascara running down my face!'

Jack smiled. 'I don't think Alex would care if you turned up at that altar with coal dust on your face,' he said.

'Nonetheless, I'd rather not,' Luci replied. The carriage came to a halt at the church gates, and Luci climbed out with her father's help, waiting whilst he lifted Matty and Theo out, too. Her heart was hammering in her chest as Ruth and Zoe came out of the gates to meet them. As chief bridesmaid, it was Zoe's responsibility to make sure the train of Luci's dress didn't get caught on anything on the way down the aisle – Luci had had a recurring nightmare for several weeks that the train got caught on one of the pews, and she ended up walking up to the altar wearing nothing but her knickers and bra.

'Ready?' Jack asked as they reached the church door. He offered Luci his arm, and she took it, glancing back to make sure that Danny, Zack and Charlie had firm hold of Matty and Theo's hands. Despite her determination *not* to cry, she could feel the tears smarting her eyes. The past year had been both a rollercoaster and a sharp learning curve. It had taken time to recover from the accident – both physically and mentally – but now she felt as though she was more stable than she'd been in years. Getting the cocktail of medications right had been an important part of the process – but Luci knew that much of the change in her had come from changing her *attitude* to her illness. Although she still worried about the twins inheriting the disorder, she knew that bipolar wasn't to be feared as her mother had feared it. Although there was still stigma surrounding mental illness, attitudes *had* changed since the 1930s – and Luci knew that there was nothing to be gained from thinking that it was some kind of curse. She smiled down at her beautiful boys and drew in a deep steadying breath.

'Of course I'm ready,' she said, as inside the church the organist started playing – not "Here comes the Bride", but something more unconventional, at Luci's insistence. "Time Warp" might not have been ideal to walk down the aisle to, but it had such a special meaning for Luci that Alex had reluctantly persuaded the aging organist to learn the song.

Heads turned as Luci and Jack appeared at the top of the aisle, but Luci's gaze was fixed straight ahead, her eyes locking with Alex's as he stood waiting for her. For both of them, this was the moment they'd been waiting for all their lives.